Orbital Sniper

A Jack Gray Thriller

A Novel

by
John T. Cullen

Orbital Sniper

John T. Cullen

Selected Works by John T. Cullen

From Clocktower Books:

Selected Nonfiction

A Walk in Ancient Rome (Ancient History, Virtual Tour of the Imperial Capital around 300 CE—release 2020/2021) First Authorized Edition.

Dead Move: Kate Morgan and the Haunting Mystery of Coronado (1892 True Crime/Ghost Saga at the famous Hotel del Coronado near San Diego, 2008).

Selected Fiction

Lethal Journey (Historical Fiction based on Dead Move, see above—1893 dark period thriller, 2009)

Doom Spore (Science Horror in the tradition of Invasion of the Body Snatchers, available)

Robinson Crusoe 1,000,000 A.D. (Science Fiction, a fresh, imaginative treatment, evoking Daniel Defoe's 1719 classic as well as the classic SF movie Robinson Crusoe on Mars).

Lantern Road (Science Fiction in the grand, poetic tradition of Cordwainer Smith, James Tiptree Jr., and Frank Herbert, *et al.*).

For a complete selection of John T. Cullen titles, see the author's personal website at [**www.johntcullen.com**] or search all major retailers.
More info at back of this book.

Maps

Island of Barra, Outer Hebrides, Scotland

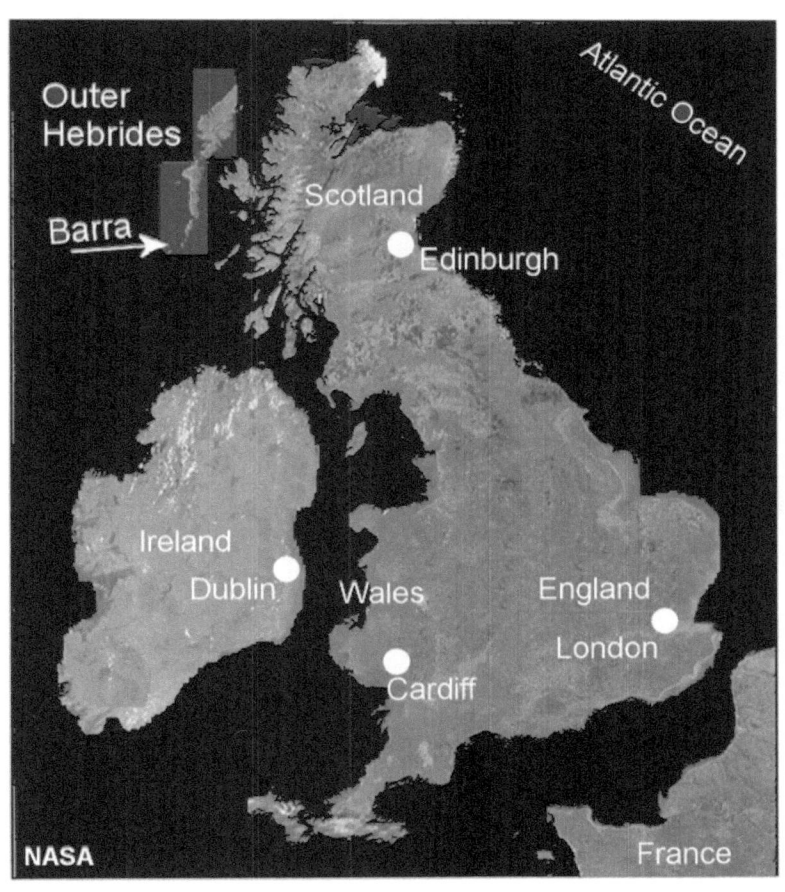

Italy/Sicily/Vulcano

Orbital Sniper

Part One: Jack Gray

<u>Big Trouble on Route 66</u>

Dysprosium Road

All hell was about to break loose in Inner Mongolia, despite a beautiful, calm summer evening over a hot, dusty Chinese landscape and industrial city of Baidu.

Jack Gray stood alone, half-hidden in shadows on a high balcony. He wore a white dinner jacket, held a gin and tonic, and packed a punchy little automatic pistol he'd smuggled in against orders.

A trade convention was in progress at his back inside the modern skyscraper. For the moment, the world looked deceptively calm and normal. Jack knew better. In his line of work, you stayed ahead of the game—or got run over by that big truck of events.

A warm, dry wind ruffled his short dark hair, like the gentle fingers of a woman with love on her mind. There was something wonderfully feminine in the air this evening, and Jack had a name for her: Xuē Siquin, his beautiful young translator and official state handler. Where was she right now, anyway? Safe, he hoped, and eager.

Alas, business first. And there was going to be a lot of shooting very soon, he sensed. The thought of much smoke, screaming, and violence roiled Jack's languid dreams of Xuē. When he'd seen her, a little earlier that evening, she'd smiled intimately, across the ballroom now behind him. Jack and she had worked together for several weeks, and it was time to cut the cards and deal. They were starting to communicate with their eyes, in that unspoken language of seduction and speculation, cutting through the veneer of professional coolness. He carried a still-smoking mental snapshot of her as he waited on the balcony: rouged lips, dark almond-shaped eyes, and a seductive *cheongsam* dress slit down one side to reveal a creamy-skinned leg (a hint that he'd see the other leg soon).

Traffic whirled around a major traffic circle below his balcony. The intersection formed a central square in Baidu. Over it loomed China's future, a modern glass and steel building in the best traditions of free enterprise, including the convention center.

Jack Gray was a dark-haired, wiry man of 37 with a California tan, an Ivy League professorship, and wealth of skills to back him up as a contract field agent. He knew all the moves of diplomacy and proper channels, but had an open charter to kill if all else failed. As Jack saw it, this was such a moment. It wouldn't be the first time in his career. But the people who signed off on his large checks weren't buying it. And Jack wasn't taking no for an answer. He knew better.

Problem was—his employers did not see things his way just now. Jack had chosen to stay, against orders, to oversee and probably assist in the Chinese military and police attack on the criminal enterprise across the way. Chinese intelligence, together with the services of several global powers, had been working for months to corner and bring down Big Yang, the criminal CEO of Sunrise Engine Corp. At stake was the world's supply in rare earths, almost entirely mined a new miles north of Baidu, and vital to the global economy. The Chinese had allowed foreign intelligence services to operate on the international aspects of Yang's global octopus of crime. Now they had ordered the foreigners to leave. They were going to handle the final military assault on Sunrise Engine Corp, Yang's front corporation, themselves.

There was only one little detail. Jack had wind of a certain amount of corruption in the local party apparatus. He did not know who, but he had suspects in mind including his own Chinese intelligence liaison, the Dragon Lady who was coordinating the coming assault. He strongly suspected that Yang had paid off the right people, and would walk away unscathed while his underlings were thrown to the wolves. Jack had a pistol that said, if Yang walked, he wasn't going any further than the front of Jack's barrel. If he ended up shooting Yang, he would be a man on the run across one of the world's largest countries. He might also miss out on a pleasant evening with Xuē. Somehow, Jack believed it would all work out. So far, things always had. Call it Lady Luck.

To get close to the action, Jack had chosen this wonderful vantage point on a balcony overlooking one of Baidu's main traffic intersections. The headquarters of Sunrise Engine Corp was directly across the street, past a central traffic island manned (or womanned) by a rather austere but attractive militia woman with nice legs and a certain rhythm with her traffic control signal on a stick.

Here in the midst of a major trade convention, Jack could also lose himself amid hundreds of celebrating men and women, including many Caucasians. It was a great cover. Passing himself as a Western trade representative (Herr Kutt of Düsseldorf), Jack had walked through the dancers and laughers and diners in the ballroom behind him. Xuē was in the building, more by coincidence than plan, finishing up some work in a computer lab. He and Xuē had agreed to meet by the hors d'oeuvres table a little later to make their escape to Beijing for a night or two in a luxury hotel, before he flew back to California and she returned to her home province and graduate studies at her university.

Now Jack stood hidden in plain sight at this perfect observation post, holding his drink like any other guest. With the index finger of his free hand, he touched his phone's ear-piece as his facilitators in the U.S. pleaded with him. Claire and Rector had called from Langley, Virginia to convince him to get on the soonest plane out of Inner Mongolia. They were both terribly worried. Jack didn't blame them, but no cigar—he was staying put.

"Jack, get out now," said Claire Lightfield, his Washington, D.C. agency interface, into his cell earphone from the opposite side of the globe. "Your job is done. Let the Chinese handle it from here."

"While you still can," added Rector, the man who signed his checks at Compass News, on the same conference line, different building, in Langley. "Claire is right. You're in the danger zone now. Get out, Jack."

He listened to their torrent of pleas, offering only an occasional nod, shrug, or grunt. When he spoke it was only a short plea of his own: "Only a few more hours, and all this will be over. I already have my plane ticket, so why don't you two relax?"

Jack didn't see getting out as part of his job description. Rather, he saw staying put as the real start of his job, when everyone else cut and ran. When all else failed, he was the agent of last resort. This waiting on the balcony for something to happen wasn't exactly an assignment, not yet. So far, it was a self-anointed gig—a footnote to a long, international espionage trawl just completed, in defense of the world's strategic supply of rare earths, located right near Baidu—but he was sure of himself, as always. He had to be. He wasn't an employee, but a self-employed contractor with his own eye for business. Danger was not a threat but an opportunity. Plenty of beautiful, intelligent women were drawn to his inner storm, like moths to a lantern at night.

He and a group of undercover international specialists had worked the Sunrise Engine Corp case for several months now, in cooperation with China's MSS (CIA equivalent). The other agencies were all packing and leaving—everything hush-hush, mission accomplished—but Jack knew better. Chinese special forces were about to raid SEC's headquarters and capture its Mafiosi-like Tong chiefs. But their *capo di tutti capi*, Big Yang, had something more up his sleeve.

Jack could taste the threat of violence in the alluring, musky Asian air. A red, angry sunset swirled over the western horizon, while cold twilight ruled in the east. It was the hour between day and night, between life and death, between love and extinction.

Claire Lightfield said: "Jack, let the Chinese mop up the final details. It's over. Come home." He could picture her—tall, willowy, understated, elegant, lightly freckled all over—in her sunny Langley office. She'd be wearing a cheery sun dress and have her straight, rather mousy hair tied back under a horn comb. If Claire wasn't jazz per se, she was the elegant silences between the notes. But she was married, out of bounds. Jack never fooled with married women, though he couldn't resist flirting anyway. He was, as a matter of record, a widower. He was a player, not by choice, but by circumstance. He played hard, and he played well.

Rector, a strong man himself, pleaded: "Jack, I have other work for you—I need you to come in."

Jack's fingertip turned white on the earpiece. His voice became a tight growl. "Sorry. The game's not over. If anything, it's about to start. I have to make absolutely sure they get Big Yang, not just his henchmen."

Claire sounded edgy and nearly impatient in her always controlled way. "How do you get so certain about things like this?"

"I can't say over the air." Would they get the hint? His phone was being bugged—of course. Jack sensed was that Yang had bought off some top Chinese brass, despite China's new drive to be a modern nation of laws—a world power instead of the amateur comedy show of its communist decades. As the Chinese liked to say—with capitalism come the best gangsters in the world. Big Yang would have done 1920s Chicago proud. Big Yang's known hero was Al Capone, in fact. Modern civilization depended on the rare earths to be found right outside Baidu for many critical components, from computers to medical equipment to the most advanced weapons. Opportunity knocked, and Big Yang answered the door.

"You're off the clock," Rector said.

"Call it *pro bono*," Jack said.

"What if you're wrong?" Claire said. She liked Jack, and did not want to see her handsome, dashing field agent become a sad memory. Jack knew all about sad memories. He wasn't about to give anyone the satisfaction.

"You're not even being paid for this," Rector ventured.

"My work is its own reward," Jack said, thinking of Xuē.

The actual order to pack up and leave for home had come from Madame Colonel Zhang Mei—his liaison with the MSS (Ministry of State Security, *Guojianbu*), China's equivalent of the CIA. The Dragon Lady had been difficult to work over the past several months.

Dr. Jack Gray, Ph.D.—historian, contract agent, master of the Win Sun fighting style, and a very eligible single man—didn't move from his perch on the third-story balcony of a glass, steel, and concrete convention center in modern, unabashedly capitalist China. From the ballroom behind him, brassy dance music wafted softly amid violins. He smelled hors d'oeuvres, fresh coffee, and sparkling champagne. Laughter and conversation bubbled through plate glass. Several hundred semi-formally dressed trade delegates and their spouses from around the world were happy about deals cut in recent days, contracts inked, and huge monetary sums deposited in good faith, billions of yen, in capital investment banks around the globe.

"Our Chinese counterparts called me and asked me to insist you be on the next plane home," said Claire Lightfield.

"That's what has me worried," Jack said. "Don't you see, Claire? I don't trust them. And they don't trust us."

"Don't take it personally," Rector said. Rector, in a clip playing in Jack's head, was a trim, smallish man of indeterminate age. Dark skin signaled his mixed European-Ethiopian heritage. His short, kinky, prematurely white hair looked just right on him, with his thoughtful mien and piercing gray eyes.

"Oh, but I always do," Jack replied to Rector. Three quick taps on the ear-piece cut the connection to Langley to terminate the conversation. "That's what makes me the best, and keeps me alive when others die."

Jack Gray—contract field agent of last resort—stood on a balcony in Baidu, regional capital. He held a gin and tonic in one hand, and packed a compact automatic under his white dinner jacket. The waiting itself was actually pleasant—there was a warm, dry summer breeze smelling of hay and rare earths blowing down from the north of formerly red (now green) China. Make that green as in money, not environment (an afterthought).

Jack smelled a rat in Chinese Mongolia. The rat's name was Big Yang, whose very human teeth were gnawing the neck of the world's commerce in rare earths, right near Baidu. Here nearly 100% of these key elements were taken from the earth for global use in computers, medical equipment, and other vital instruments that made the 21st Century world go round.

The Chinese themselves were about to strike with police and military force to kill off Yang's global criminal enterprise—Sunrise Engine Corp.—which had hijacked law and order to earn piles of yuan (red bucks), and threatened to cripple the world if the world's powers could not stop him. The People's Republic had assistance from various world powers in this crucial mission—including Jack Gray's handlers at Langley. Now the foreigners had been instructed to go home. From here on, the Chinese would handle the matter as an internal affair.

Jack thought differently. As an independent contractor, there wasn't much anyone could do to stop him, short of arresting him or killing him. As far as anyone here in power knew, Jack Gray had gone back to his home base in the U.S. But Jack knew all was not kosher at the moment, on China's northern frontier with the independent nation of (Outer) Mongolia, which formed a vast buffer between Russia's Siberia and the Chinese heartland south of there. Jack felt a moral imperative to stick around, just in case Big Yang needed to be swatted like an oversized mosquito, still having lunch on decent people's blood while his lesser accomplices took the fall to make things look good. Hopefully, it wouldn't come to that. He'd know in a short time, when Chinese special forces began their assault by land and air on the building across the street.

Jack thought to himself: *Until then, Mr. Gray, enjoy your drink and this divine sunset. Think of Xuē's sultry eyes gazing your way across the hot Mongolian plains basking in an orange sunset. Dream of her slender arms and legs tangling with yours amid clean Beijing hotel sheets. Imagine her smooth yellow features looking at you as you share a bubble bath, champagne, and fine chocolates. Always dream, because any moment may be the last in your violent and scary line of work—which someone has to do, and why not you, since you are the best?*

Jack was on his own now, as he preferred. He worked better this way, without people who thought they were his bosses breathing down his neck. It wasn't about ego. It was about professionalism. He was as hard on himself as he was on co-workers, when there were any. A pleasant, sociable guy most of the time, when there was time for it, he got along fine with co-workers. It helped if they were almost as deadly with their bare hands, a knife, or a gun as Jack Gray. If they weren't, he quickly distanced himself. Right now, he was on his own. Any moment now, he could become a hunted man, with many miles between himself and the nearest national border worth thinking about.

Like it or not, this was no bullshit. You stashed the talk, and walked the walk, even in your sleep. Otherwise, you got pissed away by some situation somewhere, when a bit of vigilance or mistrust or foresight could have saved your life. Call it the edge. Some men sharpened their knives or cleaned their guns. Jack did those things, but most importantly he practiced the still, quiet-seeing of Wing Sun, before whatever lightning moves were needed. Jack was a master of the art. You meditated with your eyes open and your senses keen, and listened to the whispering world all around you. Bit by bit, you cut out the stray information, until you were drinking in just the threat itself. You were part of it, not just a fish swimming in water as Chairman Mao had said, but part of the water itself as Bruce Lee had said. Fish gets eaten by other fish. Water closes around the empty place as if fish had never existed. Jack lives on—to meditate, fight, make love, and smell the flowers again another day. Not to mention read, think, study, understand—history, the matrix of all human life and meaning. The past, educating the future, while the present is lived just so.

Rector was right. Jack wouldn't take the job or this situation so much personally. The job simply wasn't done yet. Shrugging, Jack forgot about Claire and Rector, and stepped back into his disguise-persona as a trade representative.

Criss-cross palm fronds waved like elegant, living calligraphy over Jack's shadowy figure as he sipped at his gin and tonic and waited. Around him, corner trellises were smothered in jasmine, frangipani, and bougainvillea. Random, gentle traffic noises rose to his ears in the warm, dry evening air. A pair of high-powered, compact, night vision binoculars lay on the stone sill before him.

Down at the traffic island, that female traffic cop in dark green uniform directed traffic from her elevated platform, which was a round tower painted in red and white zebra stripes. She waved a baton with a neon circle glowing on its top end—green on one side, red on the other. Her moves flowed in smooth, bored sequences, with a certain subtle flair, as in some form of tai chi. She had nice legs, too, Jack noted, watching as she made energetic turning steps, visible in the opening above the steps leading to her traffic tower. That olive-green military skirt over her pert behind came down to a point halfway at her pale knee caps. She would turn like a ballerina, with her upper body erect and that glowing baton curving in the air. She would pivot on one loafer-clad foot, while her other leg rose provocatively, at right angles, for balance. Jack had already, briefly, studied her fine legs and slim figure through his binoculars, as a momentary appreciation of fine art. This was a necessary diversion. His interest tonight lay in Xuē Siquin, who possessed brains, beauty, and poise enough to be his traffic stop for the night—assuming everyone got through the next hour or so alive.

Traffic flowed like a dully glowing steel herd around the traffic island, where the flower of Chinese traffic policewomen practiced her butterfly dance. The illusion of law and order was hypnotic. Just a short distance beyond her lay the dark fortress of Sunrise Engine Corp. If he raised and looked through his clear gin and tonic glass, he could see her fine limbs moving, along with the glowing dot. The light was red, not green. Go figure.

Stay focused, Jack reminded himself while enjoying the dry bite of chilled vodka and skirt-colored olive. Capable of strangling world commerce. Must be stopped. He smacked his lips appreciatively and thoughtfully as he waited for the other shoe to drop, the other nuke to blow, or however many ways one could say Big Trouble on Route 66 in Inner Mongolia.

Make that Element 66—Dysprosium, a rare earth vital to the world.

Entirely in the present, he held his gin and tonic, and touched the concealed handgun under his white formal jacket. He stayed hidden in the shadows amid waving palm fronds, lush grape vines, and lightly stirring broad-leaf ivy growing on trellises.

He carried a Kimber 1911 Ultra-Covert II with .45 ACP rounds (7-clip) in a compact holster at the small of his back. He had two clips of spares in special inside jacket pockets. He hated ankle-holsters, though he owned one for rare occasions when he didn't need to run, or to wear it for long. A ribside holster, holding a cannon like his 9 mm Sig-Sauer, would be noticed at a diplomatic function. Besides, he did not have a valid local carry permit. Guojianbu had not sanctioned it. Madame Zhang, Dragon Lady of MSS, had made it clear she did not like him. He went nowhere without his personal armory—it was part of him, the way a boar had tusks, or a beetle had a carapace, or a snake carried poison. You did what you had to do, to stay alive.

The blood-red summer sunset gloried in smears of mauve and flame-yellow. The day's humidity and heat had relented, and a refreshing breeze smelling of hot earth and dry grass blew across Inner Mongolia's largest city. Nightfall brought the first quenching breezes.

At the moment, the nerve center of the city seemed quiet. Traffic was light—about one truck or bus for every private automobile, of mixed Chinese, Indian, Korean, and European makes. They sent a tinge of sour exhaust up into the fragrant air.

Among the leaves, on the travertine balcony railing, lay a compact but powerful pair of binoculars for Jack's use when the time came. Big Yang was a master of payoffs, bribes, and other corruption in high places. Crime moguls like Yang always had a back door, oiled with payola among hungry government bureaucrats. It wasn't just China. It was the Human Condition.

Yang's criminal enterprise was in a long, slow process of being busted, like dominoes falling in slow motions. There had been a tedious, covert investigation by local and extranational secret services. Jack had been working the case for three months in-country. He was ready to go home, but there were a few more details to lay to rest. The stability of world commerce rested on whether they bagged Big Yang and his bosses tonight. It might sound theoretical, but Jack was a historian, not an economist. He dealt in causes and effects, context instead of conjectures. The greed and ruthlessness of a kingpin like Yang affected small working families in poor neighborhoods from Jamaica to Kinshasa, from Chicago to Singapore. It was personal, indeed.

Jack couldn't say that he didn't feel butterflies in his stomach. He had tangled with a lot of nasty types in his day. His hands were calloused from many hours of mountain climbing, grappling with black belt opponents in various disciplines, digging trenches more for the exercise than the hole it left, and running for miles in cold rain or hot sun. It was the homework you did for this job. He'd been shot, stabbed, kicked, and left for dead in more than one dark alley around the world. He'd made his share of mistakes, but in balance he'd left more than one nasty type draped over a railing or stuck under a truck with a broken neck and a vacant gaze—never to hurt innocent people again. Jack was a soldier. He did what they sent him to do—took it personally, gave 110%, and often had to be hauled out at the last minute with his ass on fire. But he got the job done, usually better than expected.

And then it went through you, like six gallons of Tijuana tap water on fire. If you were human, you couldn't help it. You either became a dehumanized killer, no good to yourself or anyone else, or you found your own back door. The comic superhero had his fortress amid Arctic ice. Jack had his own top-secret fortress—on a remote ranch in California, a connection known only to Claire Lightfield and Rector, the only two human beings whom he trusted with his life and the lives of those he loved. There, he left his real life behind each time he came out to play these deadly games. He never allowed his mind to wander there, even for a second, when away on assignment. The D Ranch was where he went to heal when one of these gigs was over. Catherine's grave was there, on a windy, grassy hilltop. His married sister and his own daughters lived there, never knowing what daddy did for a living. Two different worlds, separated by Jack's deadly determination they should never intersect. And nobody but Claire and Rector would ever know. God help anyone who sniffed it out—Pathfinder would be unleashed, Jack's code name from a long ago and distant war. Hell was a carnival mask compared to the fury of Pathfinder on the loose, hackles out and moonlight in his crazed eyes, nose to the ground like the war dogs he had run with, seeking his doomed prey. *Leave it behind, Jack. Heal.* Get on with it. Catch the bad guys. Save the world. *Keep it light, dude.* Voice of a long-ago comrade, now deceased in the line of duty.

He set the gin and tonic aside. Enough. Time to focus, not lose the razor's edge.

Fly me to the moon... Jack whistled the tune, lightly, thinking of Xuē.

Here he was again. This was when a man really felt alive. He could savor the moment, the way a wolf on the hunt sniffs the wind and tastes terror in its prey's pelt. Yeah, only a crazy person wouldn't be feeling butterflies right about now. This was the calm before the storm. Enjoy it while it lasts, but don't get too cozy. He might have to shoot his way out, dive off the balcony, who knows what...

His phone signaled quietly into his ear again. This time it wasn't Claire Lightfield or Rector, or even the Dragon Lady. This was the call he'd been waiting for—from Xuē.

In the ballroom behind Jack, several hundred trade representatives and their spouses danced slowly while embracing. They were elegantly dressed in suits and gowns. Light jazz wafted in the air—along with tinkling ice cubes, laughter, and conversation—as did the aromas of five-star cuisine and expensive champagne fountains.

Jack had entered the premises with a phony card showing him to be a trade liaison for a German sausage company, named Herr Kutt.

It was a last-minute joke by his beautiful translator and liaison, Xuē of the sparkling smiles, dimpled cheeks, and intriguing eyes.

Upon receiving his I.D. card from her earlier that day, in order to get into the convention, Jack had told her his new name for her--Miss Chief. He'd added: "And I have some ideas for special language lessons you can help me with when all this is over."

Xuē got it. She'd watched a thousand U.S. movies, loved the culture, and understood the lingo. She actually preferred to be called Sue, but Jack insisted on going native, so she made an exception for him, as she was willing to do in matters of the heart. The best part, like toppings on taste ice cream, was her whip-crack sense for the absurd. Her humor was seductive as it wrapped itself around one's laugh button. "As your translator, I am here to help you with any tongue you require, Jack."

"Your tongue will do."

"Oh Jack, you can be so hard to swallow."

"Try, darling, try."

"I'll make a special project of you, Mr. Gray."

"You'll have me licked in no time."

In the building across the street, owned by Sunrise Engine Corp, a world-class hijack of the Mongolian economy was about to be pulled off—and, with that, control of the world's financial systems.

Poor, sweet Xuē. She was a college student, moonlighting on a government job to make ends meet. She could have ended up translating parts lists for Swedish phone makers, or customer contacts for Brazilian trade representatives in Shanghai, but what did she draw? Ministry of State Security, office of Dragon Lady, working with an American loner who smelled of danger, despite his charms, the way a match smells of sulfur before it's even lit. She dutifully listened to message traffic in her spare time, and passed nuggets along as faceless local linguists directed. The anonymity was everyone's only hope of survival, because Big Yang's Tong had infiltrated to top levels. Innocent little Xuē had passed along the deadly crypto-ultra involving Sunrise Engine Corp and an unknown mole inside MSS. Even Claire Lightfield and Rector didn't know—yet. The information was buried in Jack's soul, more to protect Xuē than himself. If he notified Langley, the coughing dragons and sickening tigers would strike in a fury to protect their unguarded rears. There would be victims. Jack must stay here, and wait.

Okay, Rector, so it is personal. Her name is Xuē. If you met her, you'd agree. If not, to hell with you.

At stake was virtually the entire global supply of rare earths or lanthanides, used in critical parts of computers, lasers, and other strategic industries by the world's powers. Half of these materials, of top quality, came from the region around Baidu. Without them, the world economy could collapse. Whoever controlled them could dictate terms to the world's leading nations.

If Big Yang and his China-based, international mafia outflanked the government raiders, who were about to strike any minute now, the entire trade convention in this building would be taken hostage by Sunrise Engine Corp's mercenary forces. Even that would be a feint. Jack had figured out, on his own, how the chess pieces were lined up for the next few moves. Yang would keep his hands clean, while his thuggish army would move in with military precision to seize this festive, poorly guarded building. Once they had hostages, especially important foreign trade representatives, ambassadors, and CEOs, the Chinese government would be in an embarrassing and helpless position. Big Yang, from the safety of some rat hole, could call the shots. The hostages would be held for a day or two and then released unharmed amid heavy press coverage and damaging negotiations resulting in a distasteful amnesty. It would all be a blind for the actual plot engineered by Yang and his secretive international finance consortium.

Play it back again: The government would blunder in, attack Yang's headquarters, and win a hollow victory. Yang would escape. Under their noses, the convention hall would be seized, and the government would helplessly surround the building in a big stalemate picked up by the world news agencies for 7/24 coverage on live networks around the globe. It would be a public relations nightmare for capitalist China and the world.

The real damage would occur at next morning's opening of world financial markets, three or four days from tonight. Yang's hidden global financial octopus, with Sunrise Engine Corp just a pawn to be jettisoned, was poised to buy up billions in tanked stock as news of the economic chaos hit stock exchanges from London to Tokyo, from New York City to Beijing, from Cairo to Sao Paolo.

Jack Gray, working surreptitiously through various guest agencies (floaters) and the host country MSS, had helped engineer the only possible counter-coup that could stop the grab—a lightning strike by the Chinese army and Mongolian police to seize Yang and his top chieftains and bog their paper-front companies down in years of litigation, while the gang chiefs themselves were held in obscure desert prisons. If the Chinese government did not get Yang tonight, the whole operation would be an embarrassment for China, and a black eye for other big players around the world.

At stake was Mongolia's near-monopoly on the world market for rare earths—critical to the world's supply of computer parts and other important industrial sectors that drove the modern world. Just an hour's drive south lay the crux of Jack Gray's investigative mission of the past three months—Bayan Obo Mining District, where much of the world's rare earths or lanthanides were produced. Without these seventeen elements and associated alloys or compounds, 21st Century civilization could virtually collapse. Despite their obscure names (Cerium, Promethium, Yttrium, etc.), they were essential in many modern industrial processes and products. They formed key components in nuclear batteries, YAG lasers, superconductors, carbon arc lighting, ceramic capacitors, neutron trapping, vanadized steel, portable X-Ray machines, PET Scan technologies—a sprawl of applications across every industry from earth to space. As in the late 20th Century world mobilization to stop Iraqi dictator Saddam Hussein from capturing most of the world's oil supply, today various nations had stepped up to the plate to prevent Yang's takeover of rare earths.

Jack hoped his lingering presence would only be an added insurance policy. He hoped to walk away from this, tonight, with his suit still looking pressed, and all those nasty little copper ladies still smiling blandly in the clip of his Kimber. He was ready for anything, but his thoughts were on sweet, tender, spicy Xuē. *Fly me to the moon…*

"Jack," said Xuē in his earpiece.

"You okay? Keeping your pretty head down?"

"I'm copacetic, Jack." Her voice was dry and self-assured like a good Chablis. It was the crisp, clear tone of a woman who knew she was smart and attractive, and comfortable in her skirt. Her command of English took his breath away. Not just vocabulary—but nuance and undertone. She spoke American idiom without a flaw.

Fly me to the moon...

He asked: "Where are you? Are you in any danger?"

"I was gonna ask you the same question, Bwana."

Xuē loved U.S. movies, and spoke West Coast American though she'd never been east of Shanghai. As with so many exploded Eurocentric myths, Jack found absolutely nothing inscrutable about Asians, especially when someone like Xuē (she taught him to pronounce her name sort of like 'chewy') signaled that she wanted to scrute, or get scruted, or whatever one wanted to call steamy, privatized romance. *Hey big boy, want to scrute?* Her family name Sechen (Siquin), to the Western ear, was just a breath away from Mandarin *she-she*, meaning 'thank you.' Jack found it fit refreshingly for his dreams of him and her. And of course he hoped she would be delighted to cha-cha, even if they weren't in Havana. He looked forward to a cozy evening for two, but alas—business first.

His ear piece made a faint tuning sound. Had he lost her? He tapped it lightly with his index finger to reopen the line. "Hello, Xuē. You still there?"

"Are you hiding, Jack?" her dusky voice teased. Jack had a theory, based on experience, that women with rich voices were exceptionally passionate in bed. He had a feeling he might test his theory, if he survived the next ten minutes. Xuē was a graduate student at Shanxi University. She'd watched endless U.S. movies, and closely studied the patois. Her U.S. English sounded educated, yet nicely colloquial. She dreamed of emigrating to L.A. (her term) for a few years of surfing, partying, and graduate studies—not a typical Chinese order of things. Nevermind—in reality, her priorities were in good Confucian harmony, she'd told Jack.

"Did you want to dance?" he asked, glancing at the colorful sea of swaying men and women in the ballroom beyond the heavy plate glass windows to his back.

"I'm on the first floor patio below you. Look and wave."

He looked over the concrete railing and saw a lithe figure in a seductive *cheongsam* dress, slit down the sides. She was very pretty, even if he could not see her clearly in this light. She had long, blue-black hair and large, serene, almond-shaped eyes. He saw her teeth in the dark as she smiled. She wrinkled her nose at him and waved.

He waved back. "Want me to come out and play?"

"When the fat lady sings, Mr. Gray. We are still on the clock."

"I'm glad at least one person agrees with me." *Tell it to Rector and Claire Lightfield.*

"We are singing from the same sheet of music, Mr. Gray."

"What do you say we sing under the same sheet, Xuē?"

"Foreign devil deal with Dragon Lady first," she said in an imitation Asian villainess accent found in ancient 1930s Charlie Chan movies. They were her favorite. As she told it, she'd once nearly died, choking on popcorn, while laughing with her friends in the Shanxi U dorm one night, watching Fu Manchu movies while wreathed in marijuana smoke.

"Ah so," Jack said in that same spirit. *Dragon Lady.* Jack assumed their conversation was being recorded by one spy agency or another, probably corporate rather than state. In modern China, corporate espionage was more intense than state espionage had been during bad old Commie days. Xuē's barely concealed code referred to their coordinator, Mme. Col. Zhang Mei of MSS, the new Ministry of State Security.

"Stay out of sight," he told Xuē. "Do we have a date when it's over?"

"You bet, Tarzan. You bring Toto, I bring Jane."

"That's Cheetah. Toto is from the Wizard of Oz."

"You Tarzan, me Jane. We fly united."

"You look delicious."

She waved. "You catch me, you bite me. I catch you, I eat you."

Jack felt a glow after he signed off with Xuē. He lifted his gin and tonic for one more sip. Maybe two…

For a few moments, time continued standing still as shadows of palm fronds waved slowly across Jack's tanned, half-hidden features on the balcony. The music played on in the ballroom behind him, while hundreds of elegant men and women swayed in a scene out of 1950s Las Vegas. *Mack the Knife…old Mackie's back in town…applause…laughter…*

There! Jack almost missed the obvious signal.

He instantly set his drink aside, and stepped close to the balcony to peer down over the travertine railing and reached for the high-powered, night-capable binoculars.

Jack snapped the compact binoculars to his eyes.

At the traffic island in the square below, it was not time for shift change. And yet—his uniformed female traffic cop—looking very strack in her dark green skirt-suit, white cross-belts, and white hat—quickly stepped down the ladder from her round, elevated island. She had nice legs under the knee-length green uniform skirt; softly muscled thighs that gleamed pale under traffic lights. Something was up, all of a sudden. Her dance was over. She was running for her life, without making it look as if she were doing anything more than sauntering in rapid little steps.

The female cop hurried across the pedestrian zone, swinging her traffic baton from one hand. Her other hand was up at her ear piece—she must just have gotten word to evacuate. She was talking to unseen superiors. The show was about to begin. She scurried on sensible shoes. Now she held on to her cap, and her pretty pale legs made urgent, blurry motions. Lovely knee caps, still…

Suddenly, the square filled with lights—white headlights behind military steel grids, and red taillights as columns of large, olive-drab mechanized infantry vehicles drove in from all sides.

Men in helmets, porting assault rifles, jumped from several lines of PRC army and Mongolian state police troop carriers. The air filled with heavy engine roaring and diesel exhaust, as well as the clatter of dropped chains. This came amid a clanking of heavy steel ramps dropping. Tanks charged down on rapidly churning treads, turbine engines whining, while their heavy bodies swiveled with surprising agility ahead of billowing black smoke.

Officers and NCOs hoarsely shouted orders as the men surrounded the Sunrise Engine Corp building.

Flash-bang grenades exploded with teeth-jarring noise and blinding lights.

Small packet charges imploded the heavy glass doors.

Assault choppers clattered overhead, aiming down darting spotlights.

Laser-like search beams darted back and forth into the sky. Muzzle flashes erupted from suicidal lobby guards a.k.a. Tong thugs in cheap, flashy suits. Raking fire of invading PRC commandos overmatched the lobby guards tenfold.

Silence ensued as Chinese commandos took the building in quick order, all floors simultaneously, one room at a time, kicking in doors as they went. They took pockets of fatigue-clad mercenaries prisoner, as they surprised them in their ready rooms before they could take up arms and fight back.

Jack's ear piece hummed, and he tapped it. "Yes?"

The cold, hard voice of Zhang Mei sounded: "Mr. Gray, I am displeased that you stayed."

"Do you have Yang Jun in custody?"

"Confidential, Mr. Gray." Her voice wavered on the last word, as if she were suddenly sloshing some new ideas around in the nutrient broth of her scheming mind.

"Don't play games with me," Jack said. "I've been here, risking my life to help you."

"You were paid to do a job. It's finished. You were told to leave the country."

"I'm just making a little detour on my way home."

She seemed to consider, pausing a moment. "There is one last detail."

"What?" Her tone made him suspicious.

She sounded velvety, false. "Yang Jun is in this building where you and I are. Meet me on the next floor up from your balcony. I have two men with me, and we'll take him."

"All right. I'll be there in two minutes."

A crowd hurried to the balcony—gaping diplomats, tractor sales persons, spouses, and waiters and waitresses—to watch the noisy, violent chaos in the square. None had a clue that, if the thugs won, all the dancers would be hostages within less than an hour. Some might die. Yang rarely took prisoners, unless for torture or ransom, maybe both depending on his whims.

Jack sidled among them.

As he entered the now-empty ballroom, all pretense about Herr Kutt was over. Jack brandished the small black Kimber. Until minutes ago, the Dragon Lady had strictly ordered him to leave the city, not to get involved in the raid on Yang's company. Now she wanted his help? He smelled a bigger rat than before. But he quickly formed an idea about the missing puzzle piece. He would move very cautiously from here on. Whatever happened, Yang must be taken down. That was a priority bigger than Jack's own safety, or—his eyes dilated with worry—*Xuē!*

The hallway outside the ballroom was dark and quiet. Soft elevator music still played from the day's conferences and shows. Jack banged on the elevator buttons, but the machine seemed stuck somewhere.

His ear piece buzzed. It was Xuē. "Jack, something is not kosher."

"Yeah—something is rotten in Inner Denmark."

"Don't joke now. I am watching Yang Jun cross the street. He's hurrying into our building."

"Is he alone?"

"Looks like it. I think he escaped into a tunnel, under the square, and came up on this side."

"I'll be careful."

"Shake that noise," she said. "Come down to the patio where I can keep an eye on you."

"Nothing would suit me better right now. Stay hidden! I'll be down there for you in a few minutes."

Tapping the connection off, he found a stairway and ran up two steps at a time. If Zhang Mei said the industrialist was already in the building, why did Xuē after that see him entering? Jack had been expecting this. The big man had a back door escape plan, which he was now executing. With any luck, Zhang Mei and her government police agents from Beijing would collar him before Jack arrived.

Or—? The shadowy, lurking realization came into the open in Jack's mind. Of course. Zhang was in it with Big Yang. This was a death trap for Jack. Yang had a score to settle, and its name was Gray. Somewhere, in the back corridors of his mind, he'd expected this as well.

Silence.

Jack shoved pushed open a door and stepped cautiously onto the hallway one floor up.

No elevator music.

No lights, just a dim reddish glow from scattered emergency exit lights.

The door slipped shut behind him as he stood cautiously pointing his gun.

An emergency light slammed on directly overhead, blinding him.

"Mr. Gray, you are a real nuisance," said the matronly voice of Zhang Mei. She walked into the hallway from a side lobby, holding a gun on him as she approached.

Walking beside her was Yang Jun, crime boss and CEO of Sunrise Engine Corp. He said something in Mandarin, which Jack took to mean "So this is that pain in the ass. Kill him. Then we'll get out of here together, Sugar Pie." Yang wore a maroon jogging suit, whose athletic implication was belied by his ample gut. The jacket zipper was open to his diaphragm, revealing an oily looking chest and a gold medallion on a golden chain. If the Dragon Lady was Sugar Pie, Jack hated to think what this beached walrus might be called on a dessert menu.

Jack could almost hear the saucy retort from Xuē: *Howzabout Peaches in Lard?*

Seeing spots before his eyes, Jack made out the muzzle of her gun as it swung toward him. So the chief of the MSS operation had been sent to arrest Yang Jun and his minions—but, instead, was in bed with Yang. It made instant sense, in the picosecond before that muzzle could flash. As with many bureaucrats, this woman's salary was modest as she moved about in a world of money, power, and influence. Yang was her one chance to throw her lot in with a billionaire, and live like an old-fashioned dowager empress, while she still clung to the last of her arachnid sex appeal.

Jack stepped back as her muzzle flashed. The gun barked, and a bullet nicked the steel frame of the door that hung locked behind him.

Jack loosed two shots upward into the emergency light.

The lights all around went dark.

"Kill this prick!" shouted Yang in mangled and marinated English.

Dragon Lady snarled like an enraged debutante in the rain without a taxi. Two more rounds escaped her popping gun, while Jack threw himself to the ground. Her shots clanked holes into the door frame where his head had been a second ago. Jack shot in the direction of her muzzle flashes.

She laughed contemptuously, as if Jack were dirt.

Jack spotted a faint glow from Yang's medallion and pumped three shots into that direction.

Yang collapsed quietly. His lard hit the ground with a heavy *plop*.

Zhang's laughs and snarls turned into bellowing. From her motion, as Jack's eyes adjusted to the gloom, she must be bending over Yang. She was trying to revive him. Jack pumped out his last round, but missed in the gloom. He shook out the empty clip, letting it drop with a hollow, metallic bouncing sound. and clicked a new one into the grip.

"You die for this!" Zhang bellowed hoarsely. "I will send someone to cut your balls off with a rusty razor!" She emptied the gun in Jack's direction. He pressed himself into an alcove. When she was out of ammo, he leaned around the corner and poured out half his fresh clip. Firing on automatic, he heard gas-pops by his ear, and the clatter of expelled shells on the hard carpet, as his rounds blasted after her.

No luck. He heard the soft soles of her sport shoes running away.

One day, somewhere, he knew he would be forced to think of her again.

Or she would send someone after him with murder in his eyes, as promised.

Jack would be looking over his back again for a while. *Sigh.*

Jack listened for a minute or two. Boots came piling up steel stairways, and doors burst open.

"Don't shoot," Jack cried out. "InterWurst!" He waved his Germanic Herr Kutt I.D. card.

The officers in charge recognized Jack from earlier contact. They ordered their men to run in the direction Jack indicated.

Emergency lights came on, and there lay Big Yang, dead as a beached sea cow after trying to mate with churning propellers in a Miami boat canal.

Now utterly ignored, Jack quietly opened the door. He holstered his still-hot gun on his way down the stairs.

In the main ballroom, he grabbed a wine bottle, two glasses, and a small box of finger foods along his way. Not to mention chocolates.

Women liked chocolates. Jack liked women. Jack and women and chocolates were the perfect combination for an all-star evening, anywhere in the world, so why not Inner Mongolia?

He found Xuē anxiously waiting for him. She had been hiding, all alone on a small patio overlooking the street. During the day time, office workers came here to drink tea, chat, and smoke cigarettes. Everyone else had just run down the street to watch the army and police trucks. Local Baidu police cars and fire engines stood by to the rear, in case they were needed. More shock troops arrived in black police vans with small, twirling blue lights and hoarse Martin's horn sirens.

Instinctively, Jack and Xuē hugged. No more need to pretend. No more office etiquette. It was the relief of being safe, after all this noise and violence. She ran to his arms, and he embraced her—their first intimate touch. They'd spent almost no time together privately so far, aside from lurid texting and colorful phone chats. She was the ideal woman: brilliant, beautiful, and sincere. They'd stayed in different hotels in Baidu, and only met in fairly public venues over recent weeks, but a considerable spark of interest had grown between them. When he'd glimpsed her earlier this evening, Xuē had looked especially lovely before the reception. He liked to imagine she had dolled up to please him.

"They are rounding up all the goons and employees across the street," Xuē said.

"I just shot and killed Big Yang Jun."

"No—really?" She was not a spy or news woman, but a translator and greeter—a very pretty young woman with a sharp mind. She looked ravishing in her stylish maroon and copper colored cheongsam—a long, tight-fitting dress with a round collar, slit sides, and subdued flower patterns. "Like dead as a doornail?"

"Yes," Jack said.

"Wow, that's frigid' cool, man."

"Right," Jack said as he handed her the wine, glasses, and provisions. The provisions were in the form of a little wicker basket with apples, cheese, crackers, and little individually wrapped chocolates—finest Belgian *Côte d'Or*, and Viennese *Sachertorte*. As he fumbled for his car keys, he leaned close and sniffed her warm aura. "You smell divine."

"It's Coco Chanel, one of my favorites."

"Mine also, as I now realize." They entered a gloomy, silent parking garage lit by wan pink fluoros. He nuzzled her bare neck. She put her arm through his, and squeezed close to him.

He handed her the wine bottle as she trotted beside him.

"Are you going to drink and drive?" she asked, swinging the bottle in one hand and the basket on its looping handle in her other.

"You just want me arrested so you can have this cheese basket all to yourself. No, we'll save the wine for later, but we'll eat on the road to Beijing."

He found his car, a gray Porsche. The car was a little perk from Claire Lightfield of Sigma 2020. It was directly returnable to a rental agency at the airport in Beijing. "The last thing I want is to be stopped by the expressway police for any reason. You're not busy the next few days, are you?"

"I have the weekend off. Back to the grind on Monday." She meant classes, until her next assignment for some government agency, as she worked her way through school.

"Good. Let's find a good hotel near the airport, take a bubble bath, and check out this red Cabernet "

"Great stuff, that wine. Genuine Chinese. Comes from Helan-Wuhan in western Inner Mongolia, in the valleys along the Yellow River."

Jack shifted and drove happily, feeling the powerful car all around him, and the woman at his side.

Across acres of tree tops, Jack spied the busy G6 Jingzang Expressway running 3,700 km (2,300 miles) between Beijing in the east; and Lhasa, Tibet in the far west. The highway itself was invisible to Jack, but the G6's heavy traffic formed a spaghetti-stream of white, yellow, and red lights that cut through forests, neighborhoods, and fields. Its light rose like fog into the sky, straight as a horizon-to-horizon fluorescent tube.

Within minutes, Jack found an entrance ramp to the G6. They were instantly immersed in a river of traffic along eight lines, bright as daylight.

A bit later he thought of a detail. "When we get to the hotel, you won't mind if we sign in under your name, do you?"

"Why, Jack? Modesty?"

"No, the Dragon Lady promised to find me and kill me for popping her meal ticket."

Xuē got herself settled. She put the wine between her knees, patted her dress in place, and unwrapped a canapés box from the basket. "I have a better idea. I use my older brother's credit card on special occasions. He's loaded—owns a motorcycle factory in Shanghai—and he doesn't mind."

"If his name is not Jack Gray or Sechen Xuē, we're both in luck."

"The credit card says 777 Motocross. That's his lucky corporate name." She grinned at him. "I could swear you planned that too, you snarky western devil." She shoved a little pumpernickel square into his mouth, loaded with crabby cream cheese, and topped with shark sushi. "Do we look like 777 Motocross?"

"Yummy," Jack said, taking an offered finger food. "Lucky family name. The Chinese will understand." He consulted the dashboard map computer. "If we take turns driving while the other dozes, we'll make Beijing in around five or six hours." According to his research online, it would be all freeway, speed limit 120 klicks an hour (72 mph) on cruise control, with no stops or tolls.

"So we made the world safe for dysprosium," Xuē said at one point as overhead lights flashed rapidly across her lovely features while she sat sideways facing Jack as the Porsche chewed up freeway miles. She began matter of factly to strip, pulling her beautiful cheongsam over her head.

"What are you doing?"

"Don't worry, I'm not going to embarrass you." Wearing only a modest pink bra and scant panties that revealed a lithe young citron body, she rummaged in a satchel. "I'm just changing into something comfy." She pulled worth a little blue jean skirt, a yellow T-shirt with a big banana embroidered on it, dripping with melted chocolate, along with the legend Hot Fudge, and warm, heavy cream-colored crew socks. "So now you know my big secret."

"What, that you have dysprosium hidden in your little boodle? Or that you are a size C girl cup?"

"No, silly, that I have an innie. I'll bet you do too."

"We'll compare later."

"Hit the road, Jack. Keep an eye peeled, or we crap out in a flaming explosion."

He grinned wryly. "You pack more drama than an action movie."

As she swiftly slid into her street clothes, she said: "We can feel good about ourselves, thinking about rare earths. We just saved the whole earth, rare or well-done."

"Good job, you and me. I can't wait to celebrate."

"We just moved the Dune clock back a few tricks."

"You mean the Doomsday clock a few ticks?"

She mock-bristled. "Allow me to be creative, okay? Keep your collar buttoned down and drive on Route 66."

"Dysprosium is one of those elements we just liberated, yes?" Jack asked.

"Right. That's a funny story. Yang was particularly trying to corner the world market in dysprosium, Atomic Number 66."

"Ah—you know more than you let on, little science student from Xanshi."

"I worked for Dragon Bitch, right?"

"So you are a secret agent, not just a translator?"

"I'm just a college student with a summer job. I had to sit in on those meetings where they talk about saving the world. I didn't actually get to save the world myself, until I met you."

"That's my job."

"Right, big boy. So you saved the dysprosium. Which is important stuff. So the irony is that this element got its name by a Parisian man who discovered it in 1886. In Greek, it means 'hard to get'. I figure maybe that old French dude was chasing some hard-to-get chick around at the time. His wurst was a lonely one."

Jack nodded pleasantly. "You're not going to be like that chick, are you? She must have been dismantling his heart one beat at a time."

"Not at all, Jack." Xuē put her harm around his shoulder and kissed him behind the ear. "I'm going to chase you around the hotel room when we reach Beijing. When I catch you, I'm going to lick your yo-yo."

"That's a relief," Jack said. He sighed and sat back. "Now I can enjoy the drive without being so anxious."

"You were anxious?" she said incredulously. "You gave me the same look you gave those chocolates and that wine. A hungry look, but the look of a man who knows where the bun is for his wurst."

He patted her thigh, all kidding aside. "I was worried about you, Chiquita. I'm just glad you are safe."

"Me too, for both of us." She curled up against him, with her head in his lap. She murmured in surprise: "That's a nice bump you have there. I'm gonna get some shut-eye. Don't wake me until we see the eyes of their whites."

"You're being creative again, huh?"

"Get used to me."

Jack said: "I see that you can be quite a handful."

"I come in handy at times."

"Are we at the hotel yet?"

"I can't wait either." She cupped her hand over him. "You really are the Wurst, Herr Kutt." She sighed happily as she rested her cheek against his throb.

Jack enjoyed the warmth of her touch. "We won't need to stop for coffee. My heart is beating fast enough already."

She murmured happily, half asleep, and gave her palm a twitch that made Jack blink.

The trip to Beijing was pleasantly boring. Jack drove for three hours. They changed seats, and he napped. Xuē took the wheel for the second half of the journey. He awoke as she was navigating into one of the world's biggest metropolitan sprawls.

They arrived at Beijing International Airport midway to dawn. They checked into a five star hotel on Xuē's brother's tab. Tired as he was, Jack had looked forward to this moment.

"You sure your brother won't mind?" asked Jack as they stood in the lobby, which seemed like ten acres of polished marble lost in a funhouse of mirror walls. House staff wore gray uniforms with various color hash marks for department designators. The hotel, with branches around the world, accepted all manner of credit services. To Jack, it was like already being in a suburb of San Diego. They did not take a bellman along, since they had very little luggage between them. Xuē held the wine bottle in both arms, as if it were their baby. Jack carried the food basket in one hand, like a proud parent.

"We'll shop and see the city over the weekend," Xuē said. "You fly out Sunday, and I'll take the train home. What a blast, dude!" On the elevator up, as they rode alone, she buried her face in his side, and ran a hot little hand up and down his back, from the knees to the waist.

In the room, they opened up the drapes to reveal a blaze of light all around—Beijing, city of over twenty million souls, and a modern world capital. The hotel was twenty stories tall, but dwarfed by giant corporate towers halfway to the horizon on all sides. Half of these were Chinese-owned, and half international, including enormous Bush Tower, topped by a Texas star, not far from Tienanmen Square. All the towers were crusted with flashing neons, running movies, lights chasing each other, even mile-long green and red laser beams, which formed crackling lines to the clouds above. The lights bounced amid the plate glass windows on both sides, and on marble and other shiny surfaces inside their suite.

While she puttered about, Jack made a sweep of the suite with his Kimber in hand and his senses alert for any sign of Dragon Lady or her slimy agents. The coast was clear, and he sat on the bed to give the gun a quick cleaning.

Xuē strutted delightedly about in a heavy white terry bathrobe with the hotel's logo on it. Not wanting to scare her (yet) in his birthday suit, Jack wore the same as he broke the gun apart and ran a few cleaning wicks through its bore. He dabbed at its lightly oiled surfaces with a dry hankie found in a glass engraved with the hotel's logo, until he could no longer feel residue grit.

"I'm tired but I want a bubble bath first," she declared as she paraded around, and the air began to smell warm and soapy.

"First things first," Jack said. He tucked the freshly cleaned gun under a pillow for instant retrieval if needed. It wasn't, and they had a great time together.

Jack appeared in the bathroom door holding the wine bottle, and watched her pour purple-grape *doucement* into the tub. "That thing is the size of a country pond," Jack said.

She winked. "Two fish can swim at once, baby."

He said. "I want to see you change from that robe into just soap bubbles."

"And I want to see you up your periscope, Commander."

"Let me open this Cabernet and I'll join you shortly."

"We will be very clean when we go home in two days," Xuē said as she splashed her hands among the suds. "We'll have fun snorkeling around in here."

"I may just decide to take you home with me, you look so cute."

"I talk too much. I can't cook to save my life."

"This evening, you are just what the doctor ordered."

He found a corkscrew in the main bedroom, and brought the open bottle with the two glasses from Baidu into the bathroom. Xuē was already drowsing under an overhead heat lamp, elbows up, with her compact, square toes poking out of the mass of bubbles. Her toenails were red.

"You must have put in a gallon of bubble bath," Jack said.

"The better to hide your submarine."

"Permission to come aboard," he said as he sat on the edge and dropped his bathrobe."

"Hairy chest," she said, wrinkling her face. She reached out to touch. "Not many Han Chinese men are hairy, like you Western apes," she told him. She delighted in pulling, twisting, patting, and petting his arms and chest. "Like hamsters," she said, giggling. But she was silent, and hungry, when they made love between fresh sheets a little later, amid the Blade Runner fire of the futuristic city.

He became intimately familiar with her stories, her family, her plans, and her finely wrought physicality over the next few days. They slept together one last time, Sunday afternoon. They were exhausted from days of making love, walking hand in hand through the city's shopping malls, and soaking in differently scented bubble baths at any time of day or night. They napped—fully dressed and cuddling—until a phone call from the lobby reminded them Jack's flight was due out in two hours. They rode down together, and parted with a lingering embrace and a long kiss in the train station.

"I hope you come to China again," she said. She had bought some U.S. bubblegum, and blew a pink balloon.

"I hope you'll come as well—to the U.S.A."

Xuē's gum exploded as she laughed. "Let's just come together, okay?"

He was acting whimsical, he knew. He did not want to part from her. At the same time, he knew that right now, in his life, nothing could work out, past pillows and bubbles.

"Be well." He gave her a last hug before she boarded her express train. "I'll send you a card."

"I hope we see each other again, Jack."

"I'll make a point next time I come to China."

She snuggled against him. "You save your point until I see you in San Diego some day soon."

"You can come study chemistry," he said. "I'll help you."

She sighed deeply and hugged him like a teddy bear. Then it was time to part company.

Xuē waved from the train window as she set off for home. Her family lived in the city of Datong, Shanxi Province, a few hundred miles north west of Beijing.

Jack rolled his suitcase onto the hydro-metro, which would speed him off to the Air China terminals for his flight to Los Angeles and an AmericAir hop to San Diego.

On the long flight, Jack sipped a cocktail or two, and read a digitized British spy novel from the 1950s—quaint historical fiction from a long ago, lost world. He dozed several times, dreaming of Xuē and bubble baths with periscopes—not to mention a tropical island, where a submarine could slip into a very, very snug harbor whose mermaid made sounds of pleasure. But he also thought of home, of the D Ranch, of his family there. He all but forgot the Dragon Lady, and her promise to find him and make him die for exxing out her sugar daddy.

Elsewhere in the world, a very different drama was just about to launch its first act, and suck into its tentacles the great powers whose economic powerhouses made the global engine go around. Where its train would stop, nobody knew—but one of the seats had a ticket on it, with Jack's name on it. Only, Jack didn't know it yet. And neither did Rector or Claire Lightfield.

Nightfall in Sicily

Villa Caproni

A milky-white Bombardier Learjet 95A from Montreal descended on a long, leisurely approach toward Sicily. Its long contrail graced azure Mediterranean skies.

Blue seas below sparkled amid whitecaps, while foamy wavelets ran onto sandy shores.

The plane had just one passenger on board—a nervous, middle-aged scientist named Louis Cartouche. He had invented a way to assassinate foreign heads of state with a sophisticated bullet shot downward from orbit.

The flight crew consisted of two pilots and two flight attendants, all in the employ of a vast corporation. Global Anaconda was about to offer Louis Cartouche a top-secret deal on his Orbital Sniper Technology (OST).

The system consisted of an orbital, death-dealing satellite, plus a control system on the ground. For personal security and negotiating reasons, Cartouche had cloned the ground control unit and formed two separate units that must work together from separate locations in order for the whole thing to work. He had named his two units for Castor and Pollux, the twins or Gemini of ancient Roman mythology.

To successfully deploy the orbital sniper system, both Castor and Pollux had to work in tandem with one another and with the orbiting satellite, Capricorn. Louis' idea was that you put Castor in one place—say in French Canada—and Pollux somewhere far from there—say in Europe. Together with the orbiting satellite, this would form a triangle of death. Louis hoped his invention would finally deliver financial wealth after years of struggle. Nevermind that he sensed Anaconda was over-confident and planned to operate the two units side by side at a small, secure facility in Montreal. It didn't matter to him what anyone did, as long as he got his money and could live a decent life from here on—maybe even become a family man, once he could afford to stop living hand to mouth.

Cartouche and Anaconda simply needed to sign some papers in Palermo first—a formality. Anaconda had already had the Castor twin in development in Montreal, under Louis' guidance, for two years. Now he would sign over the Pollux unit plans. He had a working Pollux unit in a secret laboratory in the basement of an old warehouse in Montreal—physically, it was a matter of Anaconda's movers trucking the Pollux unit a few miles from one location to another inside the city. When and if the papers were signed today, depending on how the negotiations went, the two units—Castor and Pollux—could be sitting in a secure Anaconda facility in Montreal's Technopolis by tomorrow. He imagined Anaconda's engineers would dismantle one of the units, and transfer all the capabilities to the other of the two. Having a single ground-based control unit would certainly simplify things. He'd designed the system to be complicated enough that Anaconda would not only need to buy Pollux from him, but the plans to remove the redundant, second capability (Pollux) as well.

Then it would be a matter of launching Capricorn, with the weapons on board, and Anaconda could deliver the death-dealing Project David into orbit. With its orbital sniper technology (OST), it could read the proverbial ground-based license plate or recognize a face from 200 miles up—as its Cold War ancestors Corona and Keyhole had done for the U.S. Air Force and the CIA, respectively—but more importantly, it could launch a deadly sniper bullet to kill the world's next Hitler or Saddam Hussein—or any other person of disinterest that Anaconda's paying customers happened to choose. It would be a lucrative product line.

Furthermore, Anaconda already had at its disposal the satellite technologies to launch OST Capricorn on its deadly missions, with a brace of waiting bullets (each the size of a submarine torpedo, but light-weight ceramic).

Louis felt he had nothing left to lose. He knew he was a helpless fool, riding a tiger. He was negotiating with a ruthless global corporate consortium. He would not take the unspoken threat of their vast power and merciless profit motive lightly. Corponations ruled the world, and Anaconda was the second most powerful consortium on earth, behind only its arch-rival, Camelback Consortium.

The new-model, twelve-passenger Canadian jet—shaped like a dagger with swept-back wings—was just finishing its long but comfortable flight, high above cyclonic autumn storms ravaging the North Atlantic.

The aircraft had skirted the weather by refueling at Gander, Newfoundland, and then Shannon, Ireland. The late model, twelve-seat plane flew below the edge of outer space. Under black night and calm stars, she was a glowing dot. She moved like a comet, and left a long white contrail in the atmosphere.

Louis Cartouche felt as if he were looking down into his own acid stomach and frightened thoughts. Far below whirled an early autumn North Atlantic storm. He watched as the storm ripped Iceland with Force-3 cyclonic fury. The storm's eastern edge, spinning like a giant, toothy circular saw, pushed rains and floods against the Netherlands and into northern Europe.

By contrast, the journey's southern leg seemed balmy and idyllic, as the aircraft descended into the Mediterranean, down the leg of Italy. Most men would have visions of bathing suit, snorkeling, soothing music, and a sparkling red Campari-and-soda on the beach. The world's most beautiful women would strut their bikinis at the intersection of sun, sand, and sea.

But the sole traveler on board Flight CAIT-7634 was too desperate and serious a man for such diversions. The aging, nervous inventor wore a dark suit that did not fit him well. Monsieur Louis Cartouche, age 45, was ABD-Mechanical Engineering. This meant All But Dissertation for Ph.D., a status to which he knew he'd never rise. It was not a degree, but a nebulous status like holding one's breath—and he had turned blue years ago.

He looked totally out of place in the luxury business jet. His shock of graying hair rose around his head like a thunder cloud in need of lightning—or combing, or both. He clutched his fists together between his thighs as he gazed through the small porthole. The Italian peninsula passed to the east, on his left, as he pressed his cheek against the port side window.

Louis Cartouche was a quiet, mousy man who had spent most of his life inventing deadly gadgets while on the run from the law. He'd spent his years to date huddling, so to speak, at corporate back doors for his next meal because no legitimate university would fund his research. The OST was his first viable after many failed inventions.

The next few hours would make or break his life. It all seemed like a dream just now.

Those next few hours would likely also change the course of world history.

Wars like the U.S. adventure in Iraq could presumably be avoided if one could simply assassinate a gangster like Saddam Hussein with a bullet from 165 miles (264 km) up in Low Earth Orbit (LEO).

Louis had conceived of his idea as a student and loner, clutching a mug of Labatt in a Montreal tavern, and angry at the world like many a 19-year-old. Now, over thirty years later, his dreams and sacrifices were about to become a functioning reality.

He would become a wealthy man—or a dead one.

In the right hands—like Global Anaconda's—the world would be forever safe from megalomaniacs whose few frothy apothecary grains of testosterone regularly caused great storms or wars that tore the fabric of history, dislocated economies, and murdered tens of millions of innocent people.

In the wrong hands—Louis could not begin to imagine the downside if the wrong element got hold of his Orbital Sniper Technology.

The Learjet streaked along, on approach toward Sicily.

The largest island in the Mediterranean, situated at the bull's eye of history, Sicily was a triangular football that had been kicked around by the peninsular boot of Italy since time immemorial.

Speaking of soccer—Cartouche was not a man of many luxuries or pleasures. He did, however, avidly follow the world's leading sport—*futbol*, or soccer. For many disgruntled persons and peoples around the world, soccer was the one level playing field on which a Third World nation with primo runners and kickers could defeat teams fielded by the corporate monsters who now bestrode the dinosaur swamps of history, with their vestigial nation-partners running by their feet.

Louis head a soft leakage of Brazilian soccer stadium cheers from the cockpit and found it quite soothing—like sweet cream pouring into fine coffee—along with announcer commentary in German and Arabic.

Palermo had one of the strongest soccer teams in Italy this year. From the cockpit on the Bombardier flowed a steady play by play of a FIFA World Cup playoff game just then playing in Rio de Janeiro.

The pilots, both Egyptians, cheered. They high-fived at each goal. Frankfurt was taking a beating from Cairo in a tightly fought match, 12-6.

A Palermo announcer in blunted Sicilian Italian added his excited commentary to the global, Third Millennium flavor of the moment. Whoever won in Rio would play Palermo next week in London.

For the first time, the failed engineer and dead-end doctoral candidate had something of value to offer to a rich and willing buyer. Not being a gambler, he did not enjoy the game of negotiations. This luxury flight gave him, even if for a few hours, a taste of the rich life, and he knew he'd enjoy more of that. He was starved for it. He simply must not appear desperate as he met for the final negotiation with Anaconda's agents in Palermo. That made his palms very sweaty, indeed, and his palate very parched with thirst.

An attractive young Asian flight attendant in immaculate dark blue uniform—a color hard to keep spotless, but she managed, along with sharp creases—brought Cartouche the tea he had requested. She smiled accommodatingly as she set a tiny glass of pinkish-white mirabel brandy beside it. It was his third drink on the long flight. He had hardly slept for all of his anxiety.

Cartouche's gray-blue eyes reflected the twin emotions of a man licking his lips over the business deal of a lifetime, as well as the acid-gut terror of a third string poker player about to bet his stack while knowing he was out of his league in a first-class, major casino game.

Cartouche decided that, if he failed, he would jump to his death from the Eiffel Tower, or perhaps the Arc de Triomphe. He hoped it would not come to that. Money would buy him the two things he craved most—a good woman, and a sense of accomplishment. Both had eluded him in his 45 years to date. The new money would make his heart's wishes possible at last.

The jet whistled softly to a landing at Punta Raisi International Airport (PMO), one of Italy's busiest. It lies outside Palermo, capital of the autonomous region of Sicily.

Cartouche watched from his window in the jet. A red guide jeep with twirling orange roof light shunted the throbbing jet to a private, corporate terminal directly overlooking the blue Mediterranean. Light wind ruffled tall palm trees on a nearby beach, amid colorful umbrellas. Fingernails of surf crinkled on a beach that seemed made of light brown sugar.

The main hull door opened, pushed by a flight attendant's delicate hand and blue-uniformed arm with white silken cuff.

A young man with short, curly black hair sat casually waiting below, having driven a motorized stairway to the plane. The youth's rumpled white shirt and airport epaulets contrasted with his dark tan and open shirt collar.

Louis and the flight attendant walked down those stairs. It felt good to stretch one's legs.

The young man in the orange ladder-tow motor rattled off on a black gout of diesel exhaust for his next deplaning, as it was called with industrial, saw-blade harshness.

The stewardess signaled. From a shady spot under trees, a black SUV slowly peeled loose and flowed across the blistering concrete. Its driver had been killing time near the electrified fence, which was part of the local corporate world's defense against criminal elements. There were, as well, regular patrols outside the fence, by corporate, uniformed paramilitaries with assault rifles and dogs.

The SUV pulled up, and a gorgeous Italian flight attendant stepped out of nowhere. She wore a crisp black uniform with jaunty cap. She held open the car's rear door for Cartouche. "Welcome to Palermo," she said brightly. "We will await your return for the flight home, Signore."

"*Merci*," he said instinctively, although he had meant to say thank you in English, the world's international language. On impulse, he said in his minimal Italian: "*Grazie*."

"*Per favore*," the Italian woman said. Her voice was smooth as a forty-euro glass of the finest red wine, served at a five star restaurant. Anaconda knew how to lay it on thick, and Louis loved it. Both women bowed their heads. If this was how his life would be with corporate money, he wanted more of it.

Inside the car, he felt himself sucked into luxury amid plush leather seats with all the buoyancy of air cushions. Instead of cheap, sticky plastic, these were form-fitting black leather seats anchored with black velvet buttons. Their leather fragrance filled the interior, as did the continuing stream of soccer coverage. The driver, a black man in a chauffeur suit, said in a mellifluous accent: "Welcome to Palermo, Monsieur Cartouche. My name is Pino. I am Nigerian, with all the proper legal papers and a commercial license. Please let me know if you need anything during our drive. We will be at the Villa Caproni in about thirty minutes. There are drinks and crisps in the bar before you. I believe you call them potato chips."

"Thank you, Pino. In French Canada, we call them *croustilles*.

"Crew-tee," Pino politely echoed. "*Oui, monsieur*."

"Well done, Pino. I'll just have some ice water, thank you." He made a point of being kind and polite to hired help, unlike the way he had often been treated. It was appreciated, too. Pino did not respond, but Louis could see he was pleased, by the crinkles around his eyes and his slight smile seen in the rear-view mirror.

Cartouche's mouth felt parched again. His fingers shook slightly as he took a thick crystal glass from a stainless steel holding shelf. Fresh ice cubes twinkled in a ceramic pot with a mahogany cover. He scooped up a half glassful, and filled it from a filtered-water spigot.

The Nigerian drove safely and slowly, as if he wished to avoid disturbing the gravelly roads that could pepper his precious car with tiny scratches and dings. From the crowded streets of the city, through sleepy suburbs where half-naked children ran in the streets, the car reentered a lush green coastal district in the foothills of Monte Pellegrino. The roads leading in to the wealthy suburb were guarded by stone lions and hidden paramilitaries. One was as likely to see a rubber-tired wagon pulled by a donkey, and laden with canisters of olive oil, as a passing gasoline truck still bearing the ancient Esso name, or a modern De Tomaso Qvale Mangusta purring by like an exotic blossom leaving a dust cloud.

"The Villa Caproni is just ahead," the driver Pino said.

Cartouche knocked back his third glass of water, and his fourth finger of brandy of the day, and sat back in the luxurious ebony seat leather.

The car entered the Porta Capronese along the Sea Street—a gate through high brick walls in the ancient Traianic style. The walls were smothered in ivy, from whose green profusion peered Berber and Norman *cefalue*—carved heads, from the ancient Greek *kephalos*. Along the tops of the walls stood garlanded Greek and Roman style vases of aloes and miniature feather palms. Ivies hung everywhere in redundant profusion.

The car stopped by a tall central fountain in a paved courtyard. The house was Late Palladian, in the 18th Century Jeffersonian style, with a central rotunda of clean round lines, topped by a domed, round-beveled roof like a whorl of creamy meringue.

Pino remained in the car, while several tough-looking young men of the ubiquitous Mediterranean phenotype—dark hair, olive skin, Caucasian features with aquiline nose and expressive mouth—stepped from an ogived portal to welcome their guest. The young men were all former Carabinieri, who were parachute and karate-trained, packing discreet Mannlicher-Carcano automatics in shoulder holsters. They wore sharply tailored charcoal suits, pointed shoes of fine leather, and white silk shirts with dark blue silk kerchiefs. One opened the door, while the other two bowed slightly from the waist.

Louis stepped out, so wobbly on his legs that two of the young men hurried to steady him by his elbows. He looked lost, in his oversized suit, which he had borrowed from a neighbor—a beer truck driver half a head taller than he—in Longueuil, Greater Montreal. They ushered their guest into the cool interior of the mansion.

Inside, Cartouche's eyes accustomed themselves to a marbled gloom, in which arose minutely detailed statuary with gilded fingernails, rouged cherubic lips, and improbably sky-blue eyes on glazed skin. The statues all fit together as if in frozen Baroque choral song. Their eyes turned toward heaven. Their tiny hands were piously folded.

Amid the whispering central foyer arose a carved spiral staircase, whose rosewood and pine still breathed a faint, residual essence from long ago into the cool air.

"The committee are waiting for you upstairs," said one of the hard young men, as he gestured with a fight-calloused palm toward the empty stairway.

Louis screwed up his courage, and started ascending to meet his fate.

Outside, Pino drove the Lincoln Navigator carefully in a circle around the fountain, and down a gravel path that ran along the ivied wall. He had a vague sense that unseen eyes were upon him, maybe malevolent garden spirits, but he pushed their dark touch away from his thoughts. It was too lovely a day to think of *alusi* spirits. He turned on the radio, which poured out a rich tapestry of music on multiple speakers and full range. The disk playing was his own, from the Top 40 of his homeland. The song was The Look of Love, a terakota remake by native African artists of the old Brasil 66 hit. One of those tunes, Pino thought, that will be remade again and again, for as long as man and woman fall in love on this earth.

The path was cool with the overhead shade of a row of ancient olive trees. In about two minutes, he came to an asphalt plaza coated in windblown dust from Africa. The plaza was about twenty meters (60 feet) in diameter, perfectly round as if carved with a pastry knife along its edges. On one side was the brick wall, then clockwise a semicircle of identical garage doors under red tile roofs, and, at five o'clock to Pino's right, a round waiting area with wooden benches around a gravel circle.

As Pino pulled in, he looked at his watch. There were rules for everything, and Pino himself was a stickler. He turned off the radio, having fastidiously sampled its luxury, but not wanting to overdo it. He was expected back in one hour, so he would not need to garage the car. He pulled up at a corner with water, soap, and mild brushes, where drivers could wash their cars. He soaped his prize, scrubbed her gently, and rinsed her off. Nearby at the edge of the tarmac was a shady drying spot, where the sun could not make shadowy photo-imprints of dying bubbles, and where an ever-active sirocco wind would dry the car in minutes like a warm hair dryer. Satisfied, Pino walked toward the little park, while extracting a pack of filtered *Gitanes-blondes*.

He stepped through a grapevine bower into the little park, which was a waiting area for drivers. A *Gitane* (gypsy woman) cigarette stuck stiffly from his lips, waiting for a light. Gravel crunched under his hard leather soles as he sought a cool place to sit—one of several wooden park benches provided for drivers. Pino brushed it carefully, to make sure it would not dust up his freshly dry-cleaned suit. Then he sat down, a fastidious man.

The park was shielded on all sides by thorn and brush cherry thickets. He heard bees nuzzling about. Further on, in its mysterious depths, shadowy statuary loomed under blackish olive tree crowns. Pino lit his cigarette with a gilded Zippo, which made a satisfying click as he put it in his suit pocket. The air filled around him with the first blue smoke of a fresh light that is magic to smokers, as the first phantoms of opium are to an addict. Wishing he had a radio or a drink out here, Pino tapped his foot to a remembered tune in the classic *terakota* reggae beat. He sat staring at the entrancing blue-black-white image of a flamenco-style gypsy woman dancing amid smoke with a tambourine.

Pino did not notice the dark shadow that crept close behind him on spirit feet.

Pino kept puffing; kept tapping his foot. He sat with his left hand gripped on the edge of the bench, and his right hand near his face with the cigarette.

A piano wire garrote silently stretched from one very dark hand to another behind Pino.

Pino thought of an African girl he liked in Palermo, named Efioanwan. She liked him, and he could imagine her in bed with him. He held her, as night closed around them, and she reached for him with a look of passion in her happy eyes and dazed face.

Dark hands crept from the brush like snakes, their fingers clawed for a strike.

No sooner did Pino hold his right hand away from his mouth, to flick ash carefully on the gravel by his feet, than the garrote flew over Pino's head. He had no time to react. He felt the swish of wind down his face, and heard the taut twang as it fastened on his neck. He felt the pressure of rock-hard fists on either side of his neck, as well as the edges of the device's wooden handles pressing on his arteries. In seconds, Pino blacked out, still with the vision of Efi reaching toward him.

Lucky Pino—his last look was the one of love.

On the second story of the Villa Caproni, one of the men-in-black escorts ushered Louis Cartouche into a cool meeting hall. This room contained an ornately carved oak table and a dozen matching chairs, one at each end, and five on each long flank. Louis had parted with his ice waters in a lavishly marbled upstairs lavatory. His lips were dry, and was ready for more water—more to settle his nervousness than to quench any thirst.

"Come in, Monsieur Cartouche. We have been expecting you," said man with a strangely accented voice. It took Louis a few moments to realize that the speaker was not present in the room, unlike several underlings. The speaker appeared on a large format television screen of the type used in long-distance teleconferencing via satellite relays.

Marvels of technology! The voice sounded as if the man were in the room, but of course he was far away somewhere. Flanked by a half dozen or so real-life men and women in formal business suits, the image on the screen was of a balding man with florid face and wilting wheat-colored suit at some distant, sunny location. Three men and two women rose briefly, as one of the escorts seated Cartouche and then left.

"Thank you for having me," said Cartouche, taking a seat.

"My name is George Blechstein," said the man on the conference screen at the head of the table. Louis rolled through his memories of foreign accents until he figured out that his host spoke in Dutch Afrikaans, that South African English accented with strongly rolling r's. "My esteemed associates present here, all with Global Anaconda, are..." and he introduced his half dozen colleagues, who only filled a third of the long table. The room was otherwise empty except for a large wall map—a Mercator projection of the planet Earth.

Each person reached out to shake Cartouche's hand. The two women sat on either side of him, one a fresh-faced blonde named Mademoiselle Tissy from Brussels, the other a dour, older businesswoman named Frau Eiswarzen from Berlin. The men represented peoples from around the world—Spanish, Italian, Chinese, and more. The Spaniard made sure Cartouche understood he was Basque, while the Italian was a separatist from Milan, and an Asian man identified himself as native Formosan.

Blechstein droned on: "In our little subculture within Global Anaconda, we all represent dispossessed or disenfranchised cultures, as do you do, Mr. Cartouche, coming from the Quebec nation. We welcome you. A seventh guest had hoped to join us today—Dr. James Steward of Atlanta, Georgia—but he regrettably has been detained by business matters at home. The Confederate States of America are nonetheless well represented in our covert company, which is a tiny subsidiary among Global Anaconda's myriad coils. You are giving us a powerful tool that interests our company leadership, for which we will reward you quite handsomely. Our task force related to your invention is called Project David, Mr. Cartouche, and we shun publicity. That recalls the Biblical story of David, with his slingshot bringing down the giant Goliath."

Cartouche sipped from a half-full glass of bottled water. In modern parlance, a company was a wholly owned subsidiary of a corporation, which was an independent legal entity. A consortium, of which the world had at most one thousand, was a combined governmental and corporate giant with its own passports and euphemistically named security forces. If the traditional corporation was a fictitious person in the law, then a consortium (or corponation) was a fictitious nation. One still spoke of nation states as a convenient handle. In practical terms, global corporate power had made nation states obsolete.

"Can we offer you anything more?" asked Blechstein. "A nice brandy perhaps, or an espresso?"

"I'm fine," Cartouche said. "Thank you. I had some brandy on the plane. If I have another, I'm afraid I may fall asleep."

Everyone laughed politely.

"We like to meet our business partners in person," said Blechstein. "Thank you for indulging us during your long plane trip. I trust everything went well?"

Cartouche grinned nervously. "Yes—how could it not, with Frankfurt 2 and Cairo 14 in the last minute of play?"

Light laughter and applause rippled around the table. Louis felt he was making a good impression.

"We all await Cairo's upcoming victory in London later this week," Blechstein said. "A man after my heart." He seamlessly changed topics. "Our Quebec bureau has communicated that you shared some enticing preliminary plans with them about two years ago, from which Anaconda engineers, with your guidance in Montreal, have now developed a full scale model."

"Yes," Cartouche said. He broke into a sweat so intense it was nearly painful. Yes, he was paranoid. He admitted it to himself. His life's work was riding on it. And he was sick unto death of being abused, ignored, and humiliated, being treated like a vagrant who had to practically beg for his meals while lesser, stupider men bereft of original ideas lived in palaces and dined on caviar. No matter what the implications, moral or otherwise, Louis knew he could not endure any more of that life. Here was his only chance to possess money, power, and satisfaction.

The Pollux twin, resembling the orbiting Capricorn itself, was in a Montreal warehouse. Louis had copied the designs from old Keyhole and Corona models now kept in the Smithsonian Museum in Washington, D.C. As soon as they made his money over to him, he would hand them the keys to Pollux. Let the game begin.

"Mr. Cartouche, are you are ready then to sign today, so that we can move on with your first full payment, and our first production model?"

"Yes, if the terms are as I had suggested to me. That would be quite appropriate."

"No problem at all," said Blechstein. He—or his image—could be seen looking through some charts and drawings on a portable digital work desk. Louis recognized the new 24" digital tablepad made by Global

Anaconda's wholly owned subsidiary Macrohard. Blechstein looked entirely relaxed and businesslike. After the chaos and economic catastrophe at the end of the nationalist era, the world corponational order was refreshingly efficient and beneficial—as long as one did not cross their bottom line.

Louis said: "If we sign today, I am prepared to hand over Pollux and its plans. I will join you in he operational coordination of the combined, tandem Castor and Pollux control system."

"Bravo," said Blechstein, who then read from his pad at a fast and somewhat blurry pace (no matter; Cartouche had already read a draft while still home in Montreal): "We propose to pay you half a million dollars U.S. per year, for rest of your natural life, in return for the entire, all, and unencumbered rights and your complete, unconditional, and eternal release to us, of all central, tangent, subsidiary, and peripheral plans, images, patents, copyrights, trademarks, tradenames, and trade signs, pertaining to your proprietary invention, blah blah blah, called hereafter the Orbital Sniper Technology, or OST. The sum of one million Euros annually will be deposited into a bona fide territorial bank account of your choosing. Furthermore, we propose to pay you another half million dollars U.S. per annum for your services as a consultant, at your home in Montreal, with all the staff you need for personal comfort and to accomplish your job as an employee of Anaconda."

Blechstein looked up as if needing oxygen. He regarded Louis as if Cartouche were a tedious individual who had hopefully heard enough to be satisfied.

"I agree," Cartouche said. He felt bathed in happiness—and in relief, since his lifetime of poverty and struggle appeared to be finally over now. He loved the terms as presented to him here. He felt so warm and gushy, he nearly peed with all that water inside of him. Automatically, he reached for a fresh bottle from among those in the center of the conference table, but his hand shook severely. The pretty blonde on his left heaved her shapely form, in a classic little black dress, and poured a fresh glass for him. He noticed—as she leaned across the table directly before him to reach for his bottle—that she wore a pink bubblegum-colored thong under the dress. She was so close that he could see the weave in her fine cloth, and smell faint essences of perfume and sweat in the natural folds of her perfectly taut young body. Cartouche understood that Global Anaconda, in its supreme skills at manipulation, had posted a sensuous daughter figure at his left, and a strong matron at his right.

The agreement was quickly reached. Guided by the men and women at the table, Louis signed for an electronic bank draft for half a million dollars at the table, with fingers so cold from excitement and fright that they were numb and nearly immobile. "Take your time, Sir," whispered the Belgian doll at his left ear. An unmarried man, who rarely dated, Cartouche would have loved to roll blissfully toward her, take her in his arms, and let her kisses descend on him as he closed his eyes. This moment was the fulfillment of a lifetime of dreams. He felt nearly orgasmic. He had been suffering for so long, and so lonely, that he was ready to throw his life to the winds in exchange for one passionate hug and kiss with her. He was taking the chance of a lifetime. He was throwing everything to the winds and hoping for the best.

As they finished the deal, Cartouche felt drained, exhausted, and pleased beyond measure.

"Thank you, Monsieur Cartouche," Blechstein intoned. "Your technology, the OST, is extremely powerful. It sounds scary and it is. We intend to do as we have done for many years—offer it to responsible partners for good purposes. Just think, Cartouche. Nation states are a pale imitation of their former selves, and how else would we rid the world of any more Saddams or Kim Jong Ils if they rose to power? The answer does not lie in gratuitous wars that inflict untold carnage on innocent millions, while the usual predators profiteer. Instead, we now have an advanced tool for nipping the problem in the bud by assassinating the typical dictator secretly, from outer space, with no political or judicial repercussions. You are giving the world a wonderful gift."

Cartouche grew animated. "That was my very premise from the beginning. I thought: what if a responsible consortium, in the spirit of maintaining commerce and order, were to obtain a secret injunction declaring war, just long enough to eliminate the scourge of a Milosevic or a Kim Dong Ill, and then close the books as if nothing happened? The world goes on, corponations thrive, people have jobs, and all's well that ends well."

Blechstein nodded. "Machiavelli meets Morality. My kind of man. Pragmatism wins."

"Whatever works," Louis said. He was tired, and didn't care what they did, as long as he got paid.

"The world will thank you one day soon," said Blechstein. "You, Monsieur Cartouche, will be a famous man forever in the history books." The screen went blank, signaling that the meeting was over. The men shook hands.

Valley of the Temples

As Louis stepped outside, those same imposing young Sicilian men accompanied him. On cue, the same black SUV rolled slowly around the fountain and stopped to load up Louis Cartouche for the return ride to Palermo, and a flight on that Bombardier Learjet that would have him back home in *Quebec-Nation* by tomorrow.

During a silent ride of twenty minutes, something odd began to strike Louis. He caught glimpses of the driver when the car was aimed just right, turning on tight street corners so the full sunlight beam in with X-Ray invasiveness. Sunbeams penetrated the murky front cockpit of the car, not unlike how surface light penetrated the lost world of Roman forums and villas sunken in the Bay of Naples millennia ago. The man was not the same as Pino, who had brought him here. Or was it an illusion? As the car flowed through the estate's main gate, Cartouche peered closely through a smoky glass bullet-shield that had not been there before. The driver's silhouette was stockier, and the head rounder, than Pino's had been. Louis could not become any more nervous than he'd already been all day, so he sat still and counted his own throbbing heart beats.

At the airport in Punta Raisi, the SUV did not turn right as expected, toward the corporate terminal where the Bombardier-Learjet stood waiting.

Instead, it turned left and headed toward a peripheral commuter terminal catering to local and regional flights around Sicily. It was now clear: he was being abducted. Being abducted was a common, frightening, and often deadly adventure in southern Italy. He pounded his fist on the bullet-proof glass until it hurt, but the Asian-looking driver did not respond. Cartouche nursed his sore fist, and sat helplessly back. The door locks would not open, or he might have thrown himself onto the street and asked for police assistance.

The SUV turned and entered a peripheral air strip. This had its own small control tower, no doubt networked with Punta Raisi's radars and main tower. For several minutes, the SUV cruised along rust- and fuel-stained tarmacs glistening with puddles from a recent coastal downpour. Along the runways were parked all manner of sporting and aeronautical acrobatic single engine planes in sporting colors, as well as twin-engine propeller cargo planes, and a few smaller corporate jets. The SUV rolled to a stop in a parking spot beside the tower and the field's only hangar.

Men in paramilitary camouflage surrounded the car. They wore ski caps rolled down over their faces, and peered through eye holes. They brandished compact, matte black Czech-made ČZW-438 caliber submachine guns—high performance caliber with massive stopping power, capable of shredding body armor. Cartouche, from his understanding as an armorer, estimated that whoever was employing these men possessed wealth, sophistication, and purpose at least as focused and capable as Global Anaconda's. Could it be Anaconda's No. 1 rival, Camelback Consortium, the world's largest corponation?

His anonymous guards ushered him to a small HA-420 HondaJet, capable of seating just five passengers. Louis and one powerful looking Korean guard were the only travelers on this flight, along with two pilots who might also be Korean. At roughly 40x40 (wingspan x length), the plane had a range of 1,400 nautical miles, and a service velocity just over 300 knots true airspeed.

The Korean did not converse, nor did he need to, if he even spoke French or English. He wore a dark blue blazer, gray trousers, and sturdy black Doc Martens boots over rugged looking charcoal crew socks. The Korean sat hunched a bit, with his raw-knuckled fists linked between resting knees, like a man who wished he were in a larger aircraft. As his jacket fell slightly open, the grip of a 9mm commando Glock signaled not to mess around. The Korean tried to smile. He raised and lowered his hand, palm down, in calming gestures.

Nor did Cartouche want to mess around. By his calculations, nobody could physically take the half million from him that he had just signed into his Montreal bank account. This was clearly a kidnapping, but there was no sign of desperation or violence. Instead, Cartouche caught a heady whiff of competition in the air, and decided to sit back and relax. Maybe he could find yet a better deal than that he'd just signed. After all, the plans for Pollux were still in a Montreal bank vault in his name. Anaconda had Castor, but not yet Pollux. It would take them several hours to send an armed convoy to take possession of the Pollux subsystem—the size of a small car, and shaped like a cross between a torpedo and a satellite. Emboldened by both his ridiculous gamble today, and his heady near-orgasmic joy, Louis speculated hysterically on the riches yet to be farmed from these greedy bastards. He was a misunderstood genius who would go down in the history books as a great man—as Blechstein had said—and most of these people were, after all, stupid in comparison with him. Greed and ruthlessness were their parameters, whereas lofty mathematics and impeccable engineering were Louis Cartouche's standards of operation.

The jet took off over Sicily. It stayed below its service ceiling of 43,000 feet as it slammed along at a comfortable 200 knots at half a mile altitude. The aircraft streaked over inland hills. It left its contrail across powder-blue skies. Below lay fields that had been under the plow since long before Homer's weapon-bristling warships had sailed the wine-dark sea of immortal poetry in the late Bronze Age.

A short time later, a bell in the cabin dinged softly. One of the pilots, with a sense of humor, leaned just far enough so his face showed, and said: "Prepare for landing. All cigars and other smoking materials must be extinguished. Keep your seat belt fastened or that gorilla will break your arm. We are landing in Agrigento in just ten minutes."

The gorilla gave a friendly smile, and Cartouche smiled back. What was the old saying? You catch more flies with honey than with vinegar. The gorilla was trying to smile sweetly out of a scarred, battered face.

Outside, a cloud deck flitted by. Beyond it, he could see the broad expanse of the Mediterranean ahead. Another 131 miles, and they could land in Africa—in Tunisia, to be precise, site of Rome's enemy Carthage. *Cartago delenda est,* said the arch-conservative Roman statesman Cato the Censor after every speech in the Comitium and in the Senate, some 2,200 years ago. Sure enough, invading Roman armies, wishing to finish the job after having destroyed Hannibal two generations earlier, did exactly that: Carthage was indeed annihilated. Roman forces leveled the ancient Phoenician colony, killed its men, sent women and children into slavery, and were said to have plowed salt into the ground so nothing would ever grow there again. Now that was how you destroyed a place, Cartouche reflected. Or you just shot its leading citizen from orbit with a sniper rifle, and avoided all further unpleasantness in an effective and world-changing way. *Hannibal delendus est,* might have been the simpler answer. Hannibal must be destroyed, and that would have avoided the Second Punic War that changed history.

Whoever his kidnapers were, however—their business with him lay not in Africa but right here in Sicily.

They weren't following the typical playbook of a great corponation like Camelback Consortium or Global Anaconda. They were not the Mafia; of that, he was already sure. Then who were they?

The Hondajet whispered toward the ancient city of Agrigento on the southern edge of the largest island in the Mediterranean. Greek colonists had founded Akragas (High Place) around 600 BCE, along a high ridge offering a good fortified position for the indigenous Sicel people. In coming centuries, as conquering Romans drove Carthaginian and Greek forces from Sicily, they Latinized the name from Akragas to Agrigentum.

Today, under its modern Italian name, Agrigento was home to a haunting archeological site and tourist venue, called the Valley of the Temples.

In Agrigento, the jet landed, and a small cavalcade of black SUVs carried Louis to an as yet undisclosed location.

A small fleet of U.S.-made SUVs left twin trails of dust in the air as they tooled along a country road out of Agrigento. In the back seat were Cartouche and his giant Korean bodyguard, who still made calming gestures and tried to smile.

To the ancient Greeks who first colonized Sicily, and drove its native Sicels inland, Sicily was a promised land of wine and plenty, a *Megale Hellas* (Greater Greece). It was, to the ancient Greeks, the equivalent of those promising Off-World Colonies in the 1982 movie classic *Blade Runner*. "Come to the offworld colonies for a better new life..." the ancient Greeks told their eager settlers as they left on sailing ships for this new world. Sicily and southern Italy were advertised to would-be colonists in the Greek homeland as Oenotria, Land of Wine, much as the Vikings would speak of a wonderful western land called Vineland, over a millennium later.

In classical Mediterranean style, Sicily is famous for its tuna and sardines. Its agricultural produce includes lemons, oranges, olives, olive oil, almonds, grapes, wine, pistachios, and herd animals. Its most famous wine is the Marsala, a classic fortified wine as sweet, potent, and richly moody as its Iberian cousins in Oporto ('port') and Jerez de la Frontera ('sherry'). Like its cousins, Marsala lies on the lips of Europe, but revels in the kiss of Africa as the sirocco blows in over the narrow Tunisian neck of the central Mediterranean Sea.

According to road signs in English and Italian, which Louis followed with eager eyes, this area contained a World Heritage site called the Valley of the Temples. Cartouche saw the passing ruins of a half dozen great Doric temples and tall statues, and many smaller structures, from the ancient Greek and Roman ages of Sicily's rich heritage. Each of the great temples was unique, a ghostly memory of its own period and milieu, and preserved from natural and human abuse.

These silent ruins, sweltering in a bloody egg yolk Mediterranean sunset, silently spoke of a magnificent and long-ago age. Civilizations had come and gone, wars had left their blood and gore and ghosts in the rich loam, but the countryside remained fertile. Phoenician traders, Carthaginian sailors, Greek tyrants, Roman consuls, Arab and Berber emirs, Norman barons, Renaissance cardinals, modern kings and presidents had filled the air with their bluster, and then vanished as if they never existed. Popes, bishops, and abbots had pontificated over this land, as had animist shamans, polytheistic priestesses, mystery cults, Islamic imams and muezzins, Turkish viziers, Byzantine metropolitans, and modern-day movie directors.

Sicily was so ancient that ancient Rome was a new child by comparison.

Nations and peoples came and went, kingdoms and empires crumbled into dust, armies spilled blood without their soldiers' or even their generals' names being remembered, but Sicily endures, along with the people diligently tilling its soil.

Louis Cartouche was a man outside history, wanted by no nation, himself the son of an independent French-Canadian nation-state that might or might not one day finally be independent, teetering between nationhood and oblivion like so many other ethnic blood-soil shadows Blechstein had mentioned back at the Villa Caproni—among them Scotland, Ireland, Kurdistan, and many others.

Louis Cartouche felt dazed and numbed by the twists and turns of what had become the most scary and amazing day in his life. Anything was possible, it seemed. He felt drunk with the evening sun-liquor of this enchanted place. He understood that finally, for the only time in his life, during this brief moment, he might touch the pulse of history. After a lifetime of being shunned, his powerful and terrifying invention might influence the course of human events. But now some unknown group of Sicilian assassins and Korean *dojunim* had kidnapped him—to what end?

Dr. Night

After a long drive on dusty roads, the SUV caravan entered a small, prosperous looking town in the region of Agrigento. The black cars traveled along paved roads and drowsy villages, among sunset fields full of hard-working peasants, and finally swung into a driveway.

Louis Cartouche, looking up from behind tinted windows, saw a luxurious looking, stuccoed villa with finely made, white-framed windows. Its common Italian sun awnings were of fresh canvas dyed a rich merlot. Several brawny Asian men in black suit trousers and white shirts, with crossed suspenders, sat playing cards at a table on a front lawn patio. The estate was surrounded by an innocuous wrought-iron fence garlanded with grape vines. Everything looked peaceful, except, Cartouche assumed, the men's assault rifles were probably hidden near their feet in case of unwelcome guests. Two other Asians with binoculars kept watch—one at each end of the estate along several hundred feet of street front—atop a high concrete wall that could stop a main battle tank.

The rest of the black cars peeled off and disappeared on a side road. Louis' SUV rolled down a driveway. Above, he saw the doorway had a strange figure on it: a complex and symmetrical bronze ellipse with snakes and leaves all around, and in the middle a hideous face with its mouth open and its tongue hanging out. This figure was a *Gorgoneion*, from the Greek for *gorgos*, meaning 'dreadful', as in Medusa and her sisters. The Gorgons were a somewhat different matter—female demons with hissing, wriggling serpents instead of hair. They possessed a hideous, potent beauty that turned to stone anyone who gazed at them.

A steel garage door rolled up, and the vehicle cruised into a concrete underground garage under fluorescent lighting. Several Korean and Berber guards in dark camo fatigues ushered Cartouche into an elevator. The men wore web pistol belts with police cuffs and 9mm Glock handguns.

The elevator was clean and functional, but without a trace of the opulence Cartouche had experienced at the Villa Caproni in Palermo that morning, while meeting Mr. Blechstein of Global Anaconda.

Who were these silent, efficient kidnappers? Cartouche dreaded what he might learn. He'd been quite comfortable with the Anaconda deal, on second thought.

The elevator door went *ding*, and rolled open.

Before Cartouche's eyes spread a large lounge with high, slanting ceiling. The atmosphere was functional. The materials were dark-tinted glass, steel framing, and concrete surfaces with little decoration of any kind. Very industrial. Dark-beerish late afternoon light slanted in through 45-degree tilted windows. The place could be a post-modern house of worship, or an airport departure lounge—same things, thought Cartouche.

Into the concrete walls were embossed several instances of a large emblem, brushed in brownish stain rather than paint, that Cartouche had never seen before. It was a circle, with a horizontal line through it. In the upper half was a floating eye (the Masonic symbol on the U.S. dollar bill), while in the lower half was a woman's lovely face with hideous lips and eyes, and snakes instead of hair—a Gorgon (related to, but not the same as the *gorgoneion* at the door).

"Monsieur Cartouche." An attractive young woman in a long, silvery-brown sheath dress walked toward him. The guards melted away from her, but hovered in the background. The woman did not have snakes for hair, but a lovely blue-black ball of frizz.

She represented a universal mix of races. In her almond-shaped eyes, the pupils were bluish-black. She had fine, even teeth like ivory. Her lips were just full under a slightly flattened nose, so that her features appeared balanced and harmonious. Hers was a sublime face, like the Belgian girl's in Palermo—a still pond that a man could look into without ever seeing bottom. One could gaze upon her beauty without ever seeing enough.

Her skin was café-au-lait, and invited touching, but to touch her would have meant death—Cartouche understood without being told. Her fingernails and toenails were bloody, glossy red, except on the thumbs and large toes, whose nails were matte black. She wore delicate leather sandals with decorative fringe hanging from the sides, as worn by beautiful courtesans in ancient Egyptian tomb paintings.

"Monsieur Cartouche," she repeated. Her voice was from the back of the throat, each sound a pearl or a precious stone as its echo clicked across the broad, gloomy hall amid round concrete pillars.. "Welcome to our organization."

"Camelback?" Cartouche ventured as he stood before her, awaiting direction.

"Not at all. We freelance. A brokerage, we like to think. We bring together just the right talent from all around the world."

"I was unaware that Camelback kidnaps talent from its rivals."

"Camelback!" she exclaimed with an amazed laugh. She had a fearless beauty that was its own explanation, defense, and propaganda. "Forget Camelback and all standard corporations and consortia. We are the new ball game in the world."

"I'd appreciate an explanation of why I was taken against my will."

"Soon enough, Mr. Cartouche. Come, sit here where the boss can see you. You two will converse." She turned and walked across the vast, empty floor, which still smelled of concrete from its construction. The monotony was relieved somewhat by an acre of gray, industrial indoor-outdoor carpeting. Amber columns of light slanted from high skylights onto the carpeting.

The woman led him to an island at the center, comprised of a circle of six armchairs and a round coffee table. Cartouche felt the need to water his aching throat again. He noted the presence of silvery carafes and handleless mugs on the coffee table. The walk to reach it seemed to take minutes at the woman's leisurely pace, with her runway gracefulness. The long dress shimmered as it flowed in the air around her precision-tooled figure. *Is she also Belgian?* Cartouche wondered rather cynically. Another form of seduction? He'd never been wooed by great corporations before. Was this part of the standing operational procedure, this subliminal intoxication with beauty and desire?

"My name is Alecto, but you may call me Alex," she said in her fine, flute-soft voice. "I am the Duty Officer of the Day."

"You are Alex Alecto? Is that Italian?"

"Oh no, it's a very ancient name. It inspires sheer terror in those who understand its origin. I am U.S.-Algerian-Chinese, and my personal name is Erin, yes, but that is more than you need to know. Think of me as No, to quash any male fantasies. Have you read Virgil's *Aeneid*, Mr. Cartouche?"

"Years ago, in high school Latin. Can't remember much of it."

"Not many people do, which is useful to us."

"Us?"

"Black Umbrella, the Underworld."

"Never heard of it."

"Alecto in mythology is the most savage and unrelenting of the Furies. Out of divine revenge against the impious Trojan invaders of Rutulia in Italy, nearly 1,000 years before Christ and Augustus, she stirs up a catastrophic war, which the fledgling Romans under Aeneas win after a bloody struggle. I assure you it is the only war that Alecto ever lost, or ever will lose in all eternity. "

She bade him sit in the central chair facing a large overhead viewing screen, which tilted toward him, at the same 45 degree angle as the great, tinted sky-windows opposite, and behind him.

She walked away in that same leisurely, assured stride.

On the screen appeared a static image of that same symbol, a circle with a floating eye above and a Gorgon below.

A man's voice spoke unhurriedly, with utter self-assurance. The voice had a languid coldness. Most likely, it was muffled through some sort of electronic filtering device. Somehow, it rang familiar to Cartouche, and he listened keenly to try and place it. No image of a man appeared, only that symbol.

"Good afternoon, Mr. Cartouche."

Does that voice sound familiar?

"Explain yourself. I am tired of this outrage."

"I understand your emotions. I hope we will please you with our counter offer to that which Global Anaconda made earlier today in Palermo."

I have heard that voice somewhere before.

"You seem to know a lot."

"We know everything. That is essential in our mission."

Cartouche felt conflicted. He was afraid, for one thing. He was angry for another thing—more than anything because this hocus-pocus was playing havoc with his new-found sense of financial security and all that it would buy—he had hoped. Now what was there to be?

"You are a business?"

"We are a brokerage, as Alecto already told you. We like to think of ourselves a mission, rather than a business."

Was that an Afrikaans accent?

"What is your name?" Louis demanded.

"I am Dr. Night." The name had a faint electric charge to it when spoken, breaking apart and drifting away like dread, icy ions in the gloomy ceiling light.

Cartouche sat stunned, digesting this bizarre information. Had he died and gone to hell?

"I am Dr. Night, supreme operating authority of Underworld. Or, as the world will come to know us, Black Umbrella. Blum, for short, which is coincidentally German for Flower. A very black flower, if I may say so." The disembodied voice shivered with underwatery chuckles that rippled around Louis. "We are a force the world's ruling corponations cannot deny. We represent all of the world's dispossessed, the outsiders, the defeated, the outraged, the runners in cities at night, those who sleep in forests or desert tents, those who endure the elements in hope of being restored to what is historically theirs."

Cartouche recognized the voice now.

Blechstein! Can it be?

Could this be the man Blechstein from the conference screen at the Villa Caproni? It must be Blechstein. How could this be? Perhaps he was speaking in Palermo, and his voice emerged here in Agrigento on a one-way video hookup. He could see Louis, but Louis could not see him.

"Do you recognize my voice, Louis?"

"Yes. I think so. Mr. Blechstein."

"Very good. That's rich. Actually, Blechstein was just a useful little man who died long ago. I borrow names and personas as I see fit. You will never know who I really am, nor will you ever need to. You will simply think of me as Dr. Night."

The disembodied voice paused to let that sink in, and then continued: "I see all sorts of thoughts and schemes flickering across your eyes. I have metrics all around you, to look into your soul through your eyes, your skin, your heart beating in your chest. Everything about you is being monitored." Each of Dr. Night's sentences trailed off in echoes, like ripples across chilly water at night. "I cannot be defeated, Mr. Cartouche. In case the world ever tries to rise against me—I am only one man. They can kill a thousand of me, and a new Dr. Night will always stand in the next day. The same goes for my chief of operations, Alecto."

"Erin?"

"Yes. She has many names. She is formidable in beauty and intelligence. Thou art beautiful, O my love, as Tirzah, comely as Jerusalem, terrible as an army with banners— Solomon 6:4 Song of Songs. She is terrifying and powerful like Virgil's Alecto in the *Aeneid*. Yet she can be replaced by a woman of equally wonderful capabilities. We have already chosen her line of successors. Their names are inscribed in our books—Hanne, Elizabeth, Aoi, Aleksandra, Genet—our list of names and ultra-gifted candidates is not long, but illustrious."

At that moment, in a distant maze of hallways, another beautiful woman swept by. "Case in point," said Dr. Night. "Alex Nolenta, the next Alecto if something happens to Erin Yes." The woman was shorter, but wiry, dressed in a martial arts *gi*, and carrying Okinawan style bladed weapons. She disappeared into a distant corridor. Dr. Night continued: "My principal Furies are Alecto, Tisiphone, and Megaera. They avenge capital crimes against humans, while a fourth deity, Nemesis or Invidia, avenges insults to the gods. They have snakes for hair, and men turn to stone just looking at them."

"Like Medusa," Cartouche said. Medusa (her Latin name) was the best-known of these three sisters whose collective name meant 'horrid.' He raised a silvered cup to sip water. Little Tissy from Belgium had not had snakes for hair. If anything, she had turned him to jelly.

"Yes. As with the Gorgons—who are also Underworld or Chthonic daemons—you turn to stone just by looking at them. The bite of their serpents can kill just as swiftly."

That did it. "I already have a nice contract with Global Anaconda, and I am quite happy."

"I'm sure you are."

"You brought me here to negotiate?"

Dr. Night's tone was surprised. "Oh no, Mr. Cartouche, I never negotiate. I do not ask, or beg, or bargain, nor do I spend much time contemplating what my instinct dictates. I am a decider. I simply decide, and then I do. Very simple, and always effective."

"What do you want from me?"

"Nothing, Mr. Cartouche. I already took what I decided to take."

"Me?"

"No, Mr. Cartouche. Your OST technology. It is mine now."

"But Global Anaconda—."

Dr. Night emitted a little snort. "Global Anaconda was once my employer, Mr. Cartouche, but they are one-dimensional business people, as all corponations are by nature and definition. Their best people are motivated by greed, ambition, competitiveness, and selfishness. Their perfume is the sweat of greed and fear. They embody the single goal of any corponation. Every student of business learns this. It is to maximize the wealth of its shareholders, the people who hold common or preferred stock. Legally, just as the corporation is a person—without any heart—so the corponation is a state without a soul. The corporation is a heartless entity, piloted by amoral people, who have no connection with religion, patriotism, or virtue of any sort, which are the snake oils they peddle to the sincere and gullible millions. They own the media, and massage receptive minds with slick advertising and distorted news reports. They tranquilize the masses with entertaining dramas filled with repressed sex and violence. They are owned by a tiny minority, who control the masses through their vast wealth and ownership of the means of power. They manipulate facts so that their lies become truth itself. That is where I decided to go my own way, finally, for a life motivated by my personal idealism."

"You want to save the world, is that it?"

"No, Mr. Cartouche, I want to own the world."

Louis Cartouche's jaw dropped as he stared at the six foot logo overhead.

"The world cannot be saved, Mr. Cartouche. It is composed of idiots. Why else have we had all these wars, while tens of thousands of children die from preventable diseases every day? So many horrors and evils could be cured if amoral predators did not always rise to the top in human affairs. It is the Human Condition, Mr. Cartouche. It is a law of nature, and cannot be changed, any more than a zebra can change its stripes or a spider can run from its own web. Reality is the highest ideal, Mr. Cartouche. I can do a much better job of running the world than kings, presidents, or CEOs. There will be no more predators, no more ruling class, no more wars and oil barons and liars in the media. There will only be myself, Dr. Night, and a grateful humanity. I will distribute the wealth so that every human being will have food, and health care, and freedom from fear. They will be my power base, and nobody will be able to say no to Dr. Night."

The man's filtered voice seemed to emanate from all around, from thin air. Dr. Night continued: "Your excellent technology gives me a great leg-up on my quest. With a few adaptations and technical enhancements, Orbital Sniper Technology will help me become master of the earth."

Madness, thought Cartouche. There could be no debating with this crazy man. What had he said in Palermo? *A great technology…in the right hands…but if it falls into wrong hands…*

"History, Mr. Cartouche, is filled with vanished peoples, exiled dynasties, lost causes, toppled kings, forgotten emperors, and suppressed religions burning to rise again. The world is what we know, but its shadows are delineated with phantom provinces, sleeping kingdoms, shadowy realms awaiting rebirth. Our science books speak of extinct species, lost seas, sunken continents, deserted islands, forgotten valleys, Loch Ness monsters, ghost cities like Petra, last refuges like Machu Picchu that are haunted by dead kings and queens, by spirits of what might have been.

"My intention, when I left Global Anaconda, was to found a new organization such as the world has not seen since Grandmaster Hasan-i Sabbah founded the Assassins, a secret society in Syria and Persia, around the time of the First Crusade, about 1,000 years ago. Like the Jedi masters in the movies, they were perfect masters who vanished from an imperfect world, but their name is still a synonym for divine terror. You might call it shock and awe, without the ignorance, lies, and bungling. Without the stale, fetid stench of greed on unwashed skin."

Madness, Cartouche thought, but no surprise. He should have realized that a technology like OST would attract the craziest of people.

"Your OST fits our bill perfectly, Mr. Cartouche, which is why we shall harness it to our purposes. I offer you one of two choices for your future. You must make your decision before rising from that chair. Either you turn your back on Global Anaconda and join us as a comrade in arms, or you will die before you stand up. Do not rise until I know your choice, or you will die instantly."

As a warning, twin energy beams streaked down from the ceiling, one on each side of Louis. The beams sizzled visibly in the air, stirring up fine wires of light and dust at thirty or forty feet in the air. Within the same second, the empty armchairs on either side of Cartouche exploded in smoke and flames. Had anyone been sitting there, they would have been burned alive, as if spontaneously combusting.

"A little warning to prod your logical processes. Think carefully, Mr. Cartouche."

Cartouche weakly raised one hand in submission, while crouching to one side in his seat. With his free hand, he palmed his lower face in terror. Smoke roiled around him, and he coughed with the seats' choking plastic smoke.

Powerful air conditioners sucked wounded air from the hall.

Alecto strode back into view. She walked as erectly and gracefully as ever, while holding a small but deadly looking black automatic. She aimed the gun at Cartouche from close range, just ten feet away. "What's it going to be, Mr. Cartouche? On the count of ten, live or die. One."

"It will be a quick, painless, clean death," Dr. Night said consolingly.

"Two," Alecto said.

"Good choice, either way," Dr. Night said.

"Three," Alecto said. Her lovely face was impassive, and showed no hesitation.

Dr. Night said: "If you choose to live, we'll start with a nice dinner, and company for the night."

"Stop," Cartouche said.

"Four," Alecto said.

Dr. Night said: "Or you can have a forgettable funeral right here in the Valley of the Temples."

Cartouche shrieked: "I'll do whatever you want."

"Five," Alecto said.

"You must frame your words correctly," Dr. Night said. "Correct thinking frames correct words."

"I agree. I want to work for you."

"Six," Alecto said.

"Think fast," Dr. Night said. "Four seconds before you die. Wrong thinking frames wrong words."

"I want to belong to Black Umbrella."

"Seven"

"With feeling," the hidden voice said. "Make me believe you."

"I want to give my life to you. Please accept me!"

"Eight."

Dr. Night said: "That's a good boy."

Alecto lowered the gun.

Dr. Night said: "Well done, Mr. Cartouche. You are now one of us. If you ever betray me, you face a horrifying end. Do you vow to give your life to Black Umbrella?"

"I do!" Louis sobbed. "I do!" Louis clutched the arm rests and trembled like a man with malaria. Sweat and tears streamed down his face. His teeth chattered amid quaking chin and jowls.

"Congratulations," said Alecto.

"Yes," Cartouche said, as relief flooded him. "I am one of you. I decided it. To hell with Anaconda. Tell me what you wish, and I will decide how best to help you achieve our common goal. I want to stop everything that's bad in the world. Only you should rule, Dr. Night."

"The goal, Mr. Cartouche, is for me to bring peace and prosperity to the world as the first absolute ruler in its history. We already have many allies in our fight against the world's nations and corporations. There are the shadowy descendants of the lost dynasties—Maxentian, Habsburger,

Romanovski, Napoleonic, Byzantine, the last Romans of the West, the Assassins in the east, the spirit dancers of the Great Plains. Think of the secret services of Tibet that the Chinese Reds dreaded more than anything else because they fought with spirit tools—and the Communists are gone. Stalin laughed when warned about the Pope. Stalin, who only understood terror, violence, and murder, said: *Show me the Pope's divisions*. But the Pope was playing with a spiritual deck, and Stalin had not a clue. Where is Stalin's pathetic empire now? Dust in the sands of the ages, along with so many other historically brief, crappy ideas.

"I could go on, reciting the litany of the dead and lost who are prepared to walk again and seize back the power that was stolen from them by the same ruthless types whose corporate mandate is today inscribed in the text books of business schools: There is no mission besides maximizing the wealth of corporate shareholders. There is no god besides moolah.

"Among the corporations there is no god—no morality, no truth, no higher power—than money. There is no lie too great, and no depravity too base, if it supports the corporate profit motive. But today, with Black Umbrella, we begin anew with a fresh mandate from heaven itself: there is no greater good than truth, justice, and correct leadership, under a Great Shepherd who watches over the world's people in the night."

And that, Cartouche, thought, makes you just another of history's many madmen and charlatans. He quickly banished the thought for fear that Dr. Night or Alecto could read his mind. What had he said? Metrics. All around him. He must be careful of what he thought.

He surrendered to terror, deep in the mind, where Blum reached his darkest and most intimate thoughts. Nothing could remain hidden from this Biggest Brother. Louis hated himself for it, but could not help it. Terror was the ultimate weapon of mind control, the ultimate seduction. Louis longed to grovel on the ground like a dog. He wished to crawl around and lick Dr. Night's feet. Black Umbrella had won.

Alecto put the automatic away. "Come, Mr. Cartouche, we have prepared a feast for you, and then you will bathe and party with seven lovely women." She laughed. "They are not virgins, but all the more experienced. It will be the most unforgettable night of your life—a celebration of your new happiness."

As she spoke she turned to walk away but offered a hand, held behind her, for him to take.

Cartouche lunged to his feet and took her hand, but it slipped from his grasp like thin air.

She walked away, a graceful goddess, and the screen overhead went dead with one final chuckle from Dr. Night, which echoed among the great pillars.

Blanching, Cartouche realized that, the whole time, the woman brandishing the gun to kill him had been a phantom—a holographic projection.

He had no time to digest this insight, for at that moment, from behind him, came a woman's harsh laughter.

He whirled, and saw Alecto—the real Erin Yes—standing behind his chair holding a compact, dead-black, Underworld-issued Czech-made submachine gun. As her harsh and cruel laughter rippled around him, she discharged a brief burst of .438 caliber rounds whose noise rolled around in the air, and shattered a high-hanging glass light shade.

"Welcome back to the world of the living. Enjoy your dinner, Mr. Cartouche, and all that comes with it, because you are a lucky man. You made the right decision, or you would be dead now." So saying, she lowered the weapon and came around, striding past him. For a moment, he thought he smelled sulfur. A major product of the Agrigento region was sulfur, such as lined the valleys of the Underworld in western mythology. It was a yellow crystal, like golden glass. It was also said to line the cliffs and crevices of hell. As Alecto walked, the air around her was sharp with the pepper aroma of her gunshots. "Come, but never try to take my hand or touch me. I'll guide you to the feasting room, and the dancers and flute players will take care of you for the night—whatever you wish is yours." She smiled broadly. "It's our way of saying welcome aboard, and thank you. We demand your all, but we are generous in all that we give."

As he followed her to a distant chamber with a brightly lit table, he saw stunning women there, each different from the others. The room around them resounded with conversation and laughter. The air throbbed with the music of a live six-string chamber orchestra composed entirely of beautiful women in white, elegant tuxedo gowns called she-xedos in this year's fashion magazines.

The other seven women held drinks. They chatted in pairs and trios as they stood about. A few sat on the back rests of couches. One or two leaned against a grand piano, under a glittering chandelier, where one of the musician women, in a she-xedo with back bare, played animatedly, rocking from side to side as her fingers raced up and down the ebonies and ivories. All the smilers and talkers had fine skin, lovely hair, and perfect white teeth. They wore tasteful silk dresses in colors—only one in black, the color of night, rage, and vengeance. The women nodded to each other while talking. Their eyes began to take notice of the approaching Cartouche.

Alex said: "They are the opposite of the Gorgons. These are the Eumenides, pleasant ones. They are the Roman Graces. They will please you tonight."

Cartouche felt utterly relaxed now, having faced death and come away a wealthy and fortunate man for the first time in his life. His conversion had been as sudden and stunning as St. Paul struck deaf and thrown from his horse by lightning on the path to Damascus. Paul left for Damascus as a persecutor, and, after wandering deaf and blind in the ghost-haunted desert, he arrived in Damascus not as a murderous judge, but as one of the persecuted. In like transformation, Cartouche arrived as a terrified, impoverished, exiled little man, and now strode across the hall. He was free of fear, lacked for nothing material, and felt completely a member as in a great family. If there was the faintest tingle of apprehension—that something was not right—he brushed it aside in this overwhelming bath of the senses.

He recognized one particularly beautiful, shapely girl in a black dress among the Graces at the dinner table ahead—stacked as it was with wines and steaks and ales and cakes. His heart throbbed as he recognized the Belgian girl who had sat next to him at the Anaconda conference table at the Villa Caproni in Palermo. "Mademoiselle Tissy!" he said.

She turned, saw him, raised her glass, and gave him a dazzling smile while running a smooth, tanned pinkish hand suggestively down her front. "Monsieur Cartouche, it is so nice to see you again."

He felt balmy at the beautiful, golden smile of the Belgian woman as she drifted across the floor toward him. Her hips swayed gracefully as she walked. She was meant for him. He would give himself to her. He wanted her more than anything else in the world. How had he known this earlier that day in Palermo? Telepathy? Had Dr. Night and Alecto known this, and set them up?

Tissy had intrigued him from the first, but men like Cartouche did not land women like her in real life. She had leaned close to him, over the table, while fetching his water. He'd inhaled he atmosphere of her body. She'd let him peer through the fabric of her secrets, and glimpse the untouchable in that scented conference room at the Villa Caproni. Cartouche, a reclusive man who had hardly ever been intimate with any woman, would have loved to roll blissfully with her, hold her while she held him, and trade kisses. He would give his life to possess her.

What Louis could not know yet was that Dr. Night, in declaring war on the world's powerful corponations, had opened untold new doors of war and gates of hell. The world's powers had teeth of their own—among them Sigma 2020, the Camelback Consortium subsidiary company whose masters and contractors included Claire Lightfield and Compass News' Johannes Rector, not to mention their top field operative—Jack Gray, the agent of last resort, whom they called into action when all else failed.

Dr. Jack Gray, Please

Evening at the History Club

A proper New England autumn evening had just fallen as Dr. Jack Gray drove toward the university to give a history lecture. With him was his gorgeous, dark-haired friend, Dr. Dominica Albrisi. They rode together in the sporty comfort of a dark, glossy blue Ferrari in.

Darkness spread like spilled ink around the cloistered walks and gargoyled entry ways of the university. As night fell on the neo-Gothic campus, brown leaves rustled crisply in circles, driven with a light, fingernail touch by ghostly breezes. A full moon rode among a fleet of smoky cloud galleons. Otherwise, the night sky was clear and dry. Sprinkled stars framed the night sky's darker edges.

Jack Gray drove contentedly, unaware that another, far darker drama was beginning off-stage, which would soon ensnare him in a deadly drama traceable back to Madame Zhang.

The former Ministry of State Security chief, now a hunted criminal, was a Fury in her own right, who never quit when enraged, until she tasted revenge in her blood-dripping mouth. She had gambled her career in MSS away on her stake with Big Yang—and lost everything. Tonight's target was Jack Gray, the man who had taken everything from her.

While the Dragon Lady had been a key spider in the MSS web, a thousand tangled skeins had crossed before her wary eyes. She was now a wanted person, headed for a PRC firing squad if caught. She'd lost her pension, her contacts—everything, except one thing. She had a Swiss-Chinese daughter by her first husband, a businessman from Geneva. The daughter was an attractive, deadly fixer and martial artist named Alex Nolenta.

Of the tangled skeins and black market operations, which had caught her eye while Madame Zhang was still in a position of power, one was an odd one. Alex had hooked her up with a money stream in the Shanghai underworld, involving a shell company called Project David. It belonged to a subsidiary of Global Anaconda, with a shadowy prime mover attached to it: George Blechstein. According to her sources before they dried up, Project David involved the manufacture of a powerful new sniper rifle of unknown technology.

Madame Zhang, shuttling among underworld locations—every major city in the world had its Tong or Mafia or similar brotherhood—learned from sources that this Blechstein was a ghost. He was a shadow, belonging to a man murdered years earlier in South Africa. Someone, for some reason, was using his identity. That was the sort of information Madame Zhang was expert at parlaying into an income stream among the world's many stupid crooks.

Digging deeper, beyond even her daughter's impressive new connections, Madam Zhang learned that an unknown brokerage of some sort, a global crime syndicate, named Blum was moving vast sums and countless players around on a shadow stage, under the noses of the world's governments and corponations. Whatever Blum was, Alex was in tight with them, and while there was no love lost for her mother, Alex felt an obligation to take care of her parent.

So Zhang once again had a stream of money coming in, more than enough to stay alive. It was more than enough to send a man after the arrogant and destructive Mr. Gray who had caused her so much irritation. Mr. Gray must die. She would have preferred time and torture—but she was on the run, and a swift bullet would have to do, close up, direct to the head, and a second bullet as a follow-up to make double sure. Through Alex and the money, she had stayed alive and bought enough time to start following her many leads to their dark origins, and to start making money and connections for starting a new life in the world's underbelly. She already had her first inklings of the kind of knowledge that was worth gold. She knew Blum was an acronym for Black Umbrella, and that its prime mover was a powerful and elusive player named Dr. Night. She would find out who he was, and what his strategy was so she could capture part of it for herself. She instantly understood what he was after: power. That much was easy to tell, since she'd been a key player in one of the world's major intelligence services, and rubbed shoulders with many such men who were naturally attracted to the dark services. With her experience, she was sure she could line up a new position of influence to feather her a new nest for herself.

On the borderland between worlds—quiet university campus versus noisy, secular city beyond—a man with a gun under his jacket stepped from a rented, plum-colored sedan he had just parked at the curb on a city street.

He peered about with a reluctant furtiveness tempered with a natural arrogance. Letting the car door slam shut, the man walked around to its trunk. Amid wan trunk light, he removed a paper shopping bag. Slamming the trunk lid, he glanced left and right. Then he walked across the sidewalk, carrying the bag. He stepped onto university property, climbing slightly on grassy soil, and disappeared amid dusky trees—a man on a mission, not to be stopped, with murder in his eyes.

On the opposite side of campus, expensive cars began arriving in time for a 7:00 p.m. lecture. Depending on the driver's age and status, each car was either luxury or sporting in nature, and colorful or not, depending on age and personal taste of the owner.

Students, professors, and staff had gone home. Even the dormitories were silent, with their underclassmen either away at the library studying, or in taverns around the Green.

Most campus rooms were dark, except one hall that stood open and was brightly lit for an evening lecture. Windows were framed in ogives of gray travertine. Their leaded glass panes reflected distant light, enlivened with insets of stained glass with pictures and mottoes. The insets would glow almost magically with daytime sunlight, but in the moonlight seemed duller than the thick, plain glass around them.

Lecture goers approached along modestly illumined paths and corners amid thickly ivied, Victorian brick buildings and neo-Gothic towers. Men and women in fine evening wear—formal, but casual, not quite gowns and tuxes—passed closed courtyards and hidden gardens. Some were alumni or alumnae, while most others were active or retired faculty. Some were young, socially climbing assistant professors with pretty young wives or girlfriends on their arm. Their walk was punctuated by soft laughter and conversation of the financially secure and career-assured, the crunch of men's wingtips and the clicking of women's heels. Along with the occasional whiff of cigarette smoke, the mild, cool evening air was tinged with hints of perfume and cologne, even a hint of mothballs; not from the matrons themselves, but from their rarely unearthed legacy fur wraps of a bygone age—however insensitive on environmental principles, ironically fitting for a lecture on ancient history.

The university campus was a world unto itself, while across gray-limbed groves of trees, the city glowed amid its haze of ambient light colored up with the mixed neons of pizzerias, pool halls, laundromats, and cheap inner-city hotels.

In the cloistered and guarded world of the university—in only one modest sized lecture hall that opened directly on a small faculty parking lot—fluorescent lights blazed whitish-blue and cold for the evening's two learned talks.

Surrounding lawns and tree-lined walks were full of a dusky silence, as if time stood still.

Across a darkened lawn, barely visible, the man with the gun walked. He paused amid an especially gloomy copse of trees to put down his shopping bag. He took a rouge jacket from the bag, and laid the jacket across the back-rest of a park bench next to a steel-wire trash receptacle. He unzipped his light, cotton wind jacket, took it off, and folded it into the shopping bag, which he crushed shut and stuffed into the trash receptacle for later retrieval, along the escape route after his job was done. He put on the dark red jacket of a university docent, and made sure the name tag was straight across his left breast. He checked the automatic once more—holding it up to catch the ambient light, as he pulled back the breach and closed it again—and stuffed the semi-automatic into his belt at back. Making sure his jacket hung fully down to conceal the grip, he strode on his way.

He headed toward one of the open doors and three lighted windows on slightly higher ground about 100 yards away. All other windows around him on campus brimmed pregnantly with night, as if bursting with secrets in their silence. The windows were lit only with distant city and lunar reflections.

The man's face had the hardened cheekbones, the morally slack expression, of a professional killer who did what he came to do, and left, neither with the slightest preamble or epilog of self-doubt or moral indecision. His eyes had a flat affect as they glanced about. He seemed to be awash in his own telemetry, gauging and assessing, in a constant stream of calculations to optimize the execution of his plan, and to minimize any chance of getting caught. If he had done any hard time, the casual angle of his shoulders and the loose swing of his limbs did not suggest it.

He wore an official university docent's and greeter's uniform—maroon blazer, dark trousers, dark shoes, none of which fit perfectly. And fit they shouldn't, having recently been acquired for this purpose from a retired, deceased university employee who had owed money to a certain local cash broker with connections to people who broke limbs to hasten repayment, or outright terminated the debtor if satisfaction was not to be gotten. Tonight's man even wore a gleaming brass name tag, as all such employees must, which read Antonio, which was not his name or even a pseudonym, but the birth name of the recently deceased employee (whom he had personally dispatched to the underworld, while leaving the old man's earthly remains in a Providence, Rhode Island canal about two hours' drive up the coast.

As the fake Antonio walked, he paused a moment. He screwed a matte-black suppressor onto the muzzle of his noir handgun. If he were to be intercepted by campus police, this upped the ante a thousand-fold. It was one thing to carry a gun—no matter if it was a standard US or NATO police and military semi-automatic. It was another to carry that same weapon with a silencer screwed on, loaded, and ready to rock and roll. The mercenary—who came out of nowhere, and would vanish back into thin air—tucked his newly silenced U.S. Army M9A1 Beretta under his jacket. Its magazine was loaded with nine hollow point bullets that would shred a man's insides. He kept walking at a steady, mechanical pace.

A nearby parking lot spilled full of cars as the hour drew nigh. The lot's center was dimly lit with observatory-safe lights the color of bloody-pink grapefruit flesh. As each car sought a parking space, its twin white headlights curved cautiously to a halt and went out. Simultaneously, at each car's tail, red brake lights winked out.

An expensive—-youthful-looking, though understated—sports coupe pulled in rather smartly to a far end of the parking lot. Amid loosely rolling elm leaves, the Ferrari disappeared into shadows in a tree-fringed parking lot. Its stabbing chilly-bluish headlights winked out, as did the tooled red lenses of its taillights. The sports car seemed swallowed in the night.

It was October, the time of year when the first frost moves down in a broad wave from Canada, shooting bright yellow and amber death into trillions of leaves from the Atlantic coast west into the blurry center of America. It was time for football, when the summer humidity had gone, and the days were mild, breezy, and sunny. The time of year seemed almost a false spring—promising harvest and rebirth, but bringing death and Hallow E'en. The night sky was clear ash-azure, a deep pure indigo amid an atmosphere that smelled like fresh blue ink for writing history notes, or whatever your passion inclined you toward. The air had a crisp feel, smelling faintly of wood smoke and fragile, dying leaves that circled in wind-blown spirals.

A light came on, along the lower border of the door, as it opened. Out stepped a wiry man in his mid-30s, with short, dark hair, blue eyes, and athletic features. A softened cragginess was just the right touch, the olive in the gin and tonic, for discerning women who prefer their man formal—though certainly not stiff—with just the right outdoorsy flavor for a campfire and cozy stories.

Jack Gray wore an expensively understated, dark-gray suit. His shirt was eggshell blue, starched, with a dark blue tie. The door slammed shut, but an interior light stayed on, revealing the outline of a young woman. Dark brown hair fell in rich waves over her bare shoulders and curled around her pale neck. Jack walked around the car, opened the door, and offered a hand, which she took though she did not need to. She was tall, with an elegantly beautiful face. She wore a white sheath, knee-length gown as she stepped out on high heels that became her. She wore these dangerous shoes, and her Italic beauty, with accustomed grace. Unable to resist, he embraced her. They kissed romantically in the shadows. He made a delighted sound, inhaling her scent, and she offered a sensuous, naughty giggle in return. It was a familiar giggle—they were old friends.

Nearby, a rectangle of light spilled from an open doorway. Men and women in evening wear came from all directions for the seven p.m. lecture by Dr. Jack Gray on the Flaminian Circus in ancient Rome. As the university tower clock sought the hour, a carillon could be heard winding up in its wooden framework. At the door stood a university employee in rouge and gray uniform, handing out programs. He was a slight Asian or Asian-American who bobbed his head in a friendly way each time he handed a copy to yet another beaming pair.

"Hello there!" called a woman in a red dress from the sidewalk near the door, waving her program in one hand, while her other arm was joined with her husband's.

"The Lightfields," said Minica as she detached herself from Jack Gray. They'd been expecting to meet for the lecture.

"Oh yes," he said. "I was expecting to meet them inside. They got a little bit ahead of themselves."

"Or you were getting a little behind," Dr. Dominica Albrisi, Ph.D.-Econ. said, lightly elbowing Jack in the ribs. For an elegant woman, she had a touch of the tomboy.

Jack's palm brushed her behind as he nudged her toward Claire and Tony Lightfield. "Go on, I'll be with you in a moment."

Minica kissed him wetly in his ear. "I'm looking forward to your lecher."

"I'll speak in tongues for you," Jack said.

He watched as Minica strode away—on sturdy, beautiful legs muscled from running, skiing, and surfing. They'd known each other since their college days. It had been a long, steamy, intermittent friendship. She was between husbands at the moment, and Jack was between gigs. He was on his way home from China, via this lecture at the university this evening. By tomorrow night, he would be home in San Diego County— where his real life lay. Nobody knew about his real life, not Minica or any other woman out here in the world, except his two liaisons—Claire Lightfield of Sigma 2020; and Johannes Rector of Compass News.

Jack believed in making the most of every moment, and this was no exception.

After his lecture here, there was to be some sort of surprise award for him later in the evening, hatched up by Claire Lightfield and Sigma 2020, at a secret Compass News safe house in the city.

He would spend the night with Minica at the safe house tonight, and take a shuttle plane across Long Island Sound to JFK International on Long Island. Then he'd fly off to San Diego for his well-earned vacation. Minica would be on a plane bound for Germany, where her fall semester consisted of teaching Micro and Macro Economics at the *Englisches Collegium* of Heidelberg University. How his luck in meeting her on short notice had come about: his stop in New Haven coincided with a visit home with her parents in Fairfield.

When Minica was safely beyond viewing angle, Jack opened the trunk of his late-model Ferrari. From under his jacket, he removed a holster containing his Swiss-made U.S. Coast Guard special 9mm SIG Sauer P229R DAK semi-automatic, small clip of 13 .40 Smith & Wesson rounds. He placed this in a padded plastic carrier toolkit in the trunk. He put his right foot up, and lifted his right trouser leg. He attached an ankle holster with one of his favorite secondaries—a snubby, Hungarian-made blue-steel finish Walther PPK/E compact, chambering the .32 caliber ACP round in a niner-clip. He hated ankle holsters. This would have to do for an uneventful hour or two. To his taste, ankle holsters were no good for running or climbing, nor even for walking—it was like limping around with a rock tied to one foot. Might not be perceptible to a desk-bound blob, but it made all the difference if you happened to be running for your life in some situation. He was not expecting any such situation tonight.

Jack clicked the trunk lid closed. He lightly stomped his foot a moment to settle the ankle holster. Then he joined the two women and Tony at the door, where lecture goers were still pouring into the smallish hall beyond an inside corridor.

Jack, a man of multiple hats, worked free-lance for Compass News Corporation. This was not a media organization, but an anti-terrorist, surveillance, and intervention firm headquartered in San Diego. Compass News, headed by Johannes Rector, was named for the four compass points—North, East, West, South. Through Compass News, Jack worked freelance, and almost exclusively for Sigma 2020, with Claire Lightfield as his liaison.

Claire Lightfield was a civil servant, an intelligence officer, employed directly by Sigma 2020. This was a wholly owned subsidiary company or branch of the world's most powerful corporate entity. Camelback Consortium, based in Phoenix, had over 100 major branches around the globe. Its extended network included countless lesser nodes, including many governmental offices. Claire's liaison orbit included the U.S. government in the form of Senators Bloviant and Hawgbile; the Executive branch including CIA, FBI, and OPOTUS; and MILINT offices of several 'Western' foreign corponations.

Jack worked not, as he liked to say, for Claire or with her or despite her, but with her able assistance. Ever diplomatic, while tough as an oak board, Dr. Claire Lightfield, Ph.D.-Physics, chose not to disagree, and let it go at that, as long as her mission ended up being accomplished. Claire's husband Tony was with her this evening, tall, balding, congenial. Tony was a mellowed sort of Lord Haw-Haw who had made a fortune internationally trafficking in expensive and aromatic bath products. Tony could always be relied on for cheerful and erudite repartee.

As Jack joined them to enter the lecture hall, he took Minica by the elbow and squeezed. She squeezed back, as if to say I can't wait to have you in the sack later tonight. He was sometimes tempted to make his relationship with her more solid. But that could not be. It would violate his basic principle—putting her too much at risk—based on bitter and unspeakable personal experience. Jack might be a very eligible single man, but he was not a bachelor.

Jack and Minica entered the building through a single door, which was propped open by a tilted chair. Inside was a crosswise corridor smelling of old books and carpets, as well as noodles and old hats. A double door, both of its wings open, admitted one into the 100 seat hall where Jack and another professor were due to each give a 45-minute talk that evening.

Minica had met the Lightfields on one or two occasions before—once at a tea for a newly arrived Chinese consul from Shanghai, at Camelback's glass and fountain-splashed HQ in Langley, Virginia. At the time, Minica was staying in Alexandria, and Jack brought her along as his date; another time at a resort in Vermont, where Jack and Minica stayed in a ski lodge adjacent to that of the Lightfields.

"Claire," Jack said, holding Minica tightly arm in arm, "you'll take care of her for me while I speak?"

"Of course," Claire said. She was echoed by a graying, balding, and therefore all the more dashing Tony Lightfield, who peeled a compliant Minica from Jack's arm.

"Don't worry about Minica for a moment," said Claire. The Lightfields stood on either side of poor Minica, as if she were a pickpocket who had been captured by railroad police, and was about to be escorted away in handcuffs.

Tony was a tall, robust, slightly fleshy man with heavy-rimmed dark glasses. Claire was a tall, willowy blonde with a fine, freckled face, small mouth, and too-dry strawberry hair looped in a generous but efficient coiffure. Jack, a connoisseur of freckled women, noted that she had a strong concentration of faint, lemonade-colored freckles of mostly medium diameter—not the more iconic orange freckles of the classic redhead, which was a favorite. Redheads might have a temperamental edge, usually owing to a Celtic gene pool that also gave them carrot hair, but they often had an inferiority complex, having been teased all their lives about those million tiny rust spots. His favorite line with such a woman was "do you have them all over?" and the answer, when one was given in lieu of a slap in the face, was often "oh yes, dreadful, all over every inch of me," followed in the next instant by a stunned realization that she had just revealed the most intimate secret of her private parts. From there, it was then either that slap, or else a shrug ("why not, now that the cat's out of the bag") and an intimate exploration lasting all night. Slightly lower down the interest scale were dark-haired women of all races, who sported smaller, chocolate dots amid features Jack Gray found intriguing and exotic. By contrast, the Anglo-Saxon properness of a Claire Lightfield—with her galaxy of faint lemon spots over milky skin—produced snores. Collectively, these spots were called ephelides, which Jack found especially attractive in themselves, but more so because of the tenderness and insecurity they caused many of their bearers—a source of anxiety and self-reproach with which Jack was entirely happy to help them struggle, both morally and in compromising postures that felt remarkably refreshing and exhilarating to both parties during prolonged and noisy sex. Jack never messed with married women, in any case, which left Claire Lightfield outside the realm of anything more than an occasional flirtatious remark—a fact much appreciated by Tony Lightfield as well, since he'd be no match for Jack Gray in deadly, hand-to-hand combat. That was the delightful thing about polite society, Jack found. One rose above humanity's inbred, primitive, violent impulses. A sense of humor helped, also.

Claire took Jack aside. "Great work on the Baidu event." Event was what you called a situation or a case these days, just as branches and departments were now companies, by definition subsidiary to the independent government or business entities known as corporations. At the top of the food chain were a dozen multi-industry, global cartels like Camelback, defined as consortia (plural of consortium). When these came to encapsulate entire national governments, the snide term for them was corponations.

"My pleasure entirely," Jack said. "Speaking for Mr. Rector and for Compass News, I want to tell you that we enjoy our business with you, and hope to engage in more of it soon." Johannes was the enigmatic Chief Executive Officer of Compass News, who signed Jack's paychecks.

"I never know when you are teasing, and when you are straight, Jack." Claire sighed. One some previous occasion, after a more suggestive reparté, Claire had said: "I can't imagine the things your girlfriends say to you at moments like this."

"I'm not myself when I'm working," Jack had said. It was true in more ways than one.

Just now, Claire's small pink lips pursed over straight, even teeth that were slightly grayed with antibiotic discoloration in childhood. "Tony and I will entertain Minica. You go give a bang-up talk. I can't wait to hear what the Circus Flaminius is all about."

Jack watched as Claire and Tony, still with Minica between them—all three of them about 5'8"—walked off amid the roiling crowd in search of folding seats in a row together. Jack's gaze followed Tony's jacket, Minica's pert behind in a tight white dress, and Claire's slender but more regal posterior in a red dress.

When he stood alone and waiting to be called to the podium, Jack spotted a man outside, dressed like a docent, with the most un-docentlike expression on his face.

For a moment, Jack thought it was because he fit that old adage: *qui nocent, docent*. It was a twist on words, in various ways. The old saying was 'those who can't, teach.' Before he could enjoy the word play on docent, something terrible struck him.

Instantly, Jack's hackles stood on end.

It was the man's body language.

The man seemed fixated on Jack, but was hesitant to come inside, and in fact seemed to have nothing to do with the actual proceedings of the History Club's lecture on the Circus Flaminius.

Just by luck, Jack's gaze had met his hunter's ferocious look. It was a slip on the murderer's part, for which Jack thanked his lucky stars.

From here on, Jack's moves would be tactical. He would give away the fact that he knew the man had come to murder him. But he would gear his every move to the upcoming death struggle.

Jack exchanged a few words with the event coordinator on duty, an English professor who translated classics from Latin and Attic Greek.

Jack was, however, more interested in speaking with the rouge-jacketed real docent who had been handing out programs at the door. His name tag read Larry.

"Say, Larry," Jack said as the two men stood in the center of the hall, "don't look now, but there is an odd duck out there, dressed like you."

"Yes, Dr. Gray." Larry swiveled his eyeballs at an amazing angle, while the rest of his body, including his head, remained frozen in the direction of Jack. "I don't know him, Dr. Gray. Never seen him before, and I know all the regular twenty or so docents."

"Thanks, Larry. Don't let him see you looking at him. I think he's the guy who escaped from the mental institution a few days ago."

Larry's eyes bulged. "No. You don't say. Was that in the news? I must have missed it."

"It's been all over the air waves. He killed three nurses and a doctor with an ice pick, and then he escaped over the electrified fence in great big leaps, four feet at a time. He's a veritable chimpanzee, that guy."

"Sh-should I call the police?"

"I'd wait a few minutes, and then saunter down the hall to the kitchen in back. Don't let him think you're on to him. There's a phone, and you can dial 0 for the campus switchboard. Let them call 911, and then come back here and lock the door so he can't come in. Got that? Tell them you're sure it's a murderer, because I said so, and we are all in danger. Best send the SWAT team if possible."

"Y…yessir." Larry looked at the clock, saw the time, and quickly swung both wings of the double door shut. Then he hurried off through a side door in the rear of the hall toward the kitchen.

Could it be this soon?—Zhang Mei, and her promise to find him and kill him, no matter where on earth he tried to hide.

Jack glanced at the clock. It was 7:10 p.m., and the crowd was making restless feet. The small hall echoed with their voices and shuffling. There were a few annoyed coughs. Jack hurried to the podium where he faced about eighty men and women, all of whom looked very genial, but most of whom had probably not had sex together since their last child was born, now of college age. It would not do to trifle with such people. The imaginary chimp in the insane asylum had nothing on these repressed sex fiends when they dropped their civilized veneer and started saying things like "Now see here…"

"Ladies and gentlemen," said the English professor. "It give me great pleasure…*blah blah blah*…and so, without further ado, I give you Professor Jack Gray, our visiting lecturer in History and Classical Studies."

Polite round of applause as Jack replaced the English prof at the podium. On the slightly canted surface were a small reading light, a carafe of water, an unused, upside-down drinking glass, and a note pad with pencil.

"A funny thing happened to me on the way to the Circus Flaminius," Jack began.

A mixture of affectionate sneers and howls of derision rose. They were awake and paying attention. Most had some background in the subject matter, and would be happy to flay him over the slightest misstatement, all in good sport.

"The first thing I should clarify is that there never really was a Circus Flaminius in the sense that scholars thought until not long ago. The top brains in the profession, bless them, had inked out the exact spot in the lower Campus Martius, Field of Mars, just north of the Capitoline Hill, where they were certain this enormous phantom circus existed, which they assumed was yet another chariot-racing track similar to the Circus Maximus, or the Circus of Gaius and Nero, or the Circus Bassianus of Elagabalus, but the truth lies far from that.

"So here is the intriguing mystery. Why would a circus that was never a circus be so important that is has the complete 9th imperial district named for it? It's more baffling than why name the 11th district after the Circus Maximus, which actually was a chariot racing track in its final incarnation. The Flaminian area was more of a public plaza than a sporting venue." He had their attention now.

As Jack spoke, he was on auto-pilot. His senses were wide awake and flooded with adrenalin. The gun-holster at his ankle was becoming itchy, and drenched in sweat. He noted a faint movement among the trees outside. The room had two windows on that side, and he could see the fake docent moving against ambient city light that seeped through denuded trees. The more Jack thought of it, the more obvious it seemed— this must be the payback Zhang had promised before vanishing in that hallway in Baidu, leaving her meal ticked Big Yang dead on the carpet from a hail of Jack's bullets. He continued speaking:

"You see, the word *circus* actually does not specifically refer to a racing venue, like the Circus Maximus about a mile down the road on the south side of the Forum Boarium. The word circus more appropriately means a ring, like Piccadilly Circus in London. Cicero uses it to describe the whirling stars of the Milky Way. In our case in point, it most closely refers to the ancient Taurilian Games track, which was a circular track in the Prata or Meadow of Flaminius, on which horses were ridden in religious games dedicated to the Underworld… "

As Jack spoke, his throat felt dry and constricted. He poured himself a glass of water and drank. "Stuffy in here. Don't worry, in another hour we'll all be having steak and ale, and wondering if this really ever happened."

As laughter murmured through the audience, Jack held up his glass as if appraising the water. He was actually gazing into the reflection it afforded of the window behind him. In the distorted reflection, he noticed a furtive movement, this time against the lights from the main campus clock tower. His nemesis was carefully working his way into position for a clean shot. The intention was clearly to kill Jack, and escape in the panic that would follow. His only problem was that he must make damn sure his one shot nailed Jack through the head or the heart. Not even a neck shot, guaranteed to spurt blood like a fire hydrant, would absolutely guarantee a kill. This was one shot he must not botch, or the Dragon Lady would have him flayed alive. That might buy a little time until the police arrived.

"And so," Jack said, pulling shut the heavy red drapes over the windows, "right before the Second Punic War (you know, starring Hannibal and a hundred war elephants, in 218 BCE), a wealthy and powerful Roman named Flaminius Nepos did something civically responsible in keeping with his social stratum as a Patrician—he bought up most of the lower Campus Martius. Centuries earlier, this area, then known as the Prata Tarquinia, Meadow of Tarquin, had been the personal property of the last king, before the Romans tossed the monarchy out on its ear, and declared a democratic republic in 509 BCE. For Flaminius to buy this tract of wilderness outside the city walls was seen, at the time, sort of like the U.S. purchase of Alaska in 1867—what good could it be? A waste of money! Seward's Folly! Seward's Icebox! Flaminius' meadow or circuit or neighborhood!"

The audience murmured appreciatively. Jack understood his task well. Half these people were experts who knew too much, and half knew next to nothing. He must strike a middle balance. He must keep it lively for the experts, without overwhelming the spouses and English or Music professors.

As he spoke, Jack edged backwards and peered cautiously around a slightly raised curtain edge. The crowd made a loud noise of curiosity, like a hungry beast stirring in its swamp, and preparing to be either annoyed or amused—it wasn't sure which yet.

"In case you're wondering why I am peering through the curtain," Jack said, "I'm keeping an eye on the parking meter. I may have to run and drop in another nickel soon."

The crowd rumbled, faintly amused, and puzzled at the same time. Speaking of circuses, his audience reminded Jack of those attending the games of the arena, who must be given red meat at all times or they would threaten to riot. Senior faculty and their mothballed wives would make a poor show of doddering after Jack with arms upraised in zombie-fashion.

Jack continued telling his complex topological tale, hoping for a relief force from the university gendarmes while he continued stalling for time. The audience responded with lukewarm clapping and some restive sniggering at his jokes. The low, grudging guffaws increasingly had question marks.

Jack winced as he heard a distant crash, and a tinkle of glass. That would be his car window, dammit.

He spoke faster, while backing to the curtain again. "…The Prata Flaminia also became known as Circus Flaminius—meaning not a chariot racing track, but a loosely defined district or area. It was useless land, not only as a Tiber flood plain, but outside the safety of the Servian Wall. Nobody would dare go out there and build anything useful, so why did Flaminius buy it all up? You were a dead duck out there during a siege, like Hannibal pulled off in 212 BCE."

Jack peered outside again, and saw the fake docent using a hard object to break a second window of Ferrari. What was the man looking for? Where was the SWAT team?

"Now the fact is that we have a convergence of history here. This was the area near the Forum Boarium, or cattle market, on the river's edge— the city's initial center of power to the outside world. It was on a crucial crossing of the Tiber, where two major regional trade routes intersected. It was a market center for the region as well. North of the vegetable and cattle markets was a significant Underworld cult in the form of the Dis Pater, or Underworld Father, along with the Neolithic cult of Persephone or Proserpina (the Underworld goddess connected with the miracle of the grain, with its death and rebirth every year, She Whose Name Must Never Be Spoken)."

Jack continued, while looking at his watch. Good thing he'd brought the gun.

Looks as if I am the agent of last resort, once again.

"What it amounts to, ladies and gentlemen, is a remarkable puzzle— why this feature was important enough to preempt all other names for that region, whose most famous features included the Pantheon and the Mausoleum of Augustus..."

"Flaminius would have saved us all this hoopla, including this evening's lecture, if he'd had a little more common sense and called it something like the Forum Flaminium..."

Where is Larry the real docent? Has he called 9-1-1 yet?

Unable to stand the tension any longer, and worried about the innocent people sitting before him, Jack signaled to the English professor-moderator. "Please forgive me, but it's an emergency. I'll be back in about ten minutes or so, with profuse apologies to all. Would you be so kind as to introduce the next guest, and I'll finish up later?"

"What about the Taurilian games in that area?" a woman asked.

"Precisely. I'll be back shortly to finish my talk," Jack promised.

As the English prof started speaking, a ripple of applause flowed over the audience, much like the wind-blown wheat of the tyrant Tarquinius Superbus—King Tarquin II the Arrogant—25 centuries ago. The other speaker, an aeronautics expert with a white beard and a sheaf of notes, stepped up to talk about hydrology in the modern eco-forest, and remarkable new aircraft to maintain green spaces. *Whatever.*

Jack regretted the mess his talk had become, but was more concerned about the innocent people sitting around than he was about himself or his history chat.

Striding to the back of the hall, Jack rattled the double door.

The real docent, Larry, had securely locked it as Jack had told him to do.

Jack whirled and stepped out through the rear side entrance. It was the path Larry had taken. Jack stepped from the lecture hall into a stuffy little back corridor jammed with cardboard boxes, kitchen supplies, and various odds and ends. He knelt down and took the Walther PPK/E from his ankle holster. He wished he had his full-powered howitzer in hand. The shadowy docent-who-wasn't had no doubt come with an industrial strength cannon, probably with a silencer on its muzzle. Logically, he would shoot Jack at fairly close range, to ensure it would be a silent and sure kill, so he could get away.

Within a minute, Jack found Larry's crumpled body on the kitchen's red tile floor. The poor fellow had taken a round point-blank in the chest—with a silencer, for sure. Larry's blood drained from the heart, down his white shirt and through his rouge jacket, and into the brass grating where usually soapy mop water went.

Jack's nerves were keyed to high alert. He could have worn a high tension warning as he listened intently. Wing Sun. Meditative listening. He did not see with his eyes but with his ears. A ticking clock here; a drippy faucet there; and a draft sighing through a cracked window.

There—a man breathing not far away, waiting. The breaths were large, aroused, but contained. He was a professional assassin. He'd done this before.

Larry had not made it to the phone, which hung on the wall, looking untouched.

Jack was about to reach for it, when he spotted a faint shadow from the direction of the breathing. A long, hanging curtain blocked the narrow doorway to the pantry. There wasn't room here for a regular door to swing. A curtain was easier if you had to go in and out for cans and supplies. Someone was on the other side of that curtain, coming closer. The dirty white phone hung on the wall to the right of the door.

Pocketing his gun and ducking left of the door, Jack took a broom and knocked the receiver off the switchhook to the right.

Before the receiver could clatter to the tile floor on its long, spiraling cord, a silenced but powerful round blew through the doorway curtain. The bullet streaked through the air where Jack presumably (and stupidly) was about to call 911. Jack caught sight of a rouge-clothed arm in a docent's jacket.

Gripping the broomstick in both hands, he drove it against where he assumed the man's neck should be. The damn curtain was in both fighters' eyes for the moment, disadvantaging each man.

Jack's thrust connected, and he heard an angry groan. But the fake, the anti-Larry (or Antonio), was faster and stronger than Jack had estimated. Of course, Madame Zhang was not going to send an amateur. Jack saw stars as the man's free hand slammed against his cheek. As Jack fell back against a stainless steel sink in the kitchen, his assailant popped into view through the fluttering curtain. The man's soft shoe raked powerfully down Jack's left leg in an attempt to break the knee. Jack's pant leg came apart at the seams.

Jack was off balance, and unable to reach in his pocket for the gun. He wrapped man and gun in the curtain's flapping folds. Regaining some of his poise, he used a little aikido to help the man accelerate on his trajectory. The assailant staggered across the kitchen, still pointing his silenced U.S. Army M9A1 Beretta. Gun and man hit the opposite wall, while Jack fumbled for his own Walther PPK/E.

Before Jack could focus, the man hit the wall, recoiled like lightning (many pushups, much sweat training for this). He landed on his back, aiming at Jack from the far kitchen wall.

Having no time to aim, Jack threw himself head-first through the door, and out of the other's line of fire. Two silenced shots splintered wood where his head had been a millisecond earlier.

Jack bumped against the wooden door frame. His gun dropped from his hand as he slipped and slithered and fell.

Another quiet bullet from the other's silencer whizzed over Jack's head, barely missing him. A ceiling light bulb in the long, narrow pantry exploded in a shower of fine glass.

Jack's gun clattered away, deep under a low shelf. He'd need that lost broom stick to fish it out. To make matters worse, Jack slipped on a wet spot next to a drain. To regain control of his vectoring, he did a head-over-heels roll, ending with a five-point landing by a shelf of canned goods— two hands, left hip, left knee, left foot. Well done, at least that, Jack thought—nothing broken or sprained, after landing on his hip, heels, and elbows.

"You speak English?" Jack asked, businesslike. He sprang to his feet.

Still wearing his curtain, the assassin came flailing through the doorway and waved his gun in search of Jack.

"Madame Zhang sends a message before I kill you. Pay-back for Yang Jun." The man pulled the cloth from his eyes.

Jack pitched an industrial-size can of tomato sauce. "Then stew on this a bit."

The man fired, hitting the can. Red sauce splattered all over the long, narrow space. The man said in a vaguely European accent, while wiping sauce from his eyes: "Enjoy yourself while you still can."

"Can it, pal." Jack scrambled to his feet, grabbing the next best thing—a 32 ounce jar of black olives. *Shame to waste such fine food*, his dearly departed mother's voice whispered in the back of his mind. Jack carefully spun the jar between both hands, like a basketball player aiming for a lay-up shot. He tossed the jar so that it hit the wall, a bank shot in pool, and splattered all over the man's gun, which his assailant dropped even as he rushed toward Jack.

The assailant was as splattered with sauce as Jack was. His momentum carried him forward, and now it was his turn to slip on the water and the sauce. He landed facing Jack, on his knees and forearms.

His gun landed rough, letting off one more pop. This showered the room with fine glass, pungent spices, and shredded olives.

Jack pushed over on him an entire shelf of empty glass canning jars.

The man exploded right through that glass and shelving. He'd lost the gun, but clawed at Jack with hands of steely strength. As the man lunged, Jack connected with a lightning left jab that stunned the fake docent on the right temple. As the man started to fall over forward, Jack pulled out an empty steel shelf on wheels.

Jack grabbed a firehose off the wall nearby, unfolded the first few feet, and smacked his assailant across the head with the heavy brass nozzle.

The man's head bobbed about as if he were seeing stars.

The man landed across the wheeled shelf, chest and belly down. He seemed to be body surfing, with his arms raised outward and upward behind him like wings to steady himself. Jack glanced over his shoulder, and saw their images in a dirty window overlooking a small service ramp outside, at the back entrance to the kitchen. The assailant was just coming to and shaking his head. His face was contorted in a wide-eyed, open-mouthed look of sheer terror.

Jack looked again to his left for a flight path. He saw the reflections of two tomato-smeared figures in a dirty window at the end of the room.

"Here's food for reflection." Grabbing the cart with the man on it, he shoved the cart as hard as he could.

The cart, and its semi-conscious passenger, rolled across the wet tile floor. Jack gave it another hard shove, and it smacked against the end-wall of the long, narrow room. The cart stopped dead, but the man traveled on—through the window with a loud crash, and into the night beyond. Little curtains blew in surprise.

Jack fumbled amid debris and sauce, and came up with the man's gun.

Thus armed, he staggered the twenty feet to the end of the room—near the broken window with the cart now on its side and its wheels spinning—and out through a small wooden door.

On the concrete apron of the loading dock, Jack welcomed the bite of fresh night air, after the stuffy pantry.

Having rolled upon landing, and now recovering, the assassin was back in action. He knelt as he fumbled with his own ankle-holster and backup gun.

Jack aimed the tomato-smeared gun at him. "It doesn't have to end this way." The man might be worth more alive than dead, if he had any information Sigma or the FBI could chew on.

The man swung around and aimed a small black gun at Jack, with the shooting end resting across his other, upraised arm.

Jack fired, but the clogged barrel exploded in his hand. The ruined gun flew from his hand. Jack involuntarily cried out in pain and grabbed his injured hand in his good hand.

In front of him, the man was momentarily frozen in the act of aiming across his free arm. His expression grew blank, and his eyes vacant, as a round hole in his forehead darkened, and blood trickled down his nose. He pitched over and lay face-down. His gun clattered nearby.

Jack doubled over. He waved his hand in the air to drive the jangled nerve feeling away. He felt as if he'd been jolted with a line of electricity. He hoped nothing was broken. His hand just felt numb, like a slab of cold bacon. A few days in a thickly padded bandage, he estimated, and a few gin and tonics plus some attention from Minica should do the trick.

He extracted his cell phone from his inside left pocket, and called 9-1-1. As he spoke with the emergency dispatcher, he leaned over to feel the man's pulse. There was none.

Jack lived by a number of rules, none of which contradicted each other. He had just now killed a man. He had killed before, and he would probably kill again. He never messed with another man's wife, and he never killed unless it was self-defense. Sometimes you just wanted to throw up. At other times, you were too pissed off to care. This was one of those pissed off moments. When he thought of Catherine, and Tony, Claire, and Minica, he almost wished he could kill this piece of work one more time, just for the sheer damnedness of it all. He wasn't going to puke over this bum or lose any sleep about it. He thought better of giving the corpse a kick in the head, and instead kicked the bent ankle gun out of reach.

Jack left instructions for the police not to use lights or sirens. Their dispatcher would notify campus police, and together they would arrive without noise or fuss—cordon off the area, secure the body, look for signs of accomplices, and so on. No sense getting those eighty people all riled up and scared. With any luck, this shooter would be the Dragon Lady's last hurrah, unless she wanted to come for him herself. Maybe another day.

Jack dusted himself off, and headed into the kitchen to clean up, before returning to the lecture hall.

Jack washed up as best he could at the kitchen sink. His jacket was stained and torn—a total loss. So was the necktie. He managed to wash the shirt and wring it out. He still wore a clean T-shirt under it, but he wouldn't be seen, not even at a semi-formal affair like this, wearing a T-shirt. So he put the wet shirt back on, hoping it would dry quickly. The trousers were ruined at the knees, with a total rip from the knee down on one side where the shoe had raked him, but otherwise he was still standing and functional.

His strongest urge now was to check on Minica, Claire, and Tony. As he quietly opened the small side door, a row of applause rang out. The other man, a professor of aeronautical engineering, had just told the most interesting details about a new Air Force jet that could fly backwards in a pinch. What would they think of next?

Jack walked toward the podium. He joined the innocent clapping as he walked. The English professor cocked an eyebrow. The aeronautics expert pouted in his white beard, with huge angry eyes. He looked as if he felt upstaged. Or he would start sobbing any second. To hell with him also. Jack was in no mood to hold any man's hand or indulge petty rivalry.

In their seats, Minica and Claire looked shocked. Knowing Jack, they had a good idea he had just saved everyone's lives, including his own. Minica held fingers up to stifle her gasp, and Claire had that look, which said, "Whom do we need to pay off to clean up after you?" Tony's expression was more one of "I hope the other guy looks twice as bad as you do."

Jack clapped with the audience, who were on their feet now.

Jack stood dripping before the microphone. "There was a little circus, I'm afraid."

Minutes later, Jack and his companions ducked out as quickly as they could. Claire called her office in Washington, catching an assistant undersecretary of something at a dinner party, who in turn called a local Congresswoman who knew the mayor, who was in a bar getting sloshed, but his press secretary called the police chief and explained everything. As a result, the eighty people were released immediately after giving names and other identification, in case they needed to be called. The audience separated to go to their various homes, restaurants, or watering holes.

Jack conferred briefly with a police deputy commissioner on the scene, along with the campus security chief. Jack decided not to mention his broken car windows, which the assassin had trashed more than likely to get Jack's attention and draw him out into the darkness for a quick kill, made to look like a mugging. Much simpler to let the Porsche be towed to a garage on Rector's Compass News tab, and take a taxi to the airport tomorrow. Jack got his luggage and gun out of the trunk.

Tony and Claire were driving a large, boxy government car, so Minica and Jack rode in the back with ample room. Jack cleaned up some more as best he could, and sat on an old towel. Minica was solicitous as could be, but avoided hugging Jack as she desperately wanted to do. It would have stained her white dress with reddish *solanum lycopersicum* residue.

Jack's fondest wish was to get to a hotel with Minica, soak in a hot bath, and have her fuss over his hand. He longed to snuggle with her, while watching one of those scary movies that would make her crawl deep under the sheets to get as close to him as possible, while shivering uncontrollably and seeking his sexual attentions.

Claire seemed to read Jack's mind. That was obvious from the way she regarded Jack and his beautiful, dark-haired companion.

Some time later—as he and Minica stepped from the Lightfield hay wagon on a remote city street of Colonial pedigree and elegant period houses—Claire said mock-sternly: "Your plans will have to wait a while longer. You won't want to miss this."

Minica, always a good scout under trying conditions, held Jack as if rendering bodily assistance, and to hell with her dress.

"That okay with you?" Jack murmured in Minica's ear.

She kissed Jack's cheek, and whispered in his ear: "I'm so proud of you. "

Credits, Please

Jack had been to this street, and this ornate Victorian mansion, once or twice before. He already knew, as they entered and servants took their coats, that there was a reception in progress. Unlike the reading at the History Club, however, this was a most secret affair, attended only by a very select group of guests.

His employer, Johannes Rector, came out to meet them, holding a drink and wearing a smoking jacket. "Jack," Rector said, "We had expected a fun, uneventful evening. Can't you leave it at the office?"

"I'm not really myself when I'm away from home," Jack said. It was not just a quip, but a true statement. Only Rector and Claire understood what he meant. His private life at the D Ranch near San Diego was as separate as oil and water from all that happened when he left home on business.

"Come on, let's get you into a shower and some decent clothes," Rector said. "Oh, you and" (he winked, without looking at Minica) "can spend the night here. She'll love it."

"So will I," Jack said.

"Hurry—don't keep the guests waiting. We'll only take an hour or so, and then you can do what you want. You can feel safe here. This place is a fortress, built during World War II. Under the paneling, the walls are foot-thick, reinforced concrete set extra strong, with enough rebar to support a battleship."

Rector was a prematurely white-haired Afro-American gentleman of considerable mystery to all who knew him. Jack estimated his age at around 50. As founder and CEO of Compass News Corporation, a private espionage concern, Johannes Rector was impeccable, unflappable, and unstoppable. It wasn't even clear to Jack—who after all was a hired hand and not an insider—who were the board members of Compass News, if any. The firm was small and privately held, but its clout was considerable. By far its biggest client was Camelback Consortium, which included Claire Lightfield's Sigma 2020 company.

Compass News were the go-to guys when you really needed to get a tough job done right. From Jack's perspective, Claire was his favorite co-worker—a wonder-worker, a benevolent and pretty spider at the nexus of that entire web of power and intrigue.

Jack showered in a luxuriously paneled suite with Persian carpeting and stained glass. Its walnut shelving held nick-nacks ranging from intricately detailed old Chinese vases to Art Deco lighters and radios, from Versailles ormolu clocks to Victorian Big Bennish chimes.

"Oh Jack," Minica gushed, "this is so cool."

"Secrets of the rich and famous," Jack said. It was a joke, because Minica's family were zillionaires. Her uncle Carmine was sort of a Big Yang of Neapolitan origin, with nice suits, who spoke all the various dialects of brass knuckles. Her other relatives were priests and nuns who prayed and lit candles night and day to make up for Carmine's enthusiasm.

Jack stood before Minica, naked and dripping after his shower.

She lay on the bed, languidly examining him. "If this is the house of Mr. Rector, you must be Mr. Erector."

"Get thee to a punnery, my dear little friend." He wiped himself with the towel and shivered. He'd love to throw himself into bed with her, but did not want to sleep on a damp mattress.

Seeing his discomfiture, Minica said: "Let's crank up your heat index, baby." She was not little, but nearly as tall as Jack, and as lean. She was a black belt in aikido. They shared yoga and tai chi in common—went to different schools together, as the local saying went.

She spotted a pile of fresh, folded towels in a guest closet, and fetched him one.

While he dried himself in an extra-large white towel, Minica hunted among the copious closets for something that fit him. She laid out a gray suit on the bed, along with fresh undies, a pink shirt, with matching breast pocket kerchief.

"What the hell is this?" Jack said, holding up a silky, mauve thing.

"It's a neck jobbie," she said as she sprawled across the enormous round bed on which they would spend the night. She rolled luxuriously over and over, so that her long legs peeked bare from under her white sheath dress. The sprawl became her. Jack's eyes glazed over as he relished a privileged and lascivious vision of her.

"I'm going to look like your personal gigolo by the time you finish dressing me."

"Humor me, Jack. Let me get turned on really good and hot, and we'll have ourselves a little Nevada road house right here."

"The things you say, darling."

"I only tell you what I want you to know." She sat up and fingered one arm of his gray suit jacket. "Look, it's quietly elegant. Gray goes with anything."

"Yes, but anything goes with Gray." He threw himself across the bed in a swan dive, so that he landed with her between his arms. She shrieked as they bounced, face to face. He gripped her (gently) in a bear hug.

She squealed as they wrestled. The bed bounced. When he got her into a submission hold, she laughed. He leaned over her and said gruffly: "Surrender."

"Never!"

She melted apart under him, inviting him into her car.

She shuddered so that her body repeatedly shook, while Jack groaned with pleasure as they merged.

Her red nails made claws on his shoulder blades, as her rouged lips sought the sensitive inner shell of his ear.

Her hot breath and tongue on his ear drum made him lay pipe like a lineman.

She womaned him between sweet, strong thighs as she expertly moved in practiced jiu-jitsu come-alongs. She raised first one leg, then the other, as if he were a potato rolling between her thighs. Her heels alternately banged against his buttocks. She rotated her hips and womanhandled him as close as she could, while she thrust herself up, up, up against him.

He let her.

It was a delirious ride.

He groaned like a space walker, falling into her galaxy.

Rector's guests all met on the first floor an hour later, for Jack's award celebration.

Jack and Minica came down the stairs in fresh evening dress, each on the other's arms as if they were stiff from having jogged a long distance. Their radiant smiles were met with formal applause and some hear-hears.

Over congratulatory cocktails over the success of the Baidu event, the guests honored Jack for his five years of service to Compass News, which had come upon his retirement from twenty years of corponation service with Camelback Consortium (Special Forces, then CIA, and later Sigma 2020).

The clock struck ten. The guests chatted in a sumptuous downstairs room that enveloped them in luxury—draped in crushed velvet curtains, filled with stuffy furniture that looked as if it had been stitched together with tens of thousands of dollars of antique Yazd carpeting from Persia. In corners stood glass cases showing off ivory statuettes and lapis lazuli beads and turquoise Hopi jewelry and more. Like so much of the safe house, this part was paneled in deeply gleaming, rare woods harvested when it was still legal—some native American, others exotic and foreign.

"We are going to show a little video in honor of our guest," announced Johannes Rector.

Two CN technicians had set up an extemporaneous entertainment center in the Compass News lounge, complete with multi-stereo, all around speaker system. Compass News, for all the sound of it, was not a media organization, but a mission statement: North, East, West, South— the four compass points.

The techs operated a powerful holographic projection engine, whose floor-ceiling staging chamber that made you feel as if you were inside of the action, rather than watching a flat screen.

Must get me one of those, Jack thought as he sat with Minica, Claire, and Tony among the other guests. *That would be so cool back home at the D Ranch.*

No folding chairs here—more like an enormous living room full of couches, love seats, and arm chairs. Very much your classic men's club, but with women.

Rector said a few words into a hand-held mike, drew some cheerful laughter, and worshipfully introduced his leggy counterpart at Sigma 2020. "I give you the ever so amazing Claire Lightfield."

Applause.

Claire set her drink aside, rose, and walked to the front of the audience. About thirty guests, including significant others, watched as she stood poised—a tall, pale, freckled figure. "I have the honor of making some brief introductions, to congratulate Johannes Rector"(smattering of applause)"and Compass News"(clapping, a few whistles)"and of course Mr. Jack Gray"(polite applause, since few actually knew Jack). She continued: "We call this little video Jack's Event. We think it captures some of the ambience of the world in which he moves. Consider it, also, a kind of commercial for our friends at Compass News, who richly deserve accolades for their long and excellent service against terrorists, rogue governments, and other nuisances. Let the video roll." She clapped as she walked back to her seat. Ripples of applause pattered all about her. The lights went dim, nearly dark, and part of the room came to life. The video was three-dimensional, a holographic marvel of this dangerous but exhilarating new age. You felt as if you were in the video, not just watching it.

The room filled with swelling music as mysterious shapes composed entirely of light and color rippled through the air. The music was at once sinuous, mysterious, big, brassy, emotional, and always enchanting.

As the music wrapped itself thunderously, languorously around them, a series of images roiled in the air before the guests. Amid the images, a few lines of text appeared as well—they seemed to ripple, as if underwater, then straightened out for a flat glimpse, and rippled away.

An indistinct woman dancer's cutout form writhed in a sensuous dance to the brasses and violins of the pounding music.

The theme of the presentation was: A tribute to Jack Gray, at the vortex of nature's four classic elements—earth, wind, fire, and water…not to mention the four compass points—North, East, West, and South in Compass News.

At the center, or vortex, was a stylized Roman artilleryman in a plumed helmet and swirling cloak, operating a large ballista launcher while flames consumed the horizon. When the artilleryman turned toward the audience, Jack's face appeared overlaid on his. The audience clapped.

Now the four elements appeared, one in each corner of the holospace.

Claire, or Fire, represented Sigma 2020—the consortium of federal and corporate agencies who hired Compass News to send Jack on Events, as missions were called. The music pounded on. For nearly a minute, the holospace crackled and seethed with fire as solarized visions of Jack and Claire and other players floated in hell, starfire, and points inbetween. The segment ended with Jack Gray and his gun, stalking across holospace. Claire followed in a fiery dress.

Then, a shapely dancer in a gilded bikini crossed the visual field in a leisurely, rhythmic wipe. That wipe would be repeated, in variant forms, for each segment, representing the four natural elements. The audience, almost entirely composed of Sigma 2020 and Compass News officials, clapped enthusiastically at each transition.

Rector, or Wind, Aeolus, represented Compass News Corporation, the freelance anti-terror and espionage agency working with Sigma 2020, PETO, and other 'West'-like organizations. As the four winds blew, each in its turn, the meaning of Compass News unfolded—a compass rose, by turns rippling on the four points of the compass—North, East, West, South. Toward the end of the segment, Rector and Jack met in the center, or vortex, shook hands or exchanged stylized spirits or something. Rector turned one way and strode into the wind, holding a glowing compass. Jack, wearing a dress suit and holding a gun, turned the other way, and in a sort of martial arts kata, danced out of the holospace.

The dancer crossed the entire space in a second leisurely wipe.

The audience clapped again, trying to keep it subdued so as not to overwhelm the artistry.

Neptune, for Water, was the code name of Camelback's greatest rival, the world's second most powerful corporation: Global Anaconda, representing the 'East' of modern espionage space. The great constrictor rose from shimmering, undulating water, and wrapped itself around the entire globe. As it did so, the winds of Rector grew still, blew away, and the fires of Claire fizzled away in the dying wind. Bearded Poseidon, his muscular figure wrapped in nets of sea kelp, sat on a throne at the vortex with his trident. Jack approached, waving his gun, but the trident swung broadly and knocked him down. In a scene of wishful thinking, Jack slid to the edge of the holospace on his back, fired his gun, and Neptune twirled away on his throne.

All this kept happening, in rhythm with the brassy, bold, exciting music.

The chorus dancer sensuously danced across holospace in her third wipe.

The audience reacted with a mix of clapping for Sigma 2020—and booing Gamma 2020, their Anaconda intel opposites in titanic struggles around the world.

The audience fell utterly silent on the last element.

This was the bucket for all evil as yet not known or mentioned. A mysterious bad guy, whose symbol was Earth, was the enigmatic and unknown agent at the center of the world's most diabolical compass point. The world's forces of chaos and destruction were dark matter and dark energy blended into a dark purpose. He was the unknown evil yet to come in the next Event.

The audience sat stunned, with open mouths, as the dancer did her final wipe.

The last bit of text read: Thanks, Claire, Johannes, and Jack. Keep up the great work.

Jack sat suddenly transfixed. He had a premonition about this Earth element. He did not dabble in the supernatural, nor did he hang his hat on sorcery, but once in a great while, he'd get a shiver up and down his spine, along with a vague unease, and something true and dreadful would grow out of this. His last days with Catherine Dorsey had been like this.

The lights came fully on, the magic spell was broken, and there was silence for a full twenty seconds before people rose, murmuring among each other, and headed either for the cocktail bar, or the exits with their partners and coats.

Minica shook him. "Jack! What's the matter?"

He gazed at her numbly.

"Jack, are you feeling okay?"

"Just tired," he said as if speaking underwater. She hugged him and he warmed up.

Jack took Minica by the hand. They made their way through a gauntlet of well-wishers who must shake hands (and Jack could only offer, lamely, his left hand, uninjured, while his right was swathed in a fat white bandage). Holding their drinks—Chivas, neat, in plain glasses—they took the elevator upstairs for a night of sensual delight.

Chinese Sniper Rifle

In the morning, Jack bounced for yet one more energetic hour around the bed with Minica Albrisi, his old friend. His hand hurt a lot less, and he wrapped it in an elastic bandage instead of the big white gauze.

He and Minica followed their morning romance with breakfast in a Compass News Corporation safe house. This was adjacent to a luxury hotel on Chapel Street, on a balcony overlooking the autumnal skyline with its university towers and spires. A bracing air, Jack called it. He and Minica were bundled in heavy white terry bathrobes.

There lingered between them—over breakfast of toast, orange juice, black coffee, and muffins with butter and orange marmalade—their age-old regret, that this was all there was. They had been friends since college, nearly half a lifetime ago, and they had shared passions and affections. Maybe it was a form of love, but it wasn't meant to bind them. They both knew this without ever discussing it much. They were special to each other, but Jack Gray was an affectionate man, and he could say the same—in unique ways—about several other women around the world. He liked them smart, preferably with Ph.D.s, and athletic, and beautiful. He was not intimidated by strong women, but relished them, as long as they were simpatico. As he sometimes said of the strong women in his life, and their bracing and refreshing effect on him:

"They leave me stirred, not shaken."

"Oh look here," Minica said with crumbs falling from her mouth, which she tried to catch with a handful of glossy red fingernails. "New

Chinese sniper rifle. That sounds like something you would tell me about, Jack."

"This may be why we love each other, but will never tie the knot, darling."

"You cruel boy. But I do love you."

"And I treasure you, my love. Or Uncle Carmine would have me at the bottom of Long Island Sound, wearing large concrete overshoes and sleeping with the fishes."

She handed the news tablet across the white linen tablecloth to him. He read:

(API-Evening Mail)—Special—Unconfirmed reports state that the Number Two man in the Central Asian Emirates (CAE), Colonel Osman Rulik, was gunned down while giving a speech at an outdoor rally for war veterans and widows. Rulik, 48, was considered heir apparent to strongman Hei Ho De of the formerly Communist league of small republics. Hei's whereabouts are not known at press time, and the official Hei We San government public affairs agency has not returned calls or issued a formal statement.

Foreign journalists in the capital of Kargh-i-Shaal say that Mr. Rulik had been speaking for about an hour when he suddenly fell silent and dropped away behind the podium. There was no report of any sound— neither a gunshot or any sort of cry from either the victim or anyone in the audience. Experts said this implies either a silencer used at close range— not so likely—or a highly effective new high-powered rifle, used at a great distance, with remarkably accurate optical sighting characteristics, and quite likely computerized real-time analysis of wind velocities and other atmospheric factors.

Aides rushed to his assistance, including plainclothes police and other speakers on the platform with him, but Mr. Hei was declared deceased at the scene.

A Turkish doctor in the front rows told Shanghai Daily that he had seen a lot of blood, and that the wound appeared to be 'catastrophic.' The doctor was not allowed to get close.

UPDATE: Late word is that a sniper rifle of a new type was recovered from an apartment building about 1200 feet (366 meters) away in a housing project for fish processing plant workers. The rifle, said to be of Chinese manufacture with Austrian optics and Korean targeting sensor systems, is being analyzed by a government laboratory in the landlocked Central Asian nation's second largest city, Ban-e-Melor. Initial reports say it is a new make altogether, but without patent markings—only the legend in Chinese characters, spelling Made in China; and (presumably the manufacturer) Factory 13043 of Shanghai.

Neither a search of the Shanghai telephone directory, nor calls to the postal information service, nor any other public records, indicate the location or registration of such a service. Tax registry information is highly classified, since corporate vitals are state secrets, and our news bureau could obtain no further information.

We only have a vaguely worded reply from a military department, to the effect that Factory 13043 is a small specialty R&D firm in Shanghai. This company has done limited and very selective technical research for the army, including sniper scopes, in past years, but nothing in recent times. The company was recently acquired by Global Anaconda Consortium, which is moving its assets to Germany for further R&D. Its new marketing name is Project David, which appears to be a classic Scriptural metaphor for a boy with a slingshot killing the giant Goliath with a single stone to the forehead.

JFK Traveling Blues

Jack and Minica shared a taxi to Tweed-New Haven Airport. They took a hop across Long Island Sound to JFK International on a twin-prop Bombardier 402 seating seventy passengers.

At JFK, they kissed goodbye with fondness and regret for a long time amid steel and glass terminals. Passengers and commerce of the world came and went around them. Great aircraft with tail insignia of corporate and national empires thundered in and out through a drizzly, adventure-promising atmosphere.

"Maybe one day you'll settle down, Jack." Then she hugged him fiercely, realizing what she'd said. "Take good care, sweetie."

He let him hold her, feeling dull inside.

He saw Minica safely off at the British Airways terminal, bound for Frankfurt and Heidelberg.

He was two hours early for the call to the boarding area, so he browsed the airport's digital shops for decent movies, music, or a good story to read.

Jack browsed through a literal shopping mall, which glittered with lights and wrapped a person in music. It wasn't quite Christmas season yet, nor even Thanksgiving, but the first inklings of Hallow E'en were in the air. Horrible music and chill sounds on dozens of little midi speakers filled the air. Children flew about like bats, supervised by parents or nannies.

Jack at first browsed aimlessly, just glad to be lost and anonymous among people who were not trying to kill him.

Along the way, he dropped his elastic bandage in a waste basket.

In the most expensive electronics catalog of all, he found just the right gift to ship home ahead of himself. It should arrive next day or the next day after. It was huge, and would make quite a splash. He couldn't wait for his loved ones to open the package.

Gleefully, rubbing his hands together, he went looking for a bite to eat.

Jack sat for several hours in the public lounge of Southwest Airlines. He had a ticket—carte blanche—for First Class, funded partially by Compass News Corporation and from his own personal fortune of several millions of dollars. Much as he found air travel uncomfortable and tedious, he could enjoy it under the right circumstances, which usually meant either a woman, a long poker game, or a good book—or some combination of all three.

A certain sour, existential feeling returned, and he could not shake it. He had killed a man last night, even if the man had first tried to kill him. Putting Minica and Claire at risk still made Jack want to take the man out of the morgue, and kill him several more times. Nevertheless, the act of killing in anger always left too much sick, negative energy. This very anger was a toxic quality he wished he could lose. Rage sickened a man. He thought of Master Win at Compass News, and ran mentally through the appropriate calming exercises from Win Sun.

He still felt jangled. His circuits were fried. A double Irish single grain whiskey seemed in order, so he found a dark corner in an already dimly, reddish-lit pub in the concourse. The thunder of airplanes was muffled here. A traveler could forget the noise and bustle of the airport. A waiter named Mick brought his drink, and they joked briefly that whiskey—from the Gaelic *use bertha*—meant water of life. On that note, for a chaser, Jack also ordered a mug of German Becks, not in the frosty green bottle but foamy from the tap, since the Germans religiously view beer as 'liquid bread' and sacred to human life. If you said 'thirst' or *Durst* in Germany—in dialects, *Ericht*—someone would empathize with your existential crisis and hand you legally pure Bier.

He watched the clock and kept an ear out for his pre-boarding announcement. He watched a football game on the TV above the bar. Through a remote plate-glass window, he saw huge passenger jet tails like shark fins crawling in the drizzly soup outside. He slowly savored his water of life, chased by a briskly refreshing mouthfuls of Becks—much as a gourmet, eating Japanese sushi, intersperses each tiny course with a palate-cleansing pickled ginger.

Jack had few male friends in life, save a few mentor types like Master Win at the Compass News spiritual retreat and martial arts center. He had a few drinking buddies, fishing pals, and guys he knew at the shooting range—mostly in D.C. or Virginia—but his soul mates were women like Minica and a few others around the world. He made a mental note to send a card to Xuē. Maybe she would come spend a few days with him in Southern California or Las Vegas.

Meeting his women involved happenstance, as with his male cronies, but he enjoyed a far deeper bond with them. He was solicitous of his female friends, but was afraid, with good reason, to jeopardize them by being too close too long. Some called him a lone wolf, but those who knew him better might compare him with one of those chocolate coins covered with a shiny yellow foil that you got as a kid…hard and shiny on the outside, but soft and melting on the inside.

The taste of Dr. Dominica Albrisi lingered in his soul like a fine after-dinner cordial.

Airport concourses were a great place for people watching, except that you grew tired of too many women stepping smartly about on high heels, with their luggage on rollers, too many lives in arrest as people watched screens above their seats for arrival and departure times.

Airport lounges could be melancholy caves of introspection, as well.

There she was, with her back to him, drinking coffee in a neighboring food court—Catherine Dorsey. Jack stayed glued to his seat. His heart seemed paralyzed, as if time had stopped. He could not take his eyes off of her.

There were casual women, seekers who sought him the way one steps over stones while crossing a stream (so Master Win might put it). There were a dozen or so wonderful old gloves like Minica. The ultimate was Catherine. Soon enough, she seemed to drift from her coffee shop—and appeared at his table. She was stealth, magic, love with a capital L. She was love had, and lost—come, and gone. She was the one woman for whom he would give anything, but he could not have her. She was out of his reach. Then again, Catherine was genuine—her magic was not glitzy or flashy, but wholesome and satisfying. She was the one drug that fulfilled—the meaning of life, the reason for morning, the promise of next day as night fell.

He and Catherine sometimes bumped into each other when he was alone and traveling. The waiter did not approach her, and she seemed not to need anything. She was unchangingly beautiful. A far more beautiful and elegant version of Claire Lightfield, in fact, as Jack sometimes thought. Maybe that was the basis of his deep affection for regal Claire, who was tall and blonde and could be any man's dream, and she was for lucky Tony.

Claire—for all of her pale freckles and gray eyes, and her matronly hairdo around a cute, narrow face with slightly knobby nose, small mouth, and high forehead where she crammed all those Ph.D. lectures and dissertations—was a workmanlike copy of Catherine. Jack suspected Claire was decent to him because she was that to everyone—except that she tried to sister him, if that was the word, and openly admitted her affection for him. It wasn't love or sex, which went to Tony. Tony one, Jack zero. Which was all well and good. Jack had had his chance in life, and Catherine would not let him forget it.

Catherine sat across from Jack, in the shadows, poised and comfortable. There was some borderline unease or pregnancy about her, the way a dark frame surrounds the merriest painting. She had grayish Athena eyes like Claire, but richer, more golden hair than Claire. She had the perennial tan of a rich girl amid this Northeastern autumnal gloom and splendor, but she wasn't spoiled or vapid or selfish. She was the most considerate woman he had ever known.

Jack and Catherine sat like that for a while—not a time, because time does not exist in airports. Time in airports is relativistic. It is Einsteinian, concerned with moving targets (gravitational masses, gravid histories) and their intersections along the sliding scales of relative times and spaces. Jack and Catherine sat somewhere between absolute zero and the speed of light. Each kept hands folded on the table, each waiting for the other to speak, though they did not need words to communicate during that timeless while.

"I promise to take better care of you," Jack said. "And the girls send their love."

That all pleased her. Catherine smiled mysteriously, and brushed his leg under the table. She always had that Chanel No. 19 fragrance about her, lighter than light, and the feel of her knee was soft as ever.

Her touch was light as the air itself, like a breeze scared up among people's knees as a street door opened, in the sorrows of winter, and slipped shut. He closed his eyes, inhaled deeply of her nearness, and felt his chin quaver. A tear ran down one cheek.

Soon, on the public address system, a woman's voice announced that the flight to Phoenix and San Diego was ready for boarding.

Jack did not like goodbyes at moments like this. With a last sip each of whiskey and beer, he wiped his mouth with a napkin. He felt a bit light-headed—should have remembered to eat something before boarding. He had not eaten since breakfast with Minica. That was now hours ago, here in the no-time or between-time of airport hurrying, checking screens, and twiddling your thumbs for hours.

Jack picked up his leather suitcase—Nemirovsky of Fifth Avenue in Manhattan—and headed toward that daylight, as filtered by distant picture windows. If it were a painting, it would be called Still Life in Rain and Fog, with Tail Fins.

His travels would take him across the friendly skies to Phoenix for a one hour layover, where he would relish sight of the city and its outlying deserts as a refreshing change from the darker, greener forests of the Northeast.

Land out there, in the Southwest, had eons ago been ocean bottom of some shallow, littoral sea, in which monstrous lizards and saurians basked and hunted among islands that were now mountains.

In Los Angeles, Jack would undergo the usual transformations designed to throw off any possible tailers or shooters out to ruin his day— or worse yet, to invade the sanctity of his private family life on the D Ranch near Temecula, on the borderland between San Diego and Riverside Counties. It was time to stop working and playing. It was time to go home for a rest.

He would probably never again see this particular lounge in his travels, but he would see Catherine Dorsey again. They had this habit of connecting, of bumping into each other unexpectedly in distant places.

He cast one last glance back, but she had gone.

Jack Gray, Private Reserve

Language of Dogs

"Jack—you'll be late for supper." A woman's voice echoed from downstairs through the quietly sunny, two-story Temecula ranch home. The house nestled amid pine trees, high up amid alpine meadows and stony crags.

"I'll be down there in a minute," Jack Gray called back from his upstairs back bedroom, where at the moment he puttered over a bookshelf while getting dressed. He'd been taking a little breather—a moment alone, in the safety and familiarity of the house to which he'd been born. It was his true home. He wanted to decompress. He wanted to let his thoughts and emotions float together for a relaxed and well-deserved handshake.

He'd spent the morning on the high acres of the ranch, cutting and stacking fallen oak wood. He'd transport it for chopping, a year or more drying in the mountain wind, and eventual burning in the fireplace at the main house. A powder-blue, mid-afternoon California sky presided over vast vistas of inland mountains and deserts as he chopped away, sweaty and naked from the waist up.

Nobody, aside from Johannes Rector at Compass News Corp, and Claire Lightfield at Sigma 2020, knew the existence of this place, or of Jack's family life here. Ironically, he was most paranoid about safety from assassins here than anywhere else in the world. It wasn't for his own sake so much as for his sister, her husband, and the four children who were growing up here. The smaller boys were Janet and Mark's children, while the teenage girls were Jack's daughters.

How he got here from Los Angeles, a two hour drive northwest and worlds away, was an enigma to everyone but Jack, and purposely so. Once he appeared here, he was no longer Jack Gray or Pathfinder, but Jack Dorsey…hence the D Ranch; or Dandelion Ranch.

Jack's personal domain at the ranch was an airy, upstairs corner suite including bedroom, bath, and study. The boys were down the hall, at the back of the second story, where all three single guys shared a common shower. The two girls had their bedrooms on the second floor, but on the front side—high up, overlooking the hills across the valley in the direction of San Diego. His sister Janet Dorsey-Barger and her husband Mark Barger had an apartment downstairs.

Jack's windows on two sides overlooked a Federally protected Indian reservation behind the family ranch.

Hearing dogs, Jack froze. Somewhere on the ranch a big working dog started barking. The sound came from downhill in front, where the state road passed, a winding blacktop. Other dogs joined in. Their husky hammer-blows cut across the tranquil air amid floating butterflies, skittering squirrels, and a circling hawk pair.

Standing frozen, Jack listened intently to the language of the dogs. As if he were one of their pack, he listened for any sign of danger, of an intruder, of anything at all amiss on the isolated 200 acre ranch. No dog ever raised its voice without a reason, even if it was just the joy of being alive or seeing a bird or thinking about supper. Jack, an expert on survival, had a theory that the way dogs became domesticated was not by wolves coming near human campfires and liking the food thrown to them. Rather, some form of wolf or primitive dog allowed men to hunt with them. As long as the symbiotic humans did not upset the alpha chain, and contributed to the pack somehow, they were permitted to run along at the rear of the pack with the gimps. Gradually, the human pack members achieved higher pack status, though still far below the top alpha and beta wolves. Humans made poor dogs, Jack reflected, but humans were fiendishly clever at being parasitic, as with buffalo and reindeer herds. When these gamma humans returned to their Old Stone Age clans, carrying meat, the eta and zeta dogs under them came along as if belonging to a new pack—in which humans became the alphas, and the etas and zetas were higher up as well. That was Jack's opinion about how, in Paleolithic times, the domesticated dog was born.

Jack listened intently to his dogs talking.

For a moment, something cold and terrifying crossed his eyes. His soothing equanimity vanished instantly, replaced by the survival instincts of his working life. In that instant, cause and effect blended—terrified stimulus, terrifying response. He started to reach for the fully loaded, matte black 9mm Sig-Sauer stashed safely in a locked drawer at his knee. For an instant, he saw himself with the gun in hand—running, dodging, rolling, shooting, killing on the mountain meadows to avoid being killed, and more importantly, to save his family-pack.

A feeling like battery acid spilled through his guts, so powerful it ached in the major bones where the body pivots for fighting or running. He was no stranger to the feeling. Utterly unpleasant to the point of pain, the sudden jolt of racing high voltage had saved his life more than once. But it came with a price. The adrenaline-fried emotion passed in an instant, leaving Jack shaken. He had to stand for two or three minutes— face lowered, ashen, bracing himself with both hands against the dresser. He waited for the poison voltage to evaporate from his jangled nerves. The bad movie passed in a flash, like a breakneck express train fading into night and fog.

This was sweet, balmy, blue-skied California daylight. The dogs were merely excited and pleasured. He relaxed. Three of the shepherds were former military dogs who had seen combat service. They now bounded in pensioneered glory, like retired career soldiers, bossing the ranch and everyone that crossed its borders.

"Jack?" came his sister's voice again from downstairs. She sounded worried.

"I'm just getting dressed," he called out pleasantly when his voice no longer shook. "I'll be down in a minute."

"Be sure you look nice. Mark will be here, and someone else." Janet Barger, Jack's younger sister, ran the ranch, which she co-owned with Jack. Mark was her husband, Jack's brother-in-law, a decent guy. There was a pre-nup. The ranch had been in the family for over a century, and stayed there, intact no matter who or what. Jack did not worry about leaving his two daughters at the house—or Mark would have left years ago. With Janet and Mark, nothing to worry about.

Someone else?

Herding Trucks

Jack was a sturdy, dark-haired man with intense but twinkling dark-blue eyes. Discerning women found his craggy features attractive, especially when he turned on that certain mercenary charm that went with his job. Janet liked to say that her brother was a loveable if frustrating nuisance, and who else would look after him if she didn't—when and if he did show up, once in a while, for dinner and a rest. Was she trying her social engineering again, matching him with some new friend from her social club or some of her town hall busy bodies? The irreverent always surfaced in Jack at moments when most people became earnest.

A pleasant mountain breeze, wafting through the maple and pine crafted interior, stirred curtains along its path through upstairs corridors—curtains whose pattern was neither too feminine, nor too masculine, but strong, sky-blue blocks, crisscrossed with fine white lines resembling jet contrails. The curtains represented a marriage of personalities. Janet was a work-hardened brunette who could break a horse, ride the rugged back country, and kill a rattlesnake in one quick rifle shot from the saddle if snake and horse surprised each other, and if said panicking snake seemed unstoppably coiled to strike at said snorting horse.

Jack's brother-in-law, Mark Barger, was a Ph.D. oil man and field trouble-shooter covering SoCal and Arizona. Janet and Mark were raising Jack's girls almost as their own, freeing Jack up (in a sometimes heartsick way) for his all-consuming work. On visits home like this, he tried to make it up to the girls. Luckily, Gail, 15, and Marcia, 13, were mature and well-adjusted for their ages. Sometimes Jack feared that they didn't miss him or need him at all. All four kids were, for the moment, still away at school, but due home any moment.

Jack relished both his work and his play—but this was neither. This was family. As the saying went, he left his work at the office. Each time, on arriving from the City, he'd lock away his gun in a steel safe amid shirts, underwear, socks, and electronic gadgets.

Here, at the D (Dorsey, also Dandelion) Ranch, he always came home to rediscover himself and to become whole again, often from bloody and terrible experiences, for a little time anyway, between what Sigma 2020 called—what were known in the business as—Events.

Down along the gravel road approaching uphill, all five Malinois Belgian shepherd dogs barked hoarsely. Their calls knifed through the balmy air. Jack knew them. The dogs were happy. He'd heard them in genuine fighting rage, on rare occasions over the years, as they ganged up on the occasional stray mountain lion or solo-hunting coyote under cover of night. You did not want to meet them in a dark alley in that mode. They were a wolfish combat unit of perfectly evolved, lethal savagery in that state. They hunted together and killed like one mind united by a murderous synchronicity dating to Old Stone Age times. They were three animals melded into one refined tool, like an axe twirling toward its victim. And yet, a few hours after a coyote kill—as Jack had experienced on at least one occasion a few years back—having restored law and order, they could cuddle around your legs by the fire—still licking blood and gore from between their claws, or off of one another's muzzles. One of Jack's operating philosophies was: if you didn't appreciate nature on its own terms, you didn't really live. Above all, keep smiling.

The dogs' barking and yelping at this moment was a happy sound— not quite the same as when the mailman drove by the bottom of the property around noon each day in his boxy red, white, and blue van. It was a sound Jack welcomed—just one more factor keeping his family safe. He'd resisted the urge to buy a beautiful pair of gold wolf-cufflinks one day at an expensive boutique in Las Vegas' McCarran Airport. Wolves were pack animals, like dogs. When Jack was on assignment, he preferred to hunt alone, and come back alive. Being a team player was, of course, essential—but you were still on your own at all times, and the rest was all cover. To the stalking hunter-killer, all life is just camouflage.

None of Jack's family knew what he really did for a living, and he planned to keep it that way. Uncle Jack (Daddy to the girls) simply came and went between the D Ranch and the City—a vague term for Los Angeles, with its sea of impersonal glass buildings and global wealth sifting through anonymous corporate fingers. They didn't know that his travels took him around the world. As with the Malinois of D Ranch, there were wrongs to right on his territory (the world). Agents like Jack Gray were whom you sent when all else failed. Von Clausewitz had written that warfare is diplomacy continued by other means. In the new world of low-key national governments and powerful international corporations, Jack's profession was the continuation of lawyer crap by physical means. The money wasn't bad either. Along the way, in twenty years of military and intelligence work, Jack had amassed his own small fortune, in addition to having inherited the 200 acres in common trust with Janet. His assets were sprinkled amid banking centers in Luxembourg, Switzerland, the Cayman Islands, and places in Asia.

Jack resisted the urge to pour himself a double shot of generation-old scotch from a square bottle. He did not smoke, and he drank carefully. Like wildfire, booze could get out of hand. He drank moderately, for pleasure, not from need, and aimed to keep it that way.

He felt better now. He finished dressing. He toweled his hair once more, quickly. He glanced out of his open window. On the nearby reservation, tribal police hourly drove along their electrified chain link reservation perimeter. They passed at carefully random intervals, in white and blue HummVees with shotgun racks—with good reason: three major gambling casinos reared their corporate towers on the mesas below the crags, down their other side, with archways of flashing lights advertising tens of millions of dollars to be gambled back and forth inside.

Among the patrols was a commando unit with shoot-to-kill orders if sirens and verbal warning from a loudspeaker did not suffice to deter an intruder. There were millions upon millions in cash in them thar hills, and these folks took their money seriously. Warning signs to that effect were sprinkled about. The warning signs did not mention that there was a secret bank processing facility for coins and precious metals high on a hillside above the casinos, behind thousands of feet of coiled razor wire on tall electric fences, with Dobermans racing on gravel paths. As a good neighbor, Jack had once been given a helicopter tour of the reservation, courtesy the sovereign tribal government. Chief Juan Domingo and his council had over a billion dollars' cash in the bank from combined casino operations, and counting. On a hill farther away, also, was a murky sort of corponational hive of satellite dishes, golf ball radar globes, and microwave cubes. These were guarded by Air Force and Sigma 2020 personnel, likewise with orders to shoot to kill. *Good fences make for good neighbors*, went the proverb.

Civilian families living in the area, whether Anglo, Other, or Native American, were possessive of their mutual privacy. Many of the homes belonged to wealthy, critical corporate chiefs, whose protection was in itself a government and corporate asset. A few famous film actors and rock stars had secret getaway ranches in these parts, as well. Most were fathers and mothers with children in school, and lives to live, who craved normalcy and privacy. Jack was not the only one who came and went here on the dodge.

For some residents, it was a suburb of Los Angeles, with private jets tethered at Lindbergh Field in San Diego, or Palomar Airport in northern San Diego County. Folks here knew each other, and watched each other's backs. That appealed to Jack for the safety of his own family. People here were always prepared to challenge strangers, even at gunpoint, and to call for armed backup. Units of sheriff's deputies, tribal police, and uniformed federal police would appear in minutes via range vehicle, horseback, or helicopter.

Knowing that, Jack could travel easily on his adventures, except for airport ghosts.

Hearing the dogs barking, Jack remembered what was coming.

He finished dressing in the clean, upscale clothing Janet had laid out for him—jeans, soft brick-and-wheat checkered long-sleeved shirt, and leather deck shoes. All Janet knew, or needed to know, was that her brother was often away on mysterious corponational assignments. He sometimes came home with bruises, black eyes, a broken rib, but no questions were to be asked. Once or twice he'd even recuperated from a gunshot wound after being patched up at a federal military hospital somewhere, always on the corponational dime.

He and Janet had grown up together. They owned the ranch in common, which had been passed down through seven generations. They maintained an amicable if sometimes tempestuous companionship of over 30 years. She knew better than to waste her time asking questions when Jack got 'that look.'

Despite the D Ranch's handle, the family's ancestral name had never been Dandelion. It was Dorsey on his five time-great-grandfather's side, and Leon on his five time-great-grandmother's side. In 1899 had come a marriage between two banking families, representing North and South America. In the north there was old Russ Dorsey, of Tipperary and New England vintage, transplanted to California's central mountain and desert interior during the 1849 Gold Rush, and south to the Mexican border during San Diego's financial boom in the 1880s.

From the south came Mariana de Leon of Santiago de Chile, whose extended family had owned banks in Chile and Argentina, mines in Patagonia, and shipping interests with ties to Spanish and Moroccan wealth.

Dandelion—the Taraxacum flower, from the French *Dent-de-Lion*, Tooth of the Lion—had on that long-ago wedding day covered the newly purchased mountain ranch in a wind-blown yellow carpet. The romantics at the three day bash loved it—young Dorsey's hard-fisted Irish brothers and cousins, and young Mariana Leon's rowdy part-Castilian, part-Basque, part-Gypsy menfolk. A *Gitana* card reader among them had said the flowers were a positive omen, a play on the Leon family name, and were therefore forever enshrined in the ranch's symbols.

Descendants of those flowers still covered the mountain meadows to this day. High among the dandelion fields, near the highest crest of Paawik Mountain, was an old cemetery containing family bones and ashes from before this area had become unincorporated sheriff's range, and modern times as well. The oldest tombstones were of mossy stone, including those of Russell Dorsey and Mariana Leon. Among those graves lay the urn containing the ashes of Catherine Dorsey, mother of Marcia and Gail.

As he'd done this morning, Jack had spent many a morning and early afternoon cutting firewood in the oak groves along the dry creek on the north side, with the Pacific Ocean barely a puffy cumulus streak along the horizon. It was always special to be close to her. Jack allowed nobody but himself to cut his precious oak wood, and he only harvested newly fallen or about to fall as needed. He used a medium duty industrial chainsaw, while wearing heavy leather gloves and mechanic's glasses. He brought his wood back to the barn on a flat wagon pulled by a tractor he drove. He stacked the cut logs along a breeze ridge overlooking the apple and pear orchards below. It was work for a second day, leisurely paced: cutting the logs down to foot-long tranches, clipping each in half with the nudge end of a fire axe, and stacking them in a wall to be cured by the wind and sun over a year or two. It was part of the cycle of life that kept him anchored. It was medicine to tame his inner storms.

Along the south road winding uphill from the Temecula wine country, where Riverside County borders on San Diego County, rumbled and swayed a large, dark furniture truck. The dogs chased it, barking, through the mountain meadows. As the keen ears of Jack Gray perceived, the dogs were exuberant. Maybe they understood this was a happy day, and the cargo one to bring joy to young people.

These shepherds were a type of working dog known as fenders. They were just doing what came natural to them—herding the truck along to the house, as if it would get lost if they didn't, which, but for the bumpy road, would have been quite possible. The children, and Janet for that matter, had no idea about the truck's contents. All the better.

Holographic Fantasy

Jack headed downstairs to receive the shipment and then have dinner. Along the way, he tossed his filthy work clothes down the hallway laundry shute so they'd land in the basement, which had been carved into the granite cliffside of Paawik Mountain well over a century ago.

Jack stepped outside into the gravel drive amid late midafternoon sunlight glowing strongly from the west. The house, festooned with a century's accumulation of ornaments, loomed behind him. Over one doorway was a skeletal ox skull. There were rusty, antique wagon wheel rims whose wood had long ago dried out and fallen off. Things did not rot so much as they bleached in the sun and eventually blew away in the mountain winds. Winter snows and autumn sleet did their part as well. Neither the palm tree nor the cactus were at home here, though Janet had long struggled to maintain some of both in the protective lee of the house. Apple trees like to grow fecundly here, unlike down on the coastal plains. Then again, citrus and tomatoes grew in happy profusion there, along with aloe and loquats, while this range was better suited for gnarly, deciduous pear and apple. Everything in nature had its time and place. Being here helped Jack be grounded once again.

One day, he would stay here. That day had not yet come. He wasn't ready to think about it. He wasn't sure how that went, anyway. Did you have the sense to realize you were getting gray around the muzzle and better quit playing alpha? Or did you not have the sense, and end up never coming home? Would there be an empty spot, with a little blowing grass, next to Catherine on the high range? He'd figure it out, soon enough, all in due time.

A furniture van came rumbling up the driveway, herded by three leaping, squealing dogs. Janet came running out of the main ranch house to assure two sweaty, wide-eyed Tijuana truckers that it was safe to climb out.

The children appeared from the great room on the lower floor, with its usually warm and sunny western exposure, and ran yelling to Jack. He hugged each one—Tommy, 9, and Bobby, 11. They were Janet and Mark's boys, his nephews. They threw themselves at Jack and hugged him, and then just as quickly ran off to supervise the truck mystery.

Approaching with infinite aloofness and lady-like dignity came Marcia, 13, and Gail, 15, though they kissed their father, Jack, on the cheek as they held him tightly. "Somebody smells of Chanel 19," Jack said. It was a rich, but faded aroma, perhaps coming from that tiny, brassy bottle he'd bought a decade earlier for Catherine in an arcade boutique along the Champs Elsyees in Paris. She had treasured it, and now the girls had their parents' old bedroom. Certain things stayed where Catherine had left them—the Chanel No. 19 being one of them, saved for very special occasions. Like now. Pack animals have many ways to communicate besides barking.

"Daddy." Gail touched herself behind the ear with a defiant look. Like Janet and the boys, Gail, the oldest, shared the dark eyes common to the Leon heritage. By contrast, Jack and the younger girl, Marcia, shared blue eyes from their Irish-French heritage.

"It's okay, honey. It smells wonderful on you. That's what I meant to say."

Both girls clung to him and would not let go.

"Tell you what," he said, "now that you are becoming beautiful young ladies, I'll have to remember to bring you some presents for ladies. I picked up that perfume for your mother in Paris. Now I can bring home nice things for my girls. You just tell me what you want, and I'll personally buy it."

"We want you to stay home," Gail said.

"Stay with us, Daddy," said Marcia.

He held them close, suddenly brimming with emotion. Catherine, the perfume...it was her ghost at work on him. "I do what I do for all of us," he said. He couldn't get any other words out. He lowered his face, relishing their nurturing feminine presences around him. The girls did not change their desperate grip on him. Gail gently stroked his hair to comfort him.

Janet clapped her hands and chased everyone under five feet tall—dogs and boys—in circles. "Let's get those dogs under control so the men can get out of their truck. Jack, what did you order for yourself this time?"

"For all of us," Jack emended. *I do the stuff I do for all of you.*

The Latino drivers, looking relieved, climbed down. They wore dark green mechanics' overalls with embroidered name tags on one side of the chest, and their company logo on the other. As the drivers went back and rolled up the door with a snapping sound, Jack's family gathered around in curiosity. They went *oo* and *ah* as the huge box in the truck saw daylight. On the box were images representing the latest entertainment center—a holographic TV system.

"Jack!" Janet said in mixed awe and reproach.

"We can afford it," Jack said. "It's the latest thing."

"I've seen one on demo at Horton Plaza in San Diego," she said, "but I never thought we'd own one."

"You only live once," Jack said. "Might as well enjoy it."

Gail and Marcia clung to their dad, while fascinated by the holovideo.

The drivers slid the box onto the truck's rear gate-platform. They lowered platform and box amid whirring sounds. They wheeled the enormous device into the house, followed by boys, women, and dogs.

At that moment, two other feminine personae made their presence known.

Jack immediately understood—Janet's *someone else.*

A girl of Gail's age, Roberta, came out of nowhere and hugged him. "Hi, Uncle Jack." She was a tall, light-skinned girl of Scottish and Hawaiian ancestry, with scintillatingly dark blue eyes, and thick, finely frizzy black hair tied back with a white kerchief. As Jack hugged her, along came Roberta's mother, Molly Grace. Same eyes, same hair, same captivating facial features.

"Hello, Jack." Molly's voice was a melliflous music of mixed recognition, happiness, patience, and reproach.

"Molly," Jack managed to say while all at once letting go of Roberta and accepting Molly into his arms in a continuous three-way motion.

"Janet invited me." Molly was Janet's age, and statuesque like Roberta, only filled in at the right spots, with the same penetratingly blue, almond-shaped eyes. Molly wore a red, Asian-looking comb in her frizzy hair, and a Hawaiian mumu in fiery sunset colors over her shapely figure. Molly's frame was long, without being too angular. At 5'9", he was softly padded, without being plump—she was not overly skinny, but shapely. She was…was…enough to make a man close his eyes and inhale deeply of the scented atmosphere through which she gracefully flowed.

"I'm glad she did," Jack said as he closed his eyes, and inhaled deeply of the woman in his arms. Molly pushed him gently away. As she moved, his hand inadvertently brushed along the long, soft curve of her waist, touching the wider areas at the buttocks and hips below, and her shoulder blades and breasts higher up. She could push away, but her body was hungry for him. They read each other. They were a few words and gestures away from running muzzle by muzzle on the high summer meadows of life. His touch might be inadvertent, but a woman's movements were always deliberate.

"Roberta wanted to see you so much I couldn't say no." Molly's voice flowed softly, almost husky. She was full of mischief, a great tease, and Jack knew it, as well as Jack knew she knew he knew. Molly grabbed a pinch of his waist and twisted it so he saw stars.

"What did you do that for?"

"Adults—no roughhousing," Roberta said, getting between them. She took each by the hand, as if they were children needing guidance, and towed them toward the house.

"You didn't call me, Jack"

"I'm in town for a few weeks, or so I hope. I have you on speed dial."

"Not quick enough for me," Molly said. "Bad boy."

I had to chop wood for a while first.

(He didn't say it. He didn't need to. She knew.)

"Now, now," Roberta said, squeezing their hands tightly.

Together, they followed Janet into the house.

Mark Barger already sat at the table with an unopened bottle of Temecula Cabernet Eucalyptus Leaf. Mark remained seated, and embraced Janet around the hips, while she pecked him on the lips and opened the wine bottle with a puller.

"Hey, when did you get into town?" Jack said as he strolled arm in arm with Molly across the throw rugs of the wood-hued living room. Jack and Mark knuckle-butted fists, then shook hands, loudly, each with a well-timed round-house slap to the other's palm.

"I was in LA and flew into Palomar Airport on a weekend hop," Mark said. "I hitched a ride on a resort shuttle about an hour ago."

The truck drivers efficiently—obviously, from much practice—set up the new entertainment center in one corner of the large room. It consisted of an eight by eight foot floor plate and a matching ceiling plate on fine, tubular matte-gray pillars that blended against the walls. They ran a 220 volt line to a power unit. The electrical circuit had been inactive, just waiting in the main breaker box around the corner outside. The rest of it was a matter of setting up speakers, which could flow sound to each other so it appeared the viewer was in the midst of the action. The image flickered, rolled uncertainly, about three times as many fine flickering laser lines than there were cathode gun sweeps in a standard TV. The laser beams made aurora borealises between the floor and ceiling plates. Soon there was a news program. For a moment, the presenter's head was in the air to the left of his elbow as he spoke. After some fine tuning, and signing of receipts, the image came together correctly. It was your same old Channel 12 evening news with Eddie Krafchik, except it looked as if Eddie's rear end was parked near Janet's vase of roses. And Eddie needed a new suit, because his current brown antique had visible runs in it.

The drivers packed up the stray cartons and left. Last that one saw of them, as the sun drew lower on the horizon, was their truck lumbering back the way it had come, herded by a pack of bounding, yelping dogs.

"Those are happy dogs," Janet said as with wiry arms she mixed up a large bowl of salad.

"What are we having?" Mark said. He was a compact, tough looking man with sunburned skin, who spent much time physically on oil and gas sites rather than in offices, despite his Ph.D. in Geology. Jack thought that Mark and Janice made a splendid match, and the kids liked Mark as well. The living room was full of snapshots of past family life—an array of photographic smiles in all combinations of persons. Among them were a few of Jack and Catherine, with the girls as babies.

Adults and kids sorted themselves out at separate tables. The family had form, order, and rules. Everyone understood their place in the game. It was the pecking order of family love.

Gail, Marcia, Tommy, and Bobby, along with Roberta, ate together at a long kids' table in the great room. Their table was jumbled at one end with piled school work, lunch boxes, crayon boxes, pencil cases, and wax fruits.

Mark, Janet, Jack, and Molly sat together at a square table under a low-hanging lamp. They shared salad, wine, and a promise of desert. They chatted while eating. Jack felt himself still decompressing. The day's hard work outside had done much to soothe away the stresses he carried with him 'in the City,' not that anyone really knew what he did, except that he was a security executive overseeing cyber defense and other important business for a conglomerate called Camelback Consortium. This well-known cartel was nominally headquartered in Phoenix, Arizona, but with big glass buildings sprawling across the world's twenty largest cities. Their working headquarters was at Langley, VA just outside Washington, D.C. Camelback's yearly operating plan was larger than the government budgets of many smaller nations. The world was dominated by a few hundred megakorps like Camelback, which employed a significant segment of the skilled and educated human work force. Jack's comings and goings were easily swallowed up in the immensity of Camelback, even to his family. It was just as well.

"That's really nice," Mark said, about the holo. "Glad you sprang for it, Jack."

"We must be the first private home to have one in this area," Janet said.

"I might have broken down and bought one in another year or two," said thrifty Mark.

"Cool," the boys screeched as Third-World people rode atop a tank in another of those interminable civil wars far away.

"Yeah! I want a tank like that."

"Nah, I'll take the funky bandolier and the RPG with the dents in it."

Molly ate quietly, using her fork with her left hand, while with her left hand she held Jack's hand under the table between them. This worked out splendidly, since Molly was left-handed, and Jack was right-handed. "Next time, call me," Molly said under her breath.

"Sorry."

Molly let go abruptly, and reached across the table for a hunk of crusty French bread. She tore this in half to dip into her oil and vinegar, peppered salad dressing. She had said to him a few years earlier, one time, and one time only: "One day I may not be here when you call." Those words always hung in the air between them, even now.

She seemed more relaxed just now. Maybe she had made a better peace with certain facts in life. Jack tried not to, but he could not take his eyes off her exotic features, framed in a ball of dark hair, with café-au-lait skin soft as butter. Her features were an optimal mix of lean Caucasian and rounded Asiatic, with delicate cheekbones set far apart under almond eyes. Her forehead was high and intelligent, and leaned toward Jack when she spoke, while her dark blue eyes regarded him seriously with stacks of eyemail messages. Beside each corner of her mouth was a faint, delicate prominence that made her face appealingly symmetrical. These two points were the first to dimple when she smiled. It was a face he could wake up to every morning for the rest of his life.

Only—

"Delicious," Mark said as he helped himself (again) to salad with cobbed eggs, ham, cheeses, shaved carrots, bits of bacon and potato, and sprigs of parsley. "Good job, Jan."

"Thanks, " Janet said. "I never know when I'm going to have a full house, so salad is a safe thing I can make at the drop of a hat."

"It's a modular lunch," Jack agreed. "Take out, put away, whatever you need, when you need it. Very clever."

One of the boys added: "Yeah, put in bullets, pull trigger."

"Dude, check it out," said his alter-ego. "Rapid fire. Goo-oo-oo-oo..."

The three teenage girls looked ready to gag, and rolled their crossed eyes up.

"Boys, focus on your dinner," Janet said.

Now in holovision—horrible people were doing horrible things in various places, as was the usual content of the news. With Jack's latest purchase, the family could watch in three dimensions. In the shadowy corner, as darkness fell, you could watch schools of fish swimming and tacking left-right, as if you were in the ocean. You could get vertigo flying with an eagle over snow-capped mountain peaks. Jack had promised the boys they'd enjoy the 'funnest' movies ever.

Seeing a row of men in straw hats pleading for their lives in some dusty hinterland, Mark waved his glass, belched loudly, and said: "Wouldn't you just like to go there for an hour or two, shoot their dictator, and be home in time for dinner?"

"That would be splendid," said Jack, whose job description rather matched what Mark had just said, but a lot messier. It was the human element that made everything complex.

"No fuss, no muss," Mark said, still holding up his glass as if he'd forgotten it. Ideas rippled like auroras across his face. "You just pop the top dog, their people will be free from terror, and we can keep our army home. Ideally, you'd be home in time for dinner."

"There are laws against murdering foreign heads of state," Janet said. "Wasn't it Ford and Reagan back in the 1970s or 80s who issued presidential directive against it?"

"Yes," Mark admitted. "We made some mistakes knocking off our own allies in South Vietnam. The feeling was that murder didn't pay. On top of that, we'd recently lost another president of our own, JFK, and didn't want a repeat."

"What's good for the goose is good for the gander," Molly said.

Jack ran his hand over the provocative curvature of Molly, where her slender rear met her chair. Feeling her softness, he closed his eyes. Molly demurely kept eating, and gave no sign, either of pleasure or disapproval, but Jack knew she would push him away if she did not want him to touch her. So he stroked her with his hand, back and forth, gently and subtly. The language of their touch was electric.

"Don't you think?" Mark said insistently in Jack's direction.

"What? Yes," Jack said as his brother-in-law's insistence snapped him out of his reverie.

"One of those fast new suborbital cargo planes," Mark said. "Strap in at any large airport, jet away anywhere on earth in less than an hour, drive out in a hummvee with plenty of cannons and ammo, and clean house. Be back in time for the evening news, and nobody needs to know."

Jack nodded. "Like the Mesolithic man—enjoy your campfire with the wife, but escape to the manly freedom of hunting sabertooth cats totally unencumbered by women and their nesting instincts."

"Sounds ideal," Mark said as he drained his glass. "We can dream, can't we?"

"Who would do your laundry or make your bed?" Janet said chidingly.

"It's the Walter Mitty in all of us," Jack said. "Strap on your rocket pack, fly to the asteroid belt to catch some uranium rustlers, and be back in time for a home cooked meal."

Molly ran her fingertips electrically over Jack's belly, not accidentally. "My friend here is fresh out of rocket fuel, from what I gather."

"Flying on my last breath of atomic fuel," Jack said. "But Molly will fix."

Graceful Topography

Later that night, Jack and Molly lay together in her master bedroom a few miles down the road. Roberta had stayed behind at Mark and Janet's to spend the night with Gail and Marcia, as she often did—poor kid, in need of siblings and more family than Molly alone could provide. Jack and Molly were alone in her smaller ranch home on a quarter acre.

Molly was taking her time—waiting for Jack, but not limiting herself. If there was to be a second marriage for her, she would take her time—lots of time—about it. Then again—was there time? Not if she wanted more children. She never mentioned the subject to Jack.

Jack and Molly lay loosely tangled together amid jumbled bed sheets. Gentle night wind, smelling alternately of eucalyptus and jasmine, ruffled the long drapes and played over their unclothed bodies. It was the bedroom where Molly had slept with her husband, Tim Grace, before he was killed in an ambush six years earlier. He'd been on that black mission gone bad from start to finish that every agent dreaded. Everyone on his bench had been lost in a pre-dawn fire fight in a small Congo village named Tomo, in the DRC.

Of all the people in Southern California, none had followed the irony of the evening's dinner talk more knowingly than Molly, a secret agent's widow. Jack had never met Tim, but knew of him. Tim had worked for a rival Belgrade company, Sekuritate Mondo, which some years back had been directly acquired by Sigma 2020.

Molly had come into Jack's life through Janet, who met Molly Grace at a women's club. Molly was then newly bereaved and alone in the world with a young daughter to raise. Jack met Molly again a few years later over dinner at the Navy Officers' club in San Diego, when Molly and Janet were in the city for shopping, and Jack was on layover between Tokyo and Paris. From then on, it was a love affair like *cappuccino chiaro* (light) coffee—lots of hot, dark action on the bottom, topped off by a cloud of unspoken foam and feelings.

There was always this silent calligraphy, of thoughts and gestures, in the air between Molly and Jack. That they felt deeply drawn to one another was clear to each. They'd talked about this oftentimes. Tonight was no exception, as the wind whispered in the drapes, and the air smelled of the pool outside. The breeze brought scents of citrus, of sweet night-blooming jasmin in the wrought-iron fences, and of eucalyptus bark.

Fragments of old conversations lingered in the air. They had talked it all out, and nothing had changed—not their love, nor their frustrations.

"Do you feel anywhere near ready to settle down yet, love?"

He shook his head. "I want to, Moll. I don't know if I can. That's the awful part."

"I know, baby," she said. "I'm the only person within miles of here who understands. I was married to a wonderful man like you, who never came back. He'd come home all worn out, sometimes with bruises and bullet holes, and I'd patch him up. And he kept going out there. He'd kill someone, and he'd come close to being killed. He stared death in the face every time, and screamed at night when he came home to me. Now it's deathly still around me."

"Catherine appeared to me in a lounge at JFK."

"Oh my God." Molly buried her face in her hands.

Jack put his arm around her, to soothe her.

She would not be soothed. "I couldn't bear to lose you, Jack. I'd risk everything to have you. I just can't put Roberta through it again."

"I don't want to lay that on anyone, Moll. I love you so much."

"But we found each other, Jack. Isn't that enough?"

"It's all a man could ask. One day we'll dare again."

"I love you, Jack."

"And I love you, Molly."

"I go on with life, every day, raising Roberta, talking with Janet. I meet men, but none of them is right for me. It's just—it gets lonely here at night."

He pressed his face into her bosom. "I know." He sighed so deeply it was a sob. She held his head in her arms. She stroked his forehead and whispered endearments. "Baby, you can't change the past. Quit while you still can. Leave sleeping ghosts lie."

"They are at peace," Jack agreed. "But I am not there yet." He'd been running on the knife's edge for so long, killing and waiting to be killed, that he wasn't sure he could ever again come down from that energy.

"I am prepared to be ready if you are," Molly said. "I just can't promise to wait forever, Jack."

He ran his hand gently across the tender slopes and valleys of her body. "I know, darling, I know," he whispered, nuzzling her shoulder blades from behind. He held Molly, while she curled up in his arms. With his chin on her shoulder blade, and their bodies joined at the hips, the world was at peace. They listened to one another's breathing. The gates of war were closed. They gradually fell asleep together.

Part Two: Global Anaconda

Sicily - Agrigento - Valley of the Temples - Greek (pre-Roman) T. of Concordia 5th C BCE

Launch Time

Rector: Compass News

Johannes Rector, Chief Executive Officer of Compass News Corporation, sat over breakfast on the breezy, sunny balcony of his Loma Portal hillside villa in San Diego. A small video screen on the table kept looping headline news, surrounded by sugar, salt, pepper, hot sauce, steaming coffee, and steaming ranchero omelette. A slice of beautifully cut and polished semi-precious quartz, glowing dark blue as the edge of night, lay over a small pile of paper napkins whose edges fluttered in the wind. Rector ate with gusto, while working. He'd been on the job since dawn, working from home as he preferred. He spent too many hours working on in-flight planes, and in a concrete-block office in Langley, Virginia.

Just eight blocks down the sandy street was a public beach. He could have bought closer to the beach, but he and his wife preferred the view high up in Loma Portal. They kept a powerful binocular telescope on a bipod to look over the Pacific Ocean, the beach, and the winding coastal street far below.

This morning, like all early mornings, the beach was not yet occupied by the public, who would arrive later and jam up the narrow streets with their parked cars. At the moment, its empty beach and crashing surf were still the provenance of joggers, dog walkers carrying little poop bags, and surfers in wet suits.

Rector was a slender, middle-aged man whose ancestors had been Ethiopian Orthodox fishermen and hunters on the Red Sea coast. For centuries, his ancestors took their goods to market, crossing the sea to Yemen and Oman on the Arabian Peninsula. His scholarly ancestors pursued their studies and teaching in the fabled cities of Lalibela and Axum. During the 1930s, as Mussolini's murderous troops overran the country, Rector's father had brought his wife and children to Hell's Kitchen in New York City, and from there to the West Coast. Rector was a fourth-generation U.S. citizen. He'd visited the old country after the exile of its Communist dictator, Mengistu Haile Mariam, in the 1990s. Members of Rector's family ranged from darkest African to lightest Mediterranean in skin tone, as was common along the Sinai land bridge after tens of thousands of years of human migrations between Asia and Africa. Rector himself was dark skinned, but by his more Caucasian features could pass for an Arab or Berber. His short-cut, frizzy hair had gone prematurely white, as if his potent brain had generated electrical fields while deeper than deep in thought.

At the moment, he was reading cryptonet cables from western capitals, especially from Sigma 2020. Compass News was not a news organization, but an intelligence service in a sense similar to the German BND (Federal Reporting Service). Actually, NEWS stood for the four points of the compass: North, East, West, South. Compass News was an independent intelligence brokerage, providing freelance observation and intervention to its clients. Over ninety percent of its contracts came from Sigma 2020, the security service of the world's largest corporation. That was Camelback Consortium, headquartered in Phoenix, Arizona. Sigma 2020's liaison with Compass News was Claire Lightfield, located at the nexus of government political, military, and intel power just outside Washington, D.C. That troika of powers—government, corporate, and military-intel—made Sigma 2020 one of the most powerful secret services on earth, working parallel with the CIA, NSA, FBI, and other corponational agencies. But Sigma 2020 had rivals, in a world where gigantic, ultra-national consortia often had annual operating budgets larger than those of many nations. Such corporations fought among each other like feudal kingdoms and duchies. Rector's small, highly focused Compass News helped give Sigma 2020 its spear-points. Rector liked to compare his organization's relation to Sigma 2020 with that between Markus Wolf's sharp little HvA and the huge Stasi in the former East Germany, but without the mistrust and rivalry, and without the stigma of brutality and evil surrounding the Stasi.

Rector's trained and perceptive eyes sifted through nearly 200 bulletins on his large-screen digital pad. His eyes came to rest on a CIA cable regarding a super-sniper rifle made in China. What particularly caught his attention was the attribution to separate sources in the Israeli Mossad, Chinese MSS, Australian ASIS, South African NSI, and Nigeria's NIA. He bookmarked this cable to return for later thought. He rolled through another twenty or thirty items, none of which warranted a second look. He then returned to contemplate the suspect cable.

Rector was, like any CEO, a salesman. Contracts came and went. Rector would never reveal how many men and women were on his pass-through payroll. He was always on the lookout for new work, when it was not brought to him by Sigma 2020 and its powerful North American network of corporate and government entities. Those included the Royal Canadian Mounted Police, as well as the Mexican CI&SN.

He folded his hands over his lean belly, and regarded the screen before him. He did not need to run diagnostics to see there was an exceptional spatter pattern here. Also, the dates of acquisition seemed to be very close together. If Rector had to lay odds, he would guess that this intelligence was a plant across multiple borders, which implied a large and sophisticated planter. Therefore, most likely, it was disinformation—a bit of truth, tainted by some specific grain of lie that the seeder wanted to spread, the way one fed a cat its scary pill by wrapping it in hamburger. Why veterinary pharmaceutical companies didn't make meat-flavored pills for dogs, or fish-flavored pills for cats, was one of those imponderables.

Rector put his breakfast aside. He ran several targeted searches on all the day's intel, in depth, and came up with one more item. A CIA third-stringer, a local coded as Ribeye, had been in the audience when Colonel Osman Rulik was assassinated. Ribeye had sent an encrypted message up his chain of command from the Central Asian Emirates (CAE). Rector read through a news story from API-Evening Mail, and became more puzzled.

Finally, he reached for a phone and called Washington on an ultra-secure satellite synch.

Claire Lightfield answered from her Camelback-CIA main office near Langley. "Good morning, Rector." Nobody ever called Johannes by his Christian name, not even his wife. Claire added: "I trust it's nice and sunny where you are."

"Sunny is a state of mind," Rector said drily. "I take it you're in umbrella mode."

"Rain and leaves are beating against my window as we speak. Tears run down the glass. Tell me something sunny. What can you pry me loose of?"

"Information. What do you know about a new Chinese sniper rifle?"

"I saw the message traffic, as well as the news story."

"Doesn't it strike you as scatter chatter?"

"The thought crossed my mind."

"That someone is planting this little story—not too artfully but backed by lots of money—in a spatter pattern, meaning it's a dog pill in a chunk of ground chuck?"

"I'm fighting a cold, and a little slow this morning, but yes—I see your point."

"Assassination is serious business, Claire."

"I know. Especially since it's been illegal for the U.S., since half a century ago."

"Guys like Osman Rulik are a dime a dozen. So why spatter disinformation across half the world's major intel nets, and then the press to top that?"

"You got me." Claire lapsed into one of her pregnant pauses, when you could almost hear terraflops of wetware churning in her brilliant mind. "He wouldn't seem worth it."

"My thought exactly," Rector said. "If we knew the source, we might have a juicy Event brewing."

"That's half the battle," she said. "I'd like to know what's the McGuffin." That was an Alfred Hitchcock term for the core of a thriller—the object of the quest or search, usually a lost spy message or a deadly formula or some such hot item over which characters would die mysteriously.

"I'm baffled; that's why I called." Rector hoped she would come up with an illuminating response, and waited.

"So maybe someone wants to start assassinating heads of state," Claire said. "That would explain the disinfo campaign."

Rector said: "And maybe the Chinese rifle story is a blind for the real thing, whatever that might be. I mean, clearly, Claire, this not about Rulik or the rifle, but about the concept itself."

"Hmm... maybe someone is sending a message, and the message can only be that they are putting a service up for sale," Claire said.

Rector said: "What's new about that? Unless it's a new technology."

Claire said: "We must keep all possibilities open, but I like your approach. On that lemma, if we decide it might be true, we would logically think that the Chinese have absolutely nothing to do with it."

"Right, because of all the players in this fairy tale, they are mentioned at least twice."

"Yes, someone is going out of their way to point a finger at them. They beat it to death. Who is the real source of this broadcast offer?"

"That's the key question."

Rector said: "You mentioned money. Sounds well-funded, which suggests a corporate origin."

"Right...Anaconda comes to mind," she said. Global Anaconda was Camelback's greatest rival, and number two only to Camelback's number one among corporations around the globe.

"I'll keep that thought on file, without jumping to conclusions. We'll have to track this story carefully. You have a guy on it?"

"Mmm. Now that you mention it. I'll check across channels, but I think Camelback's CIA wing has a dog in this fight."

"Fella named Ribeye?"

"Hmm, yeah. You want him?"

"Make him my asset. We'll both stay in the loop."

"Done deal, my friend." Claire rang off.

Rector sat in the sunshine and breeze, deep in thought. He sipped his morning orange juice, while his wife emerged onto the rooftop terrace in Loma Portal, San Diego, carrying a little tray of Mexican pastries. Rector's thoughts were not just about building business. The world was full of opportunities. Some jobs were much bigger in scope than they initially seemed. Rector's instinct told him this strange sniper rifle event (or case) might just be the drifting tip of a very, very large, shadowy iceberg.

Claire Lightfield: Tropic of Capricorn

Claire Lightfield was not expecting any unusual space activity that morning.

Like most midlevel intelligence officials of the West, she was on a duty roster, rotating with other desk-bound intel officers through several hours a week of what was called General Duty.

This nuisance, known as GD, was shared among midlevel officers of the Security Collective more commonly known as Sigma 2020—which included a network of agencies including the CIA, U.S. and other North American militaries, a Congressional oversight committee, a Cabinet assistant undersecretary, and the Camelback Consortium of major Western corporations.

Claire's doctorate was in Applied Mathematics with specialties in ballistics engineering, orbital mechanics, and astronomy. This coincidentally made her a perfect babysitter for the world's orbital and space industries. For her, GD was like another science lab back at Harvard.

Once a week, Claire drove to Observatory Hill near Massachusetts Avenue. She'd spend four hours, deep in a huge underground technobunker, monitoring launches and landings, as well as telemetry traffic on orbital and space (Lunar, Solar, and soon-to-be Mars) missions, after which she'd be relieved by another intelligence officer of the networked Sigma 2020 agencies.

As a fine autumn morning filled the District of Columbia with sunlight and colorful leaves, Claire sat in the special new underground wing of the United States Naval Observatory (USNO).

Established in 1830 by the Secretary of the Navy, USNO's primary mission had always been the development, maintenance, and calibration of navigational technologies. The Naval Observatory was already old by the time of the U.S. Civil War. It had always possessed a powerful refracting telescope, the most powerful generation of which, a 40" dating to the

1930s, was moved to the Flagstaff, Arizona observatory due to light pollution in the nation's capital. Still continuously in use during its third century, the USNO and its many toys continued to maintain key atomic clocks for calibrating U.S. times and zones, and to monitor certain space activities. The USNO had always been in the forefront of U.S. technological intelligence.

As a sign of the powerful corporate-government linkages in the nation's capital, USNO had become the nation's time keeper from its founding at Foggy Bottom, and as the Transcontinental Railroads spread across the United States during the Gilded Age, captained by the titans of private industry, the USNO had sold time services to the railroads. This had resulted in popular cultural and technological advances like the station keeper's accurate, personal watch—originally, a marvel of its age, the railroad watch—as well as standard time zones. That had replaced than a million local times determined by a railway station chief stepping outside at noon to set his pocket watch by a sundial or stick in the ground. The U.S. Navy's chronological and astronomic services were as much a leading-edge, esoteric network as ever in the 21st Century.

Claire sat in a sterile underground complex, whose ambient light were a mix of soft overhead biolumes, enhanced by the mingled glow of amber, green, and yellows of countless monitors. Technicians from NASA, the military, and intel services (both government and corporate security) sat at their instruments. The atmosphere smelled of coffee, warm rubber, and electronics. Long ago, these rooms had clattered with typewriters and smelled of paper—long gone in this digital age.

This morning, Claire had about thirty events to monitor on at least ten screens. Among the tools available was a digital encyclopedia on which duty officers were encouraged to look up all manner of fascinating launch country information.

Among them was a Russian cargo ship launch from Baikonur Cosmodrome in Kazakhstan.

The Indians, Japanese, Brazilians, Southern African Union, and Egypt had nothing going up today.

A Chinese bus carrying six replacement *taikongren* (taikonauts) to the Asian Space Station, and bringing home the current crew, was about to rise from CNSA's Xichuan Satellite Launch Center in southern China.

The Germans this morning were about to launch a sunspot laboratory into solar orbit from JFK Corporate Space Center in Florida, U.S.A.

And in French Guiana—on the steamy jungle shores of the North Atlantic, not far west of the Caribbean Sea—a Spanish-Portuguese-Italian (SPI) communications satellite was about to lift off from Guyane Space Centre. This was an hour's drive along the north Atlantic coast, west of the provincial capital of Cayenne. Kourou, on the coast of French Guiana in South America, was a premier launch center for the European Space Agencies. French Guyana was administratively united with Paris. The fire department at the Kourou launch center, for example, was a precinct of the Paris metropolitan fire department. Now that's centralization, Claire thought. Other equatorial nations were starting to offer competition to the old-timers as well.

As Claire hummed to herself, she skimmed through a digital white paper recently published about the state of the art regarding launch facilities around the world. Her reading would prove to be prescient, because a big fat siren was about to go off on the world's complacency.

What all these launch centers had in common was that they were each host country's best location close to the Equator. The historic irony or anomaly was that the Baikonur Cosmodrome had once been in the Soviet Union. Now it lay in the sovereign nation of Kazakhstan, Central Asian Emirate, once a Soviet Republic. Kazakhstan had gained independence after the breakup of the Soviet Union in 1991. Kazakhstan itself sprawls across central Asia being, with a population of just seventeen million, the world's ninth largest nation. By another irony, Kazakhstan's land mass is larger than that of the former Western European Union (WEU) as defined during the Cold War by the Treaties of Brussels (1948 and 1954). The West, a term still vaguely used today, in the age of Jack Gray and Claire Lightfield, had been created during the Cold War in opposition to the Soviet empire of the Warsaw Pact. The Warsaw Pact (1955-1991) had dissolved with the Soviet Union in 1991. The WEU had been officially dissolved in 2009 by the Treaty of Lisbon. The WEU's military alliance stayed in existence for decades more, amid mission creep and definition fog—the new North American Treaty Organization (NATO), a subset of the Pan-European Treaty Organization (PETO). The old North Atlantic Treaty Organization (NATO) was long extinct by now.

The Equator is so named because it is the line around the earth's surface that is always closest to the sun. The half of the earth north of the Equator is the northern hemisphere (half-sphere). Below the Equator lies the southern hemisphere.

Because the Equator runs through French Guiana, spacecraft launched from Kourou enjoy a double advantage in lifting power. Nearly all of this comes from the fact that the earth's surface is spinning fastest here, because the surface is farthest removed from the central axis of tilt—same principle as the iron hoop around an old wooden wagon wheel, whose spokes literally move faster (and blurrier) the farther one looks away from the axle hub. A tiny part of the advantage comes from a microscopically enhanced solar gravity, tending to pull the spacecraft closer to the sun.

Claire was most interested in the German circumsolar flight, but something about the Kourou launch got her attention. The spacecraft was named Capricorn. On just one occasion, a garbled exchange—perhaps at a distant tracking facility around the world—referred to Pollux. She did a few quick lookups.

The tropics are those areas of the world within a band no further north or south from the Equator than about 23.4 degrees north or south of the Equator. Since the Equator lies at zero degrees latitude, and the poles are at 90 degrees, the boundaries of the tropics are each 26% of the 90 degrees of longitude north or south of the Equator.

The northern boundary of the tropics is known as the Tropic of Cancer, while the southern boundary is the Tropic of Capricorn.

The most precise, functional definition of the tropics is that they are the region on earth where the sun rises to directly overhead at noon on at least one day of the year.

Less precisely, it is a region of eternal summer—the only other season being rainy—consisting of either baking deserts of sand or stone, steaming jungles. Off the coast of Australia, glittering seas harbor giant salt-water crocodilians and other survivors of the Cretaceous Period.

In the jungles, all manner of things slither or skulk about, from reptiles to the most poisonous vipers and serpents on earth, from colorful toads that sling poison goo to hairy spiders that bite and chew as well as they sting. Even some plants eat meat, while other plants have developed the parasitic ability to wrap themselves like constrictor snakes around trees and gradually kill their hosts. Oh, yes, and of course there are giant snakes like the anaconda, namesake of the world's second most powerful corponation.

Geopolitically, Claire knew that many of the world's Third World nations, and most of the most horrific modern dictatorships, lay within the two Tropical boundaries. Perhaps the poisonous serpents and dictators were related at some subatomic genetic stratum.

Pollux, if she had heard right, was the twin of Castor. They were the divine twins, or Gemini, of the ancient Romans, and the Dioscouri of the ancient Greeks. She must have heard wrong. There seemed to be no thematic connection. Must have been a fluke.

Claire turned her full attention to the Kourou launch of Capricorn SPI-2033F.

The two-ton satellite had obeyed its Global Anaconda and French controllers flawlessly until it reached orbit.

What was Capricorn? What were the SPI launching today? Was it a communications satellite designed to bring backward, subequatorial regions a step closer into the space age? What else could it be?

Anaconda's Moriarty: Project David

Camelback Corporation headquarters in Phoenix, Arizona was a sun-baked glass cube reinforced with steel, bearing dozens of satellite dishes, microwave cubes, and bristling antennas on its roof.

Camelback was not only the world's largest and most powerful corponation. It gave its name to the world's most powerful consortium of corporate and government agencies, ranging from the CIA and the U.S. military to the halls of Congress and the White House.

At the moment, a broker from Camelback's main rival, Global Anaconda, headquartered in Central Asia, was speaking softly on an intercom in the highly secret offices of Camelback CEO Lane Burning. With Burning sat a table full of representatives of the Camelback Consortium: CEO Burning himself; aides of Congressional oversight committee chairmen Senators Bloviant and Hawgbile; an assistant undersecretary of the Presidential Cabinet; and chargés d'affaires of several western corponations.

The human mind likes things that are binary: night or day, black or white, East or West, good or evil, zeroes and ones, Castor and Pollux. The Cold War was long-ago history, but nothing comparable had risen to replace it. In a spirit of efficiency and simplicity, the human mind still liked to think of West and East. Camelback Consortium was the leader of the vestigial West, while Global Anaconda led the vestigial East. None of this had any racial, religious, cultural—much less national—overtones. If anything, Camelback worked most of its contracts in the former North American and Western European Union, while Anaconda tended to dominate on the rest of the Asian land mass. Brazil, India, and a few other large economies fielded their own versions of Camelback or Anaconda. The rest of the world was fair game.

Today, the super-committee of the Camelback Consortium had been called into special plenary session at the request of Global Anaconda CEO Dr. James Moriarty at his headquarters in Istanbul. Moriarty spoke in a dry, self-confident voice:

"Thank you for convening today. I believe your time will be well spent. I have a proposal to make, on behalf of Global Anaconda. This should be of long-term interest to your consortium and your allies. Are we on top-secret ULTRA, CRYPTO, and BEYOND?"

Aides assured him of it, and he continued.

"As you know, an advanced Chinese sniper rifle was allegedly used recently to assassinate Colonel Osman Rulik, Vice President of the Central Asian Emirates (CAE).

"In reality, nothing could be further from the truth. This is a fiction created by our corporate communications companies to cover the wonderful new technology I am about to offer you today, for the first time in history. I caution you that this is top secret.

"I am all too well aware that the spirit of healthy competition between our two global consortia has often reached regrettable violent and bitter ends. We continue our dialog with your leadership, outside the scope of this teleconference, in order to keep competition civil, legal, and proportional. To this end, as a great leveler, I feel it is imperative that we share this new opportunity with you for the sake of world stability.

"My corporation, Global Anaconda, is now able to field what we call Operation David—a means to assassinate foreign heads of state, corporate leaders, or anyone in fact—with a sniper bullet from outer space. We call it the Orbital Sniper Technology, OST. With it, to our mutual benefit, we make the world safe from the next Hitler, the next Saddam, the next Milosevic—to name just three of the megalomaniacs who regularly rise to become our Caesars, our Napoleons, our Stalins—the list is a long one, and is no more complete than history itself."

Moriarty paused to let that sink in. A babble of voices raced around the long table, until Camelback CEO Lane Burning rapped his small wooden gavel on the table for order.

Global Anaconda's Moriarty continued: "History goes on, as do its monsters. We call our wonderful new technology Project David, for obvious reasons. With a stone expertly thrown from his leather slingshot, young David was able to kill the invincible enemy fighter, a giant named Goliath, with a single hit to the forehead. Here's the big news for us all today: Project David is good for business.

"Imagine if the world's oil-consuming nations in 1990 had been able to kill Saddam Hussein with a single shot from an orbiting sniper rifle. This is my strongest selling point today. Wars cause disruption in economies and politics. No politician wants to ride that tiger, which usually eats those who dare to harness it. Wars usually mean expenditures, distortions of GDP, inflation, and all manner of negative effects—not to mention the kind of publicity no politician likes. I am offering you a way to preempt wars by killing dictators and other Third World megalomaniacs. We can thus do much better about maintaining the stability of markets, which can only be a favorable outcome for the major consortia."

The room bubbled with excited discussion.

"Imagine if Hitler or Mussolini or Tojo could have been stopped by a bullet before they caused the deaths of a hundred million people?"

For the first time, Lane Burning spoke. "Yes, but look at how World War I was started by a sniper bullet."

"I am aware of it," said Moriarty. "It's part of the briefing videos we sent you. On 28 April 1918, in the provincial city of Sarajevo, in Herzegovina on the Balkan Peninsula, the Crown Prince of the Austro-Hungarian Empire, Archduke Franz-Ferdinand was assassinated by a sniper. In fact, the archduke and his wife Sophie were peace advocates on a mission of diplomacy. Through the tangled alliances of the time, soon the German Kaiser was agitating for war, while the Serbs were allied with the Pan-Slavic movement, which was ultimately controlled by the Russian secret service or Okhrana."

Burning heatedly cut in: "The result was a totally unnecessary war, based on the tribal and medieval rivalries of primitive German, Russian, Austro-Hungarian, and other empires. Manipulated by the usual corporate media, from Hearst to Murdoch, tens of millions of enthusiastic young men marched off to be slaughtered. Ancient generals, as usual fighting the wars of half a century ago, had these young lambs march into withering machine gun fire, and enveloped in clouds of poison gas, in an unthinkable and pointless holocaust."

"Precisely my point," Dr. Moriarty said. "Think of the religious puffery, the political slogans, the patriotic nonsense…"

"Right," said Burning, "now take another example. The U.S. President, Abraham Lincoln, in 1865 was assassinated in one of the most pointless and callous murders in political history. General Lee and President Davis of the Confederacy were seeking peace under the generous terms offered by Lincoln, even while most hawks on the Union side wanted far harsher treatment of the South. In fact, the hawks wanted the kind of crippling reparations that brought Europe from the end of the First World War to the beginning of the Second World War. The last thing Lee or Davis or any intelligent Southerner wanted was for their most generous advocate to be cut down by a mentally ill thug like John Wilkes Booth."

"Your points are well taken," Moriarty said. "These are, however, the exceptions."

"Exceptions! Presidents Gerald Ford and Ronald Reagan both issued executive orders forbidding the assassination of foreign heads of state, without a full declaration of war."

"The key word," Moriarty said, "is responsibility. Wrong assassinations lead to wrong results. But a perfectly correct, consensual assassination, after a responsible declaration of war, is simply a matter of winning the war by killing one individual. It leads to saving millions of lives by avoiding enormous battles, destruction of property, and loss of lives. You declare war, and you go after one person. This is a serious technology of immense power to either harm or do good. In responsible hands, the Orbital Sniper Technology will cause enhanced world peace and order. My sign of respect and deference for your consortium is that I present it to you as a gesture of peace and universal cooperation."

After a pause, Burning said: "My instinct is to say no. My instinct is not to trust you. However, the possibilities in your technology are so awe inspiring that I think they deserve at least some discussion on our side. That is all I can offer at this point in response to your offer."

Moriarty sounded as if he felt he'd won. "Fair enough. We can send the appropriate specifications and any other information that you wish, providing you agree that this will remain the best kept secret in the world since the United States in World War II developed the first operational atomic bombs."

Burning replied: "Dr. Moriarty, you have set a dragon upon the table. Publication of your scheme would cause panic on world financial markets. It would most assuredly disrupt world energy and other commodity spot markets within minutes. We will all do our best to keep this totally under wraps."

Neptune said: "Thank you for giving this your most urgent and secret consideration. The next Saddam or Hitler is probably a child somewhere, at this moment. We must be ready for him or her when the time comes. And I assure you, the time will be here sooner rather than later."

Burning said: "We can agree on this. The world is full of Colonel Ruliks. It is the Human Condition."

"Dr. Moriarty, I have a technical question," one of Senator Bloviant's assistants said. She was a frumpy looking young woman with a mousy, tight little hairdo and a brown dress-suit. "If I imagine this correctly, it would be like shooting a rifle into a deep pond to kill a fish at the bottom. Would the bullet not be slowed down by the hydraulic principle, since water cannot be compressed? Would the air mass of the atmosphere not slow your bullet? Would the bullet not burn up from atmospheric friction? Would the winds not carry it off course?"

Moriarty chuckled. "Wise questions. Easily answered. The concept of an Orbital Sniper bullet is quite literally true on the one hand, and a bit of a metaphor on the other hand. At the end point, your target does take a bullet directly to the torso, with catastrophic and terminal results, as happened with Colonel Osman Rulik of the CAE. The bullet itself is fired from a sniper rifle. The trick is how to get the sniper rifle into firing position, without using a human agent or sniper. That is where the fake Rulik assassination, and our proposed Orbital Sniper Technology, differ. Our technology is the ultimate in stealth."

Another Congressional aide, this time a studious looking young man in the requisite rumpled dark suit, asked: "So why not just send a sniper? Why not shoot him from a jet aircraft miles away?"

"Good questions, all," said Moriarty. "When you assassinate a foreign head of state or corporation, you want it to occur anonymously. The West, certainly, has long been lulled by its own legal niceties and legalistic suicide in the face of implacable hatred from forces of unreason. The OST side-steps the obvious issues. As I said, begin by declaring war. You can do this covertly, for the record, to cover yourself in the endless political and legal hearings that may follow, reported to death in the press. But it's the kind of thing that can also get lost in secret committees and closed door hearings. Preferably, you would make it seem like the work of some local psychopath. You do not want your fingerprints on it. You do not want to run the possibility of a propaganda disaster or media blowback. You do not want to create a strategic advantage for your enemies. A declaration of war is a serious matter. Just as dangerous is use of the OST, which must be done as surgically and precisely as a robotic mission to Mars.

"So here is how it works. You do not use cruise missiles, drones, or other air technology. Today's radars are sophisticated enough to rule out any such crude tactics—shall we say *mano-a-mano* or hand to hand combat. Radars, my friends, do not typically look upward, with one or two exceptions. They are primarily deployed to detect incoming waves of bombers, as was their design since World War II. They will look for incoming missiles, but our OST has an entirely different signature.

"For one thing, it is very small. What leaves the orbiting mother ship is a miniature ceramic shuttle, resembling a scale version of the old U.S. space shuttle, or its miniature clone, the smaller Soviet Buran design. Our model is approximately the size of a motorcycle. As it moves across the sky, it resembles a meteor, but moves slowly enough that the fire ball looks like that of an even smaller reentry mass. Every day and night, hundreds of these, maybe thousands, streak through the atmosphere, and no military or civilian observatory pays much attention to them.

"In Stage One, the primary reentry vehicle descends at a steep angle, leveling out at one mile altitude, and shatters into fragments that will land harmlessly and resemble ordinary rocks. The fragments will land far apart, and nobody will connect them with each other.

"For Stage Two, inside is a smaller vehicle, the size of an artillery shell with wings. It is a small cruise missile. It is light-weight, of ceramic like the shuttle, and designed to fly head-on toward the target. As it approaches, it aims its interior rifle. It descends to about one hundred feet in clear air space, and its tiny nose cone shears off—the size of a man's thumb, fixed on the oblique for flawless, instantaneous separation.

"Now for Stage Three, the final step. The cruise missile fires a bullet from the aperture in its nose. The gas exhausted by the round also shatters the cruise missile or sniper rifle, leaving no trace. "The bullet is essentially a .50 caliber round of fully jacketed steel, which travels a quarter mile laterally before entering its target with catastrophic and terminal results. Saddam is dead, and the world is safe from all-out war."

"And the target?" asked another Camelback Consortium aide. "How long does this all take? Won't a Saddam or a Milosevic move around in the meantime? How do you target someone like that?"

If voices could smile, Moriarty's surely did. "Now you ask my favorite question. Think, young man. What do Fidel Castro, Adolf Hitler, Benito Mussolini, Saddam Hussein, Moammar Ghaddafi, and others of their ilk have in common?"

Suspenseful silence. An observer would have been convinced by that moment, correctly, that Moriarty had his listeners eating from his hand.

"They talk too much," Moriarty's voice boomed through the Camelback conference room. "The Fidels and the Saddams are all notorious for speaking at a podium, sometimes for eight hours without interruption or pause for breath. It is a primary symptom of their psychosis and their megalomania. It is the easiest element in the entire OST program, Project David, that I can offer you today. Rest assured, psychopaths like this will stand quite still while you shoot them."

"Brilliant," Lane Burning could be heard murmuring.

The hall rumbled with excitement.

"It's a technological feat of genius from Global Anaconda engineers and scientists," Moriarty said. "OST works from Low Earth Orbit, on the basis of research dating back to the U.S. CIA's Keyhole satellites and the U.S. Air Force's Corona satellites. These were not sniper vehicles, but photo reconnaissance technologies. They could be moved upward or downward in orbit, to as low as 165 miles altitude, and back up over 200 miles. From an orbital position 180 miles high, let's say, a vehicle like OST can shoot a bullet that, traveling a mile a minute over an arc of about 240 miles, will perform through its ballistic stages from shuttle to rifle to bullet..."

Heads leaned together in excited conversation as Moriarty closed his presentation.

"...and impact the target in just four minutes. It travels, in fact, at a relatively slow speed compared to meteors and similar natural phenomena. A man-made rocket travels much faster, to achieve escape velocity greater than 17,500 mph. Our vehicle travels without undue engineering stresses, and certainly without being observed," Moriarty concluded. "The net effect is to catastrophically and definitively terminate the target, while causing observers to frantically search the grounds for a discarded sniper rifle. We thought about adding that for special effect, but canceled the idea after considering what a rifle still moving—say, a mile a minute—might do when dropping from 100 feet. We simply decided it would be best if it looked as if the sniper got away with his rifle. So the cruise missile phase is the rifle itself, which self-destructs while shooting the actual sniper bullet. We get in, and kill our enemy, without leaving a trace. For all anyone knows, the action was done by a madman with a sniper rifle, as in the Rulik scenario."

Montreal: Raiding Castor and Pollux

Even as the CEO of Global Anaconda regaled the CEO of Camelback Consortium and his top advisors with their grand scheme, a game-changing scenario by Black Umbrella was underway.

Forty commandos with their full gear, including ammo and assault rifles, lined the main body of a chartered Airbus A700M Atlas as it roared over the North Atlantic from Europe to North America.

Project Gemini of the Black Umbrella Consortium was underway.

Anaconda's Project David was about to end up dead on delivery.

The objective was to seize Global Anaconda Corporation's Castor-Pollux operational headquarters, knee-capping Project David, and appropriating the inventor's technology for the purposes of Dr. Night and his organization.

Global Anaconda had purchased an obscure Chinese manufacturer of sniper rifles, renamed it David Company or Project David. They were using it, and the Rulik assassination, as an elaborate cover for their Orbital Sniper Technology (OST).

Black Umbrella's Project Gemini was about to take over the game.

From a quarry amid sprawling, empty farm land outside Montreal, six large vehicles roared forth into the descending dusk. They were concrete mixers that had been converted to a very special purpose by a local Black Umbrella shell company. Their headlights stabbed into the growing dusk as they trucked on noisy diesel engines, led and followed by smaller flag-signal vehicles as the law required. Each of the concrete mixers had been converted to a very special purpose for just this event, using borrowed field weapons of the old Canadian army.

With their huge mixer drums slowly rotating—gray, painted with orange stripes all around—the trucks noisily barreled toward Technopolis, Montreal's city of technology.

The trucks would meet up at just the right critical moment with the BLUM commandos from Holland. The job would be over in about fifteen minutes—not much longer than the time it took to microwave a large burrito.

Immediately upon Louis Cartouche's signing the Sicilian contract at the Villa Caproni, Anaconda had not wasted a moment. Before the ink from Louis' pen was dry in Palermo, a convoy of deceptively marked Anaconda moving vans (Frontenac Movers, Inc.) had arrived at Louis' underground facility in Montreal to remove the Pollux control to join the already tested and functional Castor unit across town.

That was a top secret Anaconda facility in the Technopolis district of the city, where the last steps would take just days to complete before the Castor-Pollux-orbiting Capricorn triad was operational and ready to smash tyrants. From orbit above the Tropic of Capricorn, Anaconda's satellite—think Moon Raker with bullets—could pick off at will any tyrant the world's big corponations found convenient. If the hypothetical nation of Oilistan was ruled by a jackbooted *liberalista* with socialist or democratic ideas, some oil-loving corponation would pay a trillion dollars, euros, or intercredits to see him replaced by a more amenable lobbyist type with a fat briefcase and a fondness for wine, women, and dance music. Anaconda planned to make a killing, both figuratively and literally.

But not so fast—Dr. Night's troops were on the way. Black Umbrella was always a shadowy step behind, breathing stealthily down Anaconda's neck. The tables were about to turn, as they say in Las Vegas. Black Umbrella would seize both twins—Castor and Pollux—and change the equation completely. They already had two operational destinations waiting to receive the units and plug them in—one on a remote island off the shore of Scotland, the other on a tiny island just north of Sicily in the Mediterranean. Anaconda would not know what hit them until the game for them was over, and they would look like the impotent fools that they were. BLUM and Dr. Night were about to change the balance of world power, and the outcome of history for the next century or more.

The Atlas cargo plane—thundering more than two miles high over Greenland in late afternoon sunlight—looked like a modern update on the venerable U.S. Hercules C-130 series of the previous century. The Atlas had a squat fuselage painted dark-green for these sub-polar latitudes. Like the Hercules, it had four powerful turboprop engines, but the Atlas' prop blades were scimitar-shaped, and the two propellers on each wing counter-rotated.

The forty fighting men on board were dedicated professionals who had cut all ties with their previous lives to serve with the elite fighting units of Black Umbrella (BLUM). They had been carefully recruited from top-caliber officer and NCO corps of a number of national armed forces—the French Foreign Legion; the German Army's DSO; the British Army's regular SAS/SRR; crack Italian mountain troops; South African Recces; and Royal Canadian Mounted Police, and some U.S. Navy SEALs.

Soldiers of First Tac—officially the 1st Tactical Insertion Force, sometimes 1st TIF—sat paratroop style in facing lines of canvas seats along the bulkheads in the cargo bay. First Tac was on a straight flight from Shiphol International in Amsterdam to Montreal-Mirabel International Airport in Quebec Province, Canada. That was an air distance of 5500 km (3400 miles).

The men wore casual, dark civilian clothing. For about an hour, their officers instructed them, but for the rest of the flight, the men dozed or talked. They received one hot meal, and several cold snacks, along with each man's preference of hot, fresh tea or coffee, or bottled spring water. Ample comfort facilities made for a relaxing, refreshing flight. They would be ready for action on arrival in Montreal.

Flying at 11,000 m (37,000 feet), cruising speed 780 km/h (480 mph; 420 km), the lumbering dark-green aircraft traveled for about 8 hours against the jet stream. It crossed into Canadian airspace at nightfall.

The Atlas landed at Montreal-Mirabel after 9 p.m. local time. It taxied to a remote cargo hangar, which was almost entirely shut down at the moment. Clamshell doors opened in the fuselage, and air-stairs slid down to the tarmac.

The men emerged, well-dressed and layered for the autumn cold.

As the men filed down several air-stairs, two black buses pulled up with precise timing. The buses bore crudely painted white signage for a nonexistent local fundamentalist church. They were full-size buses with 50 seats each. The rear ten rows had been removed from each bus. Heavy chains had been welded to each bus' chassis. Loose end links lay curling across the rear floors.

As each bus pulled away with a wheeze of air brakes and a gout of diesel exhaust, it gave the appearance of carrying twenty devout young men to a worship meeting. The time was 9:30 p.m. It seemed like a late Scripture assembly indeed, but nobody would notice. Montreal was the second-largest city in Canada, and the seventh largest in North America. It was the largest city in Quebec Province (or Nation, by a 2006 act of Canada's Parliament). In a city this size, anything was possible. No police officer would think to pull them over unless they were speeding, but the two BLUM drivers and their backups would not run a single stop sign, or travel faster than the legal speed limit at any point.

Cruising down the 25 Autoroute, the buses entered the *Technopol*, or Technical City. Here was the concerted French Canadian technological initiative, sprawling across acres of Montreal's largest suburb of Laval.

Six converted concrete mixers, accompanied by two SUV-like vehicles with warning signals, roared into position on the access road that completely surrounded the Anaconda facility housing Castor and Pollux.

The grounds had six corners, and each got one concrete mixer backing up to it, with the open rear of its rotating drum pointing toward the buildings.

Lights were on the buildings, which covered only a modest four acres. They were pleasant, nondescript brick buildings dating to the 1950s, which had once housed a government run school for handicapped adults. Later, it had served as an offices and warehouses complex leased out to one company after another. Finally, Anaconda had purchased the site to house its secret Project David. Castor had been here for two years, and Pollux for two days.

Anaconda Consortium kept the presence of armed guards to a minimum, in order to keep a low profile. One or two private security rovers patrolled the perimeter at any time, inside a silvery chain link fence,

24/7. Inside the warehouses were another twenty armed security guards who stayed out of sight. They were disguised as firemen, and could often be seen training on the green lawns within the perimeter. Or they would polish their fire engines. Or shoot guns inside, where nobody could hear them.

As the six concrete mixers dieseled into position, the guards inside took little notice. Construction projects were a norm in the area. At any one time, you could see at least two or three tall cranes rising spider-like over the cityscape.

The men and women in the trucks wasted no time. First, they turned on the advanced, ultra-powerful, but quiet generators that had been built into the huge, slowly rotating mixer drums. These had been thoroughly tested, like the other system, and worked flawlessly.

As soon as each truck commander read their gauges, and saw that the right power was flowing through a complete circuit, they gave the order for the next switch to be thrown.

Inside each drum was a microwave beam transmitter of the most advanced and recent design—an improvement on old military models of U.S. and Canadian vintage that had looked good in the pages of Popular Mechanics magazine, but had not worked well.

In the hands of BLUM, they worked superbly.

There wasn't much sound, nor light. The air hummed strangely, and all the leaves fell off trees and bushes inside the four acre facility. Inside, any mammalian life form—be it guards, mice, scientists, or lab rats—was cooked to the consistency of a well-done burrito.

The two buses drove along the night-time highway, and turned off onto an industrial boulevard. The whole area was well-lit with security lights, and several large corporate buildings had private security patrol vehicles parked in their front driveways. At the far end of a small access road smothered in huge trees, was a small brick building with the legend National Special Projects in black letters on a white background. In smaller letters underneath were the words Global Anaconda Consortium. Each was repeated in French. The paint was still damp.

The site resembled a military facility. It was recessed from the main city boulevard by a large, shadowy parking lots without lights, then a silvery perimeter fence. Within that was a belt of rolling lawns, and then the low brick walls with small, opaque windows.

The two buses rolled across the parking lot and pulled up at the main gate, several guards stepped out of a large guard shack to challenge them. A man in charge leapt from the bus, looking efficient and legit, and waved to the guards as if they were about to become friends and colleagues within the Anaconda family. Several Anaconda guards, looking relaxed, stepped out to greet the busses. Inside the perimeter, four more guards with assault rifles, and a large, well-trained German shepherd dog, stood watch.

The brief interlude lasted about two minutes, during which the guards called for papers or I.D. and the bus commando told them in a relaxed voice: "Wait a moment…our supervisor is on the way. We are going to dig up the sewer line. Can you smell the stench?"

The Anaconda guards looked at each other, puzzled.

To double-check all this, a guard inside the shack picked up a land line telephone to call his superiors in the buildings, only to find the line was dead. He took out a cell phone, and found that it had no connections. He could not call out. Calls coming in, if there were any, would simply go to answering devices or else drop into the ether.

A large truck came roaring around a corner, did a quick Y-turn, and backed up to the gate. As the puzzled Anaconda guards looked on, the truck emitted a strange, low humming sound. The air flickered with a dim reddish glow, bordering on infrared. High-intensity microwaves saturated the air in a cone shape, cooking the guards and their dog in place. They collapsed into shapeless lumps that lay in the shadowless, morgue-like light of overhead security lights.

The concrete mixed backed closer, buckling the gate and ripping its steel locks out of their anchor plates. The damage was not enough to be seen from the street, but it was enough to let the commandos slip open the gate. The buses quietly drove into the dead compound with their lights off.

Three BLUM commandos had taken their place in the guard shack, wearing the dead men's uniforms.

The buses drove onto the property. Behind them, the commandos in Anaconda guards' uniforms closed the gate.

The BLUM commandos now had access to the entire one-story building, which sprawled over four acres. Judging from the sparse lights on, and small clusters of parked cars, there might have been half a dozen scientists, engineers, and other staff working late. Twenty commandos, wearing dark blue ski masks, went from room to room, ensuring that nobody was alive. They were all dead.

On an inner courtyard, shrouded in shadows, a large, slatted aluminum garage door rolled upward on its core, exposing a warehouse overlooking a loading platform.

The two buses backed up to the loading dock.

Meanwhile, the concrete mixers and their escort headed back to a specially leased warehouse nearby, where they would sit perhaps for months before anyone discovered what was inside. Their drivers would be taken to the airport to meet up with their comrades and the plane back to Shiphol.

At the Anaconda facility, work continued at a rapid, well-trained, intense but relaxed pace.

In the back of each bus, a double door opened outward in both directions. This revealed that the rear half of seats had been removed. The rear of each bus was now a cargo hold.

Within a half hour, using a heavy-duty towmotor and a steel crane, the commandos expertly and cautiously brought Castor to the landing dock and loaded it into the first bus.

Moments later, its identical twin Pollux followed.

Each unit was a gleaming cylinder broken up into functional electronic units, some with solar panels, others with mazes of strutting electronic harnesses. Castor and Pollux were each about ten feet long, and six feet in diameter—about the size of a minivan, and weighing a ton. These were the two control units that were live and able to control the orbiting Capricorn satellite that contained the orbital sniper rounds.

The commandos were expertly trained. They wrapped the units in tape and bubble wrap to prevent injury. Just as quickly, they used cranes to swing them into the buses, where they were bolted to the floor. The bolts were huge, but well-oiled and easily torqued down on their carrying bolts with special spanner wrenches.

This phase of the operation was finished within the hour.

The commandos closed the doors, left some lights on, and tidied up any stray evidence of who had done this. Thus far, the world had not yet heard of Black Umbrella (BLUM).

The two buses rolled out of the facility.

Behind them, the facility slumbered on as if nothing had happened. It might take fresh, relief security patrols another hour or two to discover the hit. By then, the stolen technology would be in the air on its way to Europe.

The commandos sat quietly on their buses on the half hour ride back to Montreal-Mirabel International Airport. The city's neighboring Dorval International now served as the primary commuter and international hub, while Mirabel had slipped to the status of a military and cargo hub. The two buses passed back in through minimal checkpoints, and soon reached the private hangar where the refueled Atlas waited.

The control units unbolted as easily as they had been fastened down.

The commandos acted as cargo handlers, using lifts to bring the two stolen OST controllers and other equipment on board.

Now the commandos split up. Only ten of them remained as crew, in khaki overalls, in the cargo hold of the plane.

All but two of the rest of the men and women donned a mish mash of civilian clothing. Boarding their buses, they split up. One bus headed toward Toronto, the other toward Detroit. There, they would further split up. They would disperse to airports across North America, and then fly back separately to several European airports, for eventual rendez-vous by car at a Blum subpost in Naples. Their ultimate duty destination: the island of Vulcano, north of Sicily. Pollux would already be in place, waiting for them, ready to join Castor in sending death messages up to the orbiter Capricorn.

The two remaining commandos drove the buses away, to be parked in that same warehouse as the concrete mixers. Those two drivers would tidy up at the warehouse, drive down to Boston in a nice company sedan with soft jazz all the way, and take a normal passenger liner to their home base in Scotland.

The TAC had successfully accomplished its mission without a hitch—and without a shot fired, unless you counted the giant burrito cookers.

Dr. Moriarty of Global Anaconda did not yet know it, but he was out of the orbital sniper business. Somewhere else in the world, Dr. Night gleefully rubbed his hands together as BLUM's Project Gemini got underway.

The ten remaining commandos, now acting as cargo handlers, secured Castor and Pollux to the flight deck of the chartered Airbus A700M Atlas.

Inspectors from Quebec customs came on board to inspect the two industrial laser measuring devices supposedly destined for a Dutch mining company with corporate tentacles in South America.

As soon as the tower gave permission, the Atlas taxied down the runway in standard civil aeronautics format. With its high and low lights twirling, and its headlights blazing, the aircraft lifted slowly, and droned away into a low cloud deck on its way toward Greenland and points east.

Project Gemini of the BLUM consortium was one step closer to going operational—and horrifying a defenseless world.

Dr. Moriarty Saves Face

Within twenty-four hours of the discovery that both their Castor and Pollux satellite control modules had been stolen by unknown forces, Global Anaconda's Chief Executive Officer called an all-hands meeting of his corporate board. Damage control was in full swing.

In a 100 story skyscraper overlooking a modern metropolis, members of the Global Anaconda Board of Directors met in emergency session. Framing them in their bench-like auditorium seats were high-level aides and executive secretaries.

The several dozen men and women, all in tasteful business attire, filled a small auditorium under a roof of greenish glass. In the filtered light, while storms raged in the clouds outside, the leaders of the world's second most powerful corporation had gathered to hear their Chairman, Director, and CEO speak.

Dr. James Moriarty was a balding man with brooding eyes and a slight stoop. He preferred conservative colors in his dress—shirts always white, never starched; three piece suit in black or charcoal; dark red or blue or brown tie his only concession to color. He had a wide, almost bulbous forehead, ringed with thinning white hair that had lost all pigmentation. When he talked, he tended to pace with his hands folded behind his back. Sometimes he turned to face his audience, but most of the time he spoke down into his collar mike, while looking down at the floor. If you happened to actually be in his audience, you tended to think he was talking to an invisible crowd on the floor below.

"Something new and dangerous is stirring in the world," said Dr. Moriarty. "I, and men and women like me, have spent my lifetime straightening out the mess left by messy democracy and the fools who ran it. We live in a new, corporate world order, a new and better econarchy, dominated by free-range capitalism. There are those who say that capitalism and free enterprise are polar opposites, which tend to attack each other in the market place, but I differ on that. My point of view is that, yes, capital kills off competition, but the way monopolies achieve their dominance is by wiping out inefficiency. I did not, however, call you here today to lecture about political or economic theory."

Moriarty, they all knew, had his Ph.D. in Economics from the Stanford University. He had published many learned papers in a variety of related fields, and was an unabashed champion of *laissez-faire* capitalism—no manmade rules or regulations, no interference in the natural order of the markets. Anything goes, as long as the profit margin gets nourished at the expense of all weak, sentimental motives. Let the chips fall where they may, for the greater public good. If the sick and the lame died along the way, that was best for them and best for the greater good of the human race. It was the true way of nature—the glorious rule of the wolf pack, for those like Moriarty and his board members, who were the alpha wolves. It wasn't about unions or protections. It was about fundamental, unchanging laws of nature. If a low-end wolf fell back, or lost nerve, or was injured, the alpha would turn the entire pack—male and female—against that member. Killed quickly and efficiently, the deceased became food for the greater benefit of the pack. There was no fooling Mother Nature. In consortium theology, lowly workers could not be trusted to handle an excess of freedom. They were not good at making effective moral or financial choices. Given the opportunity to make sound moral or economic choices, most would squander whatever was given to them, and live in lives of debt or negative-wealth sin that led to disease, poverty, and crime. In Dr. Moriarty's view, the new world order of corponations had brought about a new golden age of peace. Now it was being threatened by some dark, as yet unknown force for anarchy and destruction. This must not stand!

"I have asked you to come together for this impromptu meeting to tell you of a new threat in the world, which we and our corporate rivals must learn to master. A few days ago, two key components of Project David were stolen from under our noses. The paramilitary operation that accomplished this astonishing feat. Despite our security measures, it cannot be traced back to any of our corporate rivals. Instead, I announce to you today that Global Anaconda Consortium's internal security company, Delta, has confirmed the existence of this new threat. We know its name, but we know little else about it. It is called Black Umbrella, or BLUM. That is pronounced *bloom*, like a hideous flower in some grotesque, murky underworld spring time. More like a flowering of pale, deadly mushrooms of evil."

A murmur rumbled through the hall. As Moriarty paced on the sunken, D-shaped floor, the stands above and around him rustled with agitation.

"Ladies and gentlemen, we are at war with an unseen enemy. For now, we will keep this news within the four walls of our corporate boardroom secrecy. News must not get out, for fear of panicking lesser corporations or, worse yet, the unwashed masses. A rising monster threatens the new world order in which we pride ourselves. We do not know this Black Umbrella—which seems not to be a corporation in any form we would understand—but Delta tells us BLUM has tentacles around the world. It is not a legitimate cartel or monopoly, registered with any wholly owned, subsidiary territorial legal system such as the world has become used to. BLUM wields economic and military power like a growing corporation—and yet it is not an organization like ours at all. If anything, it is the anti-consortium. It has no respect for either national or corporate pedigrees. Call it a brokerage. That's what we are dealing with— a very powerful and secretive brokerage." He paused for effect. "It is a global terrorism brokerage."

Another collective gasp swept around the lecture all. It almost seemed as if the light in the room had grown darker—and in fact, dark rain clouds were roiling around the sky scraper as if to choke it and bring it down.

"Ladies and gentlemen, at its heart, we are dealing with a worldwide terrorism brokerage. If you are a petty criminal in Scotland, a bandit in Sicily, a thug in India, an assassin in Persia, a mafioso in Chicago, a tong leader in Shanghai, a Yakuza in Tokyo…the world is replete with such murderous guilds and recruits for their ranks…then you can buy the services of Black Umbrella.

"You may be an insurrectionist anywhere, from Africa to South America or beyond, in need of a sniper killing. Black Umbrella will cheerfully and impersonally provide you with the expert, top-notch services of a blond-haired, blue-eyed Finnish marksman, or an armorer from Peru, or a Communist from the Philippine jungles. You see what Black Umbrella has already done, under our noses, before we had a clue anything was going on? They have united all of the world's assassins, revolutionaries, separatists, and other disaffected souls into one massive killing and destroying machine.

"Where we value corporate and legal rule of law, they favor chaos, democracy, and murder. Under their notion of statehood, the mobs in the street can voice their opinions and sway their leaders. They must be stopped at all costs."

The entire corporate board rose in unison and clapped avidly. Many cheered for Dr. Moriarty, while others praised his leadership.

"It is a setback, but not a defeat," Moriarty told the board of directors who had elected him, and who could remove him just as swiftly. If there was desperation in his voice, he hid it well.

"Project Capricorn is in orbit, and performing normally," Moriarty told them. "We have only the matter of the control systems on earth to worry about—Castor and Pollux. We will recover Castor and Pollux somehow, once we can triangulate where they have been taken—but in the meantime, we must focus on damage control."

What Moriarty did not know was that Anaconda now only had nominal control of the orbiter.

With the Castor and Pollux control units in hand, Dr. Night could at any moment seize stealthy control of the orbiting Capricorn death delivery vehicle—a kind of space shuttle with a dozen or more OST 'bullets' shaped like small submarines as reentry vehicles.

The net was almost complete, weaving tightly around its victims, and Capricorn was a tender victim indeed, exposing its fair neck for the victor to take. The end game already had BLUM written all over it.

Tissy Gets A Tam O'Shanter

From Agrigento in Sicily, Louis Cartouche and his beautiful Belgian handler flew on another of BLUM's small, five-seat Hondajets to Edinburgh, Scotland via a refueling stop at Lisbon's enormous Portela Airport. As before, a Korean in a dark suit flew along—not as a keeper, but as a body guard. His name was Mr. Kim, as he introduced himself amid gestures.

The young lady's name was Tissy—a name that reminded Louis of expensive Swiss or Austrian jewelry stores, and the clear-eyed 19th Century French painter Tissot. She was a Walloon, or French Belgian, of the unhappy province of Wallonia whose citizens had struggled for many generations to separate and perhaps join France. She was from Thionville, and her family name was Fître (so she claimed).

Miss Tissy Fître had been warming Louis Cartouche's bed for a week now. She clung to his side like a wife—without the drawbacks of marriage, bitching, dissatisfaction, and all the rest of the psychoses that he saw as having prevented his meeting a suitable mate before. Tissy was opaque on this point, actually, causing Cartouche a pinprick of discomfort in his soul. He was already in love with her, but he feared that she was playing him for some reason ordained by Dr. Night. Louis was so smitten with her that he threw caution to the winds. He was nearly twice her age—but if she were faking it, she must be a world-class, Oscar-deserving actress. She clung to Cartouche as a grape clings to its vine.

During the journey, Louis and Tissy held hands as they watched sunny skies with distant cumulus pillows drift by. They looked down over the ocean, where sunlight twinkled in a million waves that seemed small from a mile up, but probably made for rough sailing if you were in a yacht or fishing boat. Tissy wore a wheat-colored sweater with appropriately Scottish looking rolled collar, a stylishly tilted tam-o'shanter, and a tartan skirt in green and red intersecting weaves on earth tones. She wore nylons and oxblood tassel loafers. Her large, pale-blue eyes and blonde hair fit in well with the butterscotch smoothness of her skin, her airbrushed nose, and faintly pinked lips.

Mr. Kim sat in a bubble of his own, nodding or smiling when Louis glanced at him, otherwise looking out the window.

"Are you having a good flight?" came the dry voice of Dr. Night. The connection was audio-only, with the usual Black Umbrella logo on the screen before them.

"Very nice," they both said.

"You will shortly be reunited with your baby, Pollux, which we have exported from Global Anaconda's clutches in the Laval Technopolis of Montreal."

"How did you do that?" Louis asked with genuine astonishment.

"No, no," said Dr. Night calmingly. "You have enough to worry about without wondering how our operations are carried out. Need to know, Mr. Cartouche, that's the guideline, and you do not need to know why or how—only what, and when. I find that the best policy for the well-rewarded and contented employee is a sense of faith that we know what we are doing, trust and confidence that we will make you continue to feel happy, and a sense of belonging so you will give Black Umbrella your utmost. It's a concept pioneered by the post-World War II West German army—*Innere Führung*, they call it even today, Inner Leadership—a total divorce from the Hitler and Kaiser eras. Back in those days, officers and NCOs shouted at the men. It was outer commanding. If a man did not obey, or if he broke and ran in battle, the officers and NCOs standing behind him would shoot him and kill him. It was one of the original reasons why such leaders carried side-arms. The soldiers were more afraid of their superiors than of the enemy. We run a totally different sort of ship."

"Very interesting," Louis said sincerely while squeezing Tissy's hand. "Thank you for the always illuminating and reassuring information."

"I will communicate further when you are reunited with your invention. Meanwhile, Monsieur Cartouche, by all means enjoy the enviable state of bliss in which you find yourself, with my hearty approval."

Tissy let Louis clutch her hands, and made an opaque, unreadable face. There was fire in her eyes.

After a four hour flight, the plane landed on a private, corporate runway at Edinburgh's busy international airport near Turnhouse.

It was a partially sunny day with occasional showers. The tarmac was puddled. The rest of the journey would not be blessed with such pleasant weather—although the company of Tissy would make anything bearable. Louis held her close to him. She was a head shorter, and snuggled her soft body against his.

Mr. Kim stood behind them, holding a black umbrella, like the black-suited butler.

They did not have long to wait. A black TX4 Fairways shuttle taxi took them to a smaller runway off in the distance. A green and white, Canadian-made DeHavilland Twin Otter stood waiting—the venerable twin-engine propeller plane that served as the world's puddle jumper.

Louis and Tissy crossed a concrete apron, climbed up a matching yellow and green air ladder, and climbed inside the plane. Mr. Kim came along, and sat behind them.

Two pilots in dark raincoats and black chauffeur caps waved and nodded from the cockpit. The plane could seat up to 19 passengers without the need for a flight attendant. The ceiling inside seemed barely high enough for a person to stand up under it.

Four older men and two women, all Scots, climbed on board. They wore raincoats and hats. Two carried umbrellas. They ranged in age from about fifty to seventy—confident, subdued, settled in life—and conversed among each other in familiar tones with many in-jokes.

One of them, a white-haired man with heavily wrinkled and sun-reddened skin, sat beside Louis. "How are you today?" he boomed.

"We are doing just fine."

"French?"

"Canadian. My lady friend is Belgian."

"Oh, it's nice to see some foreign blood out here in the wilds." The man's Scottish accent had a *Goidhealach* lilt. "Been on this leg before?"

"First time."

"You're in for a treat."

"Why is that?"

"We are going to Barra, in the Outer Hebrides." Without being asked, he unfolded a well-worn little map over his knees to show Louis and Tissy. Mr. Kim looked over their shoulders. "Here," the Scot said. He pointed to a long chain of islands, some quite large, off the northwest coast of Scotland, which itself constitutes a peninsula on the north side of the large island of Britain. The Outer Hebrides consisted of about fifteen populated islands strung in a north-south chain, plus at least fifty tiny islands abandoned but for nesting sea birds. "Barra," the man continued, "is the southernmost of the larger islands in the outer chain."

Tissy asked: "How long does it take to get there?"

The man said: "It's about 290 km, or roughly 180 miles from Edinburgh to Barra. These tin cans fly about 180 mph, so a little over an hour should do it. But the interesting thing is about Barra Airport."

"Yes?" Louis asked.

"Barra Island has the only airport in the world with an official schedule of flights based on the tides. That's right. It is the only officially registered airport in the world whose runway is the beach itself. Flights have to be scheduled in and out according to the moon tides, because half the day, the runway is under seawater."

"Isn't the sand soft?" Tissy asked.

"The sand is densely mixed with ancient seashells, so it's quite solid above the tide line."

The plane flew about 1,500 feet above boiling seas, bucking and rolling. Mountainous waves spumed and spat below. Mr. Kim made a desperate gurgling sound behind them. Louis and Tissy looked at Mr. Kim, who appeared to be feeling airsick. His face looked white, and his expression was a grimace.

The Scotsman pulled a barf bag from a holder under the window nearby, and handed it to Mr. Kim. The latter gurgled his thanks and threw himself toward the rear, where he made loud noises into the little sack. He clambered into a little perfunctory toilet in back, where presumably his agonies continued—but silently, to the relief of all.

The puddle jumper lived up to its name. It was a shamelessly utilitarian aircraft, with a plume of dirty oil fanning out down the wing behind each engine. But it was robust, and powerful, as it roared above the waves.

The plane puttered in a long curve and settled down to a landing on the broad, crescent beach. White houses nestled amid green, rocky hills in the distance. The beach was more flat than steep. The flatter a beach, the broader its intertidal zone—and here, the airstrip.

The pilots in their caps and black raincoats hustled around the cargo hatch outside, throwing bags around and pulling out several that belonged to Louis, Tissy, and Mr. Kim. These bags they left on the sand while they locked up the cargo hatch, shook hands all around, and climbed back on board.

The Scots stayed on board. They were neighbors heading home from a weekend spree in the big city, with dinners and theaters and shopping. Now they would continue north along the chain of islands on the outer banks—South Uist, Benbecula, North Uist, South Harris, and ultimately their home on the 'big island' of Lewis-and-Harris. From there, after refueling, the Twin Otter would loop back toward Edinburgh. Nice people, they all waved goodbye.

Louis, Tissy, and Mr. Kim stood alone on the beach after the plane left. Wooden markers at the ends—with attached red, blinking signal lights—were almost the only sign of the beach's double duty. On the coast road just up the beach, a small control tower and terminal restaurant held watch. As the plane taxied down the beach, its black rubber wheels threw up a fine spray of water from the tightly packed sand. The plane lifted after a short run and buzzed away into a calm, sunny sky.

A white Mercedes drove down the beach to meet Louis and Tissy. A big, pale man drove.

The driver swung around so he could holler out the window in a Scottish accent. "Right on time, I see. Hop in. I'll get your luggage. Name's Lysander. I work for the BLUM Corporation. We only just took over here."

Minutes later, the car with its four occupants tooled south along the coastal road, A888, which circled the island.

"The main town here is Castlebay," Lysander explained. "Nice sunny day, eh? In a good year, the weather stays fairly mild into early autumn."

To Louis, the area still looked foreboding. He'd grown up just a few degrees of latitude south of Newfoundland, and knew that blue look of distant mountain ranges that almost seemed to have a bit of the polar winter trapped in them year around, like the Laurentian Mountains north of Quebec City. At the moment, he almost wished he were back under Mediterranean skies on the volcanic and fertile soil of Sicily.

"Barra is about 60 square kilometers or 23 square miles and shaped a bit like a swimming sea turtle, eight miles long and five miles wide. The airport's on the north end, toward Barra Sound, just across from the bigger island of South Uist. A network of ferries connects all these islands. We've got to drive to the south end of Barra, where we'll find the largest settlement, the village of Castlebay, with a population of just over 1,000 persons."

Cartouche wondered how trustworthy this man was. "Who do you work for, Lysander?"

The driver leaned a brawny arm over the seat, while keeping a ham hand on the wheel. "Sergeant Major, SAS, retired. Now fully employed by the BLUM Corporation."

"You understand then...?"

"I understand what I need to understand," Lysander said. "I'll pass on a bit of advice. Tight lips at all times, get it?"

"Yes," Tissy said, and Louis said: "Understood."

The car came around a curve among low mountains that formed a rocky, greenish band around a blue-water bay. Nestled in the foothills all around were white houses. Sea gulls shrieked overhead. "Here's Castlebay, named after that old English tax collecting fort out there on the water." Lysander pulled over on the A888 a few minutes so they could look over the scenic bay, with its houses and castle. A large ferry was just churning out to sea, making its rounds of the island ports.

About a hundred yards offshore —300 feet or 90 meters—was a squarish stone fort nestled tightly on every available square inch of a small islet in the bay. The water glittered, dark blue, with white gulls and gray pelicans bobbing comfortably on its wavelets. What whitecaps one saw were caused by pleasant sailing winds—and there were four colorful triangles on the water just then, leaning with the air as they tacked back and forth.

"That's Kisimul Castle down there," Lysander explained. "Has its own freshwater wells, believe it or not, because it's situated on sheer, deep granite tied to the mainland. For thousands of years, the Outer Hebrides were inhabited by Iron Age chiefs and their clans. Scottish lairds had their stronghold on the little islet centuries earlier during the Dark Ages. It was the perfect place for the Elizabethan British, when they took over the region in the 1500s. The Scottish mainland went Protestant, but the islands here stayed Catholic, like Ireland. There was no love lost, I assure you. The British built an impregnable tax collection center on Kisimul."

"Does anyone live there now?" Tissy asked.

"No, it's owned by the government. They do archeological research when there is funding. Every day, depending on the season, one or two tourist boats cross over for a jaunt. Most of the time, the castle sits there empty and brooding."

"And that is the place we are going to?" Tissy asked. "My employer said so."

"You have it right, Miss." Lysander resumed the drive down into the village. "From what I'm told, BLUM Corp has leased some rights over there. All very stealthy. Built a fantastic underground and underwater facility, right under everyone's noses."

The drive took them down to a small square on Pier Road, where sturdy stone houses looked like cats relaxing in warm sunshine—though they had the look of winter on them. It must get brutal here, Louis thought.

Lysander stayed at the dock with the car and luggage, but sent his three passengers into a restaurant nearby. This was a stone fastness in its own right, with guest rooms available in season. A nicely painted wooden sign swinging over the heavy door read: *Kiltoch Arms*.

Inside, tobacco smoke roiled up from a half dozen wooden benches. Village men and women were just having a meal at three of the tables. At a fourth table under an open window framed in geraniums, a group of village men played cards over beer, while laughing, talking, and smoking. A tall, dark-haired waiter with a long yellow-and-black striped apron led them to one of the two free tables, next to the card players.

Louis and Tissy ordered beers, while Mr. Kim gestured for a lemonade. The waiter offered the daily special—a hearty beef stew with tomatoes, potatoes, carrots, and asparagus—which they ordered. Most of the smoke dissipated through the open window, but enough of it lingered in the tavern to sting the eyes of those unaccustomed to it. Laws against smoking in public were spreading around the world, but apparently the infoferry had not yet reached remote Barra.

Louis sat close with Tissy, under the window, while Mr. Kim sat opposite. Daylight played over his still-pale features. "Don't like to fly?" Louis said. Mr. Kim stared uncomprehendingly. Louis made wings of his arms and uttered a motor sound lasting a half minute, with an imaginative Immelmann barrel turn in the middle. Mr. Kim smiled in understanding and nodded. "Chick," he said. (*Does he mean chic?* Tissy wondered.) "Veddy chick." He too made wings and uttered a single-engine noise.

The stew dinners came. The men at the card table made appreciative noises at the fine aroma. As Louis ate, he overheard bits and snatches of conversation from the card players.

A very old man—who leaned over his cane, and wore a shabby old mariner's coat and faded first mate's cap with cracked, unadorned black bill—said the word Kisimul, and Louis perked up. He overheard words to this effect, rolling among the men:

"Brooding there on the water at night."

"Not fit for man or beast."

"Been sprouting antennas and satellite dishes, of late."

"Must be the damn government and the UFOs."

"It's all London, I tell ya."

"Give us complete independence, will ya?"

"You can hear strange sounds at night, though she be deserted."

"Must be ghosts of the tax collectors from long ago."

"More people go there than come back."

"Ever since the government got hold of it, it's been unholy."

The conversation shifted just as quickly to other topics. Louis finished his meal, as did his companions. Lysander poked his head in at the door. He silently gestured that it was time to go.

Back in the car, Tissy wiped her eyes as if she were crying. When Louis asked, she nodded over her little white hankie with its frilly edge. "The smoke in there," she said.

"It's all better now," Lysander reassured her.

"No more chick," Mr. Kim said.

"I remind you all of the need to keep mum and guard our secrets," Lysander said. He drove into the low mountains on winding switchback roads. Houses here kept low, with the hill slopes at their backs, to shelter them from storms and winter winds.

Tissy continued wiping her eyes with her hankie. Louis noted that her lips were quietly blubbering, her nose was runny, and her shoulders hove. Great tragic sighs escaped her melancholy breast. He held her close, and she buried her blonde head against his torso while clinging to him. Louis sensed that all was not well between Dr. Night, Black Umbrella, and this fledgling Alecto. She might be an angel of terror in training, but would she ever earn her wings? Remembering Alecto (Erin Yes) with her gunfire and cruel laughter, poor Tissy did not have it in her to be so mean or violent. Tissy was looking for a way out, and clung desperately to Louis as her only chance. Louis wondered if both he and Tissy might not wind up in the laser seat when they had ceased to be useful.

"This is Lomond House," Lysander announced as they drove up to a two-story house of granite boulders fitted together with out mortar. The front was steep and smooth, as if fortified. It had narrow windows, almost like gun or archery ports, secured under gray steel shutters. A gravel driveway curved in a long, gradual S to a hidden car port by the front door. The door itself was large, atop six broad stone steps worn with age.

"Was a farm house long ago," Lysander explained as they got out of the car. Two female commandos in dark fatigues came to fetch the luggage. Each wore a side arm and had roughly cropped hair—one blonde, the other brunette. "Don't speak to the troops unless they speak to you," Lysander said. "You stay with me. Mr. Kim and I will be your guides."

"This is where my widget will be brought?" Louis said, licking his chops.

"It's already been brought," Lysander said. "You'll be looking at it in half an hour."

They entered the ten-room lodging, which featured a kind of concierge desk with machine guns and no registry.

"We're in totally private territory," Lysander said. "BLUM Corp bought the property a few years ago, as part of a liaison with Scottish separatists. Scotland has been able to field its own national parliament in Edinburgh since 1999, so the inevitable path seems to full nationhood. With rich offshore oil fields, we will not be lacking for exports. You should sympathize with us, Mr. Cartouche."

"I do indeed," Louis said. He pondered ever more deeply the meaning of this new home he had found with Black Umbrella, and its significance for the future world developing before his eyes. Was he on the ground floor of the next great thing? Or was he on the precipice of his own demise? Louis Cartouche shuddered as he squeezed Tissy's smooth caramel paw, and she squeezed back. Louis closed his eyes and inhaled deeply of Tissy's light citrus fragrance. Even her sweat smelled like lilac soap.

Lysander took them to their suite—Tissy and Louis together in corner rooms with a U.S. style king-sized bed. Then he explained: "This was a farm house for sheep ranchers long ago. It was a dank, cold place of stone corridors where the wet winds blew freely, even with the shutters on the end windows chained shut. BLUM bought it about ten years ago and began converting it into a safe house with all the amenities. At that time, it was planned to be a strategic redoubt that could hold off government troops for days or weeks. BLUM officials were mindful of Irish, Scottish, and Welsh separatist movements even then, as potentially useful allies."

The elevator opened with a gentle *ding* sound.

As they stepped inside, Louis saw that the elevator was pleasantly done in gray and maroon carpeting, with lit buttons and mirrors just as in a luxury hotel in a big city.

On the ride down, Lysander continued: "We knew that the black islet, where Kisimul stands, had its own natural wells. They deliver fresh water from the adjoining mainland, below the salt water table. That led us to explore further, and the result is as you'll see." As the elevator continued its slow descent, a good ten stories under ground through solid granite, Lysander said: "Today, we lease space on top to keep our satellite dishes and antennas for your device, Mr. Cartouche, and Black Umbrella's Project Gemini.

After a long ride down, the elevator stopped with a final *ding*. Its door opened on what looked like an underground garage, lined in massive banks of concrete. Fluorescent lighting flooded the air, almost too garishly, over asphalt surfaces among round pillars about eight feet in diameter. "We followed the water channel from an underground stream. This took us under the town, under the beach, under the bay, and to the granitic footing of the islet on which Kisimul perches. The authorities have no idea we have this underground—or should I say underwater— facility going on. Scotland will declare her total independence soon. She will form a powerful alliance with other Gaelic or greater Goidelic speaking states and islands, including on the French coast and in the Pyrenees. BLUM Corp will be the benefactor of a powerful new contra-nationalist confederation that can start swinging its own weight with the global corporations. The work we are doing here at Kisimul is an important stepping stone."

So saying, he led his group to a cart seating up to eight passengers under a colorful canvas roof. Mr. Kim, surprisingly, took over as driver, as if he'd been here before. Louis and Tissy held each other as the wagon lurched into motion. They whizzed along an underground tunnel lit by wire basket lights. Louis could hear water dripping noisily as they passed under the bay.

In ten minutes, the vehicle emerged in a small concrete tomb under Kisimul Castle. Several armed guards in black commando camouflage patrolled the roughly circular open space. Several doors led off at tangents into the bedrock of the islet. A door marked *Lift* opened as Lysander brushed his hand in the air. "Welcome to Gemini West," he said as he led his charges into the elevator. After a short ride upward, they emerged in a jarringly, pleasantly sunlit room.

"We are in the bowels of Kisimul," Lysander announced. "Nobody outside BLUM knows that this facility exists. From here, we will soon begin ruling the world."

The windows were narrow slots looking low over murky water penetrated by wan sunlight as coppery-golden as fish scales. Directly outside were wet, barnacled rocks overgrown with dark green slimy seaweed. Here and there, through thick plate glass windows, one could see saltwater fish swimming about with stubby copper bodies and huge lower lips made for scooping up stray nourishment.

The floor was of gleaming concrete covered with a syrupy sheen of dry, hard shellac.

Technicians, engineers, and scientists purposefully moved about. All wore variously hued lab coats or surgical scrubs. Some sat before wide banks of computers, while others worked on high banks of electronic equipment. The walls were covered with monitors offering both digital readouts and analog images. Some of the images appeared to be of outer space, while others were orbital and looking toward the earth.

All of this swirl of motion and importance focused on one central object: Louis Cartouche's invention, Castor, which sat bolted, like a small extraterrestrial minivan, to a steel laboratory table in the midst of the control room. From it sprawled a network of cables, relays, and monitors onto surrounding work tables amid heavily reinforced steel shafts and studded girders.

Louis understood completely. Somewhere else in the world, BLUM had already installed its twin, Pollux.

Working in tandem as Louis had designed them, the two control units would manage the deadly Capricorn satellite in orbit over the Tropic of Cancer. Its targets would not so much be Third World dictators as First World corponational CEOs plus popular civic and religious leaders or heads of state.

Dr. Night was all set to rock and roll.

Ribeye

A third-string freelancer—whom Camelback Consortium code-named Ribeye—stopped into a yellow Bundespost phone booth in the train station at Kaiserslautern, Germany, to call his contact with Compass News in the United States. He had no idea, nor did he care, who the slightly African-American sounding voice was at the other end, code-named Zephyr.

Norwegian by birth, originally a young street tough from Oslo and later Berlin, he was a young man with dark blond hair cut short around his head in soft, straight lines. He had a very thin, bony face with beard bristles. He wore a khaki raincoat over a fine bluish-gray wool suit. Despite the expensive clothes, his rough and tumble upbringing was reflected in old gang signs tattooed on his knuckles—l-o-v-e on the right hand, and h-a-t-e across his left knuckles. Under his coat dangled a shoulder holster, and in it a small Norwegian-made Union automatic with a six-round clip of 6.35 ammo (.25 ACP). Ribeye preferred it for close action, especially inside buildings. For him, this so-called street weapon was light, easy to hide, easy to ditch, and caused the least spectator notice. If found, it suggested amateur rather than professional, and thus attracted less investigative effort from police agencies.

During his teenage years, he had experienced a religious conversion, switching from messenger money drops to snitch for Oslo detectives—eventually working with the Kripo's department for cases of national criminal importance. As a former petty hood with a savvy brain, he was useful in special ways, until he was nearly killed in a shootout in Berlin, and decided to go on his own. For the past two years, he had gone freelance with this U.S. outfit he knew only as Fire Department. His contact was this mysterious voice (Zephyr) somewhere in North America. The man sounded faintly African-American, as Ribeye could identify from the G.I.s still stationed in Germany, and more importantly, he sounded almost fatherly. It was a quality that evoked in Ribeye what little loyalty he was capable of maintaining. Fire Department always paid on time, and the jobs were more of the brain than the gun.

Ribeye approached the train station in Kaiserslautern, Germany—about a 45-minute drive north of the French border of Saarlouis in Lorraine—with a woman at his arm. She was a cute, tough little broad he liked, from somewhere in Sicily. She spoke good Norwegian, having lived in Oslo as a child—but went by the name Meg Aera.

With a throw-away phone card, he used a land line to call his employer. The phone call instantly became one of millions fleeting across fiber-optic cables among hubs and over backbones in Europe. Lost among myriad other voices, his transmission connected with a man sitting on a sunny patio in San Diego, over 9,000 miles away. Data cannons along the English Channel fired enormous bursts of energy skyward, where high capacity satellites relayed the data among their orbital network. The data streaked down to earth-based transponders, and thence to Johannes Rector's patio table in Loma Portal.

"Zephyr," Ribeye said in Germany, speaking good English with a Norwegian accent.

"Ribeye," Rector said on a sunny hillside in Loma Portal, overlooking the broad expanse of the Pacific Ocean as waves rolled in toward the beach, and surfers darted over the water.

"I have located the Anaconda cell associated with Project David."

Speaking across the heavily encrypted line, Rector said: "Is it what we thought?"

"It appears to me that the sniper rifle is a blind, but I don't know for what."

"Keep working it. Do you need more backup?"

"So far not, but I will let you know."

"Don't take any chances. We can provide plenty of lifting power if you need it."

"I'm not crazy. I take no chances."

"Call me twice a day at this number."

"I will."

Ribeye hung up. He dropped the phone card in a slot designed to shred and dispose of any credit type cards as a public service from the Bundespost, trying to minimize identity theft.

Meg Aera smiled as he emerged from the booth. She was a small, slender woman with long black hair tumbling in waves. Her features could have been Mediterranean, except that her eyes looked faintly Asian. Her dark eyes were large and luminous in a triangular face wide across the forehead and tapering slightly down with an even nose, over a generous and red-painted mouth, down to a narrow chin. He had met her just two days ago, traveling on an express train from Vienna to Frankfurt, and they'd become inseparable lovers.

She was on vacation, returning home from Turkey to Oslo via the former Austro-Hungarian empire. She said she'd lived in Europe most of her life. She was good with languages, and Ribeye believed her.

Ribeye was on a much longer journey. He'd traveled to the People's Republic of China to begin his quest. He was tracking a company called David, which been founded by two entrepreneurial Szechuanese partners. Those two had recently sold the company to Global Anaconda, which was transferring its assets and capital stock from a factory in China to an undisclosed location in the Rheinland-Palatinate of Germany. Ribeye and his handler, Zephyr, thought it might be in Speyer, on the Rhine River, which was less than and hour north of here. Ribeye's mission was nearly complete—to find Anaconda's secret headquarters for Project David. All Ribeye knew was that Project David was about making sniper rifles, and that the technology was important to the military and security forces of the West. It was all he cared to know. More importantly, there would be a large check waiting for him at a Norwegian bank in Paris. He would spend a wild weekend with his new girlfriend—and they'd return to Oslo to plan their engagement. He was falling head over heels in love with her.

Ribeye had never met a woman like her before, and already he knew he wanted to marry her. Meg Aera was gentle, humorous, and always ready to cuddle. She had family in Oslo, she'd told him, but her grandparents lived in the town of Scala, in the province of Agrigento, near the south Sicilian coast. Since they had fallen in love so suddenly, she had changed her travel plans to stay with him. She was a computer consultant in Oslo, and she spoke excellent Norwegian with an Italian accent. She was on her annual, six week vacation—which native Europeans enjoy at full pay, in addition to many holidays. She had nothing better to do than make love with him in first class railway cars. All she asked was that they spend a long weekend together in Paris. Kaiserslautern was on the direct train route to Paris.

She opened her arms for him, and he embraced her after stepping from the Bundespost booth. She whispered over his shoulder: "I think this is the longest we've been separated since we met."

He held her in both arms, but stepped back. "I think I have lost my mind. I am falling in love with you."

She raised a finger to stroke his chin, while her eyes looked soulfully into his. "I think I have always been in love with you. It was just a matter of waiting to meet you."

They each raised a hand, palm open, and touched fingertips—*soul mates*.

"This is so romantic." She took his hand and kissed his palm.

He held her tightly to him.

Minutes later, Meg and Ribeye walked arm in arm, two lovers, down the drizzle-slicked streets of Kaiserslautern. A faint whiff of coal or wood smoke hung in the air. From the small square at the top of the hill at the train station, on the Bahnhofstrasse, they walked downhill on the Richard Wagnerstrasse among the few older buildings that had survived World War II. Many were narrow, two or three story purplish sandstone buildings with antique, ornate fronts.

Ribeye and Meg Aera came to a small, triangular square at the Beethovenstrasse. The square was just big enough for a bench or two, a yellow Bundespost telephone booth, and a public bicycle rack. The square was sheltered on two sides by mundane modern concrete-block buildings with glass store fronts, forming a corner. According to Zephyr's instructions, this was a Sigma 2020 safe house. Somewhere near here was the Anaconda technical center where a new sniper technology was to be developed. The two super-corporations kept an eye on each other everywhere around the world. The corporate details did not concern Ribeye, only the money—and he had not told Zephyr about his new girlfriend.

"We'll spend the night here," he told Meg. "Tomorrow we'll go back up to the Bahnhof, and we'll be in Paris by noon." He kissed her tenderly, holding his fingers in her rich hair. She raised her head, his lover, eyes closed and mouth open, to accept both the rain drops and his kisses. She radiated devotion to him, and to him alone.

Ribeye ran a grimy fingernail up and down a vertical row of rusting door bells and scrawled names. When he came to the name *M. L. Sombra*, he stopped. "There it is." He pressed the button.

"Ja?" came a middle-aged woman's voice in German.

"Ribeye."

"*Komme' sie hinuff*," the woman said in the Palatinate or *Pfälzisch* dialect.

A buzzer sounded, and a dark, heavy door popped open an inch or two.

"Is this where your friends live?" Meg asked in her girlish voice.

"Yes, darling. Hurry on up with me—we'll have a room to ourselves, nice and cozy..."

"I can't wait," she said sweetly.

Ribeye pushed forward into the dark landing.

Meg moved in the shadows behind him.

He hardly noticed her as he concentrated on pushing the door shut. He went to lock it, to keep out the chill, moist wind. He fumbled with the light switch. "Must be burned out," he muttered.

"Yes," Meg Aera said behind him, "all burned out."

He felt the garrote on his neck. It looped over itself behind his head, cutting off his breathing. He clawed at it with his blunt fingernails, but the fine piano wire of the upper octaves was buried deep in his skin and cutting into the flesh in his neck.

Meg Aera—Relentless Megaera the Avenger—climbed up his back on her knees. She planted her knees firmly in the small of his back, supporting herself with her wiry arms on his shoulders. She held the garrote tightly, while balancing her elbows on his torso.

Helplessly, Ribeye felt his body go slack as the light faded and eternal night rose in his blood. *There is a cozy bed for us upstairs...Meg darling, will you marry me?...* was his terminal thought as the car rushed down a tunnel of lights, toward a spiraling Milky Way galaxy over a sunny meadow and then black, empty space. Why was he alone?

Claire Lightfield: Tropic of Cancer

Claire Lightfield glanced at the wall clock in her bunker under the U.S. Naval Observatory in Washington D.C.—11:00 a.m. Her half-day shift would be ending at noon, and with it her nuisance duty for the month. She planned to take a long lunch, do a little shopping on the way to Sigma 2020's headquarters in the new CIA Annex in Langley. She had a husband and a little boy at home, who would love a little present. Of course, she also had her eye on a darling new purse, all black and shiny patent leather, shaped like a long book, with a matching pair of black suede gloves.

As she was reveling in these thoughts, at 10:59, one of her encrypted land lines buzzed. She leaned closer to the wide, banana-shaped desk, which bristled with monitors, keyboard, speakers, and telemetry equipment. She picked up. "Duty Officer." It was a required succinct statement, designed to give nothing away, even though the line was nominally secure.

"Claire, it's Johannes Rector." He sounded harried.

"Yes, Rector?" Nobody ever called Johannes Rector by any other name, even his beautiful wife. Claire pressed a button on a bank of lights, which switched the line to the highest degree of encryption as well as digital security.

It was called ULTRA/BIN/CRYPTOMAX.

There was only one higher security status on the building's phone lines: PRESIDENTIAL/BIN/CRYPTOMAX/ULTRA. *We aren't there yet,* she thought. It was a type of conversation you never wanted to have, because it might mean that a comet the size of Connecticut was hurtling toward earth, or the planet was breaking in half, or terrorists had seized Palm Springs, California, and were holding top corporate executives and U.S. Senators hostage.

Rector crackled: "What have you got on an Anaconda launch from Kourou?"

"Nothing special." At that moment, as a chime through the building announced the eleven o'clock hour, on the dot, something changed at the French/ESA launch center just east of the Caribbean coast of South America. "Wait," she told Rector. "Hold on."

Among Claire's many monitors, a small one for launch anomalies began blinking orange in warning, then red for total alarm. The same gadget made a low rising and falling whine, very low, which she tapped off like an unwelcome alarm clock.

The other thing that caught her attention was a rise in pitch among the usually calm voices of European controllers at Kourou. Her hearing was confirmed by a wine-red square that started blinking on and off, signaling distress had been detected in the launch engineers' voices.

Claire's duty desk monitored, in rotation, the voices of the world's launch centers. The software on this specialized telemetry system was designed to look for certain key phrases like *explosion, abnormal, deviant, abort*, and the like. Engineers at Kourou were speaking some of those words in French and in European-accented English.

"What's going on?" Rector asked.

Another secure line started burping and flashing. "Hold it," Claire said to Rector, and spoke into the other phone: "Duty Officer."

As she spoke, the consternation of Capricorn's handlers became more evident. They seemed to have lost control of the Capricorn satellite.

Claire did a double-take as she looked up the GASS acronym: Global Anaconda Space Services Company. Now what did Camelback Corporation's primary commercial competitor have to do with this satellite?

"Special Agent Lightfield, this is Colonel Howard at Sigma 2020, liaison with the Pentagon. We have a situation."

She switched that line also to ULTRA/BIN/CRYPTOMAX. "Yessir?"

"Can I get you on a conference call with Senators Bloviant and Hawgbile?"

"I'm—" *—handling about ten things all at once—* She swallowed her objections and said: "Go ahead." *The world is blowing up. There go my lunchtime shopping plans.*

"Rector, I'm talking to the Senate Committee."

"I'll hang in there a few minutes. I just need you to confirm: is it an Anaconda mission? Is something going wrong?"

Colonel Howard said: "Claire?"

She told Rector "Yes, and yes."

"Call me when you can." Rector rung off.

"Yes, Colonel Howard?"

"Quick briefing. Anaconda gave a speech this morning, offering some new technology for assassinating Third World nutjobs before they start wars. We're not sure how they plan to execute the jobs, but the Consortium is seriously considering buying in, and there is consideration of making OPOTUS Copy G on the briefings traffic. To put it mildly, Anaconda has our full attention with their Project David as they call it."

As Claire sat before her blinking, crawling, whining instruments, she waited with earphones over her blondish helmet of hair. She heard rustling, coughing, papers shuffling, bodies dropping into roller-chairs, fingers tapping the flying saucer mike in the center of the table as the crisis conference got underway.

Meanwhile, she watched a remarkable visual unfolding on a large display screen high up under the ceiling. Technicians and intelligence officers, male and female, gathered before Claire's station to witness the event.

In her monitoring speakers, the normally phlegmatic, calm controllers at Kourou sounded extremely edgy, cutting across each other with verbal outreads and statuses.

On the screen, a diagram of landing and descent trajectories cut across a virtual globe. The globe was dissected into longitude and latitude lines in fine green. Ascending or launch trajectories showed in blue—at the moment, there were two, one from Kourou, the other from JFK (the German solar satellite). There were no descents shown, which would have been in yellow. If a shot were in trouble, it would be blood red. At the moment, the Kourou shot officially switched from amber alert color to vivid red.

Orbital trajectories could be seen on another screen, but they were the responsibility of the Astro-Propulsion Laboratories in Pasadena. At least six duty officers monitored the earth's busy orbital traffic on other screens.

On the big screen above Claire's head, two dotted lines appeared. One was the Tropic of Capricorn, just over 23 degrees south of the Equator and parallel to it. The other was the Tropic of Cancer, just over 23 degrees north of the Equator and parallel to it. These were the official boundaries of earth's tropics, or tropical zones, spanning the globe between them. Tropical meant those areas on earth where the sun reached a point directly overhead at least once each year. About half the world's population lived between the Tropics of Capricorn and Cancer, as did most of the dictators and tyrants—a hunting ground for the OST.

As Claire watched, and as others gasped around her, the wayward Anaconda satellite deviated toward the north. Its intended orbit had been on the Tropic of Capricorn, for which the Capricorn satellite was named.

On the diagram glowing above, the craft itself was a pulsing dot, like a blood clot moving along a straight artery. The trajectory behind it was solid red. The apparent frontal trajectory was a dotted red line.

Barring any major course corrections by the unseen hand that had taken control of the launch vehicle, Capricorn would soon cross the Tropic of Cancer.

Whatever the satellite's mission might have been over the southern tropics, in the Third World—as defined over a half a century earlier by France's President Charles de Gaulle—it was now to be executed over the First World in the northern hemisphere.

We don't even understand who the players are, Claire thought, *much less what their mission was or has become.*

As she listened to the meeting—with the spidery mike before her, branching from her headset—she spoke to nobody in particular. It was a reflex, as if she were explaining the inexplicable to her own mirror self. Or it was like an autopsy, spoken by the medical examiner to a microphone as she cut out parts of a corpse, seeking the cause of death. "It traveled as far as a position about 1,400 miles south of the Azores on acquisition orbit, then Kourou and Toulouse lost control. The craft deviated on a fifteen minute burn, vectoring northeast at 45 degrees to its planned trajectory. Traveling at a velocity of 17,500 mph US, the craft is now over Mongolia and…making one more course correction…" An audible outcry rose from the men and women standing around her, independently echoed by French controllers in Kourou, Toulouse, and the South Pacific. "…now dead on the Tropic of Cancer."

The craft continued pulsing red for a minute or two as it stabilized in orbit at the northern edge of the earth's tropics. Already, it would be streaking at about 200 miles (320 km) altitude over Venezuela. In this orbit, it would be visible at night to the helpless controllers at Kourou, who could only watch it passing overhead like a blinding little pinprick in the tropical night sky, and wonder *why*?

At this altitude, it would not survive long. Atmospheric drag would pull it down and it would burn up in the atmosphere. For what?

As Claire watched, the screen cleared. For a minute it was blank. Then a refreshed image returned. The Capricorn launch was gone, into the hands of APL trackers as well as those of ESA and the *Centre National d'Études Spatiales* (CNES)—France's government space agency of industrial and commercial purpose application.

She sat back in her chair and pulled off her earphones for a moment. Dabbing her brow with a tissue, she heard APL duty officers cursing and groaning as the renegade red dot pulsed on their orbital monitoring screens. That was two rows of cubicles away from her own. The clock read 11:29, and she wondered if she might yet make it out of here on time. She could monitor the conference, incoming only, on a secure ULTRA/BIN/CRYPTOMAX line in her car.

An idea was forming in her mind, driven home by the satellite's Low Earth Orbit (LEO). As she sat waiting for her replacement to arrive for the noon to four shift, she did some public searches on the Keyhole and Corona satellite series. This was a top secret series of what were today called Digital Intelligence or DIGINT satellites. Famously, it was supposed they could read a license plate in a Moscow parking lot from a LEO of 165-180 miles. The craft could, in fact, be lowered with thruster rockets to run a series of photos or a stretch of film, then pushed back over 200 miles altitude to avoid atmospheric drag and an unplanned, catastrophic reentry.

When a segment of exposures was in the can, so to speak, the satellite ejected them to fall gently into the atmosphere. Once past the troposphere, on average under 50,000 feet, a small parachute would open. The increasingly thick and humid atmosphere would slow the capsule's descent. A specially rigged interceptor plane would scoop the descending canister out of thin air, and return it to the CIA (Keyhole) or USAF (Corona) for processing.

Was it possible—had someone adopted this ancient Cold War technology to a new, sinister 21st Century purpose? Was this what Holmes had just spoken about? A special satellite that would change history, as happened with the shootings of Abraham Lincoln, James Garfield, JFK…and as should have happened with the likes of Saddam Hussein, Slobodan Milosevic, or Adolf Hitler? Claire did not want to leap to conclusions, but her conjecture made some sense as she considered it in depth. It was her only working hypothesis for the moment.

Screens across the tracking center showed the red downward trajectory of the ESA satellite as it plunged toward its death. At the same time, a fine light-blue dot began pulsing—the insidious parasite satellite, belonging to an unknown force of great power and wealth, with an agenda that would soon become manifest. The Anaconda host satellite, Capricorn, had just been sacrificed for this new killer object in orbit on the Tropic of Cancer.

She donned her headphones again, just in time to hear someone coughing and making a boring speech full of ah's and um's and other filler sounds as people began attempting nervous explanations, when nobody really knew anything yet.

On a separate ULTRA/BIN/CRYPTOMAX line, Claire privately called Rector to discuss her Keyhole-Corona hypothesis. Someone had reinvented the wheel, but with teeth.

Dr. Night: Underworld Triumph

There was quiet jubilation in the Black Umbrella (BLUM) space control center under Kisimul Castle in Castle Bay on the southernmost of the Outer Hebrides—Barra, a rugged island in the North Atlantic within the coastal boundaries of Scotland.

Dispassionately, a launch control announcer said: "Acquisition is now complete."

The sixty technicians in the shining space center clapped politely. Dressed in surgical scrubs of varying colors, they were bathed in the curiously peaceful greenish waters of the kelpy bay. As wind outside the heavy plate glass windows moved water, foam, and seaweed about, flashes of yellowish sunlight cast hypnotically calming patterns around the walls and people of the underground nerve center.

"You see," Dr. Night's dry, calm voice said, "we have achieved our objective through calm, focused discipline and attention to detail. I congratulate each of you, and will award each man and woman a significant bonus in their pay."

There was ripple of pleased laughter, punctuated with enthusiastic clapping.

"The former Project David of Anaconda is now Project Gemini of the Black Umbrella Consortium."

More clapping.

"This is only the beginning, ladies and gentlemen. Now begins the hard part. The bird is now safely in our hands, and orbiting over the Tropic of Cancer. We will refer to our wonderful and exciting new cause as Project Gemini—after the divine twins who saved the Roman Republic in a great battle just a few years after its founding in 509 BCE."

He added: "Keep your eyes and ears open to ensure absolute secrecy that has made our organization so successful. We have grown to a global power under the noses of our opposition. We are too big to fail, too powerful to crush, and too successful to be acquired or destroyed by the corponations that rule the world. They are obsolete, and we are the New World Order."

As the techs and engineers clapped each other on the back, he added:

"Remember, we are not like our enemies. We are of the night. We are the earth, the underworld. We are dark and stealthy. Our power lies in silence, while they peddle all their blather to billions of gullible victims using the media they control. They are about talk—we are about action. We walk silently and conquer in darkness. Even the light of our victory is a black one. For every day, there must be a night. We are Persephone—the Korē, the virginal daughter of the grain goddess Demeter. Like the Neolithic grain itself, Korē the pure maiden was abducted from a meadow where she played with the feral child Artemis and other virginal huntresses and she-warriors. Hades, the king of night, abducted her to be his wife, which made her debased and defiled. Korē in her other life, this dark life, became the fearsome queen of the underworld. Her name as queen of the underworld was Persephone—she whose name must never be spoken, so dreadful was she. With the help of the sun and other daylight gods, Demeter found her beloved daughter. Zeus decreed that for half the year, Korē the maiden would run and play with her sisters on the sunny wheat fields when they are ready for harvest. Then, as the grain falls to the earth, dies, and lies entombed until its resurrection in the next crop cycle, Korē once again becomes the most dreadful female in the cosmos, the queen of the underworld, Persephone—whose terrifying name must never be spoken, as if the very sound of it could kill the speaker or the hearer of it. She is our model and our guide as we take over the world, along with the Furies Alecto, Megaera, and Tisiphone who serve her."

He added with relish: "Alecto, relentless fury, an anger without reason or bounds, rage that exists purely for the sake of rage, chaos, and destruction, death to humans. And her sister Furies:

"Tisiphone, limitless Revenge; and Megaera, boundless Jealousy."

In the underwater (and underground) nerve center, the late afternoon sunlight played in chaotic but pleasing patterns all around the walls and over the faces of those in the domed chamber. They did not laugh or clap, but regarded each other with a mix of fear and awe.

The power of Dr. Night, and the forces he mustered, seemed beyond all natural boundaries. The irrational ruler of the ancient physical world was back in the saddle: Fear, and only Fear itself.

Nowhere Man

Jack Gray: Man from Nowhere

In a certain amber city of American mythology, a dark knight waits in a marvelous urban villa until called to duty. His secret mansion in an unlikely inner city section looks plain and ordinary from the outside. Its graffiti-smeared brick walls are dark with moss and decay on the outside. Inside, the superhero's fortress is filled with the latest luxuries and defenses.

The hero has risen from nowhere to become not only a financial prince and benefactor, but also a caped crusader to right such wrongs as bedeviled his childhood. Like Everyman, he is not some vapid fop, raised with a silver spoon in his mouth, but a hard-scrabble child of the gutters who made it big—but never forgot his roots as a common citizen.

The city fathers—corporate and governmental—have only to display his logo atop a light beam, projected as a signal upon the highest building on the skyline.

A garage door briefly opens, shedding a rectangle of buttery light into the darkness outside. A powerful dark automobile roars up from the light, flies like a shadow down a leafy driveway, and roars out onto city streets that have once again grown lawless (though not leafless). The season is, more often than not, autumn—or Fall, as the Americans call it so evocatively. Night and day are equal near the October equinox.

The hours of night and day are measured in strokes of the master clock in the entrance hall. The hero leaves his carpeted library, gleaming study, and Gothic hallways ornamented with leaded glass windows inset with stained glass.

There is a princess in his life—a shadow who moves languorously among heavy maroon drapes, which frame windows as dreamy and bleary as if they were perennially covered with rolling rain drops. Her shoulders are bare; her hair hangs in heavy waves, her figure is a delicacy in a sumptuous robe; her movements have a wounded musicality in a minor but intriguing key (like one lingering, broken piano chord); her lips are lush, and her eyes are filled with meaning. Whatever her name is, she does not just look, or drink in, with her eyes. She emotes, or radiates outward from her brain, through her eyes, as the ancients thought vision must function. She is all about our hero, and he is all about her. When they make love, they are a poem in one of his books. Action is everything. They never speak of love or sex. Ellipsis or omission is the most fitting enjambment in illustrated quatrains of *amor* (passion, sex) or *caritas* (loving, caring). Perhaps only a warrior like Jack Gray—losing himself in his post-doctoral Classics and History studies to forget the world outside his castle, or ranch—would appreciate these delicate nuances of the ancient Romans and their lost world.

The hero must once again rescue mankind from that small, predatory minority of its species who, in all places and all ages, manage to rise to the top through constant manipulation, ruthless backstabbing, false accusations, and downright sabotage or even murder. Some of these, like tame and noble stallions, eventually become the civic fathers of both finance and city hall. Their untamed siblings are lords of crime and corruption, ever filled with self-justifying ambition, boundless corruption, and salivation over power and wealth. Both types of men and women are united in their lack of self-doubt. Their shadowless egotism is the clockwork that drives the hands of crime around the clock of destruction. They give long-winded, rambling speeches whose focus is entirely on themselves. They are adults who never outgrew the infantile boundary—the narcissopause—where I end and others begin. Like Narcissus, they fall in love with their own reflection in the water. Like an infant, only they exist, and the universe is their suckling breast.

The ancients posited that all things in the universe are composed of four smallest, indivisible particles described as *atomai* (from Greek *a-*, without + *temenos*, a cutting or separation).

The thinkers of long ago—including brilliant *heterae*, women who were neither slaves nor wives, but an exalted gender—suggested that there were just four types of atoms, each representing one of the four elements. These are earth, wind, fire, and water. All things are built up of these, in endless combinations.

In human nature, one might imagine that some long-dead Athenian probably once sat on a *stoa* or porch (school) with his students, and taught that human nature consists of a fifth element, a universal compound forever blended from two qualitative atoms: good and evil. Whether anyone actually said this is not known, but the wisdom of the Athenians was eclectic and daring.

Our dark knight, shining hero, the Classics and History professor, would have pondered these things in his gloomy and heavy-curtained study full of books and globes and scrolls. He might have scribbled in ink over parchment, or stylus over digital pad, while dawdling over a glass of claret and perhaps a pungent cigarillo.

The two halves of human nature are an indelible part of human nature and cosmic law. Opposites attract. Computer language is binary—zeroes and ones. For every action there is an opposite and equal reaction. Examples are boundless. They are yin and yang, left and right, sweet and bitter, up and down, gravity and levity. Either-or. *Ad infinitum*. Castor and Pollux.

As long as the two viral strains of human nature remain separate, the hero knows there is hope for the world. Full of idealism, and reenergized by a good rest after his last adventure, the mysterious crusader sets forth once again to right wrongs and rescue honest citizens, including fair damsels who find him to be ruggedly handsome, charming, and intelligent—*heterae* who are neither wives nor slaves, but an exalted gender. Their name means *other*, because they are not of the household, but a curling smoke of dreams wrapping around the linearities and curvatures of the logical imagination.

Jack Gray's call to action came in the form of a signal from Rector.

Jack had only minutes ago down to lunch with his sister Janet. The kids were at school, and Jack's brother-in-law, Mark Barger, was away at work. Molly was out of town to help an ailing aunt in Napa County, some 500 miles or 800 kilometers north, beyond San Francisco. Jack and Molly had made their peace once again. They loved each other, but neither dared to push it any further than their current arrangement. If either found someone else, they agreed it would be for the best. Molly did not want to lose another husband in the line of duty, as she had before. She vowed that Roberta would never again have her loving heart wounded by the loss of a father figure. Jack was not ready to call it a day being a secret agent, and Catherine still loomed in his life, *amor interruptus*—better yet, *caritas interrupta*—an unfinished business.

Jack and Janet ate the meal she had prepared—a beef stew with red wine and new potatoes among the ingredients—along with a glass each of local Cabernet Sauvignon. Janet was no doubt thinking about the kids, about her husband, about the ranch. Jack was thinking of Molly and Roberta at the moment.

It was possible he might come home one day and find Molly embracing with some other man. Still, he thought of him and her as a planetary love. Would the moon and the earth continue in their long embrace around the sun, or would the earth awaken one day, and find that Selene had drifted off, run away, with some darkly handsome star from out of nowhere? The odds were totally against it, both literally and figuratively. So Molly—a long, slender figure in semi-gloom, on her bed beside him, sleeping while night wind and moonlight stole in past moving drapes—remained the moon in his life. Her kisses and embraces, shining with light borrowed from the sun and the moon, said the same to him. She would be his moon, as he would remain her earth. She would remain beautiful and beyond reach, but in his orbit; while he continued hunting, and worshipped her. So went the metaphors of their dreamy reveries by moonlight, stroking one another's strong limbs.

But anything was possible. Each time Jack went off on another mission, he might never return. The hearts of Molly and Janet, as well as his daughters Gail and Marcia, and Molly's daughter Roberta, would be broken; not to mention Janet and Mark's two smaller boys, Tommy, 9, and Bobby, 11. Jack had gone every day up the hill to talk it over with Catherine. She had long ago released him from his self-imposed mission. She wanted him to quit, and live a normal life, and care above all for Gail and Marcia. The two girls resembled Catherine, in fact, as much as they resembled Jack. Not to play favorites, of course, Gail looked more like Catherine 's daughter—as the saying went—while Marcia looked more like a young Jack with softer, feminine lines but the same stubborn eyes.

As Jack and Janet ate, a hilltop breeze pushed Janet's softly checkered kitchen curtains in and out. It was the same breeze that stirred the meadows and dandelion fields. An airplane droned innocently in the blue sky amid big white puffy cumulus clouds.

Then came a chime of twelve hours on the living room wall clock. Jack glanced over at the antique Junghans in its ornate oak case. The time on the tin face read 12:32. Clearly, this was not the time for the full chime set, followed by twelve *bong*s. On cue, his wristwatch began to buzz. It tried to pull his hand around on the table. There was no mistaking the signal from Johannes Rector, which no doubt meant that Claire Lightfield needed his services once again.

"I have to run," he told Janet.

"Ja-a-ck," his sister groaned.

"Gotta do it. Work calls."

"What about the kids?"

"I'll be gone before they get home from school. Please give them big hugs and kisses for me, will you?" Though they stayed at their places around the table, he wrapped his arms around her. He nuzzled a kiss behind her ear, but she made a sour face. "C'mon, Sis. Help me out here."

"I give them lots of love every day."

"I know you do. One day, when I am ready—"

"—or dead, Jack—"

"—I will come home, settle down, and sit in the rocker on the porch. I'll hunt quail, and track my investments. I'll go for walks with you and the dogs."

She rose, in a huff, and took her plate to the garbage. In two rapid, angry moves, she forked her unfinished lunch into the pail. Then she stormed to the sink and began doing dishes. She turned her back, and did not look at him, but he could see her shoulders were heaving as she cried quietly. As designed by evolution, a woman's crying is more terrible and powerful than the squalling of an infant, which is a language unto itself, whose cues parents pick up. When a woman cries, her keening is like a dreadful wind from beyond. Her agony is like broken glass that cuts the skin and tears a man's heart. Jack wanted to rush to her and hold her, but he was the cause of her anguish. He must not make things worse with any clumsy words or gestures.

When she was upset, she could not eat, or she'd throw up. It had been like that when they were little kids, not yet ten years old, riding in the back of mom and dad's station wagon, to the movies or a restaurant or whatever. On a few occasions—like the time they'd driven past a dead dog on the road—Jack had held a garbage bag open while Janet spent twenty minutes on and off sobbing, hiccupping, throwing up in to the bag, and crying some more.

He went upstairs and changed into street clothes—very unassuming: cowboy shirt, blue wind breaker, denim trousers, cowboy boots. Not a ten gallon hat or even one gallon, but a San Diego Padres baseball cap.

By the time he came downstairs, Janet had cleaned up, done the dishes, and poured both their wines back into the decanter, which sat with its crystal cork on a shady shelf in the living room. For a moment, he thought she would not say goodbye, but before he could exit by the rear door, she came flying out of a corner where she had been dusting, and wrapped him in a tight embrace. "Take care of yourself, okay?"

"I promise, Sis." He stroked her hair as she closed her eyes and breathed against his neck. With her head resting on his shoulder, she looked as if she were asleep. Her skin was pale, except for a tense flush in her cheeks.

"I want you to come home to us," she whispered, barely audibly. Tears dribbled from anguished eyes. "The girls love you so. The boys too."

Ten minutes later, a casually dressed man, obscured by heavy sunglasses, stood by the chain link fence near the house on the D Ranch. He carried a small handbag with the San Diego Chargers football team logo on it. In a holster under his jacket, he wore his compact, Swiss-made U.S. Coast Guard special 9mm SIG Sauer P229R DAK semi-automatic, which carried a short clip of 13 .40 Smith & Wesson rounds. In the bag were his toothbrush, spare underwear, a tie he liked, and his backup with ankle holster. The secondary was a snubby, Hungarian-made blue-steel finish Walther PPK/E compact chambering the .32 caliber ACP round in a niner-clip. He hated wearing an ankle holster, and preferred carrying it in his trousers, under the belt, at the small of his back.

He waited at the chain link fence separating the D Ranch and other properties from the Federal reservation with its casinos and assorted defense facilities. He found the miles of coiled razor wire atop and along the bottom of the fence intimidating, as were the warnings about high voltage, sentry dogs, and shoot to kill orders. All that was as scheduled.

The next patrol was not a scheduled jeep or hummer. Instead, it was a dark blue sedan with U.S. Federal plates.

Jack showed his badge, and a scanner atop the car looked at his credentials. From experience, he blinked his eyes shut, without looking away. A light flashed over his features. His digital image was relayed to local security. He touched his fingers to a reader, and looked into a retinal scanner. Only then did a gate open in the chain link fence, and he stepped into a twenty-foot corridor between the outer and inner fences.

Jack got into the back seat.

As cameras recorded every move, the car sped up and took him deep into the reservation. With the windows tinted all around, including the bullet-proof safety glass over the front seatback, Jack never spoke with the driver—never saw him or her, and vice-versa.

They stopped at a round, black-top landing place, where got out and boarded a light Sikorsky S-434 chopper. The pilot, a civilian wearing a GS badge, flew him away toward the west. The pilot was a skinny little man of about 50, hiding behind sunglasses, a raised windbreaker collar, and a low-seated Navy cap weighed down with headphones. The flight to the federal air strip took about fifteen minutes over a maze of hills, canyons, casinos, public and private streets, and some suburban neighborhoods.

At a back runway on Palomar's secure airport, a curious maneuver happened.

A black Lincoln Town Car with tinted windows and California livery plates pulled up as soon as the helicopter landed. Jack, carrying his little hand bag, stepped from the chopper. The limo driver, in his black suit, held the rear door open as Jack got in. A minute later, the limo was rolling across the airport toward the main passenger terminal building.

In the back seat, Jack sat beside another man dressed similarly, except for the logo on the hand bag, the color of the wind breaker, and the baseball cap. Jack's double was the same size and weight as Jack—a member, in fact, of the security force at Camp Pendleton, the huge U.S. Marine Corps installation some miles north along the coast.

Jack and the other man switched places in the back seat. The double must exit on the same side that Jack entered, in case anyone were tailing and observing Jack. This was all part of Jack's deal with Rector and Claire—he worked for them, but his family life stayed top secret. Jack and the man switched caps, jackets, and hand bags. Jack transferred his weapons and other paraphernalia to the new handbag, while the other man would carry in Jack's old Chargers bag a half dozen oranges to equal the weight.

Minutes later, the limousine pulled up at the rear entrance to the main terminal. Without comment, the double stepped out onto the runway. He wore a San Diego Padres baseball cap and heavy sunglasses. His windbreaker was light blue, while his denim trousers were a darker blue. He wore a cowboy shirt and cowboy boots. The double carried Jack's San Diego Chargers hand bag, full of oranges the special security staff at Camp Pendleton would enjoy. The double walked smartly up the broad concrete stairs to the main lounge. There, he would walk around for a few minutes to check if he'd been watched. Then he would walk outside, step into a waiting taxi, and be driven back to the vast Marine Corps base, to be swallowed up amid its security.

Jack, meanwhile, was driven to a remote runway. There, he hustled on board a one-propeller Piper PA-28 Cherokee (one pilot, capacity three passengers, but dedicated to Jack alone) waiting with the engine running. As soon as he pulled the door shut, the plane began to taxi.

As he buckled up, the plane lifted him off on the next leg of his reentry into Compass News' and Sigma 2020's world reference. Jack was often the secret field agent of last resort. He was the hot dog when they ran out of hamburgers at life's barbecue. He was their hot dog, period.

The aircraft flew for about fifteen minutes in the direction of Los Angeles, at an altitude of about 3,000 feet. Encountering a dense coastal cloud bank or marine layer, the pilot took advantage of the visual disruption—should anyone be watching from the ground or in a tailing aircraft—by spiraling upward to 5,200 feet or about a mile high. The pilot—again, anonymous—flew due north, northeast in the direction of Las Vegas. This was a distance of 330 miles, or 538 km—a good six or seven hours by car through heavy traffic and ridiculous heat, with drifting dust devils, on the alkaline flats at the edge of Death Valley. By air, in this craft, at about 140 mph (230 km/h), it was a little over 2.5 hours. Jack sat back, sideways, and dozed with his outstretched legs crossed at the ankles, his hat pulled down over his eyes, and his arms crossed over his ribs.

As the plane descended to a landing at Las Vegas' McCarran International Airport, Jack awakened. He yawned, pulled open a compartment built into the back seat, and pulled out the clothes he was going to wear upon landing.

The Piper Cherokee flew into the same back strip from which the federal government flies top-secret passenger jets to desert locations including Tonopah Test Range, which includes such tantalizing installations as the fabled Area 51 of UFO fame, or its less famous but even more exotic neighbor, Area 52. Some of the most secret air and space technologies of the U.S. had been developed here during the 20th Century, including the U-2 spy plane, the SR-71 Blackbird, the F117-A Stealth aircraft, and others. It would not be his destination, although the OST was the type of science that could easily have originated around Groom Lake.

Jack Gray's little one-engine plane taxied to a halt. It was lost among the giant aircraft standing around it on the tarmac at McCarran, one of the world's busiest airports.

Out of the plane climbed a man in a dark suit, white shirt, and merlot tie. He carried a charcoal suede executive briefcase that matched his soft shoes and gloves. That man was Jack Gray.

He walked briskly into a building, through a checkpoint manned by Air Force security personnel in fatigues, who held assault rifles. Nobody even looked at him, except Jack knew he was being intently watched by multiple special duty officers on closed circuit video.

His path took him out into the free air and sunshine of a low-security government services airport. There, he found a U.S. Navy Gulfstream G280 executive jet waiting for him. As soon as he was on board, the plane began taxiing. It had a crew of two, and seating for up to ten passengers, usually top GS civilians, Congressional delegations, or flag officers. Instead, there was only Jack—and one young enlisted airman to provide services. When the plane had reached its service ceiling at 45,000 ft (13,716 m, well over eight miles), Jack ordered from the menu—a tuna salad sandwich on toast with lettuce and tomato, pickle on the side, complimentary desert pack with chocolate pudding and vanilla ice cream, and a chilled root beer along with a companion bottle of lightly chilled spring water. The tuna was mixed thickly with chopped celery to take away any excess fishiness, and to make the excellent tuna even more steak-like. The root beer was one of the wonderful range of crafted sodas produced in the U.S. these days, with a butterscotch richness added in; not too sweet or cloying, not too spicy or biting; just nice, balanced, and rounded without any edges to its flavor. A chasing drink of bottled spring water further smoothed its effect on the palate.

Cruising at about 500 mph (circa 800 kph), the aircraft took about three hours to reach Kansas City, Missouri. There, at a military field on the periphery of Kansas City International Airport, the plane refueled. Jack stepped off onto the tarmac in the fresh evening air to stretch his legs. As expected, a man and a woman walked steadily toward him. They waved—Claire Lightfield and Johannes Rector—and Jack returned the greeting.

As they stood in a circle of three, Jack said: "Must be a big blow."

"It's a Force Five hurricane for sure," Claire said. She wore a business suit in earth tones, and carried a matching field green raincoat over both arms as they stood together beside the waiting jet. A long tanker truck was just now engaged in a mating ritual with the jet, coupling by means of a main fuel line.

"I lost a man in the field yesterday," Rector said. "I need you to pick up the trail where he left off. It's critical." He wore a more casual outfit, with a dark green pullover, brown slacks, and gray leather shoes. He carried a ski parka, dark blue, with furry white collar, slung over one shoulder. The airport was, at this hour, a bit windy, a bit warm, a bit humid, and generally comfortable. With the smells of rubber, avgas, and oil in the air—not to mention a host of secondary artificial aromas of industry and transport—it was not the great outdoors. It was not the clean air of the D Ranch. But it was livable. And to Jack, it had that comfortable safeness one found in a civilized democracy, where there weren't knocks on the door at three a.m. and unexplained trips to prison, resulting in one's disappearance or transport to a gulag. Having worked around the world, often at the risk of life and limb, Jack exerted a certain amount of paranoia about his surroundings at all times. It was a walking stress-trauma that went with this line of work.

"And what are we after?"

Rector and Claire explained that Anaconda, the world rival of Camelback, was fielding a new sort of sniper rifle that could kill people from orbit. If that wasn't bad enough, it appeared that a new, shadowy power had risen out of nowhere, and stolen the satellite with which Anaconda hoped to offer its services. They could only be up to no good.

"Not a bad line of business," Jack said appreciatively.

After some minutes, as the fuel truck drove away, they boarded the plane. They sat in plush leather chairs, at a conference table, in the midsection. The young airman brought his menu out, but they now ordered only fresh-brewed coffee, variously with sugar and cream.

"What is this new organization nobody has heard of before?" Jack asked.

Rector said: "They've been around for some years. I would describe their core business as murder and terrorism. They are the world's first global terror brokerage. No matter if you are a guy like Osama bin Laden, sitting in a mud hut in Afghanistan, or a young anarchist in Tokyo, or a militia nut in Kansas, if you can ante up dollars, Euros, or gold, you can buy any service you need. Want to assassinate your country's president? They will send a blond, blue-eyed guy, looks like a church pastor, and he'll garrote or shoot or poison your target. Whatever suits the occasion."

Claire said: "Their agents could be an Arab, a U.S. citizen, a Congo bushman, a North Korean fanatic, or an L.A. gangbanger—no longer limited to any typical own ethnic, religious, or other homey group. Police profiling won't work anymore."

Rector added: "As a secondary effect, the crime rate goes up. A lot of these nuts will rob banks and murder people locally to get the money they need to pay Black Umbrella."

"They're not all nuts, Rector," Claire said. "Black Umbrella, from what we're able to tell, is now actively recruiting among what they call the disaffected. The world is full of lost causes, dispossessed kings, downtrodden ethnic groups. The world is run top-down by imperial consortia, who see common people as an ant farm to be exploited or stepped on as the bottom line optimizes itself—on autopilot, running on programs and routines, on indices and parameters, often without human intervention. That leaves not only billions of victims, but also a lot of lost souls looking for revenge or justice in whatever crooked way BLUM offers."

"To kick things off," Rector said, "it looks like they hijacked Anaconda's new toy during the launch and first orbit. Anaconda was symbolically placing their pet, called the Orbital Sniper Technology, or OST, in orbit over the Tropic of Capricorn, which forms the southern boundary of the tropics." He opened up a creamy clamshell computer, built into the bulkhead, to show a 24 inch screen. He brought live a series of informational sites and maps.

Claire interrupted and pointed at a world map on the screen. "The northern tropical boundary runs through central Mexico in the Americas, while the southern boundary runs through northern Chile, northern Argentina, and south-central Brazil. It totally avoids Europe, but passes through the southern Sahara of Africa in the north, and northern South Africa in the south."

"And most of the land in-between is jungle," Jack observed. "The Amazon, the Congo…"

Claire finished: "…the southern half of India, much of southeast Asia, and northern Australia."

"More jungle," Jack said.

"Right," Rector said. "Home to a lot of dictators where someone with an OST can earn a fortune popping them off. Think about it—some tinpot Caesar happens to control huge oil fields, Anaconda can be hired to silently kill him and put someone in place who is willing to be bribed."

"I get it, stop with the drama," Jack said. "What am I supposed to do in all of this?"

"Find the spider at the center of the web," Rector said in a hard tone. "We know he goes by the name Dr. Night. Learn all you can. Stop them. Kill if you must. And destroy the technology."

"The usual," Claire said sympathetically. Her tone suggested she meant that Jack could have a desk job anytime he asked for one. "Your insurance is maxed out."

Jack ignored her.

Rector said: "I was running a lowball agent in Europe, trying to follow the tracks of Project David from China to its new home in Germany under the wing of Anaconda. I think my man, code name Ribeye, found out more than they wanted him to know."

"Do you think you'll get him back alive?"

"Rector shrugged. "Pity. Nice young man. Unless they want to ransom him, I'm afraid he'll turn up dead. I'm just waiting to see how imaginative and creative these Black Umbrella people are in handling their victims."

Siegrid Unger: Nights at the Tiergarten

In Frankfurt on the River Main in Hesse, Germany, a pretty young blonde woman named Siegrid Unger, age 23, rolled out of bed in the gray hours of dawn. She moved silently, so as not to wake her live-in boyfriend Wolfgang. Wolf worked nights as a taxi driver. He came home after three in the morning, when the two usually made passionate love, before Siegrid left for work at seven a.m. Wolf slept most of the day, leaving for work before she got home.

She tiptoed around the apartment, brushing her teeth while wearing only skimpy pink briefs. She dressed while spooning strawberry yoghurt and sipping hot instant coffee. She had made her lunches last night, including a pastry and a bit of ham for the midmorning, a liverwurst on a slab of good brown farm bread, and a small white sausage with mustard and a roll for midafternoon.

Wearing jeans, a dark blue pullover with high rolled collar, and soft brown hiking shoes, she carried her purse and her lunch bag as she made her way to the nearest U-Bahn (Underground metro, subway). She and Wolf shared a small apartment in the Henning Tower district near the Südbahnhof (South Railway Station). Being young people, they were pleased to get away with a relatively small rent on a somewhat cramped, almost industrial street with some crime and noise. They were enjoying life together, though their hours were conflicted. On weekends they were inseparable. They went out often, either to their favorite hangouts or to the movies or whatever. Wolf was a kind young man, and she found him good looking. She was a nice blonde girl for him, slender, with long legs and small breasts, and blue eyes. Like all men, he simply needed a bit more parenting to grow up so they could talk about more serious things in life.

Siegrid boarded the U-3 subway at the train station. This took her north over the Main River. Near Hauptwache on the north side, she switched to the U-7. This took her almost directly to the Frankfurt Zoo.

There, in a locker room for women, she took her hot morning shower. Afterwards, she changed into a fresh work uniform left for her by the laundry service. One had to look good for the tourists. Her outfit consisted of black rubber wading boots up to the knee, really cool khaki jungle fatigues with a blue military style belt with the zoo logo for a buckle, and an Ami-style baseball cap of dark, felty blue. On it were the red colors of her home Fussball heroes, Eintracht Frankfurt. *Los gehts, Adler!* Go, Eagles!

Siegrid left her lunch locked in her locker, and headed out to her work zone. Along the way, she picked up the ring of keys required to open the section gate for visitors, who would come in starting around ten a.m. She took pride in her work, and hoped to make this her permanent job.

She was very conscientious. She picked up scraps of paper and put them in the trash can, and looked about for any signs of disorder. Everything was in order. *Alles in Ordnung.*

It was going to be a sunny, breezy day with blue skies and happy tourists. She could feel it in her bones as she slogged across the smooth concrete of her zoo section.

Whistling to herself, she unlocked the heavy steel doors and entered the main crocodile house.

Instantly hysterical, she stopped and screamed.

Somebody had let out three of the mature male Australian sweetwater crocs, which get to be three meters (just under ten feet) long. There they were—Rudi, Willi, and Franz—curled around their meal which was totally off schedule.

And therein lay the real cause for screaming.

Somebody had fed them a man for breakfast. There was actually little left of him. His clothing was in shreds and was mingled with the bloody piles of bone and meat that had been a human being. The man's head was a ball of exposed bluish-white bone, pinkish-gray brain matter, and ghastly red circles where eyes, nose, and mouth in a face had been.

The disaster still managed to look toward Siegrid as if asking for help.

One of the crocs was just now chewing on a rack of his ribs. Blood and gore covered the entire concrete apron, while other crocs looked on wistfully from behind thick glass and armored steel doors.

What really made Siegrid gag were the man's hands. They had come loose from the body, and lay detached at her toes as if ready to chase her. On one set of knuckles was a tattoo *Love*, while the other hand had *Hate* written across its knuckles.

Siegrid screamed again.

The crocs looked at her.

She ran so fast that her boots stayed behind.

One of the crocs lurched after her first, followed by the other two. They'd had a taste of human flesh, and seemed very enthusiastic about having more.

Breathless—retching, terrified—she stood in stocking feet and fumbled the padlock shut to save her own life. The gate slammed shut just as the leading crocodile's snout crashed against it. Another second and it would have been Siegrid's turn for a lurid and gory death.

Too blind and breathless to scream, she was a blur, running for a nearby emergency phone.

Message for Mr. Gray

In the air above Virginia, the white U.S. Navy Gulfstream G280 executive jet with black markings descended for a landing at Reagan International Airport in Washington, D.C.

Rector took a call on the cabin phone system, which tied in to the cockpit communications systems. "Yes," he said. As he listened, his eyebrows rose way up. Claire and Jack watched with mystified fascination as Rector listened to a phone message. "Thanks," Rector said after about two minutes. He rang off. "Oh dear God in heaven."

"What is it?" Claire asked.

"That was about Ribeye." Rector looked a bit sick around the gills. "Poor kid. I just learned that Black Umbrella is highly creative indeed. Jack, you're going to need to fly to Frankfurt, and work your way back from the crocodile cage at the Frankfurt Zoo."

"They fed him to the reptiles?" Jack said.

Claire looked pale.

"Yes. He called me from Kaiserslautern the night before, so this all went down very fast. Let's see..." he searched on the computer "...the A6 Autobahn runs between K-town and Frankfurt, a straight shot of about sixty miles, or 100 klicks. The body was still fresh as a pile of hamburger an hour ago. The zoo keepers found his wallet, and my blind contact number. Langley forwarded the Frankfurt Police chief's call to me—he speaks great English, and left me a detailed message, which Langley was kind enough to forward. That's what I just heard."

Claire observed: "Usually when something like this gets done, the doers are sending someone a message."

"I get it," Jack said. "Message received."

BLUM: Introducing Black Umbrella

Game Show: Ultimatum 1

In three hundred of the top corporate boardrooms around the world, each was filled with a rapt audience of core executives and top shareholders. As of yet, the press had not gotten hold of the story—but the world was only one leak away from hysteria. The executives, who looked darkly at each other, knew fully well that the man about to speak was proving them to be helpless. They understood they were becoming a power vacuum. In history, some megalomaniac—Caesar, Napoleon, Lenin—always stepped in to take the reins of state. In this case it might well be the reins of world.

Dr. Night introduced himself and his organization, Black Umbrella, to the corporate world. His style was to utter a brief speech, and then pause for a full minute or two while his listeners absorbed and discussed what he said.

In an utterly self-assured, dry, almost mocking voice, Dr. Night followed the initial pleasantries thus: "You all have professional corporate and government intelligence organizations. You have heard of a shadowy organization that sells terror and death to anyone willing and able to pay for our services. Now I wish to announce to you—the world's leading corporate-government entities, or CGE as your dueling lawyers like to say—that a new world order is in place. Ladies and gentlemen, the world is no longer your playground."

People sat stunned. As he spoke, men began to twist their ties loose as sweat poured down their faces. Women dabbed at dissolving facial makeup. Staff rushed to turn thermostats down in some of the world's highest and most massive steel-and-glass towers.

"Yes, ladies and gentlemen, you are no doubt feeling the shock that happens, in evolution, when an animal that has enjoyed unchallenged supremacy suddenly hears the thunderous foot steps, hears the mile-wide roar, sees the bloody claws and teeth, of the next great thunder lizard.

"You three hundred CEOs and chair persons employ half the working people of the human race today. Your power is unprecedented. The biggest world governments are merely departments within your corporate structures. When you speak, they fall all over themselves to obey. Senators, prime ministers, presidents, and parliamentarians come running. Using the media, you have turned their own constituents into mindless, blabbering fools who unwittingly promote your corporate line under the guise of fake religion, fake values, and fake patriotism. You have no more use for morality or patriotism than a snake has. You add tea bags of lies to the already tepid water of their nonexistent grasp of history, geography, and even basic logic skills. Your hate-media demagogues made fortunes feeding their listeners' petty and unreasoning rage toward their fellow children in the sandbox of life. *You're lazy. You're stealing my cookie, and I won't let you. You can't climb into my sandbox. I'm going to hit you with my plastic pail. I'm better than you. I can cut in line ahead of you because the voice on radio or television said so.*

"Once you mix the potent brew of lies and rage in a moron's head, it can never be pried loose because to do so would require reasoning—and too many of your human tools—your useful fools as Lenin called their type, your urban mob as we speak of ancient Rome, your sans-culottes as we call the mobs of the French Revolution—do not possess critical thinking skills to accomplish that. This has happened time and again in history, as the masses are manipulated by liars who claim to be the opposite of what they really are—ruthless, greedy predators who let nothing stop them in clawing their way to the top. Your media manipulators will convince the mob that anyone trying to help them is the enemy, and the mob will tear the good guys apart while selling their souls and their children to their new corporate owners in the name of empty slogans. Guns, nationhood, Jesus, Mohammed, whatever is the hollow and misappropriated cause. Now, ladies and gentlemen, all that is about to change. Did you really think that your rulership by unreason would last forever? Your abdication from responsibility was the final step in proving that the limits of democracy begin where the average person's grasp of facts and logic ends. I, Dr. Night, have come to declare that 1984 is over. Newspeak is no more. Your day is over.

"Now about you, CEOs, individually—as of this moment, each of you is a hunted animal. You will always look over your shoulders. You will prefer to remain indoors with your families. Nobody on earth is immune from our awesome and growing power."

He paused while babbling broke out in penthouse boardrooms across the world's skyscrapers in the world's twenty-five largest and most influential mega-cities.

"This is only the beginning, my friends. I am about to offer you a proof of concept."

On large viewing screens—usually reserved for self-congratulatory stock charts, video clips of corporate achievements, and annual awards— Dr. Night's technicians preempted the circuits and broadcast from the orbital communications network a specific BLUM feed.

The test signal, lasting a half minute, was of the BLUM logo—a circle with a line bisecting it horizontally. Over the line floated a powerful eye. Below the line of the earth was a beautiful but foreboding Gorgon face surrounded by an image of wriggling, hissing snakes. Then the live streaming video feed cut in, along with a soothing stream of orchestral music with violins, brasses, and piano.

"Please forgive the elevator music," Dr. Night said. "The designers of our program wanted to emulate one of your eminently successful television game show in every way, including the thematic and thrilling music. Now please give a round of applause for our leading lady on the show, Miss Megaera Spite. She prefers you just call her Meg. She is a member of what I call our Alecto Circus of key feminine Furies who put the *oom* in to BLUM—Black Umbrella! She is a real, weaving spitter!"

Laughter at Dr. Night's pun rumbled amid a wave of hand-clapping by an unseen audience—probably BLUM staffers—a beautiful blonde in a flouncy white dress stood before a large board in what looked like a game show set. The board had squares, to be filled with letters or numbers—it wasn't clear yet.

The blonde waited, holding an old-fashioned school-teacher pointer with rubber tip. She smiled dazzlingly.

"I thought it would be more dramatic if we organized this like one of your mind-numbing corporate game shows," Dr. Night said. "To avoid world panic, we will keep this among ourselves, *d'accord*? Ten billion ants in your ant farm don't need their day ruined all at once. It would lower their efficiency in your Fritz Lang *Metropolis*."

He paused to let the boardrooms bubble with shocked and angry commentary.

"Ladies and gentlemen, this will be a brief show without commercial interruptions."

The blonde went to a large wheel and spun it. Inside, what looked like rectangular chits, of white plastic, the size of large plastic credit cards, tumbled and glittered amid the ambient stage lights. Each chit had a man's or woman's full name and city of record on it in black ink.

Meanwhile, on a side panel a list of names and addresses scrolled for all to see.

"You see, on the side, the names of ordinary citizens of the world's cities. You'll note, for example, Mr. Yao of Beijing, an electrician. There is Mr. Yamato of Sapporo, a truck driver. There is Miss Brahma of Delhi, a jewelry expert and buyer. We see here Mr. Bonyo of Brazzaville, an accountant. And there is Mr. Chavez of Lima, a school teacher. And Mr. Thompson of Dallas, a policeman. And so on. I chose not to begin with something more spectacular like assassinating the chairman of the United Nations General Assembly, or the president of the United States, or someone far more important, like the CEO of Camelback or Anaconda. In our next game show, we will step up to the big time, but for now, this is just a proof of concept."

He paused again. Board members summoned aides, who frantically ran from the room with scraps of phone or digitexts listing the names of potential victims.

"You will not have time to contact police around the world, even if you had the phone numbers and addresses as we do. From among a thousand names in that bin, our Miss Spite will draw one unlucky name.

We are about to demonstrate proof of concept by terminating that individual. Ready, Megan?"

The blonde strode about with a great gleaming smile and one happy arm raised high, while, with the other hand, she hiked up her long dress to show off full, pale legs.

As applause rippled through the air, and while the audience in the corporate towers gasped and booed, Megan Spite spun the big drum. The plastic chits tumbled and sparkled for a full minute before the drum came to rest.

A ticket popped out and flew into a silver tray.

Miss Megan Spite flounced by, picked it up, turned, and strode off to the right. Her arm was up, holding the ticket to present it to someone off camera.

"Good job, Miss Spite," said Dr. Night—whose face nobody outside Black Umbrella had knowingly seen to date. That information in itself would have been both invaluable and dangerous. The person knowing who Dr. Night really was could earn a large reward from the world's corporate consortia, led by Camelback in the west and Anaconda in the east—and a quick assassin's garrote, bullet, or crocodile.

"Let's see what it says. Oh! Unfortunate man! Let's watch the clock."

For the first time, the video recorder on the set shifted to an enormous clock, which had a white face as tall as Meg, and black hands ticking off the minutes and hours against a circle of simple black numbers. "The computer on board Gemini has received the information, and the program is executing. Oh! I am informed that the shot has been fired. Four minutes, folks. In about two minutes, I will read off the name of the unlucky winner."

Words like *outrageous* and *amoral* and *psychotic* floated around the 300 corporate boardrooms forced to participate in Dr. Night's elaborate and bizarre show.

For over 100 seconds, the music swelled in lifting fugues.

Through the music, one could hear the giant clock ticking on the set.

At the two minute mark, the music softened and Dr. Night cut in. It seemed the clock was ticking louder.

"Our unlucky winner is…Mr. James Dooley of London, U.K.

"Folks, don't try this at home. Our sniper bullet from outer space orbit is on its way to terminate Mr. James Dooley, a sidewalk artist, who is at the moment painting in chalk on the sidewalk on the southeast corner of White Tower on the grounds of the Tower of London. What a terrific choice! It will be too late for anyone to warn him, especially since only you leaders of the world's 300 top corporations are aware of our little demonstration. This should prove beyond a shadow of a doubt that we mean what we say, and that we are capable of killing anyone on earth, at any moment, with this Orbital Sniper Technology."

The screen cut to London. On the grounds of the Tower of London complex, by the Thames, the satellite video from the Keyhole-Corona based cameras on the Gemini space craft picked up a young, long-haired man of about 25 years old. He wore an easily targetable white T-shirt with a rock band logo on front and back. He was crouched over a large sidewalk artwork—one of a line of such artists permitted the rare honor, on the queen's anniversary day, to work in chalk. Immediately below the brownish-gray, white-streaked walls was a strip of grass, hemmed in by a nondescript little iron fence. Before the fence ran a row of black iron benches. Today's festive street art exhibit was taking place on the concrete surface before the benches. Throngs of tourists walked slowly by, or stopped to examine the portraits of flowers, the queen, and passers-by.

"Ten...nine...eight," Dr. Night counted.

One heard sobbing in the corporate boardrooms. They knew that any one of them could soon be next.

"...Three...two...one..."

James Dooley finished a line in white chalk on his drawing of a vase of flowers. He straightened his back and tilted his head to one side to inspect his artwork. A small circle of bystanders clapped.

"Great job, Mr. Dooley," Dr. Night enthused.

Abruptly, the target's T-shirt made a violent fluffing motion, and in the same split second, he was thrown several feet forward. A cone of bloody ejecta spewed ahead of him. His corpse bounced once or twice, so violent was its crash into the concrete surface.

There was an outcry in the corporate boardrooms.

"You profess disapproval," Dr. Night said, "but think about what your corporate policies have done, and continue to do. Think about how you sold cigarettes, and used your media to lie about how good smoking is for people. What about healthcare in the U.S.? Evil! Communism! Socialism! The useful fools preferred to kill their own children to avoid common-sense health care that every other industrialized nation on earth long ago delivered to every citizen. Your outcome was mass murder, a holocaust of banality, happening one child at a time without undue notice in the media that you controlled. With the lessons learned from those early experiments in New Think, right out of George Orwell's *1984*, you could convince people of the most absurd falsehoods. What lie have you not promoted for your profit motive? What murder and outrage have you not perpetrated?"

He chuckled drily and appeared to clap slowly. "Really, let's put all pretense aside and agree that this is a wonderful technology. Too bad it's not under your control any more. You will have to negotiate with me, with Black Umbrella, to establish a new world order. It will be so much better for everyone."

He cleared his throat modestly. "So, you ask, what do we, BLUM, have to gain from all this? It's very simple, ladies and gentlemen. Why did nobody think of this before? You will turn over 25% of your common or preferred stock to a special account that can be accessed from any one of thirty major world financial institutions. It will be registered in the name of our consortium, on behalf of the world's lost causes, desperate rebellions, deposed kings, waiting princes, and struggling poets to name just a few. We'll provide social services and win the masses over. We'll restore the decent, middle class life that you destroyed. We'll provide universal health care even to the poorest soul, because it is affordable and the right thing to do. You have created a vast new class of former middle class families now living in their cars and lining up at soup kitchens. They'll hate it at first, because you taught them lies. When they realize their families will be healthier, happier, and more productive, they will vomit on your and your lies. History will piss on your disgusting grave

"Think of it—the number one law—in fact, the one and only law that exists—in the corporate universe is to maximize the wealth or equity of shareholders. That's the people who own stock, and therefore own your corporations. Of course, most are tiny stake holders, who have no real vote. Like the world's industrial democracies, you permit fake proxy votes, but really, ladies and gentlemen, you are to be congratulated on the hermetically sealed and perfect little world in which you have enshrined your absolute power amid smoke and mirrors. Now the rest of the world is going to take a large piece of your action.

"And if you do not pay up, we will begin whacking your leadership, one by one, until you tire of running and hiding. We can pick you off while you stand on your balcony, holding your spouse in one arm, and raising a martini to your lips with your other hand. We can pick you off as you go sailing on your twelve-crew yacht. We can pick you off as you board your private jet. There is no place on earth we cannot reach you. That's food enough for thought today. I give you five days to comply.

"Those that sign over 20% of their equity will continue business usual. Trust me, you won't miss it, so vast are your holdings. But the poor and working classes, and the disappearing middle class, they will appreciate the health plans, the road projects, and the jobs we will create right under your greedy and ruthless noses.

"And—lest you think we are the imaginary leftists your propaganda has denounced for generations to secretly promote a corporate, post-nationalist, global agenda—I will admit that we are a for-profit organization, interested in our own wealth and bottom line.

"We are not do-gooders, and we do not sing Kumbaya. We are business people, only far better than you are. You are amateurs. We are professional killers when it comes to having our way. We never lose, because we do not waste time with lies and contradictions. That is why we will bury you. You will soon be in the dustbin of history. I have established a new world order that will last for a thousand years or more.

"We have a new product line, and we are tougher and smarter than you. We have more coils than Anaconda, more ripples than Camelback, and more tentacles than an octopus. We do not pretend to be a democracy, nor do we pretend to be a legal entity. We are, in a nutshell, going to eat your lunch. Actually, we are going to eat you for lunch, and spit out your pathetic bones.

"Either comply, or get your final affairs in order. Your days in the board room are numbered.

"Ta-tah, children, until we talk again."

Part Three: Black Umbrella

Outer Hebrides, Scotland - Kisimul Castle, Castlebay, Island of Barra

Kisimul

Jack in Frankfurt: Message Received

Jack Gray arrived in Frankfurt on a drizzly day, typical for the maritime climate of northwestern Europe. He rode a shuttle across the tarmac, amid light rain gusts, to a leading hotel chain at Rhein-Main International Airport.

Over a light breakfast of coffee, rolls, butter, and a selection of fruit compotes, he met with his assigned assistant from Sigma 2020. Miranda Coldstream was a British woman from the southeastern city of Exeter, Devon. She was young, pale, and pretty in a bland and severe way. Jack almost felt as if he had a school marm along.

She wore sensible shoes, shimmering nylons, and a brown skirt-suit. She wore a greenish, military looking windbreaker, and carried a chocolate colored umbrella. She seemed nervous.

And yet—she wore a large, sexy rhinestone ring on the fourth finger of her left hand, and she would look beautiful if she let her honey-colored hair down.

She introduced herself and joined him at a small table for two, with white linen and stainless steel service, in the first class dining room overlooking the runway.

"Nice view," he said, as huge tail fins of various airlines shifted around them.

"It is, Mr. Gray." She seemed nervous.

"Have you been read in?" he asked as he buttered a fragrant roll.

Her eyes moved left and right. "Here?"

"We're bug proof."

"How do you know?" She sat darkly glowering, hunched, with her fists between her knees.

"You new at this?"

Hesitantly, she replied: "Graduated from the new SIS Academy at Sandhurst just three months ago."

Jack Gray spread a dark berry compote on his roll. "Still wake in the middle of the night shouting slogans and standing at attention?"

She cracked her first smile. "Not after the first month back to normal life."

"You can smile now," Jack said. She did look pretty in an unadorned, rain-swept way, he thought.

She sort of fell apart in embarrassment, smiled, and looked down. "But the table might be bugged."

He made an allowing shrug. "Could be. But they'd have to bug every table at the airport, because I picked this restaurant and this table at random."

"Still…"

"Here, if it makes you feel any better." He leaned under the table to look for bugs, noting how her nylon knees were pressed together and pointed away from him. That was not an SIS or MI6 instinct, but a female one. Jack finished his search for bugs and straightened up. "Not a bug in sight. But here, if it will reassure you." He took his small carafe of water for breakfast tea—not used, because he preferred freshly brewed coffee— and dumped it over the condiments tray. Miranda jumped back. "There," he said. "If I were hiding a bug on this table, I'd do it between the salt and pepper shakers. I don't see anything sparking—do you?"

She shook her head, three feet from the table, where she had pushed herself, and now sat hugging her upper body, and pointing her knees away from him at the perpendicular.

A waiter in white top came rushing with a bunched towel in his hands.

"Sorry," Jack said, as he led Miranda in changing to a less western maritime table.

"I can see that working with you will be interesting," she said in a brittle tone.

Jack leaned sharply closer and said in a flurry: "Listen, you twit. I've been in this business since you were in puddles. Don't you go pulling academy or girdles or attitudes on me. You exist for one reason and one reason only. You are here to help me, to serve me, to do as I say, so that I can exercise my mature and superior judgment and make sure we do not both end up dead. Do you comprehend that, Agent Miranda Codfish? Or I will throw you back in the sea, and ask for another helper."

She looked pale for a moment. He thought she was going to cry.

Jack resumed fixing his roll. "Am I clear?" He took the first bite, and it was delicious.

"Yes." It was a simple statement, full of just the right meaning. He was proud of her at that moment. She got herself together, and looked at him with a steady gray gaze. She folded her hands on her purse on her lap, and waited for him to say more.

"Have a roll," he said. "The berry compote is exceptional. The coffee is dark roast, crisp without a hint of bitterness, and a faint buttery roundness effected by hints amount of turbinado and fresh light cream."

She smiled again, moved closer, and put a breakfast together for herself. "I'm sorry. I was so nervous I didn't sleep much, and I didn't have time to eat before I rushed to meet you."

"I'm touched. Now your number one mission will be to relax and not be nervous. It leads to mistakes. It's essential to get a good sleep every night."

"You're right about the coffee. Mm, that's good."

"The cream does it. Can't you smell the meadow grass?"

She laughed. "I think I just heard a cow mooing.' She set her cup aside and buttered a roll. "I'm to brief you on what Sigma knows, which is not enough."

"It never is. But shoot."

She told him what he already mostly knew about the new player—a shadowy organization named BLUM, which stood for Black Umbrella. They had hijacked an Anaconda technology for killing people with a bullet fired from Low Earth Orbit, or LEO. Near as the analysts could figure, this was based on some rather old-fashioned spy satellite technology, only instead of shooting film, it shot bullets."

Jack said: "When you say bullets, I assume you mean some kind of delivery vehicle to low atmosphere, because a bullet would get lost or burn up."

"Right, that's what we figure. They assassinated a young artist just yesterday at the Tower of London, for proof of concept."

"And their bottom line—?"

"Anaconda wanted to sell us the ability to assassinate tin horn dictators in the tropics, and avoid costly wars. Now that BLUM have hijacked the technology, they are threatening to kill corporate heads and government heads of state unless the corporations all ante up 25% of their stock ownership."

Jack sipped at his coffee. "Hmm…that would give them a leg up on a controlling interest in the entire world economy."

"They must be stopped," Miranda said. "Lord knows what would happen to us all if they gained control."

Jack set his cup down with a rather precise little *chink* of white glass on white glass. "Miranda, since we risk our lives at this, we always have to consider—is this something I want to die for?"

"But…our orders…"

"If you do not think for yourself, and think outside the box, and think independently, you aren't ultimately much use in this business. Yes, we have orders—but we can either resign our commission entirely, or ask for a desk job whenever we feel it's getting over our heads."

"But…"

"I know, orders. I decide to go in on this, partly because I'm not ready for a desk job or a permanent shady spot fishing at a lake I know, and partly because BLUM doesn't sound like a savory organization to me. The corporations are just another term for feudal baronies, but—well, think of that poor kid at the Tower, painting his flowers in chalk as you say, when they snuffed him out. Understand, Miranda—once you're in, you're in, to the hilt. You can't hesitate or have second thoughts. Once you go in the field, ready to kill or be killed, the lives of your fellow operatives will depend on you, and your life on their integrity."

"I got all that at the academy," she said drily.

He paused a moment. "Maybe I'm trying to psych myself up, more than you."

She laughed. "It's okay, Mr. Gray. We must think on the same wavelength."

"Oh yes, and call me Jack."

"You Americans."

He put his hands over hers. "Let me explain. We are as class-oriented as you, but with slightly different underlying assumptions. Anyone can be hey-you one day, and sir or ma'am the next. When we call each other Jack or Miranda, it's just a different way of saying Sir or Ma'am."

She had a nice, bubbly laugh like a forest stream. "Okay, Jack Sir. I'll try to wrap my English skull around your folkways."

"Yes, Miranda."

"I see what you mean. It's not the familial Jack or Miranda. They are more like titles."

"Exactly," he said, squeezing her hands and letting go. "If you look in a typical corporate org chart, the boxes usually have either titles or names in them; sometimes both. The knife work is the same."

Newly comrades in arms, they walked together in the damp breeze on the vast airfield, where giant planes like singing whales moved about among terminals, continents, and great cities.

Miranda drove an unmarked tan Mercedes belonging to the German federal government.

"Glad I have you to navigate through all this," Jack said as she expertly maneuvered the powerful car through massive traffic arteries.

"Frankfurt is the most important business center in Hesse, and one of the largest in Germany," Miranda said. "I've lived here on and off for several years."

"I take it you read the CIA country guides, or their MI6 equivalents."

"I read myself to sleep at night," she confessed, blushing at the hint of intimacy.

"So do I," Jack said. "Mostly either romantic suspense thrillers, or very dry books on topics like ancient Roman topology. Frankfurt has a large Roman ruins section in the old city."

"I know. Sounds intriguing. Now you want to travel to the zoo?"

"Yes. The crocodile section, to be exact."

Approaching the Frankurt Zoological Gardens, Miranda parked in a reserved government space outside the ornate, two-and-three-story headquarters, built in a somewhat severe looking Italian Renaissance style in 1876. Like most of Frankfurt, the spacious building, with many offices and several roomy halls, was destroyed in the Allied bombings during World War II. Like many historic buildings thus destroyed, it was restored over a period of decades.

They met a Herr Udo Grün in office on the first floor, after walking through sunny corridors of closed doors to find him as prearranged. Grün was a tall, odd looking man with the hunched posture and opportunistic eyes of a vulture. His narrow, beaked face and longish brown hair— combed strangely downward and forward across the ears and cheeks— radiated what Jack would describe as office politics radars of the finest attunement. But Herr Grün was helpful, as evidenced by his dropping everything, by his firm dry handshakes, and by his determined stride as he led his visitors out the back of the administrative building into the zoo itself.

He explained fondly as they walked through his domain: here was the great lake, with islands and a bridge over it. On the lake's north shore was the ape house with gibbons and other primates, while its surface was covered with ducks and more exotic birds. In a farther, smaller lake were pelicans. Other areas of the zoo included a jungle for big cats (jaguars, panthers, and the like); an African savannah with horned, ungulate grazers; a taiga for owls; a veldt or bush for African birds; an *Affenhaus* for more primates; and so many more reproductions of native habitat for camels, elephants, flamingos, without an end to the list, it seemed.

"The young lady who discovered the body," said Grün, "is too traumatized to ever work in the Exotarium with the serpents and reptiles again. She is on medical leave just now, and will return in a few weeks for new duties in a less ominous environment. Shame, because she did well with the reptilians."

"Any idea who brought the victim in, or when, or how?"

Grün shook his head. "Obviously, an inside job. Our security and the Frankfurt police and Hesse Landespolizei are working on the premise that whoever murdered the man must have had access, keys, all that sort of thing. What I am wondering is why?"

"So are we, Herr Grün," Miranda said. "So are we."

"We have reason to believe that he was last seen in Kaiserslautern, the day of or before his death," Jack said. That got no response, and he dropped the line of inquiry for now.

At the Exotarium, they met a smallish woman, aged about 50, with gray curly hair, a business suit, and a white lab coat over that. She had her hands in the lab coat's wide pockets, and extended her right hand to shake hands with the visitors. "Zweig," she introduced herself with a faint dip of the head.

"Frau Doktorin Professorin Hannah Zweig," Grün said formally.

"An honor," Jack said, and Miranda mirrored the head-schnappen along with the knickser.

"Frau Doctorin Professorin Zweig is the chief clinical officer of all veterinary operations at the zoo. She also knows a fair amount about operational fields including human physiology, criminal forensics. And she is the director of the small infirmary for staff and guests."

Zweig laughed in a friendly manner. "A Czech of all trades, a master of one or two." Her English was quite good—the kind of German-accented British most Germans learn as school-children. "Giraffes, crocodiles, humans—they are all animals to me."

"Very noble," Miranda said.

"Did you get the autopsy results on the victim?" Jack asked. He'd already seen a report passed along to him by Rector, while flying across the Atlantic during the night.

"Ja," Frau D-P Zweig said, "what can I say? Lividity showed that he was dead hours before he arrived here. He was garroted so severely that his spine was broken, and his neck was nearly bisected. And so the poor girl found him when she unlocked the Exotarium to prepare for the morning rush—typically, classroom tours from schools around Frankfurt and Darmstadt and the *Speckgürtel* (fat belt) around the Zentrum, meaning the suburbs and exurbs where the wage earners live who commute into the city each day for work. Our tax income."

Grün added: "Our city detectives, who have been directing the investigations, keep me informed as well as Dr. Zweig and the top officials of the Zoological Gardens. They have so far neither motive nor weapon. We do know that the dead man was a Norwegian national, living in Oslo when not traveling on business for a company that makes retrofit luxury automobile interiors—you know, mahogany, ebony, fine leather, that sort of stuff."

"Sounds intriguing," Jack said. That was obviously a cover for Sigma 2020 field operations. Ribeye had been tasked with finding a connection between the Chinese source firm and the Anaconda technical bureau in the K-Town area, intended to continue the R&D on Project David before it was hijacked by this BLUM organization.

"All I can really show you is the spot where Fräulein Siegrid Unger found the victim." She brought them inside the rounded Exotarium—house of exotic animals—where, on a rear walkway, several concrete paths converged. Crocodilians, with dark tan bodies, and black striping, lingered behind heavy gates and thick glass panes. They were nowhere near as huge as Australia's sea-going saltwater crocs—whose mature male could exceed 6 meters (20 ft) in length, and weigh over 1.5 tons. These ten-foot sweetwater cousins from Australia were motionless. They were coiled springs of sudden frenzy and violent, frothy pink death. They lay on slimy artificial embankments, on which they could launch instantly into their pools, just like on semi-arid river banks and washes back in northern Australia. The water, visible in some of the windows, was dark mossy green in the shade of large trees above, and bright mud-color where sunlight penetrated. It was a dreamy study in terror, fueled by an inbred human revulsion against snakes, spiders, and reptiles.

"Obviously the crocodiles were not able to call out for lunch," Jack observed.

"And with a half-severed neck," Grün said, "our man could not have let himself in and laid down for his friends to make a bloody mess of him."

Grün and Zweig tittered between each other. Miranda looked reserved and unsure of herself.

Jack saw dark stains on the central crossing, where zoo keepers must have hosed, scrubbed, and hosed again for hours to clean the mess.

Miranda asked: "No sign of forced entry?"

Grün shook his head darkly. "We are looking into the matter, I say to you very confidentially, of an insider in our organization who let the party or parties in with the victim, sometime in the early morning hours yesterday.

Jack nodded to Miranda. "Make sure someone is working that angle, and we get any reports forthcoming."

"Will do," Miranda said. "Herr Grün, would the people who did this have parked their car in front?"

Grün nodded thoughtfully. "Yes. I know they did not come on foot. Nobody noticed them. And if it was an inside job, as seems the case, they must have been quite bold and come in through the main administration building—where you met me at my office."

"Then," Miranda asked, "would there be any sort of video record of license plates coming and going?"

"I think we have something," Grün said. He used a collar dot to call his offices. He put a small earpiece in his ear, and turned away for a private conversation.

Frau Zweig, meanwhile, shook hands all around. "I must go back— many matter await me. Call me if you need to consult with me further. I will be happy to help in any way I can." She put her hands in her lab coat pockets and busily strode off, with tension in her shoulders.

Grün concluded his call. "Security says that they record license plates during the work day, mainly to prevent repeat offenders of illegal parking. They say sometimes the system is left on accidentally all night, usually recording only their own security vehicle making its rounds. They will run a check and get back to us."

Miranda said: "The clue we have to work from is that our victim was most likely murdered in the greater Kaiserslautern area."

"Do they have special license plates?" Jack asked.

Miranda explained: "Germany has a complex but revealing system of license plate codes. The vast majority of cars are privately owned. When a

German moves from one address to another, they always have to register with the local police *Revier*—or precinct."

Jack said: "Sounds...er...efficient."

Miranda made a *shoosh* face, not to offend Herr Grün.

Jack studied Grün's expression—the vulture had immediately caught on. No matter.

Miranda said: "When a German family moves, they must re-register with the local police. If they are moving from one license plate district to another, they have to buy new plates with the appropriate city markings."

Jack said: "Assuming the car was German, it could be owned by anyone of eighty five million people, counting infants and the aged."

"We're trying to narrow it down," Miranda said steadfastly.

"Good for you," Jack said, remembering their conversation in the dining room at the airport a few hours ago. "Thinking for yourself—love to see it."

"Thank you. So, a car registered in the greater Frankfurt area would have the standard broad, narrow white German plate with the prefix F followed by a multiple digit number.

"If the car was registered an hour's drive south of here, it would be KL for Kaiserslautern."

"Brilliant," Jack said. "If we get a digital image, we can follow the car to its owner in greater K-Town—assuming it wasn't stolen. But one thing at a time. "

Grün said: "I have the information. The Security lieutenant says they have some grainy films, aimed mainly at bumper level. The lighting is bad, and the shadows are uneven, but they can see shapes in this one car. Thirty cars pulled in and out during after-hours. Some were just turning around on Thüringerstrasse or Brehm Platz outside. With KL plates there was one dark red Simca, a French-built car, driven by a small, dark haired woman. She had two men with her, one blond and the other dark-haired, both young—in their twenties—and athletic. On the left, there is a small white D for Deutschland on a blue background with a circle of stars, so the car is German-owned within the European Union. We have two snapshots—one coming in the main entrance, the other departing. Security was already looking at it yesterday, but we did not have the KL lead to go on." He handed over a slip of paper on which he had scribbled a name and address. "An M. L. Sombra on the Beethovenstrasse in K-Town."

"Thank you," Jack said.

"There is one more thing," Grün said.

"Yes?"

"The official police register for that precinct shows twenty names in the little apartments there, above a hair salon, a travel agency, and a baker of wedding cakes. None of them is M. L. Sombra. Frankfurt detectives, speaking with Kaiserslautern detectives, have conjectured it is either a false name or a false address."

"Interesting," Miranda said. "You know what? Sombra is a Spanish word meaning shade or darkness, and I would bet that the initials are not those of a name—."

"I agree," Jack said. "Coming from the Southwest as I do, and having some Hispanic ancestors, I'll bet you any money that M. L. stands for *Me Llamo*—my name is. You remember the old book jokes? *Yellow River* by I. P. Daily? *Rusty Bedsprings* by I. P. Nightly?"

Miranda snorted with laughter. "Americans—too much time on your hands."

"Danke, Herr Grün," said Jack, and they all shook hands and made snappy little head-bows to each other.

My llama Sombra....My name is Darkness.

Charming.

Actually, scary as hell.

Jack in K-Town: M. L. Sombra

On the A6, flying southwest toward Kaiserslautern, Jack drove Miranda's powerful German sedan. There were no federal speed limits on the Autobahn. The system was a Hitler-era strategic highway system that had served as one of the models for Dwight Eisenhower's U.S. Interstate Highway System in the 1950s. The invasion of Europe, starting with D-Day in June 1944, had been a logistical universe of myriad moving parts, and Ike, as a five-star general overseeing the entire galaxy, had come to admire the German highway system. Grafted onto existing U.S. patchwork road systems, Ike's neo-Germanic highway network became the world's longest highway system when substantially completed as late as 1992. To the overpopulated and disciplined Germans, freedom of the Autobahn was a national relief valve. To impose speed limits would be like dictating limits on gun ownership in the United States. It was culturally unthinkable. Drivers throughout the world were obsessed maniacs, with U.S. drivers in torpid last place for speed and recklessness. In Germany, people drove at 135 kph (81 mph), which were not speed limits but polite government suggestions. They drove at rocket speeds, stacked on one another's bumpers, often just a few feet apart, looking for the slightest opportunity to accelerate their powerful machines over 200 kph (over 120 mph) and pass on the grassy shoulders if necessary.

At a leisurely 100 mph (160 kph) on the A6 (a.k.a. E50, or European highway 50), the drive from Frankfurt to K-Town took about forty minutes. Jack kept to the right lanes, while streaks of white (German) and yellow (French) headlights grew in his rear view mirror, and just as quickly formed passing red taillight rockets before his dizzied eyes.

Much of the journey alternated between rolling industrial farmlands, cultivated urban forest parks, a few German military installations including residual Cold War jet airfields, and the ubiquitous castle ruin clinging to a vine-overgrown crag.

Jack, the History and Classics professor, hummed to himself, treasuring his hoard of professional, enjoyable, and half useless information. As it would turn out, his knowledge of Roman history would prove useful as the situation at hand wore on.

Today, the German Autobahn (meaning car-runway) system was the fourth-longest in the world—after roads in the U.S., China, and India—totaling around 12,800 km, or 8,000 miles.

As Miranda primped, Jack said: "You know, something about this bothers me."

"Oh?" Miranda said. She was looking this way and that way into the mirror on the back of her window visor. She was carefully applying the faintest bit of makeup—barely visible blush on her cheeks, and a nearly translucent pink that Jack thought looked good on her rather lush, pale lips.

"It's too easy."

"What do you mean?"

"The people I work for said, as they sent me here for this job—that crocodile business—someone is sending someone a message."

"And what would that be?"

"It's a come-on. Just be careful in this job. You always have to out-think your potential adversaries by several steps, as in chess, even if you can't see them. Even if you don't know for sure that they exist. Every move you make, think—how can I be blind-sided or checked when I go here or I call that person or I do this?"

"Good pointers," Miranda said. She teased a few minims of mascara up her eyelashes. As she looked at herself, left and right, the tip of her tongue wiggled out and stuck in the corner of her mouth.

"Trying to keep us out of trouble," he said. Being on a Sigma 2020 mission on German soil, he was authorized to concealed-carry like any host nation detective or federal agent, but only as long as he had a German or other authorized handler along. That would be Miranda, still on a U.K. passport, but hauling BND and NATO papers.

"Next time, let's take the scenic back road through Speyer and Neustadt," she suggested.

Jack saw his opportunity to lay some groundwork. "Maybe, after we're done with work and business and all that, you can show me around a little bit."

"We'll see," she said, carefully hedging.

It's not a flat 'no,' Jack thought hopefully. One had a right to be enthused.

When they came into the city, Jack took the first exit in the eastern part of the city. Refueling at a gas station, he asked Miranda to take the wheel. She expertly navigated along the city streets across town to the Bahnhof district. Together, Jack and Miranda cruised until they found their way down Richard Wagner Street to Beethoven Street. The street signs in this part of town were blue and white enamel, dating to the French occupation of 1919-1926. Everything in Europe was layered with histories upon histories, Jack thought. While Miranda waited with the engine running, Jack memorized the information given him on a slip of paper by Grün at the Frankfurt Zoo.

He soon found the small, dingy high-rise apartment building on the inner corner of the triangle formed by the two streets. As in places like this the world over, he found a rusty vertical row of name labels, each beside a round white bell button. A few of the labels were neatly typed on yellowing paper. Several had the names printed or scrawled in various colors and stroke-widths of ink. One or two were empty, although in one of those someone had written a barely distinguishable name on the spotted brass. Only the typed labels were mostly covered with little transparent plastic shields. One was of glass, as they must long ago all have been.

One label caught Jack's attention. It was brand-new, typed in 10-pitch Pica on an old-fashioned typewriter, and read Muller. Something puzzled Jack, until he realized that the standard German name, equivalent to the English Miller, was Müller or Mueller. Not only had this label been newly inserted into its tiny, age-speckled brass frame—but the writer must be foreign. Who was this alleged—maybe phony—Muller on the third floor?

Jack pressed the buzzer.

While he waited for a reply, he took a fine-point pen from his pocket and picked at the label. It crumpled up, like a snail racing across a leaf. Sure enough, underneath on a slightly older label, was the legend *M. L. Sombra*—'My name is Darkness,' in Spanish.

On the second buzz, a man's voice replied in accented German: "Hallo?"

Jack said in English: "Sorry to bother you. I am looking for my cousin, Mr. Sombrero."

Pause.

"There is nobody here by that name."

"He called me yesterday and said to meet him here. It's urgent. I have money for him."

Money changed the equation. After a pause, the voice said: "Just a moment."

The door buzzed, inviting him to push it open as the lock was momentarily disengaged by a press from Muller above.

Jack signaled for Miranda to drive around the block.

Then he entered the narrow, dark hallway. He caught a faint, foul smell, as if a mouse had died in a corner. With a tiny keylight, which ran on one AAA battery, he examined the hallway. On its walls, he noted there were small black spatters. Leaning close, he sniffed—and nearly gagged. It was the smell of decaying blood. If Ribeye had been garroted, chances were good it happened right here in this passage.

He checked the 9mm automatic in its holster under his left arm, hidden by his wind breaker, as he climbed the stairs one creaking step at a time.

A pair of young men in stocking feet awaited him at the third floor landing. Behind them, an apartment door stood half open, admitting gray, rainy light from an alley window beyond. Down the street, he had noted, were some sex clubs with strident neon signs, with English and French words meant to entice either U.S. or French soldiers, or Turkish or Arab workers.

The two men were casually dressed, each in jeans, one with a white T-shirt, the other with a maroon pullover. They were dark-haired, probably Mediterranean, perhaps Arabs or Berbers.

"Guten Tag," they said in unison, offering handshakes.

Jack shook hands with them, noting that one had soft hands like a student or teacher, while the other had calloused hands like a man who worked with his hands—but his horn-covered knuckles suggested someone who practiced heavy-duty karate.

"My name is Sombrero," Jack said. "Alberto Sombrero, cousin of M. L. Sombra."

"Like the Mexican hat," said Knuckles, with an evil grin full of malice and self-righteousness.

"You have money for him?" the one with the soft hands said.

Jack heard the hatred in their voices. Their German sounded resentful, learned by force of circumstance—the tongue of an enemy.

"Yes, indeed. A month's pay. So just now you happened to remember that you know him?"

"He is right in here," Knuckles said with malignant sincerity. His dark eyes radiated meanness. His contemptuousness showed like a flag.

"In there?" Jack asked lightly.

"Come on in," said Soft-hands, with the same sincere face and loathing eyes.

"I don't need to come in. Why don't I just give you the money for him?" Jack said. He reached into his pocket, extracted his wallet, and began counting out Euros.

"Yes, yes," said Soft-hands.

"No, no," said Knuckles, "we'd like to sit and talk. Come in. We'll make coffee."

"I like coffee," Jack said. "Here's five hundred, and I'll bring the other five hundred later to day. The ATM ran out of twenties."

Impatiently, as if dealing with a retard, Knuckles grabbed Jack, bunching the windbreaker in a steel grip. "Come in right now."

"Oops," Jack said, stepping down the stairs backwards one step.

Knuckles tightened his grip, while staggering along to regain his balance.

Jack took another step backward and down, while unleashing a punch into Knuckles ' ribs under the arm. The man looked surprised and crumpled a bit in that direction, but his right hand came at Jack's head in a close round-house punch like a broken brick. Jack blocked the punch with his left, while turning his arm to free himself of that steel vise grip. In the same motion, he turned, swept Knuckles over his back, and sent him flying three stories down, head first and screaming. The scream stopped abruptly about halfway down. The last second of sailing time was silent, but ended in a bone-breaking thud and clatter. He struck a projecting corner at the lowest landing and snapped his neck.

Soft-hands, no stranger to violence, ran back to the open door.

Jack raced him to the apartment. Soft-hands was faster, but Jack wedged himself in the door. Soft-hands tried to push the door shut, but

Jack got in a low jab to the man's kidneys, which dropped him in tight sprawl on the dirty linoleum floor. Jack took out his SIG-Sauer, while closing the door and stepping on the man's hand so he was pinned.

Jack clipped him across the carotid artery to stun him. He left a dazed Soft-hands on the floor and made a quick tour of the small apartment. This was no college dorm or love nest. It was a terrorist dormitory lacking sentiment or care. Dirt was shoved into corners. Trash cans overflowed. Bed sheets looked gray and dirty in the two bedrooms. The kitchen was stacked with filthy dishes around which squadrons of huge black-green flies practiced takeoffs and landings. The food was Arabic. A Koran in an ornate green leather binding lay on the table, along with bomb making equipment.

Jack's lightning inventory took in something else—a locked wooden bathroom door, and next to it a small bedroom with a woman's bra slung over a chair. He detected a faint whiff of some citrus Parisian perfume.

Behind him, he heard Soft-hands rising with effort. Jack stepped back into the kitchen, shoved Soft-hands against a wall, banged his head on it several times to get the man's attention, and then inserted the barrel of his gun into the other's mouth. "No time to play games. Who are you?"

Soft-hands stared at him defiantly, ready to die rather than talk. Jack felt a sense of rage rising in his gut—not cultural, not religious, not buying into their fanatical nonsense, because every religion and every culture had fungal infestations like this. He thought of Ribeye, so horribly murdered and then subjected to a grisly crocodilian taunt against all decent and humane persons on earth.

"You want to die, so you can enjoy your seventy-one toothless old whores covered in syphilis pustules?

Soft-hands nodded, then shook his head, then nodded again.

"Which is it? You want to live to eat couscous tonight, or you want your worthless life snuffed out if I shoot your brainstem off, assuming you have one? "

The man went cross-eyed, staring with wide eyes at the machine-oiled barrel stuffed painfully into the soft tissues of his palate. A thin rivulet of fresh red blood ran from one corner of his mouth.

Jack looked over his shoulder at the bathroom door.

The grainy pictures on the zoo security cameras had shown two dark-haired young men who could have been these two. Driving, and probably in charge, had been a small woman with dark hair. Iranians? Mediterranean? Useful fools, fanatics for sure, whatever these creatures were—in the employ of Black Umbrella.

"I know I'm on the right track here," Jack said.

As Jack glanced over his shoulder toward the bathroom door, Soft-hands telegraphed a move, but Jack was ready. In his state of adrenaline intoxication, Jack was a human rocket. His reflexes, in this condition, were unequaled.

Soft-hands made his move, twisting his head away to free his mouth of the gun. He raised his left hand to push aside Jack's gun. With his right hand, he reached in his belt and pulled out a six inch Austrian hunting and gutting knife with a handle of a carved antler.

Jack pulled his gun hand away. In the same lightning move, he stepped back and kicked the other in the gut. The knife kept coming, but Soft-hands' tempo was slowed down. Jack shot him in the right shoulder, and the knife tactic was over. Soft-hands tried to toss the knife to his good left hand, but it fell short and rattled on the floor.

"Enough is enough," Jack said. "You won't talk? Here's a little head space for you." Smacking Soft-hands to stun him, Jack took the man by the belt in back, and walked him away from the window. To make him bend over forward, Jack smacked him with the gun on the top of his spine under the neck. Half unconscious, Soft-hands allowed Jack to speed up the walk, until they were running. Jack stopped, but Soft-hands kept going in an Aikido-like motion.

Head first, Soft-hands smashed through the bathroom door and landed on tiles.

Inside, a fully dressed woman rose with a gun in her hand, aiming straight at Jack.

She was tall, thin, and blond-haired. She got off two rounds that crashed through the wall inches from Jack's head.

Jack ducked and emptied his gun into both Soft-hands and the woman.

As the deafening noise rang in his ears, and gun smoke drifted through the narrow hall between kitchen and toilet, Jack was still wired on energy. Dropping the empty clip in his right pocket, he pulled a fresh clip from the left pocket and reloaded.

But there was no need.

Sprawled over each other in the doorway were a dead man—Soft-hands—and a dead woman, both covered in blood. Their eyes were half closed, their mouths half open, as they stared into eternity. What were they about to say? What were they seeing there, on the other side, that made them look so languidly surprised? Seventy-one toothless old men in rumpled suits, licking their abscessed gums as they reached out, with passion in their rheumy eyes? Whatever awaited fanatical murderers on the other side, it must be a disappointment, to say the least.

No time—Jack hurried down the stairs three at a time, brandishing the gun and ready for another attack any second.

But none came.

Knuckles sat dead at the bottom of the stairs. He had tumbled violently. His head hung down over his chest at an unnatural, twisting angle, as if he was trying to put it on to go to work in the morning, but it wouldn't seat properly. It was like a morbid joke. How many lunatics did it take to screw in a light bulb for a head? The punch line was silence.

Jack pushed heavy glass, wire-grid door open and ducked outside.

Miranda was just pulling around the corner.

There were no passers-by to witness anything unusual. The building's occupants apparently had all gone to work for the day. It could be hours before the mess was discovered—or minutes.

Jack put the gun away, pulled the door locked, and dashed across the little triangle of interlocking concrete tiles.

"Go go go," he said as he jumped and pulled the door shut.

Miranda efficiently gunned the car into motion, and the door closed of its own accord. "I missed all the excitement."

Jack was in no mood for levity. "Do your job. Get us out of here."

Miranda did not seem fazed. *Good for her*, he thought.

"Bear with me, Miranda."

"I've got your back, Jack."

"Let's get out of this cell range, and I'll call my home office."

Miranda drove back toward Speyer on the Pariserstrasse (Paris Street, a main city artery). For twenty minutes, they raced along a winding, two-lane blacktop among sighing trees. Jack placed a secure cell call to Rector.

Jack explained: "Looks like they weren't quite expecting us, but they lured Ribeye to his death in that building. They attacked me, and I killed all three of them."

"Is Agent Coldstream with you?"

"Yes, she is safe. Driving the car like a champ."

"Very well, Rector said. "I'm sending a team of cleaners from our K-Town safe house. They will make it as if nothing happened. Meanwhile, I can't bring you in. You'll have to hide out for at least a day or two. Get a hotel room and bill me."

After a brief Internet search by Miranda, the two settled on a clean *Pension* (bed and breakfast). The large residence, with four guest suites, was situated in the tiny, picturesque village of Frankenstein some twenty minutes east of K-Town along the back road to Speyer on the Rhine.

The rail line to Darmstadt and Frankfurt ran on elevated tracks on the right as Jack drove toward Neustadt. Most of the route was deep in one of Europe's largest forests, the Pfälzerwald. Frankenstein was a village dating to the European middle ages.

Frankenstein was a tiny hamlet among abrupt, tall hills smothered in dark pines and wreathed in fog. The main drag was a short, single loop on a blacktop road, joining at both ends with the main road. As Jack drove into the village, the road seemed to sink down a bit, and massive pine forests rose all around on steep hills.

"So much oxygen," Miranda said. "I can breathe better."

"Looks like nasty weather moving in," Jack said.

As he pulled up at the *Pension Adler* (Eagle), he looked up and saw wet clouds, darker than cigarette smoke, ominously clinging to the very cliffs. Fog roiled like smoke among the pines. High up sat a jagged ruin.

"There's a ruined castle up there, too," Miranda said.

"We'll stay in something more modern," Jack said.

Miranda said as she unbuckled her seatbelt: "Okay, let's wish ourselves luck."

"Guarded optimism," Jack said. "Always."

Shoes crunching on wet gravel, they walked up to the main door and rang. The doorway was rounded at the top, recessed between twin lanterns, and cozy looking. A woman came to the door, middle aged and wearing an apron. Frau Lentz took them to a small concierge desk. Everything inside the building was clean and sparkling. She looked at the guest register and said in good English: "You are in luck. We have just one suite left for the night."

Jack did not look at Miranda but asked: "Is there an extra cot available for me? My wife has back pain and requires a lot of bed space."

"We can put in a futon for you at no charge," the woman said.

The building's layout was simple—two central corridors intersecting in a cross shape. Floors polished to a high luster. On the first floor, there appeared to be the desk and a waiting room in the front half, and in the rear half, a recreation room with ping pong and billiards table on one side, and a laundry room on the other side. Similar layout on the second floor, with four corner suites.

As they unlocked the door to their room, Jack said: "If you are uncomfortable with this, we can change to a hotel and get separate rooms."

Miranda folded her arms together, as if forming a fortress to fight off enemy warriors, and shook her head. "I'll take the futon, and you get your beauty sleep."

"I'll flip you."

"No."

"Yes."

"My coin."

"Deal."

She produced a thick U.K. one-pound coin and flipped it. She slapped it on the back of one hand, and covered it with the other palm. "Call it."

"Heads."

She lifted her hand way. The coin's tails side was up.

Miranda looked pained.

Jack said: "Listen, no games; no wasting time. I'm going to make a command decision." He turned the coin over. "You win. Take the bed, and don't say another word about it."

She smiled. "If you insist. You Yanks can be gentlemen sometimes. Are you hungry?"

"Famished. Do you realize we haven't really eaten since breakfast at the airport?"

"Find us a restaurant, and I'll pay."

" John Bull pays."

"A girl can pretend."

"Money is money."

The suite consisted of two rooms and a bath. The front room had a kitchenette, a coffee table with two armchairs, and a computer desk. The bathroom was sparkling clean and smelled of fine soap. The back room had a large bed in it.

There was a knock on the door.

"Come in," Miranda said.

The husband of Frau Lentz, a heavy set man in his 50s, came in carrying a large object wrapped in a clean bed sheet. It was the futon, consisting of two long upholstered sections. Herr Lenz head to the bedroom with the futon.

"Please put it in near the kitchen," Jack said. As Herr Lentz made a shocked face, Jack added: "My wife screams at night. I need my rest, so I always sleep in another room. When it's real bad, I spend the night with neighbors, or in a bar."

The Lentzes departed, casting horrified looks after themselves, before quickly pulling the unit door shut.

Jack called Rector on a secure line, which was shunted to ULTRA/BIN/CRYPTOMAX on a U.S. Air Force satellite relay. He described where he was, and asked for instructions.

"I will call you tomorrow," Rector said. "Someone from BND will show up during the night and replace Miranda's government car with a different model, color, and plates. Nothing you need to worry about." He added: "Just as a note, if I wanted to recall you to CONUS, this would be the perfect opportunity, since you are a few miles from HQ USAFE and NATO Air Forces Europe."

"Oh, Ramstein AFB," Jack said from long-ago memory of being stationed with Military Intelligence in Germany.

"Yep. Sleep well, Jack."

"Out here, and thanks. My regards to Claire."

"Done."

Jack and Miranda drove out to find something to eat, and wound up in Neustadt for an excellent meal of Szechuanese. The owners were authentic, as was the fare. Faint moon lute music tinkled through the comfortably gloomy air as Asian servers in white shirts and black trousers hurried about. Jack shared with Miranda a generous portion of Mu Shu Pork with purple duck and plum sauce. They had brandies after dinner.

Miranda yawned.

"Been a long day," Jack said.

She looked at him strangely. In a very low voice, she said: "You killed three people today." She blinked, dazed. "I'm sorry, I must be overtired."

"You'll kill a few of your own if you decide to do this for a living when you grow up."

"I'm sorry, Jack—I know they attacked you first."

"That's the game plan for us good guys. We don't shoot innocent young artists, from outer space. We don't try to kill strangers who come looking for some shade."

In a blue twilight, they walked down the picturesque streets. Neustadt (New City) was a barometer of German history. The small city was spared the bombings of World War II. Its picturesque half-timbered buildings, medieval alleys, and 18th Century cobblestones survived into the 21st Century. It is located on the famous Weinstrasse (Wine Road) established in 1933, highlighting the region's world-famous wine production—the year Adolf Hitler was appointed as Chancellor of the dying Weimar Republic in its final months. The Weinstrasse runs through the Rhein and

Palatinate historic districts of Germany to the French border of Lorraine near Haguenau.

Miranda somewhat absently thrust her arm through Jack's arm as they walked leisurely on cobblestones, where long ago the ornate carriages of 18th Century barons rolled into the elegant center of theater and opera—in the age of Baroque, of powdered white wigs, of low-cut bodices and running footmen with elegant hunting dogs.

Other couples sauntered along the curving sidewalks, and Jack Gray and Miranda Coldstream did not look out of place. As Jack glanced at her, she seemed to be romantically mesmerized by the setting, the brandy, the dinner.

She took her arm from his when their car came into sight, perhaps remembering their mission. He held the door for her as she climbed in. She thanked him in a whisper.

Within a half hour, traveling at the edge of the headlights along dark roads, through forests interrupted by small, neat towns along the rail line, the arrived back at Frankenstein. Though this was most likely not the particular village from which Mary Shelley in 1816 picked the name for her Promethean hero, Victor Frankenstein, the medieval ruin presented a grim and fearsome atmosphere. Illumined from the corners and below by spotter lights, the ruin had a House of Usher look amid the black carpet of pine trees and the rolling clouds of fog. Though the area was well-populated today, Jack could well imagine that wolves must have howled in the neighborhood only two hundred years ago—not to mention the fierce wild boar rooting about, favorite of German hunters and local emblem of nobility.

Pension Adler was busy with three other sets of guests who were just settling in for the night. There were a French family with three small children, an older German couple from Bavaria, and an attractive young Italian couple with business in the Frankfurt financial district.

Jack checked the grounds. All seemed in order.

He parked the car under a shady willow in a corner of the gravel lot. That way, German intelligence operatives could switch cars unnoticed later in the night.

By the time Jack got back to their suite, Miranda had already turned the lights down. Her clothes lay across the futon in the front room, and a steamy shower was in progress. Good idea, Jack thought, as he locked the door and hard-bolted it. Extracting his 9mm Sig-Sauer, kicked his shoes aside and padded on stocking feet to the main bedroom in the building's corner.

He'd given her the bed, but she apparently was insisting on the futon.

He would just rest for a moment.

As he landed, bouncing, on the bed, he fell asleep fully dressed.

A while later, he half-woke to pull the cover around his upper torso without opening the bed.

Then, when it was dark, a clock somewhere chimed eleven p.m., and the bed bounced a bit. He opened one eye, to see Miranda's blonde hair coming toward him. She had undone it, and it fell in a straight silken pageboy around her face. She tugged at him, until he woke enough to sit up. She pulled the covers down, and they both crawled inside.

"My god, you're cold," Jack said. Her naked body felt like a bag of peas and carrots in the freezer.

He opened his arms to her, and she snuggled, shivering, against him. He rubbed her long, soft curves to generate heat—in himself as well as on her skin.

"I can feel your goose bumps," he murmured as he slipped his clothes off.

She snuggled even closer, with her arms crossed against his chest. Her teeth rattled in his ear. Her icy knees pulled up as high as she could force them in a fetal position. Jack reached down and pulled up another layer of blankets. "Get in here with me."

"Brrrr," she said. "Futon is impossible."

He pulled her arms apart, and she slipped them around his back. Her breasts were small, but firm against his chest.

Miranda cuddled even closer, if that was possible, especially for a tall woman. She thrust her icy hands, folded as if in prayer, between his thighs. "Hold me," she murmured.

She rubbed her hand provocatively against his throat, large ring and all.

"Raspy," he said.

"Wake you up," she murmured. Her hands moved upward to play. "Mmm," she murmured contentedly.

"Mmm," he echoed. His voice tapered off into a long groan as he threw himself on his back and let her have her way. She was passionate and imaginative.

After a few minutes of drowsy, intoxicating snuggling, it was so hot that they thrust all blankets aside.

He rolled on top and held her arms down. Her eyes looked up at him, half closed with pleased surrender. He found her, and her eyes opened wide and hard like diamonds. She stared at him, wanting him, and her mouth worked in silent phrases until his lips covered hers and their tongues found one another.

Naked, sweaty, and noisy, they made love on the firm bed.

Jack awoke about three in the morning. As he opened his eyes, he felt Miranda beside him, and touched her soft curves. She made *mmm* sounds in her sleep and made herself smaller in a fetal position. He pulled the blankets up to her chin, and stealthily rose.

Hearing a distant car coming close somewhere outside, he remembered the intended switch of vehicles. That would be coming off on schedule.

He bent down to pick up his compact, German made .32 caliber Walther PPK/E spare. Holding the little black semi-automatic, he went into the front room. In the gloom, which was relieved only by a little night light inside, and a street light somewhere in the parking lot, he padded nakedly into the bathroom. He locked himself in and laid the automatic on a glass shelf under the main sink mirror. Her bath towel still lay on the floor before the tub, and there were still nice, fluffy, fresh towels and washcloths on a chrome rack. The shower enclosure was in a corner, phone booth style, all glass. Using her damp towel for a foot rug, he turned on the shower water. Steam came out of the enclosure, and he made the necessary adjustments.

Jack took a long, leisurely, steamy shower.

He almost fell asleep standing up, and resting against pale tiles in the booth.

Somewhere, a door slammed. A car door? Had this not already happened half an hour ago? As he awoke from his reverie, he got an awful feeling in his gut.

There it was again—a slamming noise. Was it a car outside, or a door inside?

He thought he heard an animal or a woman scream—briefly, as if suddenly truncated.

Jack turned off the shower so he could hear clearly. As he stepped to the sink to retrieve his PPK/E, the damp air in the bathroom magnified sounds. He heard a scuffle, and touched the wall. He could feel the vibrations, meaning it was in the next room.

Miranda!

He instinctively grabbed a towel to cover himself, and tore the door open. As he walked into the front room, he twisted the towel around his waist. Still dripping, he advanced cautiously behind his outstretched gun hand. It took him half a minute to take in the disaster.

The lights in each room blazed. Gone was the cozy atmosphere. It was as if a comet had crashed through the roof.

In the bedroom, the sheets had exploded all over the floor during her struggle.

There were faint smears of blood on the sheets—no splashes, no puddling, but they were rough on her—whoever 'they' meant.

In the front room, her possessions were gone—purse, clothing, even those prim grayish nylon stockings. Her shoes, her makeup kit, everything had been taken—including Miranda.

Jack ran into the hall, still holding the gun.

The hall was quiet, except that the young Italian couple's door stood open. He dashed down the hall and looked in. Their suite looked as if nobody had ever set foot in it.

The sombreros had struck again. He felt no humor about it—just rage.

His heart ached for sweet Miranda.

Jack took a back stairwell down to the first floor. A back door on the stairway stood open to the cold, damp night outside. Drizzle dripped down the door frame, running down his face like tears.

The government car had been replaced—he could tell even in the wan street lighting, under drifting tendrils of fog, that it was now a light blue Volvo, again of recent and sturdy make.

Hearing a motor receding, he stepped onto the wet concrete outside in chilled bare feet, and rested his hands helplessly on a wrought iron railing. His gun dangled uselessly.

Through bushes, through trees, through fog, he caught one or two glimpses of red taillights rapidly receding. Jack's heart pounded in his ears as he tried to hear if they were turning right (toward K-Town) or left (toward Speyer) when they reached the main road. He could not be sure, and that defeat brought tears to his eyes. He so wanted never to see another woman killed while under his protection or affection.

He hurried back upstairs, closed the door, and started packing. Meanwhile, he paced up and down, holding his cell phone, until he had another secure connection, and Mrs. Rector got Mr. Rector out of bed.

"Mmm?" Rector said sleepily in California.

Jack explained the circumstance, struggling to control the shaking in his voice. He could not confess to Rector that his relationship with Miranda Coldstream had gone beyond bounds, and that it had been wonderful for one fleeting hour.

Rector was quickly awake. "I think someone has compromised our secure crypto lines."

"About the Italian couple," Jack said.

"You get out of there. I'll have the cleaners over to sift through every shred of evidence. Meanwhile, I'll have BND send you another national." He meant *handler*, Jack understood. Rector continued: "We'll put out a bulletin on Miss Coldstream, and make every effort to recover her—dead or alive. Every cop in Europe will be looking for her as of right now. I have my contact at BND in Berlin on the line as we speak."

"She is a great agent," Jack said. "Was. Is. I hope she's okay."

"We'll do what we can," Rector said neutrally. He sounded like a doctor, speaking with a patient, before discussing biopsy results. *Dead or alive.*

"Drive over to Ramstein Air Force Base. Building 2560. It's Sigma 2020. Small building behind massive amounts of barbed wire. I'll forward a map to your Volvo's GPS."

"Get that secure line cleaned up," Jack said angrily.

"We will." Rector sighed. "It's an ongoing struggle. The good can never rest."

As he gathered his few belongings, Jack found a calling card on the kitchen counter by the little steel sink. It was a business card with a nice design on one side: Overnight Pizza and Bier Taxi. That was how these goons came in—under cover as deliverymen. Miranda would not have fallen for it. They would have jimmied the lock and come in, maybe three or four of them, in overwhelming force, with ski masks and silencers.

On the plain white back of the business card was a variation of the BLUM logo in plain, purplish rubber stamp ink. By now, Jack recognized the circle with the horizontal line through it, the all-seeing and invincible Nazar eye floating above the line of earth and the beautiful but deadly Medusa below. Next to it, scribbled in a fine hand, was a note. It read: "Second warning, Mr. Gray. Third strike, you're out—cold and forever. M. L. Sombra."

As Jack walked out of the building by that back door on the first floor, a van pulled up and four men in hoodies and dark clothing—Claire Lightfield's BND cleaners, provided to Rector of Compass News on request—were already climbing out onto the gravel with mops, buckets, brushes, and evidence satchels.

Jack and the cleaners did not nod to each other.

They mumbled in German or French among each other.

He unlocked the light blue Volvo, using the same keys as for Miranda's former car, and drove west toward the city of Kaiserslautern and beyond that to the village of Ramstein.

His emotions were raw. His thoughts were chaotic and angry. He'd done it again.

Catherine would chide him next time they met in some airport or far-distant, foreign restaurant, always when he was alone, tired, and vulnerable.

Within forty minutes, as he drove along winding side roads, with a small village at every turn—Vogelweh, Einsiedlerhof, Landstuhl—the brightly lit runways of the supreme NATO and USAF-Europe command and airbase stretched from horizon to horizon. He was in pain.

U.S. Air Force security in fatigues and black berets checked his papers and waved him in. The two strack-looking women troops pointed the way to Building 2560. After a foggy, drizzly crawl, blinded by runway lights, he arrived at the small compound that almost looked as if the entire thing had been constructed of razor wire from top to bottom. On top were dishes and antennas.

Waiting for him was a USAF Security patrol with two German shepherd dogs, and four young airmen armed with assault rifles. Also waiting were two civilian men in bulky windbreakers. One, blond, was the taller, with the legend LPRP (*Landespolizei*, actually Rheinland-Pfalz state police) front and back. The other's windbreaker read U.S. FBI. The four uniformed airmen stayed to guard the entrance and his car parked before it. The two plainclothesmen ushered him into the building. As Jack stepped into the dry warmth and fluorescent lighting inside, a trio of supersonic fighter planes roared down a nearby runway and pounded away into the clouds. The moist air magnified their thunder.

Jack might have been more impressed in years past. BLUM was an organization like no other, capable of penetrating through walls, into top secret crypto message traffic, and into locked Pension Adler rooms. It was an enemy like none he had ever seen. It was unlike the clumsy apparatus of national and corporate bureaucracies, which formed the ponderous operating framework of even the best organizations like Camelback Consortium's Sigma 2020 or Global Anaconda's Delta spy company.

Their hit on Miranda now made it deadly and personal. Jack was going to take them out—and he was prepared to die doing it.

BND Karl: Night Jump

The van carrying Miranda Coldstream turned left on the main road toward Speyer, heading toward Frankfurt as its ultimate destination.

Miranda lay handcuffed on the carpeted back deck, while four kidnapers sat in front, including the driver and the Italian couple.

Curled in a fetal position, Miranda was glad to be alive, though bruised and battered. The men had not handled her gingerly. She hoped Jack had made it alive—why kidnap her and not him? It seemed they were creating leverage. That was her best guess, and the next statement seemed to confirm it.

The driver was in charge, as far as she could tell. "Sombra wants her alive," he said in heavily accented German. Miranda guessed that he was southern Italian, perhaps Sicilian.

So I am destined to be a bargaining chip, Miranda thought. She felt enormous relief, knowing that she'd had a reprieve from death. Perhaps, if she survived, she would go back to university and pursue a medical career or something else rewarding, that would not put her life in constant danger. A few months out of Sandhurst, and here she was. Rum deal.

In Darmstadt-Eberstadt, on the southern rim of greater Frankfurt, a phone rang in the dark.

A young man's bare, lightly hairy arm reached out of a warm bed and lifted the receiver.

"*Jawohl?*"

"*Herr Sipinski, hier ist Kontrollamt. Ihre Dienste werden benötigt.*"

Agent Karl Sipinski of the *Bundesnachrichtendienst Einsatzgruppe 34* (Federal Information Service, Action Group 34) sat up in bed. His beautiful young wife Anna slept on, wreathed in long dark hair. In the faint moonlight penetrating their bedroom, a smile played across her pale face, amid some lovely dream. Their two-year-old daughter Beate slept in a crib in the corner.

Karl listened to his instructions, then rose. He was the alternate night duty officer this week. Only about once a year did anything happen worth getting him out of bed. Luckily, he had watched a Krimi show with Anna and gone to bed early for a change. Beate was suffering from a little kiddie cold—her snorkeling, uneasy sleep could be heard in the quiet of night.

Karl went to the bathroom, brushed his teeth, combed his short brown hair, and looked for a clean shirt. His suit hung in the hall closet. Like many good German homes, the Sipinski house had a shoe rack in the front entrance. People entering took their shoes off and donned black felt house slippers.

As he dressed, Karl made himself a little breakfast of salami and ham on buttered bread, along with a few pickle slices, and some cold black coffee left from yesterday.

He loaded up with four clips of 9×19mm Parabellum rounds for the SIG Sauer P220 in his belt holster.

Within 30 minutes of the call, he kissed his sleeping wife and daughter goodnight, and walked outside. He walked down the stone stairs in front, down a narrow flagstone path between patches of lawn that he never sufficiently mowed or watered, down another flight of stone steps along the property wall, and onto the sidewalk. There, parked at the curb, was his unmarked Porsche 997X hybrid. The police pursuit car was souped up to reach Autobahn speeds beyond 200 mph (320km/h) in seventh gear overdrive on a PDK double-clutch transmission system. Though most Hesse police used locally produced Opel cars, this was a test model in a federal program, designed primarily for use with unmarked highway pursuit units—and in anti-terrorist units like the world-famous Bundesgrenzenschutz (BGS, or Federal Border Defense).

The black car started up with a throaty *blarrr* so deep it was almost inaudible. On broad steel-belted tires with heavy gripping surfaces, the car pulled away onto the quiet street. Under streetlights, over circling leaves, the Porsche crawled like a hunting panther—in search of a highway entrance.

Once he got onto the brightly lit Autobahn, the A661 tangent *Taunusschnellweg* (speedway named for the Taunus Mountains), he opened up. The car's GT2 538 twin turbo horsepower engine pulled him past 60 mph (100 kph) in 3.4 seconds, so that his lips curled back like in one of those old science fiction movie space launches. It was the part he loved best about this car.

It was to be a short ride, however, in more ways than one.

Ten minutes down the road, he pulled over into a reserved area for police and military units only. Decelerating to a crawl, he waited as a gate guard in a lighted shack raised a red and white metal barrier. He drove through, parked in a well-lit row of spaces immediately to his right, and jogged from the car to a circular helicopter pad.

When the ground crew—and two men aboard a waiting, unmarked, black BGS chopper—saw him coming, one jumped out and held the door open for him.

As he jogged toward it, Karl recognized the configuration: an older model Bölkow MBB Bo 105, with a crew of two, capable of carrying four passengers. It could reach a service ceiling of 5,180 m (17,000 ft) and travel up to 600 km (360 miles) at a cruising speed of 200 km/h (120 mph). The maker, designated Messerschmitt-Bölkow-Blohm (MBB), had long ago been subsumed by merger with Eurocopter. Karl, who at age 28 liked speed and risk, knew every machine on earth capable of going higher, faster, and further. This was still a very good aircraft.

The pilot, while waiting for Karl, revved the feathering blades up to flight speed. As with the Porsche, the result was a low thunder that rocked gravel on the pad, and created a wind that would blow a man's hat and briefcase away.

As soon as Karl was on board, even before he finished strapping in, the chopper tilted forward and arose in a slow turn to seek its flight trajectory. The pilot up front sat amid banks of amber, blue, and green lit instruments. He spoke with a nearby control tower as he rose. Soon, his flight plan would be shifted to a control tower at a military airfield closer to Kaiserslautern, and ultimately to a tower associated with the great US-NATO base at Ramstein.

He was to meet a U.S. agent named Jack Gray; codename: Pathfinder.

The helicopter rose to a cruising altitude of 10,000 feet—a tiny dot of flashing lights, passing over the towns and sleeping villages of Hesse and Rheinland-Pfalz.

Karl was the replacement for Miranda Coldstream.

But other plans were afoot.

About ten minutes into the flight, as they were passing over a black stretch of dense forest stretching from horizon to horizon, the man to his left suddenly moved forward into the co-pilot seat. This caused Karl only mild and momentary curiosity.

In the next second, however, a black revolver muzzle prodded Karl's left temple, like the cold kiss of a cobra.

"Stay still, Mister Sipinski," said a woman's voice in perfect U.S. English.

Karl looked out of the left corners of his eyes and glimpsed an attractive Asian face. Whoever she was, she was dressed in a dark blue jumpsuit.

"Keep your hands where I can see them, Mister Sipinksi. The last thing I want is to accidentally shoot you in self-defense. Stay very still, and do not do anything until I tell you to."

She kicked a bundle of something with her left foot—she wore dull, suede brown combat boots. "Pick it up."

He bent slowly, picked up a round nylon bag. Inside was a red-white-blue striped sports jumping helmet. "Are you here to brief me on the details?" Karl asked innocently, still hoping for the best.

"Don't worry, this is part of the mission," the woman said. "My name is M. L. Sombra, and I work for someone similar to your boss. We are partners in crime, so to speak."

"You must be joking," Karl said.

"Of course I am." She laughed openly, as if it must be obvious that she was just an incorrigible and slightly crazy kidder.

Karl felt confused. "I don't know of any crime."

"You are an innocent participant. I understand. I feel for your inner turmoil. Get up, Karl."

Hearing the steely edge in her voice, Karl rose under the cramped ceiling.

"Bring the helmet, and step back here."

Karl stepped into the cramped rear platform, where she must have been hiding.

On the deck sat a parachute in field-gray German army nylon.

"Suit up, Karl. No time for talk.

"But—."

"No time to waste. Germanic efficiency, please. Oh, and you'll need to hand over that cannon hanging from your belt, any spare rounds, and your wallet."

"Now wait a moment." From this point, Karl had no illusions. Somehow, this insane woman had hijacked a German federal police helicopter, and was about to make him jump into the dark forest four miles below.

"No waiting, Karl. Please don't make this difficult. I'm so pleased that everything is going according to plan. Now don't make a mess of things by being a bad little boy."

Karl thought about shooting her while taking out his gun, but he felt a restraining hand on his back. The co-pilot had clambered back here to help Fräulein Sombra.

"Good boy," Sombra purred as he donned the parachute. The co-pilot, with firm and experienced hands, tightened the harness so it fit just right. Sombra kept the gun pointed at him. The man handed him heavy, clear goggles, which Karl donned over his helmet.

Behind him, Karl felt wind and heard the roar of the open door.

"Turn and jump," Sombra said.

Karl donned the helmet, fastened the clasp of the chin guard, took one last look at her—the situation was hopeless—and stepped into thin air.

He had jumped before with the army, and knew the drill. It was just—this was so unplanned.

The helicopter clattered and roared away toward Ramstein.

Karl was in the middle of a beautiful four-point drop, with his hands and feet spread.

The cold wind of high altitude tore at his face, his hair, his suit.

The goggles protected his eyes from fogging or freezing up.

Distant city lights came into view on the horizon. He wondered if that was Kaiserslautern.

Couldn't be Ramstein—no C-17s or other huge aircraft in sight, nor long runways that should have been illumined in the night—just darkness. *M. L. Sombra.*

Karl was within 2,500 feet of the ground when he pulled the cord.

It felt wrong. Instead of a solid tug and a pop-pop, he felt a sickly lurch and then a loud rattling sound. Clutching the air around him, he realized that the perfectly packed main shute was flying in tatters above him. Above it, the reserve shute wasn't doing much to help.

Karl screamed in fear as he realized he had less than a minute left before he would impact the granite cliffs, the impaling trees, and the walking paths below.

Ever a practical man, he used his last minute to think about Anna and the baby Beate. He remembered how Anna had looked in the moonlight, with that smile on her pale, lovely face, and her dark hair spread in swirls around her as if she were underwater. "I love you," he said through fluttering lips he could no longer control in the savage air. He pissed and shit his pants, but that didn't matter now. "Baby Beate, I hope you get rid of your sniffles."

The last thing he sensed was how cold the damp, foggy air of the forest was as he slammed ass-down into the smells of leaves and moss. He embedded ten feet into a boggy patch of squishy earth, deep in the woods. Bubbling water and silent debris closed over him. The helmet and harness tore off and bounced away, leaving the impression someone had left an empty outfit in the woods. His head and body were buried, so deeply that he might not be found for days, weeks—or centuries. The world would search for missing Agent Karl Sipinski, without any luck.

Ramstein: Jack Meets Karla

The Sigma 2020 building at Ramstein AFB was a nondescript structure inside, made entirely from U.S. building materials including drywall and sheet-paneling. That made for a sort of dentist-office look, with faux blonde wood walls, a water cooler, and kitchenette with coffee and tea service. A small refrigerator stored milk and other perishables. Off to the sides, he saw

The two federal cops bade him take a seat and offered him coffee.

As Jack waited, a middle-aged man in U.S. Air Force fatigues hurried in, along with several enlisted aides including a sergeant-major. "Lieutenant Colonel Bing Loway," the man introduced himself with a firmer grip than Jack expected. "I'm the FOD for base operations including security tonight." FOD meant Field Officer of the Day. His complement—

at a major headquarters in the largest U.S. community outside the United States—was the office-bound SDO or Staff Duty Officer manning critical communications networks.

"Nice to meet you," Jack said. "Major Jack Gray, U.S. Army Reserve, Special Forces and M.I. background."

Loway, a man of strong, stabbing words and actions, bade his staff sit in the comfort of the central lounge. Loway poured himself a cup of coffee, and checking that Jack already had his own hot, comforting mug with the logo of some tactical fighter wing on it. Together, he and Jack entered a dark room full of winking server lights. Loway flicked on a switch and closed the door. "I'll be with you as long as you need me. I've turned over the shift to my assistant, an Air Force captain, so I'm sure the base will be in good hands."

"And watchful eyes," Jack said as he stirred his coffee—not the craftsman brew he liked to make, and a little watery, but it was better than nothing.

"I'm also an intelligence chief," Loway said. "In my real job, I work with Sigma 2020 and NATO intel. I have received some need-to-know from the Lightfield company."

Jack was startled. It was sort of comical. Old Claire. So she was the 'Lightfield organization' or 'Lightfield company' out here in the real world.

They sat in a cramped little corner, which contained two small bucket seats and a little coffee table. Normally, drinks were not allowed in a server room, but Jack guessed the zigzag line of blue duct tape glued to the floor meant that some airman had measured the precise specs to the inch—and probably smoked marijuana in here as well.

"Mr. Gray, we have some preliminaries in from Sigma's forensics team in the city." He meant the cleaners who had gone to the M. L. Sombra house. "The three assailants you neutralized all had their fingertips etched with acid to destroy their fingerprints. Their clothing had no labels. There was no intelligence-worthy paperwork on the lease, although apparently an M. L. Sombra rented the place about seven months ago for a one-year stint. Very orderly, quiet, no complaints from neighbors. It's a downtown apartment complex for students, waiters, shop keepers, that sort of person. They said the residents on the third floor looked foreign, kind of dark, maybe Mediterranean or Iranian."

"There was bomb making equipment," Jack said. "And I saw a Koran."

"Those details could be real or a setup," Loway said. "You never know for sure. It appears that our new-found friends at BLUM recruit from all the world's disaffected groups. They will even bring in elements who hate each other, like a handful of Israeli and Palestinian hardliners. But here's the thing."

"Yes?"

"Our cleaners found some fibers in the woman's bed." Loway held up a phone pad, on whose viewing screen was displayed a document. "They were able to trace it back to a very common line of textiles made in China."

"What else," Jack said dourly.

"Right. But this is a special weave, such as one finds historically associated with Scottish clan tartans. We were able to easily determine that it is the specific tartan of the McNeils of Barra, the titular heads of the entire clan throughout Scotland and the world. Their seat is a small island at the southern tip of the Outer Hebrides, called Barra."

As Loway spoke, Jack brought up the names he mentioned on the Internet on his phone pad.

Loway continued: "The minute we got that information—hell, what other straws do we have to clutch at?—we had our SIGINT people start scouring the airwaves around Scotland, Ireland, and the Outer Hebrides for evidence of any related message traffic. At first, we got nothing but the usual ships traveling through fog on GPS, local radio stations, the BBC, and so on. Then—bingo."

He showed Jack a readout on his own phone pad. "See those sine waves rolling through the general fog of signals? That's a steady carrier wave emanating from a very precise point in the south bay of Barra. It comes from a 16th Century Elizabethan taxing stronghold called Kisimul. It's a small but impregnable fortress on a rock offshore in Castlebay."

Jack felt exasperated. "What if BLUM is trying to lead us around by the nose, like prize fools?"

"We thought of that," Loway said. "But we are flying you there tonight, Jack."

"Why?"

"We received one more clue in the past few days, which we put together with this info."

Jack sipped coffee, and said nothing. His mind was on Miranda, and his stomach churned.

"Look at this," Loway said. "See this pattern? Look again at the carrier wave."

Jack saw a dark welter of signals captured over a period of about an hour.

"That was the exact launch time of Anaconda's Project David satellite, of which we believe BLUM seized control, with code emanating from this location."

Jack nodded. "Now you have my interest."

"We did a little more research," Loway said. "We looked for any signs of internecine conflicts among the factions of House McNeill. There have been some rivalries over the supreme chief's title over the years, particularly with a branch called the Macneils of Colonsay. But all those have been peacefully resolved through the Lord Lyon, the supreme arbiter of Scottish peerage, at the Heraldic Register house in Edinburgh. So they have nothing to do with this, and probably do not have a clue that there is a BLUM terror base located right on, in, or under their Castle Kisimul on Barra Island."

"That's comforting to know," Jack said.

"For the Scottish authorities, and for the clan system, yes. They are as much the victims of Dr. Night as anyone."

There was a knock on the door.

"Sir," a muffled voice said, of one of the airmen.

"Come in," Loway said.

The door opened, and in stepped a pleasant woman of about thirty years. She wore a field-gray German Army jumpsuit, and a soft cap over her short-cropped black hair. "Karla Sipinski," she said. "I'm actually liaison between CIA and BND. I'm your replacement agent."

Jack Gray stared at her. She was beautiful—flat face, slightly upside down triangular, with wide, gentle, low cheekbones; broad, full lips; and very much almond-shaped eyes that crinkled with laughter. Probably San Francisco Japanese-American or something. Her humor had a harsh edge to it, which Jack detected under the camaraderie. What was it about her?

He rose to shake hands. Her grip was firm, her hand small, with differing sets of calluses—at the top of the palms, indicating lifting heavy free weights; on the knuckles and edge of the hand, martial arts. Or, as the boys in Wing Sun used to say before adults took over, martial tarts.

"I thought they were sending a Karl Sipinski," said Loway.

"Probably just a typo. Karla, not Karl. How silly."

"Thanks," Loway said. "Welcome on such short notice." Loway smiled without a care in the world; which made Jack's paranoia hackles crawl up and down his spine.

"Glad to be of assistance," Karla said. Where are we heading to?"

"A place you will find intriguing," Loway said. "A fairly desolate North Atlantic island in the Outer Hebrides off the west coast of Scotland, called Barra."

"I look forward to the trip—and conversing with Mr.—."

"Jack Gray," said Jack Gray. He wasn't telling Miss Sipinski a thing more than he had to, until he got the lay of the land about her. "You sound American," Jack said cautiously.

"Absolutely," she said with a broad, almost manic smile that chilled him. "Lived in Santa Rosa, north of San Francisco—but my great-grandparents came over from China as coolies—the dreaded Yellow Peril, huh?" She laughed with a wild toss of the head, so the short, thick, and rather beautiful bluish-black hair flew around her face. Then it hit Jack. The thing that had started setting off alarm bells in him. A man who could kill three enemy agents recognized the crazy light in the eyes of another agent—whether friend or foe—who had only recently killed another human being, and walked away unfazed from the act. It was one thing to kill in self-defense, and push aside regrets. It was another thing to kill people who got in the way, as some people shell peanuts to eat the meat. That was the flavor he sensed around Karla Sipinski—sheer peanuts. Killer peanuts. Just nuts. Having just lost his dear Miranda, Jack was frazzled. On edge. Paranoid, hyper-alert. He must calm his instincts, and watch her carefully. Lt. Col. Loway moved things along by saying: "Time to get you on your flight to Castlebay and Kisimul. We're searching for Miranda, Jack, and hoping for the best. Meanwhile, great luck to both of you."

Castlebay

Barra

On the world's only registered airport whose runway was a beach, an unusual event happened. Because it was night, the control tower was shut down—and so nobody would ever spend the rest of their life telling about it.

In the partial moonlight, which gleamed on the turbid water, two shadows descended from the clouds, and crept across the sea until they hovered directly above the inter-tidal zone. Each had a powerful searchlight under its nose, shooting foggy light onto the beach below.

They were Royal Air Force Harrier II jump jets—capable of vertical take-offs and landings (VTOL). Clearly marked with RAF insignia, including the classic blue-white-red roundels with a red dot at the center, they had just spent the past two hours flying from Ramstein USAFB to Barra Island in the Outer Hebrides of Scotland, a distance of 760 miles (c1,200 km). The two jet fighters had stopped for refueling on a U.S. aircraft carrier exercising in the English Channel. Operational Harriers have only one seat in the cockpit—for the pilot. These were training jets, with a second seat in back for the instructor; or a passenger, as in the present case.

The tide was out, and a long fingernail of hard beach, mostly sand and seashells, was exposed. From each aircraft silently dropped an articulated, rope-like wire ladder. The planes were at minimum thrust, with their wheels down and lightly touching the sand. Still, grit and wind blew up as each plane's sole passenger clambered over the side. Down each ladder came Sigma 2020's two troubleshooters sent to investigate the possibility of BLUM activities in the late medieval tax enforcers' castle at the island's south end.

The moment Jack Gray and Karla Sipinski touched feet on the beach, the ladders rolled back up into the rear seats of the two trainer jets. The canopy slid shut, the pilots waved, and off they went upward and sideways to thunder away into dense cloud cover.

"You okay?" asked Karla as they hurried up to the road.

"Been better, been worse," Jack said tersely.

Each of them carried a compact rucksack with basic clothing and toiletry needs, plus equipment including cameras, listening devices, and a powerful transponder that could relay a cell phone message directly to an orbiting satellite without need of a local tower. Each carried a cell phone with GPS tracking, to be monitored constantly by Sigma people in the U.K. and Germany.

"Maybe a drink at the local pub will make you loosen up a bit," Karla said.

"All closed by now. I don't really drink much. A good night's sleep would be more like it."

At the edge of the A888 road, which circled the island, stood a parked car. It was a small Mini Cooper, burgundy, with a dark moon roof. Under a round stone near the front tire was a valet key that unlocked it and enabled driving it.

"You do the honors," Karla said as she tossed her rucksack in the back seat and took the front left passenger seat.

Jack dropped his rucksack next to hers, and took the wheel. On the driver's seat, before he got in, he found an envelope with a full set of keys, plus a simple map prepared by a local MI6 plant, and two separate room tickets at the Kiltoch Arms in Castle Bay.

The drive was only about eight miles. Before long, Jack found himself tooling over a rise and down a winding road. Before him lay a splendid sight.

Karla, who was being very quiet, commented. "Oh, how beautiful."

The rugged hills all around were spotted with the kind of short, green growth Jack had seen in Iceland and Greenland. There was a nearly full moon overhead, which illumined the bay as if a flash bulb had gone off. Squat and menacing on a tiny island off the coast, dominating the bay, was the old British tax fort—Kisimul. The stone islet under it was Innse Chisimul, according to an obscure reference Jack had found online, while traveling on the Harrier. Innse meant Islet, and Chisimul was a combination of old Gaelic words meaning a place where taxes are gathered. More than just the Elizabethan IRS, it had been a way of openly leaning on rebellious Scots and reminding them who owned the shop in those days. Castles like this were sort of fixed warships, with cannon overlooking the local town. To Jack, the fact that they needed to sit in an impregnable fortress showed there was no love lost between the British Crown and these remote subjects. The island itself had been inhabited since the Stone Ages, and there had been a fort here, of some sort, for thousands of years, since the Iron Age.

Karla said: "I can't wait to start nosing around here. I hope that BLUM, if they do have their tentacles here, will try to reach out and touch us."

"Probably means another go at trying to kill us," Jack observed acidly. The K-Town trio of goons came to mind.

"That would work splendidly," Karla said. "I can't wait to open a line of conversation." So saying, she flashed a wicked-looking, gravity operated four inch knife with a wide, curving, serrated blade.

"Put that away. You're scaring me."

"You're not easily scared, are you, Jack?" With a flick, she made the gutting knife disappear.

"Let's say that, if I were a girl, my middle name would be Prudence."

"Jackie Prudence Gray. How cute. I always wanted a girl."

"Got any kids?" Jack asked conversationally.

She shook her head. "I'm a career girl. Never had time."

"Neither have I. We'll just die as spinsters." Jack did not let the thought of his two young daughters enter even his own mind while he was in the field—much less share the faintest details of his highly secret personal life with an unknown woman he did not trust or even like much.

"You are quite negative," she said.

"Don't mind me. I get very focused on my work."

She shook her head. "Not the legendary Jack Gray that the girls talk about."

"Must be my ribald twin."

She ignored him as the town rolled by. They headed downhill, toward the bay, on a mix of smooth asphalt and bumpy cobblestones.

"There is the hotel," Karla said. She pointed to a sign hanging under a street light.

As they got closer, Jack read: *Kiltoch Arms*.

They found parking on a side street.

A sleepy young man answered their knock. With hardly a glance at their papers, he let them in through the main entrance. "We knew you were coming," he said. "Welcome to Castlebay."

"Thank you," Karla said.

"What a nice little place," Jack said.

"Aye, we like to think so." The gangly youth introduced himself as Rudy Chantray, the owners' son. His mum and pop had owned the business for over twenty years, and done well with it. The island got enough tourists in season to make it work, so he told them as he led them through the first floor.

The main restaurant and bar were gloomy. They smelled of stale beer, stale tobacco smoke, and stale beef. Chairs were up on tables, and stainless steel counters gleamed. Hanging glassware glittered dully.

"I'll show you to your rooms. Not married, are ye?"

"We're brother and sister," Jack said.

"Oh, of course." That explained everything, except her Asian features and his decidedly Caucasian looks.

Jack made up a story. "Her great-grandmother was a granddaughter of Pu Yi, the last emperor. She was kept prisoner in the Forbidden City for several years, until my great-grandfather crashed there in a Sopwith Camel from the last war. He was a creationist missionary who came to his senses and converted to Buddhism. Together, they practiced Shao-lin martial arts and fell in love during the hot ashes carry. Then the commies took over, and our great-grandparents escaped with Chiang Kai-shek to Taiwan, but got student visas to the University of California at Berkeley. They worked nights as bus boys in a Chinese laundry until he won the lottery, and thenceforth they were able to finish their doctorate degrees in marine sciences. With his lottery winnings, he also kicked off a small family fortune in cooked shrimp, whose benefices we continue to enjoy today."

The concierge soaked all this up, but had one more sort of sideways quarrel with them. "Most of our visitors have more luggage."

"Our suitcases will be delivered," Karla said.

Fresh out of objections and buts, the curious concierge took them to the second floor, where a comfortable corridor with red carpeting and low lights made a small square around a central utility room. "We have eight spacious rooms," he said proudly. "You are pre-booked into Numbers six and seven—opposite each other, if you forgot your toothpaste or something."

He did not linger for a tip, but simply unlocked the two doors, handed each a key on a small plastic triangle with the hotel's name, address, and phone number on it, and bade them good night—or good morning.

"Would you care to come in for a drink?" Karla said.

"Honestly, I'd love to, but I'm about to pass out from exhaustion."

She had the look of a beautiful woman who always calls the shots, and is not used to being spurned. "Strange trip this is turning into. You are a legend in the service, Mr. Gray. I thought I would see if you like a foot rub or something. Instead, separate flights, and separate rooms."

Jack oozed between the door and wall into his room to get away. "Those were training jets, and these are training rooms."

"Well, I hope we graduate from our training some time soon."

"I'll let you know, Grasshopper."

Jack left her in the hallway, and quickly closed the door. He locked it, and propped a chair against it. He recognized a woman with fangs when he saw one. She was beautiful and tempting, but she put him off. And he still had Miranda on his unsettled mind.

The room was compact, and totally framed in deeply shellacked, caramel toned wood. Gun in hand, he checked out the small bathroom with shower—clean, simple, nice. Without undressing, he lay on his back on the narrow single bed. He laid the gun in the top drawer of a night table, and just pushed the drawer not quite shut for a quick grab if need be. There was a folded spare blanket at the foot of the bed, which he pulled up to cover himself. In a second, he was fast asleep.

Sweet Dreams

At first, Jack did not dream.

Then, in his sleep, there was a knocking at a door.

He squirmed in his sleep, too tired to rise.

But the knocking was elsewhere—at a door in his dreams.

The door opened, and a man and a woman stood in it whispering to each other.

Go away, he told them in his sleep. *Too tired to move.*

They did seem to recede, but kept murmuring like a brook that never stops.

Were they the ghosts of dead people?

Jack awoke, to find himself on the floor in a tangle of sheets, drawer open, and gun in hand. He was sweaty, and shaking. But there were people talking in the hallway outside.

He swallowed hard, talked to himself, got calm, and silently came to his knees.

The room was still except for the whisper of a wall heater in the bathroom. Could that have been the source of murmuring in the black corridors of his nightmares?

But there was whispering in the hallway outside. He wished the damn heater would cut off so he could be sure.

Tiptoeing to the door, he pressed his ear against it and listened.

Then he looked through the spy hole at eye level.

There was Karla in her open doorway, talking with a burly Caucasian man in his forties. She wore white flannel pajamas with tiny roses on them, and a fluffy little red-rimmed collar. Her visitor wore dark corduroy trousers and a heavy pullover. He had a slight gut, and brawny arms.

"I'm not working for nothing," the man was just muttering rather crossly.

"Of course not, Lysander. We'll front you five thousand, and deposit one large per week to your account with BOS." That would be what, Bank of Scotland? Jack surmised.

"That will be agreeable to me, but don't fock me around."

"I didn't fly here, all this distance, with my associate, to fock you around, Lysander. If we wanted to fock you around, you'd be dead and focked long before now. Watch how you talk to me, or I'll gut you like a focking duck, do you understand?" Jack caught the flash of a knife blade in her hand.

"Yes, Mum," said a chastened Lysander, though the brown grip of a pistol peeked from his belt in back.

"Now run along and do your job."

"Yes, Mum. Long as I get me money that's due."

"You'll get paid. Now run along and be a good boy."

Lysander creaked away down the corridor, and she closed her door.

Just then, a floor board under Jack's feet made a loud cracking noise as he shifted slightly.

Her door opened, and she stood staring at Jack's key hole.

They were almost eye to eye.

He still held the Sig-Sauer, and had to restrain himself from emptying it into her through the door. His skin crawled as he met her beautiful face and dour gaze, as on the BLUM medallion.

Slowly, still staring, she slipped her door shut.

Jack released a pent-up gust of breath as he decompressed. He leaned with his back against the wall, letting the gun dangle so it nearly fell from his grip. He could almost hear a fading hiss of snakes in her hair.

"What I don't do for God and Country," he whispered to himself as he prepared to resume his sleep—hopefully, with more pleasant dreams. His mind raced for a short while…

As he settled back into uneasy rest, he turned to a long-standing project that existed not on paper yet but only in his mind so far. He was forever getting ready to write a historical analysis, a book about the fall and rebirth of democracy in the world's major societies over millennia, but driving and running and shooting and fearing armed women had thus far kept him from setting quill to parchment…

So the muscle's name was Lysander—the name of an ancient Spartan general who defeated Athens in 404 BCE, and became its first dictator in centuries, having destroyed the Golden Age of Athenian culture and democracy. Athenian democracy had already destroyed itself from within, through special interests and lies, and the Spartan vultures had merely picked it clean. Demagogues had harassed Pericles in parliament, small men with deep pockets and venal ambitions, who falsely accused him of corruption on the navy contracts required to keep a strong fleet to counter the Spartan menace, as well as on popular building projects that gave work to the common men. Any lies and distortions, as long as they served one purpose—to bring their rival down, even if it meant abusing democratic institutions and destroying the entire country. Athens never recovered. A few centuries later, the ancient Roman Republic had fared about the same, as the *Populares* factions and their corporate sponsors and larger than life heroes (Sulla, Pompey, Caesar *et al*) destroyed her democratic institutions in their unbounded greed for power and money. Jack believed that history did not repeat itself, contra urban lore. Human nature itself never changed—the Human Condition, which had been fixed in our genes since the Stone Ages. The same outcome was always inevitable. Tyranny always rose from the ashes of democracy. But tyranny, usually in the form of some megalomania who first saved the people from themselves, and then destroyed them using themselves, had a way of quickly dying. The fire that burns shortest burns brightest. The dictatorship of Caesar had lasted two years. The eternal empires of Napoleon and Hitler had lasted less than a decade. From the ashes, guided by wise people and secret agents, it was possible to build a new consensus. Jack looked forward to the day when he could sit at the D Ranch, in the glow of Molly and their children, and write that book. But it was a long way off, and she might get other ideas in the meantime.

Today, the ruins were governed by giant corporate consortia. Triumvirates had already come and gone, as in ancient Rome.

Dr. Night wanted to become a modern what? Alexander the Great? They all did, the megalomaniacs and tyrants, but most ended up being Nero or Milosevic and their ilk, a blend of rank libido and ostentatious grossness. Or unwashed peasants like Mao and Stalin, whose morbid sickness filled the room around them with the power of their monstrous personality and the stench of their murderous paranoia.

But history was also filled with good leaders—usually none with the black supernova force of a Mussolini or a Pol Pot in their moment—but more often leaders by consensus, using reason and morality to persuade other good citizens to join in a bond and declaration for liberty…

Jack Gray was composing his book during the twilight between wakefulness and sleep, year by year, one bad dream at a time, one shining ray of hope a day.

Castlebay

Someone knocked on the door.

Jack opened his eyes, thinking about the handgun in the drawer nearby.

"Mr. Gray," said the young concierge. "Breakfast is being served downstairs if you are of a mind, sir."

"I'll be down shortly."

"Yessir. Thank you."

Jack yawned, sat up on the edge of the bed, stretched left and right, and yawned again.

For the first time, he noticed wooden shutters opposite, indicating a window.

He padded barefoot across the room and gently opened the wooden shutters. Twist one, and they all twisted, revealing a strong grill of sunlight that momentarily blinded him. As he got his first glimpse of glorious blue bay, twinkling sunshine, and a shady alley below, he also got a glimpse of a man in corduroys and pullover standing at the far, dark end of the alley—Lysander. When Jack finished rubbing his burned eyes, and looked through floating spots, the man was gone.

Karla was already at a window nook, sipping black coffee and working on a plate of scrambled eggs, little fried ham steaks, toast, and orange juice. "Good morning, Sleepy Head."

"Good morning," Jack said as he slide into the bench opposite her. "Wow, that's bright." The window overlooked a cobblestone street that descended into a square.

"Feeling better this morning? You were grouchy last night."

"I like to stay focused and keep things businesslike."

"Oh-kay. I'll just think of you as Jack Gloom."

"Why, Karla, do women never cease trying to remake a man to their own ideals?"

She grinned wryly. "Point taken."

"I have an idea for a TV show," he said. He signaled to a waitress. "You know how there are all these home makeover shows? You know— contests to see which toilet outshines them all? We could have a show called Make Over Your Man."

"MOYM," she said. "Nice acronym."

The waitress came, and Jack pointed to a ketchup bottle. "How about tomatoes, Britannic style?" Nothing like fresh sliced or stewed tomatoes all over your eggs, instead of red chemical paste.

The waitress brightened. "You like your tomatoes the Scottish way, sir?"

"Scottish tomatoes are spanking good."

"Coming right up, sir."

Karla said to him softly, glancing about with a wicked look, so nobody could overhear: "The tarts come highly recommended also. Meat pies especially. I've heard the Asians especially—."

He ignored Karla: "Imagine this. Women everywhere are glued to their TV sets, with their slob plastered in a corner chair with his beer in hand. Now the show starts. A panel of four experts—with one grouchy Brit thrown in as they always do—makes cruel remarks to four sobbing contestants. Who will be out today? Whose show will be canceled? Who will be sent home? Who will lose the competition to make over Mr. Slobbarooney?"

Karla laughed. Jack paused as the waitress brought a steaming bowl with stewed tomatoes in it—the original British sauce that morphed into U.S. ketchup. Jack slathered it all over his eggs, along with a sprinkling of Parmesan cheese.

He continued: "Got that? There are segments where they buy his underwear. Others, where they buy new pants for him. The woman who buys him loud, checkered golf pants is out the first day. Next one out is a woman who buys Mr. Made-Over a brilliant red shirt with a giant yellow parrot on it. And so on."

Karla nearly choked on her orange juice. She set the glass down and doubled over. "Stop, Jack, please."

"I hear that a lot." *Oh please don't stop!* "I become smoother once I've had breakfast," he told Karla.

"Mm...you're right, Jack. I do enjoy a nice tomato." She added: "A saucy one," wrinkling her face and nudging him with one toe under the table.

They were interrupted by a hubbub. Outside, on the narrow street, was a delivery van. A man came in carrying two suitcases—one, as it turned out, for Jack, the other for Karla, and both from Onkel Niederweg (Uncle Loway) in Jolly Good Deutschland.

Jack and Karla began their investigations with a walk down into the village. She was investigating Jack, and he was investigating the entire situation starting with her.

He wore jeans, hiking boots, heavy gray crew socks, layers of shirts, and a sweater. He topped it all with a tweedy hat with the brim turned down. Karla wore a yellow rain slicker clipped *gamine* just below the waist. Below that, she wore short dark-gray corduroy shorts. Her legs were bare, except for cream crew socks and hiking boots. They each wore a fanny pack with essentials.

In autumn, the island was cold and breezy even on a sunny day like this. Pennants fluttered briskly, including the McNeill standard raised on a flagpole above Kisimul down in the bay.

A tourist ferry hooted long and hard. Its cry echoed around the hills like that of a primeval sea monster. The ferry chugged toward a dock on Pier Street—an ocean going motor vessel of the Caledonian MacBrayne line, named MV Clansman, whose lower hull was black, and its superstructure white, with a large red stack on top. It traveled between Barra and the larger Uis isles north of there. Barra was the southernmost and one of the smallest of the Western Isles, forming a small island group of its own.

On a hilltop sat the island's Catholic church. While a major part of Elizabethan-era Scotland had been forcibly converted to the Anglican Church, headed by the Queen of England, the Celtic realms had stuck to their older allegiance to Rome. The McNeill, of Irish origins as far back as the late Roman Empire age, remained of the older persuasion. While various of the northern isles converted, those closer to Ireland did not. *It's now all ancient history of little modern warrant,* Jack thought as he strode along with Karla. Each side had been as bloody, cruel, and unreasonable as the other. The little people always suffered. It was as true today as in the superstitious and clan-driven fiefdoms of the past.

"We probably look like a fairly standard tourist couple," Karla said as they reached the square at Pier Street, where seagulls paraded around looking for hand-outs, while keeping an eye toward the sea. "Cousins out for a lark in the park."

Jack said: "Unless some bright soul notices that you look Chinese and I look Caucasian."

"You already explained our lineage to Rudy Chantray last night."

"Oh yes, if I can only keep it all straight. It's hard living a lie, isn't it? You have to remember all these odd little details as if they were from another person's life. Could get dangerous."

She smiled opaquely and changed the subject. "Then again, to most people around the world, anything is possible with the Americans, so nobody would expend much energy on wondering about how we got to be a sibling duck-and-swan."

"You can be the swan," Jack said pleasantly. "I'll be the duck."

"Quack."

She had a great deal of charm for a killer, Jack thought. No matter how she played his inner strings, he always came up short before that glacial interior, that heart of cold, that breath of ice, and that crazy laugh that widened her eyes when she looked at you. Was the gutting knife ever far from her fingers?

"Back to the strong, silent type," she murmured in his ear. She strutted alongside him, imitating a stiff gait. "Let them think we are a couple. I get high just thinking what they imagine we do in our little hotel together at night."

She didn't look half bad in those shorts, Jack thought. She was a half foot shorter than he, with flying dark hair and perky almond eyes in a well-shaped face the color of light custard. She even had a few cinnamon freckles on and around her small nose. He began to fantasize in the unfenced and weedy back forty of his otherwise fairly orderly imagination. What would it be like, on a dark and stormy night, to have those thighs wrapped in a death grip around his head, while he stared at her twitching navel, and she flattened herself against the hotel room wall and wailed in ecstasy? Was she capable of such humanity?

They went on patrol around the market square overlooking the bay.

From the sidewalks, they looked in the shop windows, and even prowled through a small supermarket west of the village. From there, armed with spring water and cookies, they clambered up a network of trails into the hills, until they reached the highest point on the island.

Having climbed Ben Heaval (Mt. Heaval, 383 meters, or 1,257 feet) they rested side by side on a lichen-covered yellowish boulder, and looked across the wild and beautiful scene while birds circled and screeched around them. Other boulders all around were liberally coated with guano or bird poop. The wind here blew almost continuously, making a tattering noise in the ears that almost made a person feel deaf. The air smelled freshly of rain and salty sea and green vegetation including stunted bushes and krummholz.

"Glorious breeze and sunshine up here," she said wrinkling her nose with pleasure.

Barely 1.5 km (.9 mile) below them, to the southwest, lay Castlebay and the round blue bay itself. "Wish I had binoculars," Jack said. He glanced at his watch. It was 11:00 a.m.

"Here you go." Karla took a small pair of matte black opera glasses from her fanny pack. She sidled closer, sitting beside him. He felt her warm body against his. She held the glasses up for him to look through. He took them and scanned the bay below.

She rested against him, fondling his shoulders lightly.

"You make me an offer I cannot refuse," Jack said.

"Oh, what's that?" she teased. Her mouth was so close that he could faintly smell coffee on it from the morning meal.

"I would be too hard put to run away right now."

"Let me see." She reached down and cupped his corduroys. "Yep. I'd say so. Admit it, strong and silent Jack. You are helpless in my clutches."

He sighed. "I can think of worse things." He remembered the Dragon Lady in Baidu shooting at him point blank and—luckily—missing in the dark.

She rested her chin on his shoulder, while hugging him around the neck. "Am I a worse thing?" she purred.

"I'll tell you what." He shook her loose and rose. "Let's make a deal." He took the Sig-Sauer from his holster, walked ten paces away, and placed it on a small rock shelf. "You put your arsenal here, including knives, throwing stars, poison darts, and anything else you're carrying."

She shrugged and rose, dusting her shorts off. "Okay, Jack. I don't blame you for being cautious." She walked to the rock and laid down her gutting knife and a small but deadly Smith & Wesson double-action .45 ACP semi-automatic compact pistol.

"Is that it?" Jack asked. "No brass knuckles?"

She laughed delightedly. "No, sweetheart. You must take me for a street tough. I prefer the velvet touch."

"I'll remember that when I'm up against the wall."

"I'll be by your side, Jack."

"Okay, Karla."

"See, look?" She picked up the gutting knife and hurled it with all her strength. The knife arced up in the air, paused for a moment as if thinking what to do next, and then remembered to fall with gravity. "No more knife. No need to be scared."

"You had me wetting my pants," he said. As the knife landed, out of sight over a low rise, it made a different sound than Jack had expected—more of a metallic clang, than a dull thud or audible sound at all. In fact, he heard it hit metal several times as it fell down a well of some type.

"You can check my clothes, Jack." She stood with her arms upraised. "No hidden machine gun nests."

"I believe you." He sat down on a mossy spot and gestured.

She came close and sat on his lap. "This is where I wanted to be last night," she whispered in his ear. "I didn't know if I was coming or going."

Jack gingerly felt her body with both hands.

"Go ahead, Jack, check me all over. I'm cool."

She swiveled so that she sat astride him, with her ankles at his back. She wrapped her arms around his head and kissed him firmly with her tongue in the forward position.

Jack got his hands up her shirt and felt about. "Any weapons up there?"

She nodded fervently. "Mm-hm!" without relenting in her osculations.

Jack felt her weapons. "There they are—well-hidden, Karla."

"Mm-hmm!"

"Good job, my little tart." He rolled, taking her beneath him. With his hands, he pressed her wrists down onto the moss. She was his prisoner now. He instinctively knew she'd enjoy a touch of dominance. He pressed his mouth on hers. Her tongue stabbed deeper than ever. She took little nips at his lips. It grew painful, her chewing at him, until he head-butted her, forehead to forehead, and she lay back with a flushed, pleased look. Her eyes went momentarily in circles, as if bells and choir angels were doing a carousel around her vision. "You are good," she whispered stressfully. "Come on, show me you are a man. I don't meet many men these days."

He pursued some aggressive kissing, while she freed her hands. With a lot of wriggling and pushing, she got her shorts off, and pushed his trousers down. The touch of skin on skin made Jack crazy, amplified by the cool wind blowing between them. Where they touched, sweat bonded them, and when they came apart, the wind was colder in those regions than on dry skin. Karla wrapped her legs behind him, and wriggled her arms down there to bring him in. They rocked rolled together while the gulls grew still and observed. He rolled onto his back, and she rode him as she would ride a stallion. Her lips parted, and she keened while holding her small breasts. Her eyelids fluttered, closed, except to open slightly so that he saw her eyes roll up in delirium. She threw herself up and down on him, as if the stallion were not fast enough, but they fit together well. He provided the slow, long, powerful strokes that made her little body fly up and down, while she straddled him and could not go fast enough. Somehow, her sine waves and his long amplitudes made just the right sparks. It was a wonder the whole mountain was not lit up.

Eventually, they collapsed together and gasped in unison: "Wow, that was great."

There was still fire left—for Jack, all the more pungent because she was a dangerous, forbidden partner. They clashed again, several more bouts over the next hour.

Finally, Jack lay sprawled on his back. He was too numb to feel any more. Karla lay over him like a casualty. "Thank you, Jack. I needed that. You are really great—word on the street was right about you." She ruffled her fingers through his hair, and crawled closer to plant a hundred little kisses from lips that looked round and red like little cherries. Throwing all reservations aside, he hugged her close to him, knowing it was like hugging a hand grenade.

"Want more?" she whispered. "Here." She rolled on top of him, and moved her torso down so that she took him easily. She pumped away, but he could no longer feel much. Nevertheless—once more in to the breach—he rolled on top of her and came to one last shuddering, rockets-to-the-sky, fulfilling train station along the route to utter exhaustion.

They lay together for a while, stroking each other. He enjoyed the electric feel of her skin. He glanced at his watch—1:30 p.m. They had dallied for over two hours.

"Join me in my bedroom tonight," she said.

"What about your friend?"

"Hmm?"

"Lycurgus. Lysander. Whatever his name is."

"I heard you cracking the floor boards. You were listening. I found that very exciting."

"Who is he, Karla? Why was he at your door at oh-dark-thirty, half-past-late?"

"He's a disgruntled Anaconda employee who has decided to work with Sigma. He's a retired BAF sergeant major with the right tactical skills. Short on long term plans and strategies, but good in a bar fight."

"And you chose not to tell me about him. Why?"

She rolled over onto him and placed a finger on his lips. "A girl has her secrets, just like you have yours."

Jack groaned as she found him again and trapped him in that wonderful grip that seemed to have a life of its own, without any hands necessary.

"I am holding you hostage, Jack Gray."

"I feel like the earth's gravity just doubled. I don't know if I can ever get up again."

"I'll walk on your back tonight. Good massage. Get you back in working order."

"Your little girlfriend knows how to hold a guy's head."

Karla wiggled her hips. "She says thank you."

"Tell her I said I want more of that when I'm recovered."

Karla made that crazy face, laughing like a Mongol going zero to sixty on his pony with spear and shield in hand. "I'll never give you time to recover."

Gradually, however, they helped each other up. Both were limping. They hopped around, and nearly fell down, while tugging pants up and zipping zippers. Jack slipped and fell on his side. She piled onto him to wrestle. They laughed like children.

Arm in arm, lovers now, they walked in a circle around the peak.

"Now where did you throw that knife?" he asked.

"I got rid of it," she said. She laughed, an abrupt little hiccup. "Mutually Assured Distraction. You destroy mine, and I destroy yours."

"How about Mutually Assured Sea levels," Jack suggested. "I see yours, you see mine."

She laughed all the harder. "Bad, Jack, bad!"

He spotted a large metal grill in the ground. It was square, a meter by a meter, its steel bars about an inch apart.

"Here it is," he said.

"Here's what?"

"Where your knife went. I could have sworn I heard it hit metal and bounce around on its way down somewhere."

"What do you suppose it is?"

He let go of her and knelt to probe around the steel frame. "Ever drop your car keys down a thing like this on the street?"

"I think I have." She uttered a small peal of laughter. Her eyes grew wider.

"We didn't see it before, because of those boulders all around it." There was a circle of stones ranging from the size of a human skull to that of a motorcycle gas tank. A quick look told Jack that the mosses and lichens were wrongly positioned. These boulders had recently been maneuvered into place, within the past year.

He sat down and took out his phone pad. With a few deft manipulations, he had a cartographic survey map open in PDF format. He zoomed in on a relief map of Barra, and panned around. "The bay is just a mile from here, and it's about 1200 feet down to sea level. Kisimul is out on its little islet right there, at the end of the passenger terminal pier. Panning around, I see that it's on a dark shelf, while the waters around the bay are lighter."

"What does this tell us up here?" She sat beside him and stroked his hair.

"It means that Kisimul is on a rock shelf that stick out under water. The surrounding water is much deeper, but it's sunnier to a greater depth close to the surface. I read that the little island has its own fresh water supply from one or two wells, which means it must be connected to the mainland, while sea water can't get in. And this shaft must be an air exhaust for some huge structure underneath the mountain—maybe stretching out as far as Kisimul. That would help explain why Sigma detected a carrier wave coming from Kisimul along with transmission bursts, like the one that coincided with the satellite launch that BLUM intercepted."

"Jack, you are way over my head."

"It's all logic, my dear."

"I am passionate. You are logical. Opposites are a perfect match."

"We should have a closer look," Jack said. He knelt and pried at the steel grid. "I'd love to come back to investigate further, but why waste another climb?"

"We could make love again," she suggested.

"I'm going to take you up on that other offer later," he said. He collected their guns, handed her the silvery compact, and put the more massive black Sig-Sauer into his fanny pack.

"You name the time and place, and I'll bring the whistle and the funny hat."

With effort, they got the heavy grate to swing up. It was on twin, rusty hinges. There were bright spots on the metal, suggesting it had been recently assembled or at least painted. With the grate open, he could look down.

"Spooky," she said.

"It is somewhere between claustrophobic and roomy." Jack looked down into the gradient darkness. A set of rusty iron D-rings formed a utility stairway up and down the pipe, which was about six feet in diameter. "Got a flashlight?" He had one of his own, but he'd tease something more out of her.

Karla reached into her fanny pack and pulled out a small pink flashlight, run on two AAA batteries. He shone it down the shaft, where its beam soon lost itself in darkness. The ladder headed straight toward the center of the earth. Perhaps it came out by another shaft on the other side—that would be around New Zealand in the South Pacific. Hopefully, there would be a stop at sea level on this side. He handed the pink flashlight back. "Bravo for you. Let's go down and take a look."

"After you," she said.

Jack climbed down to shoulder level. Cautiously smelling the air, he caught a whiff of what seemed like paper…furniture…copy machines…

"There's an office somewhere down there. The air is quite nice…I smell women's perfumes…"

"Then it should suit you perfectly."

"Coming?"

"Not again just now, thanks." With a mighty heave, accompanied by a martial arts *heeyahh!* yell, Karla slammed the grating down.

Jack had just enough time to duck his head, or he would have been brained, and would have plummeted to his death a third of a kilometer below.

As he stared upward, he saw her rolling boulders on top of the grating. "I forgot that your empty hands are a weapon too."

"I told you to check me thoroughly, Jack."

"I did, to my utter delight."

"I'll give you a hint, lover. This is neither Anaconda nor Camelback territory. This is BLUM, and you are the star of the night today."

"You are M. L. Sombra." He'd suspected it, but *amour* had blinded him.

"The one and only, sweetheart. Actually, I am one of the Alectos. But you'll learn more about us, depending on how Dr. Night feels about letting you live—or not. Go on down, before you get tired and fall to your death. It's a long way down, and you'd best start right now. Don't worry, you'll have company. Thanks for a good time, sincerely."

As Jack gave her an angry look, she whooped—with that crazy laugh and the wild eyes—and took off running to do somersaults on the meadow above.

Nocturne in Barra

Descent into Hell

As Jack descended, he reflected that he had once again exceeded the speed limit with this one—if Karla Sipinski was even her real name. Certainly, *Me Llamo Sombra* (My Name is Darkness) could only be a code name. Her English was perfectly American, so she must have grown up in the States. She could not fake that. On the bright side, she could have killed him—so by letting him live, she was setting him up for something. But what?

He stopped some distance down, hanging on by one hand, while his feet uncomfortably perched on a narrow iron step in hiking shoes that suddenly seemed larger than they needed to be. Fumbling in his fanny pack, he ascertained by blind touch that she had left him his gun, his flashlight, and his phone pad. "That's so thoughtful," he said out loud. His voice echoed deadly about him in the shaft. "How cheering."

He continued down. As he climbed, the rush of warm air became more noticeable, as did the smells of offices and aftershave and perfume and electronic machinery.

He began to realize, as close as the smells seemed, how far their source really was.

The climb grew tiring. He did not count the steps, though he realized he should have. He hung on and pressed the button that made his wristwatch glow foggy bluish. It was 2:05 p.m. He'd been climbing since about 1:50, by his best estimate, and he was descending steadily at a rate of about…he timed himself…one rung every five seconds. That made for 12 rungs a minute, and in fifteen minutes he must have descended about 180 rungs. The rungs were spaced about a foot apart, so he had descended 180 feet. He had maybe 1,000 more rungs to go until sea level.

Good luck with that.

His hands were beginning to swell, and his legs were getting wooden. All the exercise with poison pill up on the meadow should have suggested a nap, had he known what he was in for. She must be psychotic, he decided. That had to be it. *God, forgive her, she knows not what she is doing.* She could make some lucky guy very happy—if she didn't kill him first, or eat him during sex like one of those female spiders that eats her mate just as he is climaxing.

Stopping to rest, Jack descended for another fifteen minutes.

By now, maybe 400 feet down, he was beginning to ration his movements. He was getting fatigued. He began to consider strategies—like using his fanny pack to tie himself to a step, and rest a few minutes—but what if the fragile nylon strap broke, plunging him to his death far below? Okay, Jack, one step after another, one rung at a time. He recalled his SEALs training in Coronado. He had already proven himself to be as motivated as any human being alive. Now was the time to pull that energy back out of its inner well—no pun intended.

At 600 feet, he began to get dizzy. The air seemed warmer and to be streaming more powerfully. It was becoming harder to fight the increasingly powerful counter-stream coming up as he went down. He was getting hot too, and thought about shucking his jacket.

At 700 feet, he slipped his jacket off, one arm, then the other, and let it fall.

He looked down.

Was it getting brighter down there? Was it hell? Was it the underworld in which BLUM committed its crimes and atrocities?

The jacket seemed to spiral down, like a man falling with his arms outstretched.

Was it spinning slowly on its way down, or was he hallucinating?

He dropped the fanny pack to lessen the weight on him.

He'd give anything for the bottle of spring water he'd left on the meadow.

The wind grew warmer, and stronger—and brighter.

And noisier. Like a big blower.

Of course—it would take a huge blower to push a constant volume of air up a tall shaft. Cool air near the top would form a heavy plug pushing down on hotter, lighter air, which would cool off and grow heavier. There must be a hell of a fan pushing upward.

At 800 feet, he figured he had 400 feet left until sea level. There must be some break in this monotony.

At 900 feet, he felt something odd.

Or rather, he felt nothing as his left foot probed for the next rung.

He looked down, and was instantly blinded by a bright light. The light seemed to come from something like thirty stories below—with luck, maybe the equivalent of twenty stories.

No matter—he was out of rungs. He had no way up, and no way down.

He cried for help several times, but there was no sign of life—only that incessant din of the blower, and the rush of warm air. Dehydrated, dizzy, and weak, he finally let go.

He'd heard a man tell once of how he'd been whitewater rafting in an Arizona canyon. When the man's boat capsized, he was thrown into the foaming, seething rapids. One of the other men on the ride tried to aim for a boulder along the way, trying to clutch it between his arms, and was smashed to death. The story teller said he had simply resigned himself, let go, and hoped for a painless end. Instead—he being relaxed like a man who's drunk a pint of whiskey—the water shot him along at about fifty miles per hour, around turns, over bumps, into dips and back out again…only to land belly up, and breathing calmly, on a beach in a huge cavern, where the water practically stood still.

In much the same way, Jack let go and hoped to find peace. He was carrying entirely too much baggage. What would Catherine say? He thought of the girls—Gail, 15, and Marcia, 13—and of Molly, and of her daughter Roberta—as he plummeted toward the Underworld. He felt himself spinning, like that jacket he had dropped.

Barra Nocturne—Ultimatum 2

"Good afternoon, Mr. Gray," said an invisible man.

Jack opened his eyes.

He shook his head and wondered what had happened.

He lay on his back, spread-eagled on a very large, comfortable bed.

"You were out cold for a little while. Don't worry—our senior duty sister checked you out—what you would call a nurse practitioner in the United States—and you have nothing wrong with you. Nothing at all. You made a soft landing on our special blower cushion."

Must have been quite a sight. Jack pictured himself, unconscious, spread-eagled, spinning slowly atop a maelstrom of warm air scented with the perfumes of secretaries. He imagined people stopping work to gather in a circle and point upward at him under some cavernous dome in the earth, whose *oculus* was the mouth of the shaft he'd fallen down.

This bed was firm, and stable, and smelled faintly of oats or a warehouse or something; still pleasant. He sat up and looked around. He wasn't tied down. His fanny pack lay on a nearby table, with all of his possessions intact—even the gun.

He was in a round, spacious bedroom with a low ceiling of bare grayish rock glistening with silica. The walls leading up to it were of the same material, but had been painted a faint, sunny citron up to about eight feet all around. The cavern was illumined by indirect lighting. On the floors were thick rugs in happy colors, matching the bright and cheery bedspread.

"Go on, Mr. Gray. Explore. Just don't shoot anyone, please. I left your weapon for you, in case you encounter any large sea animals. That's right, you are two stories under water. Under Kisimul, to be exact."

Jack looked up at the invisible voice. "Who are you?"

"I am your host, Dr. Night. Welcome to our world. I trust the Alecto treated you well?"

"I had it made in the shade." Jack rubbed his sore wrists, remembering his long climb down.

"Ah yes—*Sombra*. I asked her not to break your neck as you achieved orbit. She can be very impulsive. But always imaginative. And deadly, the way I prefer my women. You too, I see."

Jack briskly rubbed himself around his head and body, trying to fully come to. "The funny thing is, she is so loveable."

"Despite all her instincts on the rash side and so forth. I agree. And I am impressed at your magnanimous spirit."

"So who is this going to be a message to?"

Dr. Night chuckled, a dry sound that echoed through adjacent hallways. "Very perceptive as always, Mr. Gray. The more I get to know you, the more impressed I am. You may be a fool with women, but you are a disciplined thinker and doer otherwise."

"Why don't you come out so we can meet man to man?"

"I would love to, Mr. Gray, but I am over a thousand miles away, watching you on closed circuit video."

"And Sombra?"

"She will be on her way to me shortly. To your question—you had three warnings, the last of which said that if you did not relent in your pursuit of the Orbital Sniper Technology, you would die. That was my message to you."

"But you've kept me alive. Why?"

"Because now you will be the medium. And you will be the message. You will be our second warning to the world powers. When I am ready, I will snuff you out—very visibly, across a thousand board rooms and parliamentary committee rooms. The first warning was our deletion of a young art student, who had nothing to offer the world but some chalky pipe dreams. The second warning will be your spectacular death here in the underground command center of Castor."

"Castor oil?" Jack said. "My aunt used to feed me castor oil when I was small, when I was constipated—stuffed full of crap. Is that your problem too?"

Dr. Night laughed softly. "I like your spirit, Mr. Gray. I like spirited, lively, passionate people. That is why I surround myself with women like the Alectos—the ancient Roman Furies, unstoppable, unquenchable, relentless in their rage and their hunger for vengeance. "

"What about your boy Lysander. Is he around?"

"Pardon me, Mr. Gray, but I have just opened a conference call with the world's corporate and government leaders. This time, it will still be secret. I keep offering these fools olive branches and soft landings. They have enjoyed absolute power for too long to comprehend their new reality. They are like the mighty polar bear, the world's largest mammal predator at nearly one ton—suddenly drowning for lack of ice floes due to atmospheric hyperthermalism, or AHT. My Ph.D. is in Applied Sciences, so I perhaps understand the metaphor better than someone with a Ph.D. in History. You have the advantage on me, Dr. Gray, in that you are thus a better student of human nature. Yin and Yang. The balance of all things."

"That's right," Jack said. "Folly never changes. Absolute power corrupts absolutely."

"Precisely," Dr. Night said in an admiring tone. "For example, take those dinosaur corporate governments who pay your check. What are they called these days, now that they have destroyed any meaningful democracy? Corponations? Hybrids like that are an abomination, and do not last long in nature. You should really think about joining me. We'll change history together. What do you say? Maybe I won't kill you, and you'll live out your life amid your books in…where is it now? Southern California?"

A chill passed through Jack as he thought about exposing his family to such madness. He dreaded the idea that he might have outfoxed himself in a yet bigger way than he'd done in letting Sombra run rings around him. He had thought he could manage her, but she'd manhandled him.

"I will give you time to think. Please, by all means, take a look around. You have one hour in which to either die, or pledge absolute loyalty to me and to Black Umbrella. Meanwhile, you can listen in while I address the top 1,000 corponational leaders of the world."

Jack donned his fanny pack, and put the gun, the flashlight, and other paraphernalia from the table into the little satchel. His heart leapt when he saw his phone pad. He used the predial for his satellite transponder to an encrypted line to Claire or Rector.

Nothing.

"Oh, Dr. Gray," Dr. Night said, "I almost forgot. There is a telephone on the marble table as you enter the main control room. By all means, use it to call your superiors. Don't worry, we listen to all their SIGINT and ULTRA/BIN/CRYPTOMAX traffic, so nothing is lost. Your little phone pad can't reach an outside cell from here. Please tell Mr. Rector and Ms. Lightfield that I said hello."

Brazen son of a bitch, Jack thought to himself. *Arrogant bastard.*

"Now please forgive me as I turn to important matters. Remember—the clock is ticking, and you now have just fifty-five minutes to decide if you want to live or die."

Jack began to encounter the first few men and women in white lab coats as he walked around the facility. He knew this place was bounded by the postage stamp of land on which the castle sat. At the same time, there was at least one passage between here and Barra Island, with the mountain on top of it.

The Castor control center under Kisimul castle was a large, low, dome-like chamber about fifty feet across. This was surrounded by a circumferential, arched corridor some twenty feet wide, from which rooms and smaller corridors branched off. One main corridor about twenty feet wide with a rounded ceiling led toward the mountain, but it was sealed off by a heavy steel door.

The outer perimeter consisted of a massive submarine sea wall, punctuated by eight thick plate-glass portholes. These cast a dappled, dancing, sunny light around the chamber that was downright soothing. It was like working in a swimming pool, minus the wet and chlorine smells. Or, here, the saltwater smell. Jack sat by a porthole—each had a little bench or shelf seating up to four persons—and looked out at the water. What must it have taken to construct this massive project under the eyes of so many people? He was more impressed with BLUM's technological capabilities than ever.

He saw many small fish and other sea life, and the occasional larger grouper amid drifting kelp. The surface appeared to be about twenty feet above the upper rim of the window.

Turning on his seat, Jack surveyed the command center, looking for an opening—anything to destroy this operation, and escape alive. A wall legend read *Castor*, along with a BLUM logo and the words *Project Gemini*.

If this was Castor, where was its twin Pollux?

The room was a quiet hive of activity. At least twenty technicians of all races and both genders sat at computer terminals in a circle broken in two places by open passages just wide enough for a person to sidle through. About half of the staff wore white lab coats. The other half wore the kind of scrubs his dentist back in Temecula wore—just covering the torso, and either reddish, greenish, or bluish, with dark scrub pants and nurses' clogs or tennies underneath. A few wore yellow or purple tops. He wondered if it were a random selection of fresh scrubs when you came to work, or if it were a deliberate color code.

He also noticed that those wearing scrubs all wore little blue phone attachments on their ears, while the people in white did not.

As he frantically studied the place for details—so he could rescue himself and maybe stop this madman from continuing to assassinate people—he recognized the squat, powerful figure of Lysander skulking about. The man wore a purple scrub top, and a blue earpiece. As he spotted Lysander, so did the man make significant eye contact with Jack. Was he an angel of death now? Had he been sent to kill Jack when the hour struck? Jack had forty-five minutes left before Dr. Night's death threat was to be carried out.

Jack went out into the circumferential corridor. It was lit by long lines of bioluminescent lights along the main vault of the arched ceiling. Men and women in lab coats or scrubs passed him in each direction. They seemed silently preoccupied with their duties. Many carried lap-pads or other digital devices.

The main gate out of the underwater facility, and into the mountain on the main island of Barra, was guarded by four persons in dark gray uniforms that might have a touch of taupe or mauve in them. The two men and two women carried side arms and wore peaked caps like Austrian or Italian border guards. Loitering about at the periphery, Jack studied the door as best he could from a distance of thirty feet. The door looked strong enough to contain the sea itself, should this place ever spring a leak. *Claustrophobic thought.*

Then Dr. Night's conference call with the world's corporate governments went live, and resounded against the background noise of the busy Castor control hive under Kisimul.

"Ladies and gentlemen," said Dr. Night, "my patience is long, but not endless. Because I plan far ahead, I anticipate a measured response to your inertia. You have become beleaguered tyrants in a thousand bunkers. Black Umbrella is the enemy at your gates. As the Goths seized Rome in 410 A.D., so we will seize your strongholds. But I still hope for a peaceful and reasonable takeover of 25% of your equities. I am now increasing that number to 33.33%, or one full third. If you do not heed this warning, the next message will ask for 51%, an absolute controlling majority. Please consider acting in your best interests before it is too late.

"I did not expect that you would understand my first message. The young man at the Tower of London did not die in vain. Now Black Umbrella will snuff out a more convincing target. In one hour, the clock will begin ticking on the life of some globally famous and important president or prime minister, yet to be determined. If you then do not get it, we will start targeting members of your elite corporate CEO club—that should hit home."

Instantly, in Jack's mind, images of President Helen Cameron flashed—a former Senator's wife from Colorado, who had gone from being a corporate lawyer in Denver to state governor, and then to the U.S. Senate, and finally—with overwhelming support from the Corporate Oversight and Direction Administration (CODA) governing civil affairs— to her party's nomination. She had won the last presidential election with over 60%, and was judged very likely for a second term in office. Since CODA had replaced the Electoral College, and the nation's powerful and crucial corporations were able to openly exercise their (considerable) proportionate governing power, the media had become muted and the stridency of the old democracy had faded. The chaos was gone, replaced by strong and sensible central rule that created jobs, kept issues simple and unconfused, and blurred the lines between parties to a point that everyone was just having one big, happy time. Helen Cameron was a businesslike, attractive woman who liked to say she got her hair done in New York City, her nails done in San Francisco, and her clothes tailored in Chicago. It was her way of saying that she traveled around the country a lot, listening to the common people as well as the heads of corporations, and always tried to deliver the best solution for everyone involved. Capitalism and free enterprise, which were naturally and logically diametric opposites, enemies, oil and water that could never mix, had achieved stasis—monopolies on top, free enterprise somewhere down in the murk below. The chaos of ideas and competition had given way to the well-regulated market. The optimistic view was that the best men had won. The pessimistic view was that predators, as always, rose to the top—the Human Condition, the problem that Dr. Jack Gray, the historian, was making his life's intellectual problem to solve or at least write about.

Dr. Night continued: "We represent the disaffected, the downtrodden, the deposed kings waiting in the wings of history. We oppose the corporate takeover of the world, and our legitimacy is absolute. We count among our numbers the legal descendants of the last Byzantine emperor, Constantine XI Palaiologos, last seen on Easter Sunday 1453, in full armor on his horse, waving his sword as he plunged into a mass of Ottoman Turkish besiegers, just hours before the end of a more than two thousand year Roman empire. Among our numbers are the princes descendant from both the French Bourbon line, and the Napoleonic line. We have among us the descendants of Confederate President Jefferson Davis. Among us is the current crown prince of the Stuart line, descendant from King James who was ousted in 1707 in favor of the Germans who ruled the British monarchy for over 300 years. But also among our numbers are the ninja of all cultures—those who just wanted to till their fields, but the samurai could kill them or their families on a whim and get away with it. So the ninja moved into the mountains and learned new martial arts that made them the best fighters in Japan, so scary and skilled that even ruthless killer samurai feared them. That best describes Black Umbrella, ladies and gentlemen. There are other metaphors from history. But this is not metaphor. It is reality. We are the ninja, and you are the daimyo in your feudal castles. We come at night—like the ancient Mediterranean deities of the Underworld—to eat your lunch."

As Dr. Night spoke, Jack sat down to ponder his next move. Lysander sat near him, facing him defensively, but twirling his fingers together comfortably over a solid belly. "Mr. Gray, are you thinking which way to go?"

"Yes, out of here," Jack said.

Lysander smiled thinly and shook his head. "There is no way out. You're wasting your time if you're still thinking about escape. Join us or die."

"Have you been sent to kill me?"

Lysander laughed. "Oh heavens, no. Dr. Night will kill you. It will be a big, wet surprise for you and most of these people here in the Castor company."

Jack stared at him, shocked. Lysander had just given away the scenario. So Dr. Night planned to blow up his underground facility in the next forty minutes or so, drowning all the technical people like rats at their computers. So much for his love of the downtrodden masses—or, as it turned out, given the number of women working here, the sodden lasses.

He was offering Jack a chance to join him, so there must be an escape group. Judging by the earphones on the colored scrubs people, they would most likely receive a warning when it was time to leave. That would almost certainly be either by that heavy door on the main corridor—or some smaller escape hatch, if there was one. He could call Rector to warn him, but Dr. Night would have thought that through. What if he joined them, with the intent of sabotaging…wait a minute. Project Castor…if Dr. Night planned for some reason to abandon this facility, did this not mean….Project Gemini….did this not mean there must be a Project Pollux somewhere. Was Castor a blind, a false front, to cover for Pollux? The name Gemini had to mean something…the Twins, in Roman mythology.

"Tell me" Jack asked Lysander, "what does it take to get on board with these people?"

Lysander eyeballed him with cold speculation. "Sincerity."

"What if I just want to be paid better? Camelback pays poopoo, and Rector takes half before I get a few peas on my plate."

Lysander shook his head. "I don't know what you just said, but Dr. Night is waiting for your answer. I'm here to relay your answer, if you're ready to give one."

"Tell him that I'm just a hired gun with the Camelback Consortium, and I'd be willing to hear some options coming from BLUM."

Lysander rose. "Is that a yes? There is only time for yes or no, not maybe."

"Yes."

"Very well. Dr. Night is busy, but I have been deputized to receive your answer. Let's take a walk."

Overhead, Dr. Night began speaking again. "Ladies and gentlemen, you have forty-eight hours in which to commit that you will sign over

33.33% of your equity to Black Umbrella, on behalf of the world's downtrodden masses and their deposed, legitimate rulers—all of whom now work for me."

Castor in Eclipse

As Jack followed Lysander, he noticed that a number of the ubiquitous Black Umbrella screens came to life along the high walls, even the ceilings in some places. The screens turned on as one approached, and faded into blackness as one passed. Dr. Night never showed his face, but was always the voice behind the monologue for his captive audiences around the world.

This time, the screens did not simply display the BLUM logo. Instead, they displayed the underwater control center at Castle Kisimul.

Remarkably, Jack saw images of himself, in real time, walking behind Lysander.

"Ladies and Gentlemen, I have a special message for all espionage and insertion group commanders in their headquarters. My consortium has captured one of the world's top field agents, Major Jack Gray. For academics, make that Professor Jack Gray. Let his fate be an example to all of you. Within this hour, as Project Castor ends its final phase, Major Gray will face his ultimate decision. Should he die here, a loyal fool for you corporate sharks, or will he see the light—I should say, will he see the darkness? Will he abandon his fruitless allegiance to his cold-hearted masters, that being you, and will he switch his loyalties to my organization? Or will he die here for no reason other than his own stubborn blindness? It will be entertaining to see how Major Gray handles his final assignment for Camelback Consortium. Let's give a big hand of applause to Dr. Jack Gray as he squirms in the same moral dilemma you are all about to face in regard to your sovereigns." He added contemptuously. "Your owners, you serfs."

"Hell of a speech," Jack muttered.

Lysander overheard. "Everything on plan, Mr. Gray. No stone left unturned."

"What made you switch sides, Lysander?"

"Oh...common sense. For one thing, I was retired after wasting my youth on the U.K. military, when in fact I am a Scotsman and deserve to march to my own piper—if you see the twist. There I was, still vigorous, as I am now, but without much gray hair yet. I didn't want to waste the rest of my life sitting around with old farts wearing stained black suits covered in medals, glad to march at the rear of a parade full of young cannon fodder for His Majesty the King, damn his soul. My pension wasn't bad, but nothing spectacular. Along came Dr. Night and his lovely project, and my pension money doubled overnight. Plus I get to continue doing interesting work, for my people and for the people of the world."

"That's how I see it," Jack said. "Well spoken. I get peanuts for risking my life so the corporate fat cats and their wholly owned governments can live like medieval barons. I think BLUM is the best thing to come along since...oh, the U.S. Constitution."

"There you go precisely," Lysander said. He showed Jack in to a small room that looked like a medical infirmary. Two attractive young women in white lab coats stood working over a laboratory bench. "Mr. Gray is here for his truth test," Lysander announced.

Meanwhile, Dr. Night had shuffled the video to show images of Washington, D.C., London, Paris, and other world capitals. "Within the next two days, we will eliminate one of your world leaders. Most likely, it will be either the President of the United States, the British Sovereign, or someone else of a high symbolic stature in the brave new corporate world. If you do not sign over one third of your stock ownership to Black Umbrella, we will start aggressively targeting not heads of state, but heads of corporations. If nothing else gets your attention, that should."

The scene switched to a somewhat blurry image of Jack, with his shirt stripped off, being led into a machine resembling a metal detector door at buildings or airports.

"Dr. Gray is being strapped into the truth machine. He has offered to hear more about the wonderful benefits of switching allegiance to BLUM."

Jack patiently waited as the two white-coated women strapped him into this truth-archway by his ankles and wrists. Half-naked, spread-eagled, his image must have rippled through corporate boardrooms around the world.

Next, the women attached a network of EKG wires to his body in a pattern much resembling the map of body energy in Chinese traditional medicine, called *chi*.

"Think of this as an advanced and sophisticated lie detector," Dr. Night said. "We do not relish liars or traitors. We smash spies and enemy agents if they were insects crawling up our leg.

"While we wait for Dr. Gray to be fully hooked up and interrogated, I would like to regale you with one last bit of information. As you know by now, Black Umbrella hijacked Global Anaconda's Project David. This is the Orbital Sniper Technology (OST) developed by Mr. Louis Cartouche of Quebec Nation. When Mr. Cartouche developed his fabulous technology, he knew he would need to sell it to someone like Anaconda— where he hit pay dirt on his first try. Congratulations, Mr. Cartouche, who thought better of it, and now works for me."

As Dr. Night spoke, the screen showed a beaming Louis Cartouche with a pretty little blonde close and purring at his side.

"Don't they look like a happy couple? All of our employees enjoy marvelous benefits and salary, as well as European style vacation plans unequaled in the sweatshops of American serfdom. All that will change as we apply fair employment laws across the world. We value our employees. They are not tools or assets or 'human resources,' to which the corporate world has reduced human beings. They are citizens of the new, free world that is being built by Black Umbrella. But I do go on, gushing so, as I display my unbridled enthusiasm for all we have yet to accomplish."

Jack was now attached to the machine in this little room, by his ankles and wrists, and several dozen wires attached with round, white tape terminals around his torso and head. There were a few wires attached to his extremities as well. Two men entered the room, consulting digital tablets. The women technicians kept adjusting a tape dot here or there.

As Lysander guarded the door, a woman in a white lab coat entered. She was a middle-aged, perfunctory brunette, without makeup or jewelry but a healthy, tanned complexion. "I am Dr. Witswot," she said (or something, maybe Nitsnot) in an Afrikaans-sounding dialect of English. She laid her tablet aside and took control of the truth machine. "We'll begin with a few test questions. Is your name Jack Gray?"

"Yes."

"Do you teach history?"

"Yes."

"Are you an expert on ancient Roman topology?"

"Yes."

"Is the Forum Magnum the same as the Forum Boarium?"

"No."

"Was Julius Caesar a German king?"

"No."

"So far so good, Mr. Gray. I have some more foundational questions before we narrow in on the big question of the day."

Dr. Night, meanwhile, continued his monologue. "You know that Black Umbrella has taken over the Anaconda David Project. Our code name is Gemini, the twins. Being of a practical and safe mind, bless him, Louis Cartouche built in a safety factor that we much appreciate. Didn't you, Monsieur Cartouche?"

Cartouche's face flashed on the screen. He and the blonde nodded happily.

"Mr. Cartouche divided the functions of his delivery vehicle, an orbital satellite, between two stations—Castor and Pollux. He sold Pollux to Anaconda, while wisely keeping its Castor twin in a secret location in Montreal. Finally, when the price was right, he sold Pollux to Anaconda as well. We were able to liberate Castor from Anaconda's Delta Company in Montreal without incident. It is now located at Kisimul. However, progress is ever ongoing. To survive and get ahead, a successful company, corporation, or consortium must think on its feet, look at all the alternatives, and plan far ahead.

"My point is, Ladies and Gentlemen, you should understand that our capabilities are on a par with yours, and in many cases superior." He flashed images of southern Barra bay, then Kisimul Castle, and then three large dredging barges. "It took us just one year, working under the noses of the corporate authorities, to finish our secret facility at Castlebay. Those barges were more than they seemed. We had over 400 workers on shift, night and day, excavating the underground facility and building a command and control center.

"Now before you decide to send your military minions along with jets and ships, think about this. We anticipated that you would launch missiles, or even orbiters, in an effort to destroy the Pollux satellite. It is fully functional already, as we have proven. We already used it to delete that art student in London, and with which we are about to kill one of your most important symbolic leaders.

"But wait—before you do, consider this. On board the Capricorn station, as we call our Pollux weapon, is enough dirty radiological material to destroy a large city and kill several million men, women, and children. It's a little frill we added to Mr. Cartouche's more rudimentary design. If your military assistants were to take out our satellite, it would rain death over thousands of square miles. And if you decide to get sticky about it, we'll relay it to your wholly owned mass media. It's a story even they won't be able to suppress for you, or twist into yet another propaganda tool to fool the world's hordes of Stupid People."

In the booth, Jack's interrogation was reaching a climax. With the two women in white lab jackets hovering around him, he tried to control his breathing, think Zen thoughts, and appear convincing.

"Are you sincere, Mr. Gray?"

"Yes."

Pause.

"Do you wish to join Black Umbrella?"

"Yes."

Pause.

"Are you lying, Mr. Gray?"

"No."

Pause.

"Do you love Black Umbrella?"

"Yes."

Pause.

"Very good." She stared with furrowed brow at her readout. A call came in, and she touched her earpiece. As the test administrator listened, she nodded, and brightened, and nodded more brightly. "You passed with flying colors," she said.

"Congratulations," said Lysander and the doctor in one voice.

"I heard that," said Dr. Night. "Everyone around the world, a round of applause for Mr. Jack Gray, who has renounced his allegiance to the west, and to the corporate world, and his joining the great cause of Black Umbrella. Welcome to the Underworld, Mr. Gray!"

It was not applause, but stunned silence that came in response to Dr. Night's pronouncement. If, as he had just amply demonstrated, a key western agent could fall to the charms and threats of Black Umbrella, then who in their organizations was safe?

Jack saw a brief shot of a corporate boardroom somewhere—people were looking at each other suspiciously, wondering who the next betrayer would be, and hoping they would not be the betrayed.

"Excellent," said Lysander, patting Jack on the shoulders. "Come on, let's visit with Louis Cartouche."

As they left the testing room, Jack said: "I thought he was at the Pollux location."

Lysander laughed softly. "Dr. Night and his theatrical team like to spice things up. They bend the truth a bit when they have to. Come, Mr. Gray, I'll introduce you to the real hero of Project Gemini.

In a smaller domed room, across the main corridor from the central control center, they found a tall, graying man with the pasty skin of a heavy smoker, in the company of a beautiful young blonde with exquisite features—introduced by Lysander as Miss Tissy Fître, though it came out more like Hissy Fit in his situational rolling brogue.

As he shook their hands, Jack noticed that Cartouche wore a long white lab coat and no ear piece, while Tissy wore a purple scrub top and a standard blue phone jacked to her ear. She was a finely burnished woman, about 23 Jack estimated, Nordic—Belgian, Lysander at some point specified—with golden-blonde hair wrapped around her head and held in place by a barrette decorated with strawberry motifs. She had clear blue eyes, a tiny ski ramp nose, and a rather pouty, distressed little mouth touched with light pink lipstick. Her facial tone was an appealing light café au lait color (one sugar and at least two creams, no doubt). She had a reserve around her that made sense to Jack, though Louis Cartouche seemed impervious to the obvious.

"We are aware," Dr. Night said, "that elements of the European Strike Force based in Aberdeen and Dundee are already en route, top haste, to seize our headquarters. Anticipating this rash behavior, we have planned well ahead. As I was saying, we are shutting down Castor company, because with the successful launch of Capricorn, we no longer have need of the redundancies created so wisely by Monsieur Cartouche.

"To see us lightly discarding an enormous investment like Barra should give you a clue as to our scope and capabilities. You do not stand a chance, so please, for the last time, before we start eliminating kings and presidents as well as CEOs, sign over a third of your equity to Parapluie Noir Financial Corporation in Geneva, Switzerland, and its subsidiary companies around the world. No need to become instantly desperate and frantic—you can't trace the money. It's a blind, you fools. With that, I leave you to some spectacular viewing, and I hope some very sober thinking."

Sunset over Barra

"Come this way, Mr. Gray," said Lysander.

"Wait," the truth machine doctor said, chasing after them. She held a purple smock in one hand, and an earpiece in the other. As Jack and Lysander waited in the hallway, she worked the scrub top over his head. While he smoothed it down over his trim form, she placed the earpiece in his left ear. She tapped on it a few times with her fingertip, and Jack heard clicking sounds.

"I think it works," he told her.

"Welcome to Black Umbrella," she said.

"We have to hurry," Lysander said.

The doctor gripped Jack's clothing anxiously. "Be sure to keep listening, or you'll miss the boat—literally."

In the earpiece, the voice of an old acquaintance—Karla Sipinski, a.k.a. My Name is Darkness—said: "At the sound of the klaxon, all color coded staff will leave their work immediately and proceed to the underground submarine dock. Do not—I repeat—do not talk with your neighbors. Not a word to the white coats. Repeating…"

So Karla was a highly placed person in BLUM's organization. Jack thought he should feel flattered that she and her thugs had paid so much attention to him. First, they had lured him to the Frankfurt Zoo. Second, they had waylaid him in the Beethovenstrasse apartment, where he had killed two men and one of her female cohorts. Third, Karla herself had lured him directly into her seductive arms on Barra—to make a worldwide display of him, showing BLUM's power to turn the most loyal, capable, and proven agents.

There was at least one major flaw in Dr. Night's organization, Jack thought. For all their talk of the masses, they were cold-blooded murderers who showed no regard for human life. If you controlled the media and the ruling powers, and had all the money, it was an unbeatable hand at the poker game of life. It was an oft-proven exercise from history. Control the medium and you own the message. Pack that message full of your lies, and the medium becomes the massage for millions of gullible small fry. The corponations had used that strategy well in gradually but surely taking all the teeth out of the U.S. Constitution.

The explosion was just minutes away, if the threat to Jack was any guide. He had twenty minutes left, on Dr. Night's game clock—unless Dr. Night bought into Jack's lies about willingly joining BLUM.

Lysander stopped at a metal office door, which he opened, and showed Jack inside.

There was only a chair, a table, and a lamp in the room—nothing more. And just enough room to stand up in. "Are we on our way to the submarine docks?" Jack asked, suddenly suspecting the answer was no.

Lysander closed the door, turned in a rapid, blurry wheel, and punched Jack in the head. It would have been a knockout punch, with those massive shoulders and brawny arms, but Jack's reflexes were quick enough so that he deflected most of the force with one shoulder. Lysander kicked him in the back of one knee, forcing his leg to fold, and shoved the chair under Jack.

In the ear piece, Dr. Night spoke. "Mr. Gray, I was disappointed, but not surprised, to learn that you failed your truth test. The fact is that you remain utterly loyal to mankind first, the corporate system second, and the west last. There is no place for your heart in our organization. Pity. Nevertheless, we managed some very convincing theater, didn't we? No, Mr. Gray, you will die here along with the nonessential personnel, but the lie will live on. For years, as the corponations look over their shoulders, they will expect to see the great Jack Gray, agent of BLUM, coming for them in the dark. I have invested a fair amount of capital in you, Mr. Gray, and it appears the investment will more than pay for itself. Good bye now, Mr. Gray, happy afterlife to you. I must move on to those who will live on with me."

The ear piece went dead—totally dead. He was cut off from the BLUM apparatus.

Lysander slapped him across the back of the head, so that his ears rang.

"Bloody focking turncoat," Lysander said. Evidently, Dr. Night was speaking to him. "Yessir, I'll take care of him right now. Nossir, he won't cause anyone any more trouble."

As Lysander focused the last of his attention on the phone call with his demigod, Dr. Night, he gripped Jack's other shoulder in a death grip. It was clear that, any second now, he would apply the other hand, and strangle Jack to death, to drop dead on the floor in just minutes.

Jack moved his elbow up and around, trapping Lysander's arm for a second. The other man was quick, but not fast enough. As Jack rose, he kept the turn going, and brought his left fist against Lysander's temple. It was a relatively weak punch from a disadvantaged position, but the man was momentarily stunned. He looked down, dazed, and gave his head a shake.

Jack got behind him and held Lysander with a left arm choke around the neck, while repeatedly pummeling him around the temple and carotid artery with his right fist, traceable to Brazilian jiu-jitsu. In a BJJ competition, he'd be on this back on the floor, with a stunned opponent helplessly tangled above him in some leg or arm hold, while the free hand sought soft spots to beat or choke for an inevitable win. This was life and death. Jack estimated that Lysander died with the third punch to his temple—but he twisted the man's head until his neck snapped. "Welcome to the Underworld," he muttered as he peeled off Lysander's ear piece. He already wore a purple smock, signifying the non-technical inner circle—probably the goons or enforcers or, as so euphemistically termed, Security. Lysander's name had been embroidered over the left side on his chest.

Jack—now someone named Lysander—turned off the light in the room and left it locked as the door swung shut.

In the hallway, men and women in colored scrubs hurried past him.

Men and women in white lab coats looked up from their stations, mildly puzzled. Many had not heard a word of Dr. Night's speech to the world, much less Karla's earpiece instructions to the chosen survivors.

Jack wanted to leave the facility with this submarine, but he also wanted to save lives if possible.

The first and final alarm klaxon sounded, coming from the submarine parked below.

Jack heard the diesels revving, and smelled a strong aroma of diesel exhaust coming up the stairwell.

Jack ran back to the control center, where puzzled white-coats were gathered in the initial throes of panic. "You need to get out," Jack yelled. "Dr. Night is about to blow the windows and drown you all."

They stared at him uncomprehendingly, as Jack thought they should. Who on earth would dream up an insane and murderous show like this—except the sort of world class, industrial strength megalomaniac who only comes along once or twice a century?

"Find a way out right now!" Jack yelled, but they looked paralyzed. They knew something was wrong, but they were still blinded by those large paychecks from BLUM that kept them in hot and cold running Porsches.

With minutes to go, at most, before the submarine sailed, Jack ran out into the main corridor. The guards at the heavy door were gone, but they had linked heavy chains through its brackets. It wasn't going to open again. There wasn't time or manpower enough to see what lay behind that door, if anything—maybe just a long corridor in which they would all drown while trying to escape.

In a corner of the runabout, on the ceiling, Jack spied an odd looking square vent. Now where did that lead? To the main vent he had so laboriously climbed down? No time for long deliberations. Not only that, but there was a small D-ring series of stair steps going up there. Jack, seizing a heavy red fire extinguisher from the wall, clambered up the stairs until he was jammed under the ceiling. The air here was hot, since hot air rises—so couldn't be a vent. Might as well find out. He swung his fire extinguisher, back and forth, holding it by the steel wheel on its top. When he had a good swing going, he added some body English to it, and brought it dead on the flimsy looking grate. He lost his grip on the fire extinguisher, and nearly lost his grip on the top D-ring. While stabilizing himself with both hands, avoiding a nasty fall, he watched as the fire extinguisher fell and bounced on the floor. On top of it landed the crumpled vent screen cover, which had come loose. To his amazement, the vent had covered up a hatch like that in a submarine conning tower.

An emergency exit? But to where? Jack remembered reading that the grounds of Kisimul were now part of a national historic preserve, and covered with archeological digs. He half expected to see a crumbling Iron Age corpse in chain mail fall from the ceiling. Instead, there was this steel hatch, with a broad steel wheel that surely unlocked it. Must be BLUM's work. He reached over as far as he could, and pushed on the wheel. It barely budged. Leaning even further into space, while holding on with just the fingertips of his left hand, he gave the wheel another push. It turned with a loud creak.

Jack lost his grip on the D-ring, and barely managed to grab the steel wheel in the above hatch with both hands. Thus, he dangled and swung about fifteen feet above corridor level. He supposed he could drop down, hoping not to break anything, climb back up the D-rings, and try again.

Instead, he pulled himself higher. Like a spider, he clutched the wheel while planting both boots against the ceiling. In this pose, he tried to walk in a circle with his feet against the roof, taking the wheel with him.

To his amazement, someone or something knocked on the other side.

"Yes, dammit," Jack shouted. "Yes, unlock it."

A man's voice cried faintly: "Unlock it from inside." The voice echoed through the metal of the hatch.

Jack renewed his efforts and went another three full circles. His hands still hurt from his long climb down. "I'm losing my grip," he shouted to nobody in particular. As he let his feet drop, and his hands were starting to tremble a minute away from letting go, the hatch screeched as someone gave a yank.

Jack was within seconds of letting go, when the hatch swung upward. It carried him up with it. Amid a gust of cold, bracing, sweet fresh air, a dozen hands held him, and almost as many strong arms lifted him onto grassy ground under a half moon. Several gun barrels pointed at his face.

"I'm Major Jack Gray, U.S. Army Reserve, Special Forces."

"He looks like his picture," one man said.

"Bloody defector, I hear" said another.

Jack said: "No, no, that's Dr. Nut with all that looney chatter." He brushed their confusion aside. "Listen up, you guys. That was all a fake. BLUM is going to blow the whole show down there any minute now, killing a hundred innocent people. I'd love to stay and bullshit with you, but I'm on a mission. Can you handle the rescue?"

Two young officers in cockade berets leaned forward among the multitude of helmeted, heavily equipped, and well-armed U.K. Special Forces. One officer saluted and said: "Ensign Terry McDougal, Royal Navy Special Boat Services, Sir." The other saluted and said: "Chief Warrant Officer Douglas O'Donnell, Special Air Services."

"How many people have you got?" Jack said.

"Ten men on the island, two launches standing by with twenty more in the shadows behind the island."

"Just get these people out," Jack ordered. "You are not to interfere in any way with my mission, which involves staying with the pack they are going to evacuate. Trust me on this."

"Yessir," they both said. "We do have a cruiser and a frigate en route, along with a parachute regiment."

"Negative on all counts. Put them on standby off shore. Stay away from Kisimul, in case she blows."

"Yessir!"

Everyone was making command decisions under cover of night, in the fog of the situation. They trusted him, and he must trust them. He thought of Miranda, and thought: *I still have business with Dr. Deadhead.*

"I will go back down and herd them over here. You get them up here by hook or by crook, and then beat feet out of here in case the whole island goes up. Got that?"

"Yessir."

They lowered him down on a rope ladder. Then several of their men followed to look for victims to evacuate. Jack stuck his head in the command center door and yelled: "There is an escape this way." The panicky men and women ran toward him, smart people all, and readily understood what he was saying—especially when they saw heavily armed commandos of two renowned British commando units waiting for them.

"Run for your lives!" Jack yelled as he dropped back down into the doomed command center. He saw the way down to the submarine by following men and women wearing color coded scrubs and earphones. He was one of them now.

If he had to guess, Jack thought as he took the stairs two at a time, the compact submarine about to leave its underwater dock was an advanced, 21st Century version of the venerable Brazilian *Tupi* class diesel attack submarine for coastal warfare, based on the highly effective modern German HDW 209 and 214 Types. He remembered a lot of about the specifications, since he'd been involved in a German naval operation on Somali pirates a few years earlier. Her name was posted in public spaces around her interior.

BUS Nightingale had four powerful diesel engines, generating 6,100 horsepower to turn one worm gear and one propeller. She was approximately 60 m (200 ft) long. Her tapered cigar-shape was, at the beam of her outer pressure hull, about 7m (23 ft) wide. Her submerged speed was about 22 knots (40 kph, or 24 mph), while her surface speed was half of that. She could stay at sea for nearly two months, above a crush depth of half a kilometer (1,640 ft).

Typically, her type carried five officers and 22 sailors on a fully equipped cruise. Jack supposed this boat had been stripped of weapons and supply cargo to carry all these people.

As Jack approached, *BUS Nightingale* was just pulling away from her dock in a quadruple gout of black diesel smoke that lingered in the claustrophobic underground docking chamber, despite the efforts of noisily banging exhaust vents in the walls all around.

A man on the sail spotted Jack, with his purple colors, and hollered for Jack to hurry.

"What is your name?" the officer shouted.

"Lysander," Jack shouted. "Hootmon."

"Right, we were looking for you."

"Well, here I am, begorrah." Jack made a running leap, landed on the steel-grilled deck with its rubberized gripping surface, and ran as fast as he could. A hatch in the rear deck was already closed, leaving only the sail hatch for entry by now.

He climbed up a steel ladder to the top of the sail, while the officer on watch pulled him up. They clambered down into the conning tower. The officer shut the hatch and rotated its wheel shut.

Below decks, the boat was full of passengers in colored scrubs. Four merchant crewmen in nondescript jeans, soft boots, and stained shirts formed a skeleton crew.

Jack spotted Karla in the control center. She sat next to the civilian captain, and was busy issuing orders. She looked wild and lovely as ever, with her black hair flying around her ears and curving spider-mike. On a lark, she wore a Soviet-style garrison cap tilted rakishly forward.

Jack retreated to the rear, along semi-dark corridors. With about forty persons on board, the boat was crowded. He sidled his way down the machine room gangway, and found a corner in which to sit down, near the sectional hatch leading to the engine room toward the bow.

As he sat, resting, he could hear every detail of sound in the water around the boat. The metal hull transmitted and even magnified sound, not to mention the water outside under pressure at about seven fathoms or about 42 feet depth.

With her engines growling, the sub nosed slowly out of her docking bubble. She crawled down a concrete tube. Jack could feel her grating gently has her metal hull bounced against smooth concrete.

Then, the engine pitch changed as she entered open water in the bay.

"This is your chief of station speaking," came Karla's voice over the P.A. system. "The captain wishes me to welcome you on board, and promises a safe voyage. Our trip will be brief, only about thirty minutes. Once we are safely out of Barra's southern bay, on the open North Atlantic, we will board an aircraft that will bring us to Project Pollux in the Mediterranean." She added: "There are British warships in the area, and more rushing to the scene. I must ask you to be very still—do not talk, do not laugh, and do not make any noise."

A profound silence descended within the submarine.

For all the noise at dockside, her powerful diesels throbbed. As soon as she was fully submerged, she switched to batteries and truly ran silently.

As her sonar woman read out soundings, a navigator softly uttered a constant string of soundings and coordinates. These were confirmed by the map officer. The skipper frowned with concentration as the boat steered through the bay entrance and into open sea.

"No enemy vessels in sight or on radar," announced a chief in a thick brogue.

"No visual," said the first mate at the periscope station.

Nightingale whispered along just under the surface, shadowy as the blackest fish.

"Incoming aircraft," said the sonar woman.

"Special Flight One calling," said the radio man.

Someone handed the captain a set of earphones. He put one side to his ear. "Aircraft, this is *Nightingale*."

"*Nightingale*, this is SF One. We see you on radar. Coming in for a landing."

"We'll be waiting for you." With that the captain handed back the earphones and took a seat in his throne chair. Men and women around him quietly and tersely guided the boat into the pre-planned configuration running south-southwest in the general direction of Ireland.

Overhead, Jack heard a distant thundering sound that grafted itself onto the throbbing of the sub's four diesel engines, the wet and oily turning of her long worm gear in its grease-packed shaft, and the whirring of the propellers outside in the dark, cold waters of night.

The submarine rocked wildly for a moment as the rescue plane set down on the water almost directly above her sail.

"All passengers, prepare to transfer," said M. L. Sombra. "We will be exiting through the main hatch on the after deck. Deposit your earphones in the container as you reach the gangway up. You will not need the phones again."

Everything had been planned to the least detail—except his substitution for Lysander. Perhaps these eagle-eyes would not notice that he was slightly taller and lighter than Lysander.

Jack grew beads of sweat. Should he try to hide here indefinitely? Should he try to hijack the submarine? Of course not—those were silly options. He could have escaped with the Special Services men on the island much more easily. No, he had to see this through. Karla might spot him. That was nearly certain. It was a risk he'd have to take. He rose, and joined the queue of men and women in colorful scrub tops who were filing toward the rear of the boat.

He averted his gaze as he walked through the command center. Karla, or Sombra, or whatever her name was, sat on a chair beside the captain's, and gave more directions than the captain did. She was clearly in charge, and too busy to notice Jack.

As the line sidled down a narrow central corridor, Jack overheard conversation about the next big thing that puzzled him. It would take several De Havilland Twin Otters, or comparable float planes, to haul all these people off. But only one plane had landed—a massive one, judging from the engine noise and vibrations.

Nightfall at Kisimul

The evacuation of some forty technicians, abandoned by Dr. Night and intended for a watery death, required several squads of elite Special Air Services (U.K. Army) and Special Boat Services (Royal Navy) commandos.

It was hurried, desperate work, lifting the men and women one by one. They threw aside their white lab coats, and either climbed up the rope ladder, or were lifted by mountaineering ropes.

For the most part, two or three human beings at a time flew upward. Strong arms lifted them onto the grass. Other men, dressed in fatigues, and having thrown aside every ounce of extraneous equipment—guns, coils of rope, web gear, back packs, fanny packs, and even helmets—guided the running specialists along partially moonlit paths to a small squadron of waiting inflated military boats and commandeered civilian craft.

Over a period of fifteen minutes, several boats chugged away on powerful motors. They were laden with passengers, whose scared faces looked pale in the moonlight as they stared back toward the ominous castle.

The last dozen live ones came up the hatch as the first set of prepositioned dynamite charges went off. The noise was deafening.

The underground corridors filled with flat, bitter smoke.

The air became gray and translucent.

"Up up up!" shouted the last boat master.

The final passenger climbed up the ladder, and ropes dropped to take up the three SAS men left in the corridor below. Each held his rope, and rose, his mates pulled overhead.

In the last fleeting second, they glimpsed the end of Project Castor.

Rows of charges exploded in reddish-yellow sparks amid thick black smoke.

The very granite foundations of Kisimul rocked.

The terrified men, and their rescuers above, barely had time to haul ass together toward the last waiting navy speed boat.

A cloud of dust and smoke hung over the black island.

But bedrock held, as it had for tens of thousands of years. Castle Kisimul would live to see another day—many more days, or even centuries.

The commandos' last glimpse was of the plate glass portholes imploding, and sea water rushing in like a circle of Niagaras all around. Thundering greenish-white foam, laden with ripped kelp and stunned sea life, smashed over the fragile control equipment, pulverizing everything as massive waves crashed about the central underground dome. The men did not wait to see the former halls of Dr. Night become haunted underwater grottoes beneath the ghostly walls and parapets of Innse Kisimul. Soon, fishes would be swimming and nesting down here, where humans had once worked over their computer stations.

Without loss of life, the abandoned staff were rescued and taken to the Pier Street square. There, a series of large Royal Navy Merlin helicopters of the Fleet Air Arm took the survivors and their rescuers away. One by one, a series of Anglo-Italian built AgustaWestland AW101 Merlin choppers set down, picked up, and lifted off in the direction of an aircraft carrier some 100 km (60 miles) northwest of Barra. Each chopper could hold a combination of either up to 45 standing passengers, or up to six U.S. or short tons of equipment. Brawny young troops boarded the rescued workers first, sent away several choppers loaded with gear, and finally clambered on board the last flights themselves.

Within thirty minutes, except for the drifting dust heading out to sea from Castlebay, it looked as if nothing had happened. The market square was empty except for a few cars parked along the peripheries.

Many house lights had flicked on around the hills above the bay, as the explosions wakened people. The helicopters made plenty of racket, but then sea rescue operations were a familiar element in island life, and the lights soon went back out. There would be plenty of rattle and tattle in the local stores and taverns in the morning—no need to waste good nighttime sleep.

The last chopper pounded away, northward, under a veiled partial moon.

Another of Barra's mysteries thus joined the ages, and who knew what tall tales would be told over pipe and brew in taverns like the Kiltoch arms, by retired old sailors who had not yet been born today.

Aboard BLUM Flight One

As far as Jack knew, the age of flying boats was long past. The difference between a float plane and a flying boat was that the latter were far larger than any plane taking off or landing on built-in pontoons under the wings. A flying boat's fuselage, on the underside, was like a boat's hull, complete with a slight keel and a huge bull-nose on which it landed or cruised on water.

He heard the hatch open overhead, further down, and felt a cool sea wind rush through the corridor. Dozens of voices *oo*ed and *aa*ed at the fresh smell. Then a collective *oooo* passed down the line. From what he could gather in snatches of whispered conversation, the huge object wallowing adjacent to the submarine was a genuine flying boat.

He clambered out onto the deck, under a clear, starry night sky. To the northeast lay a bank of clouds, enshrouding the Outer Hebrides. Ireland lay somewhere west over the horizon. A few scattered islands spread across the eastern horizon, visible mainly for peaks of guano on their exposed high points. Those would be the trailing end of the Barra island chain.

Looming on the starboard side was a plane unlike any Jack had ever seen, but he remembered reading about it. The BE-200 was a multi-purpose Russian aircraft manufactured for the venerable Beriev Aircraft Company. The company had been founded in Stalinist Russia, and was approaching its century mark. Its various revolutionary designs had broken various air records, and received many globally recognized awards.

A totally articulated, flexible ladder—like one of those rope ladders over jungle chasms in adventure movies—stretched between stanchions on the deck, and the side cargo hatch of the great plane. Jack joined the column as it swung and bobbed across the chop just six feet below. He heard gasps from people before and behind him, and understood why when cold splashes of water crawled up his trouser legs and soaked his shirt.

The machine sitting on the water nearby was magnificent in every way. The BE-200 was painted black, like the night, with reflective silvery markings as required by international law. On the tail fin was the BLUM logo—circle, earth, eye-nazar, Medusa. The markings glittered like cold steel in partial moonlight. Her nose was long and pointed, more like a rocket's than one of those ancient Blohm und Voss flying boats of World War II with their high, blunted, impossibly large snouts recalling dinosaurs.

The BE-200, in its latest incarnation, was a 21st Century wonder machine. The plane was designed to carry up to 72 passengers, as shown in the long row of windows on each side. Towering above its long fuselage were the wings.

On each wing was a turbofan engine as big as full-size furniture vans. Under each wing hung a large, torpedo-shaped pod carrying extra fuel.

Her length and wingspan were each 33m (108 feet). That made her more than half the spread of an Airbus A-330 jet passenger plane. Like a passenger jet, the Beriev's flight range was continental—more than 1,600 miles, or 2,575 km. It was designed to leap across the sixteen time zones of the former Soviet Union, either carrying cargo or passengers, or as a hospital ship of 30 stretchers, or as a fire fighting plane capable of landing on lakes and soaking up twelve tons of water in fourteen seconds to drop on forest fires.

Now, the vast aircraft sat high on the sea, upon her boat-like hull. Like all flying boats, this hull design tapered quickly into an aerodynamic airstream fuselage. When her passengers were aboard, and she was low to her Plimsoll marking, she would be a sight to behold. And she was.

As Jack watched from a window seat, the submarine silently disappeared under the waves nearby. The boat would slowly diesel its way hundreds of miles to the same destination, but arrive days later.

A red light message board inside the plane ordered all passengers to buckle up—in Cyrillic letters. No flight attendant came out to make a pretty little pantomime for safety. In the pouch on the back of the passenger seat before him, Jack found a little blanket folded into a square, a barf bag, and a plastic-coated book of safety instructions as well as aircraft performance specifications.

The plane's powerful turbofan engines revved up to earsplitting noise levels.

The aircraft began to roll, so to speak. Actually, it became a giant motor boat.

Looming like a full-sized passenger airliner, she roared across the North Sea leaving a 100 meter-long wake of white turbulence. Reaching a takeoff speed of just over 220 kph (137 mph), she rose steadily. Like a powerful horse in harness—pulling a heavy wagon without effort—she climbed at 13 meters (43 ft) per second. Her flaps tilted at an extreme 20 degrees in the hands of two cowboys piloting. She rolled upward and pitched to the port side at such startling angles that Jack's stomach rose in his gullet. Her passengers turned white and hung on for dear life.

Must be Russian or German pilots, Jack thought. *They fly as they drive on European highways.*

The aircraft passed through a high cloud deck and leveled off at 8,000 m (26,000 ft), traveling due southeast at 550 kph (340 mph), under starlight in clear heavens.

Jack kept his face down as Sombra passed through the aisle and disappeared in the cockpit area.

The P.A. system crackled, and Dr. Night spoke: "Welcome aboard. Thank you for a job well done on Barra, and I look forward to an even more exciting collaboration with each of you on our new destination: The island of Vulcano in the Mediterranean. It is off the coast of Sicily and the Italian peninsula. Until then, happy flying."

Jack sat squirming in his seat. On the one hand, he was happy to be alive, and to have thus far escaped the clutches of Sombra. On the other hand, he wanted to do something. He consoled himself with the knowledge that neither Sombra nor her employer knew Lysander was dead, and that Jack had taken his place. He still had the phone, and no doubt Rector and Claire were tracking him via the GPS module inside. A bead of sweat prickled under his collar—although, perhaps, Dr. Night was on top of that as well as all else.

Beside Jack sat a sleeping man, who looked as if he might be Latin American, judging by the Indio shape of his upper lip and long nose. As the man snored, Jack noticed that he had a cell phone in the pocket of his smock.

Gingerly, Jack extracted the phone and eased out onto the aisle. The middle-aged woman on the end seat was curled over, fast asleep as well. Jack casually strode back to the toilets. Both were available, so he picked one and closed the door behind him. In the narrow space with bowl, sink, and mirror, he first relieved himself. Then, leaning against the amenities tray with its tissues, hand soap, and other small amenities on folded white towels, he flipped open the clamshell. Using his own phone was foolhardy. This might do nicely. He dialed a number and waited for a response on the other side of the world.

"Elmer's Pizza," came a young woman's voice."

"This is Pathfinder," Jack said. "I'm starving to death. Can I order the works?"

"Let me see if the chef is in. Yes, he is."

Rector picked up. "Mr. Badliner, we've been waiting for your order."

"Well, I'm so hungry it feels like I'm flying to Italy."

"What will you be having with that signal we got?"

"I'll take a large Vulcano, with the works—pepperoni and extra tomatoes, light on the anchovies, extra olives, and heavy on the parmesan. Sicilian crust."

"We'll get that out to you as soon as possible."

"Park in front, lights off. My landlord is a jealous dog. He no like-a de pizza boy."

"I understand. We'll be careful not to disturb him. We'll call when we are close to your location, but we'll need help finding the apartment."

Jack clicked the phone shut, ending the call. He stopped to erase the call history.

He made his way back down the aisle, sidled past the woman, climbed over the Indio, and resumed his seat. It was still warm, and cozy. He slipped the cell phone back in the man's pocket.

Checking the time on his watch, Jack snuggled up against the window with one cheek on the little blanket from the seatback pouch.

As the plane droned on, Jack grew weary and slipped away in to sleep. He thought about turbofans as he drifted off. What a wonderful, efficient invention. In most jets, the propulsion created from burning fuel pushes the plane forward, so that air is forced into the intake at the front of each engine. This air is then compressed, accelerated, mixed with fuel, lit on fire, and blown out the back. Much more efficient if you put a powerful fan in front to suck air in at higher speed, cram it down the compressor's throat, and the rest is essentially the same—except now you can build a slightly smaller jet engine in back, and burn less fuel. *Wonderful*....

In the midst of his snooze, Jack felt the urge to sneeze.

He rumpled his nose in the dark, but couldn't quite sneeze. Nor could he make the explosive sensation in his upper nose go away. As he opened his eyes in the dark, without moving, he saw what was causing his sinus distress. It was a fresh pillow, just taken out of its hypoallergenic plastic bag, and covered with allergens.

Jack's sneeze went away as a bath of acid churned in his stomach.

Inches from his face was a large black gun in a dark brown hand.

There was a generously large silencer on the muzzle.

Jack felt his eyes grow big as saucers in terror. He felt as if acid had been poured into his gut and was filling up the insides of his legs. He clutched the arm rests and prepared to die.

The black, beautiful female flight attendant holding the gun pressed the pillow against the face of the Indio, pressed the muzzle into the pillow, and pulled the trigger.

P'p.

Everyone in the passenger section slept blissfully on, except for Jack, who was terrifyingly awake, and the man beside him, who was tragically dead.

The African woman wore a crisp blue and brown uniform with jaunty cap over one eye, and gleaming brass wings on the front corner of the cap. She reached around and stealthily extracted the cell phone from the man's pocket.

She went away.

Two goons in black suits appeared. They lifted the corpse out of its seat, and carried him away.

The flight attendant returned with a small bucket and a sponge. She had now donned yellow rubber gloves from the galley toward front.

She pushed the pillow against Jack's face.

Jack wondered if he should kill her before she killed him.

"Sleep," she murmured to him, "sleep, darling, everything is just fine."

Jack lay frozen, unable to see much. He could smell cordite in the pillow. In a pinch he might have used the bullet hole to breathe if tried to smother him. He heard her sponging...wiping...squeezing...sponging...wiping....squeezing...

The rhythm of her cleaning almost put him to sleep.

After five minutes, she pulled the pillow away and slipped a fresh one in his place. "There you go, sleepy head. Sleep on, darling, you are in dreamland."

Jack pretended to have a slight apnea event as he turned his back toward her, and the dead man, and faced the window. Snoring and snorting softly, he clutched the pillow with both hands. Moving it to his left cheek, he puffed it up between himself and the window. For a second, he saw the woman holding the bucket with her gloved hands, and a goon standing behind her, aiming the silenced gun at Jack.

A dark man in a black suit with black gloves, built like a steel girder with cross piece, sidled in. The steel man easily manhandled the Indio as if he were drunk. With the dead man draped over one shoulder, he sidled back out without waking the woman on the end.

Jack stopped looking through a corner of one eye. He squeezed his eyes shut, squirmed to look as if he were getting more comfortable, and pretended to be asleep.

When he next peered through slitted eyes, two minutes later, they were all gone.

The empty seat next to him smelled faintly of Happi-Kleen, with faint undertones of chlorine and fresh scent.

About an hour later, Jack had to go again.

The woman on the end had put her armrest down, and was happily snoring on a pillow. Her face hung over the seat on her left, where Mr. Indio had just been murdered.

Jack yawned and feigned absolute innocence as he strolled back to the john.

Along the way, he glanced at dozens of sleepy or sleeping faces. Among them, he spotted the two men in black, who ignored him as he ignored them. He'd just as soon (or goon?) not tangle with them tonight. The flight attendant, a tall black woman, sat on a stool at the back. He looked at her. She looked at Jack. He prepared to run. She nodded languidly and smiled. Jack smiled back and ducked into the john.

When he came out a few minutes later, the woman had her back to him, and was deep in an animated conversation with another flight attendant—this one a pale blonde with almond eyes and round cheeks, who might be Russian or Finnish.

Jack sidled down the aisle. He stepped over an ankle here, a foot there. Every passenger on a long flight likes to stretch his legs. Nothing to it. He glanced back and saw that the two flight attendants were not watching him. Neither were the two goons, who sat back in their seats with earphones on and eyes closed, perhaps listening to the latest installment of Azerbai-Johnny and his Central Asian Rollickin' Fools, or some such stirring soul food for men who help killer stews dispose of dead Guatemalan physicists—*whatever*.

As Jack moved down the aisle, he spotted two familiar looking heads in a pair of seats on the aisle side, a few rows ahead of his own. The aisle seat itself was free. In the middle seat was the little blonde he'd seen on Dr. Night's latest game show—Tissy Fître. Beside her was a larger, older, grayer head, that of Louis Cartouche, inventor of the Cosmic Douche, or whatever he called his Orbital Sniper Technology.

Casually, not knowing what to expect, Jack leaned over the empty seat. Tissy looked up with blue eyes and a guilty look. Poor thing, she looked half-blind, like someone who needed to wear glasses but was too vain. Cartouche himself looked ravaged—now that was interesting. Why was he all gray and dripping sweat, like someone who had been given money for mom's medicine, but spent it on a lot of candy instead. "I admire your work."

"Thank you." Cartouche looked as though he wished Jack would go away.

"I'll just rest for a few minutes," Jack said as he sat next to Tissy. She shrank from him. Cartouche put an arm protectively around her.

"Long flight," Jack said. "Have you been back to the toilet? It's quite modern for an old Stalinist plane. Where do you suppose Dr. Nihil got a hold of this thing?"

Cartouche shook his head.

"We were about to doze off," Tissy said primly.

Jack nodded. "Me too. Long flights like this just kill me. I like to stretch my legs. I'll go back where I belong in a moment. Say, aren't you Mr. Cartouche? I saw you on the TV with Dr. Nail's pop show. Nice music, huh? You must be—."

"Tissy Fître," she said in a soft voice, dragging one lip over the other as she spoke. So cute—and she was probably as much a cold hearted killer as Sombra. Jack fully expected that, the minute Dr. Night gave the high sign, she'd pull the plug. Maybe have the stewie come back with her pillow and that gun.

"Nice to meet you," Jack said. "Say, Cartouche, are you okay?"

Louis Cartouche looked a sight from hell.

Tissy put a hand protectively over his hand. "Louis is not feeling well."

Cartouche fairly sobbed. "What I suffer from, I wish I could talk to my priest about."

"I'm sorry—I haven't had Holy Orders," Jack said. "Could it be flu? Or guilt?"

Tissy gently slapped the hand she was protecting. "What's bothering you, darling?"

Cartouche nodded. "Mister, I feel trapped. I take it you are not a fan of Dr. Night either?"

Jack took a huge chance. "Public enemy number one. Keep smiling so nobody will notice us. Do you want out?"

Cartouche nodded miserably, while Tissy clung to him. "We want to get married," she said. "We want to escape."

"Miss Tissy, I thought you were an Alecto."

"In training," she said, "but I failed my first big test."

"Oh?"

"I was supposed to kill Louis before we left Barra. But I fell in love with him, and want us to run away together. I failed, and now D. Night will deal with both of us when we get to Vulcano."

"Honestly," Jack said, "they are so much fun. I saw them murder the man sitting next to me less than an hour ago."

"They are taking their time with us," Cartouche said.

Tissy said: "When he pulled the plug on Castor, their need for Louis was finished. Maybe they need him as a consultant for Project Pollux."

"If they didn't, you'd both be dead already. My name is Lysander Black. I am a secret agent for Camelback—rivals of Anaconda, to whom you entrusted your machine before BLUM stole it."

"What a mistake it has all been," Louis said. "I am a miserable fool. If I am going to die, at least I had the most happy hours of my life with my little darling." He raised her hand in both of his, like a precious bird, and kissed it several times. Tissy moved her free arm across her little full bosom, and laid a soft, caramel hand over his upper arm.

Jack said: "I'll help you if I can, but I need to know what's going on. Where are we going?"

Cartouche glanced around in fear. "We can only speak for a few minutes, and then you have to return to your seat before anyone notices. Lysander, is it?"

"Yessir." They shook hands. Tissy offered a firm paw, and Jack shook it too. "Help is on the way. We'll do our best to extricate you."

Cartouche said: "As far as I understand, Dr. Night has Pollux—the main OST unit now that he's eliminated Castor—on an island called Vulcano."

"We've gotcha covered," Jack said to save time. "I know a fair bit about the Med, too. I have a Ph.D. and teach Classics as well as ancient Roman topology—the rocks, the docks, the whole nine blocks of the imperial capital."

"How wonderful," Tissy said admiringly.

"I enjoy it, Jack said."

"We must talk sometime when all this is over," said Louis.

"Let's make it over then as soon as we can," Jack said. "What's this main unit thing?"

Cartouche said: "When I invented the killer satellite concept, I knew I would have to offer it—clandestinely, because it's not the kind of thing you advertise on Roberto's List online. So I devised it so one needs two compatible units that co-processed their programs as well as their encrypted keys. That's how I sold it to Anaconda. In fact, the chief engineer on the project for Anaconda is George Blechstein, an Afrikaans or Dutch-speaking South African. He is Dr. Night, or at least his voice is."

Jack whistled softly. "So he's a traitor, working within Anaconda, while moonlighting as Today's Most Horrible Man on Earth."

Tissy gave a fleeting, teary smile.

Cartouche nodded. "Blechstein forwarded a million $US to my bank in Montreal, in return for my final plans on both machines. "

"What's the next step, Louis? How can we stop him?"

"That is usually a death warrant. Once the Capricorn satellite reached a stable orbit, Dr. Night lost interest. He no longer needs Castor, and he no longer needs me. Things that are extraneous are a liability to him. Like myself and Tissy now."

"So he can just operate the single unit on Vulcano, without needing the other?"

"Right, and it's under Vulcano, not on it. You know he prefers all things Underground."

"Yes. Okay, hang in there." Jack extended his hand. Cartouche shook it in a strong, if damp, grip. Sweat continued rolling down his gray features. Tissy added her hand, as if they were the Three Musketeers.

"Mr. Cartouche—" Jack said.

"—Louis—"

"Louis, consider me to be your priest. You have just confessed your sins, and sincerely offered an act of contrition, and I bless you and forgive it all. You can die in peace now, but Tissy and I would prefer you live happily ever after together."

"Or die together, if must be," she said with gusto and determination.

"Tissy, tsk tsk, you must never talk like that. Bad girl." Jack touched her forehead with his thumb in what he thought was probably a good priestly gesture. *Every day is Ash Wednesday on Vulcano.*

Tissy laughed—a happy gurgle of relief, a sparkle of teeth and eyes.

Cartouche still gripped Jack's hand, and pumped it all the more profusely. "Thank you, Mr. Black."

"It's actually shades of Gray."

"You give us new hope, " said Tissy sincerely.

Jack left them and returned to his seat. For a moment, he felt as if there had been hostile eyeballs on him from a distance, but it was probably just a delusion. What was not a delusion was that the first hint of dawn was breaking, and the Mediterranean lay below.

Part Four: Orbital Sniper

Aeolian Islands-Vulcano Island, seen from Lipari looking south toward Sicily

Vulcano

Forge of Vulcan

By the time the Beriev sea plane nosed down over the Balearic Islands east of Spain, and the blue Mediterranean, Jack estimated that about four hours had passed. Passengers began to wake up from their exhausted sleep.

Jack guessed that they had already dropped the spare fuel tanks over the Atlantic, off the coast of Portugal. In all, the flight had spanned 1,400 miles, over 2,300 km.

As the BE-200 circled ponderously looking for a landing site, Jack recognized a tantalizingly familiar coastline. Somewhere north along that brooding coast line lay the Bay of Naples with Mount Vesuvius stewing behind it, ready to blow again one day in a thunderous Plinian eruption casting many thousands of tons of molten stone toward the stratosphere. Today, the area looked calm. Every island on this sparkling Tyrrhenian sea had a continuous history dating to ancient Rome and far more ancient times. The waters off the coast of peninsular Italy basked in moonlight. The Tyrrhenian Sea, one of many coastal divisions of the Med, looked calm as the massive aircraft nimbly streaked down toward a landing.

The BE-200, steadily descending at a slow, smooth rate, headed south toward Sicily.

Jack remembered the Aeolian Islands off northeast Sicily, named after the god of winds.

Ah yes, Jack thought, Vulcano, chimney of the Underworld. Every so often, Vulcan cleaned his forge, according to ancient Roman mythology. Gouts of smoke flew up as Vulcan pounded on his anvil, in stories told by Roman grandmothers to big-eyed little Romans at bed time.

Whenever it went boom, sending shockwaves hundreds of miles across Italy, the ancients had made the sign of the nazar, the Evil Eye or *malocchio*. They said that Vulcan, smith among gods, was hammering in his workshop again.

Could Dr. Night be hammering at that forge this morning?

The Beriev BE-200 headed south toward Sicily, in a grand downward spiral ever closer to the blue-green water with its myriad foam caps now visible, in the same breezes that long ago blew Homeric sails across these waters, during the Bronze Age, before there was a Rome or a Greece.

Jack spotted the Straits of Messina on the eastern horizon. That was the narrow sea channel between the toe of the Italian boot, and the island of Sicily that it forever kicked westward. He sat back with his eyes closed, and let bits of history and memory drift together by association.

Sicily was the Mediterranean's largest island, followed by Sardinia, Corsica, and not in order, Crete, Cyprus, and Malta, plus thousands of large and small islands from Gibraltar to the Aegean Sea and the Black Sea.

To the immediate north of Sicily lay the Aeolian Islands, named for the Roman god of the winds. Of these eight islands, the largest was Lipari, population over 10,000, and about 37 km square or 14 square miles, as Jack recalled. He had done his Ph.D. thesis on the Forum Boarium as archaic Rome's initial commercial center, and along with the Aventine wharves, her first exterior window on the larger world.

He'd had done copious research on the islands from Sicily to the French coast. He could visualize a map in his head, and the other names came to him. The more he could remember now, the better off he'd be—and he had nothing better to do while waiting to land..

Jack sat buckled in, with his hands folded, and racked his memory for information—between his study of CIA country books, and his Classical studies. He remembered the eight little Aeolian Islands as forming a Y whose foot pointed south toward Sicily, and whose eastern or right arm pointed toward the mainland of the Italian peninsula. The islands were small, but well known, especially to the tourist trade and glamour set.

On the left arm of the Y were Alicudi at the top, and southeast of it, Filicudi.

On the right arm, from left to right running northeast, were Panarea, Basiluzzo, and Stromboli—the latter being one of the world's most famous active volcanoes. Along with Vesuvius at Naples, up the coast, and Etna in the center of eastern Sicily, Stromboli was one of the world's most active volcanoes. In fact, just as the sliding tectonic plates around the Pacific created a huge ring of fire extending around the Pacific, so there was a line of fire extending from Sicily up the coast, through Naples, to the Rome area and slightly beyond. Italy's volcanoes, and copious underground thermal and lava activity, were caused by friction between the African and Eurasian tectonic plates—the enormous crackers floating atop the molten rock soup deep under the earth's crust, which appeared to ordinary mortals as the continents.

At the crux of the Y lay Salina, which had the second largest land area at about 27 sq km or 16 sqm, and 4,000 souls.

South of Salina lay Lipari, the largest island at about 38 sq km or about 10.5 sq miles. It had a population of over 10,000 that doubled in the tourist season to over 20,000.

Vulcano formed the foot of the Y. Small as it was, it was the third largest Aeolian island, lying south of Lipari, and just 27 km (16 miles) from the Sicilian coast.

There were four other very small islands whose names Jack could not recall.

Vulcano, the third largest of the Aeolian Islands, was well on a line extending from mighty Etna, a few hundred km south, through mighty Stromboli, a few miles north of Vulcano.

"Good morning," said Dr. Night over the public address system. "I trust you napped well. I want to welcome you to the Black Umbrella headquarters for Project Pollux. We won't need the names Gemini or Castor any longer. With our bird safely in orbit, and Castor gone, we can focus all our energies on the live controls for Pollux, which are underground in an ancient Roman gallery on Vulcano. If you have any worries about the volcano, don't. Our facility is inside an old, abandoned

NATO secret air defense base. It is inside the mountain, and thickly reinforced with concrete and steel."

"Briefly, Vulcano is a small island with one of the region's most violent histories. Although it is only 21 square kilometers, or 16 square miles, it contains several volcanic cones, including a baby that erupted in 183 BCE, and is called Vulcanello. You may recall that nearby Stromboli and Etna remain two of the most violent and active volcanoes on earth, and the extremely violent Vesuvius last erupted in 1944.

"The largest volcano on the island is Fossa, whose cone today towers to 500 meters. That's half a kilometer, or one third of a mile, or roughly 1,600 feet. Fossa is still considered active, giving off constant smoke and gas, though it last had a stratovolcanic eruption 1888-1890.

"Vulcano gives its name to the world's volcanoes, named after Roman Underworld god Vulcan, the Smith, same as the Greek Hēphaistos. The ancient Romans had mining and lumbering stations here, but not a real town to speak of. The island was a rich source of sulfur, as well as alum compounds used for laundries, cosmetics, and many other purposes. The island's rich volcanic soil was in those days covered with trees, which the Romans harvested. Over the centuries, little more has come of Vulcano. There were some vinyards and mines, but they were wiped out in the eruptions of 1888 to 1890. In recent generations, it has been a tourist resort reached from Lipari or Sicily. It has healthful sulfuric hot springs, mud baths, and a few luxurious hotels. People come from Lipari and Sicily to enjoy fine cuisine, healthful bathing, medicinal drinks and potions, massage, cool night air for healthy sleeping—in short, a wonder world of Mediterranean delights."

Descending at a steady, smooth landing speed of 220 kph (137 mph), the aircraft became once again an oversized motorboat leaving a beautiful white wake in the morning sunlight.

Sombra's voice replaced Blechstein's on the p.a. system. "Good morning, ladies and gentlemen. I trust you slept well on our chartered Beriev BE-200 aircraft. After dropping us off, the wonderful pilots will fly their craft back to the Black Sea, where it performs tourist charter service along the northern coast between Istanbul and Trebizond in Turkey, plus famous places like Yalta, Sebastopol, and many others. That's a few thousand miles east of here, and not on our plate today. Let's give our wonderful flight crew a hand, shall we?"

Laughter and applause rippled across the passenger deck.

Jack raised one eyebrow while clapping, as he glanced at the still damp spot where Mr. Indio had breathed his last nostril whistle during the darkest hours before merciful dawn.

"Welcome to Vulcano. Naturally, you must not speak with any local or tourist not part of our mission. You should always expect enemy secret agents to be in our midst. Report any suspicious activity immediately, so that we can deal with it before it becomes a threat to Dr. Night and the Black Umbrella mission. Thank you, and we'll be chatting again soon."

Jack thought: Dr. Night's idea of a chat is he does all the talking, and listeners either live or die according to his whims. Love those downtrodden masses!

If there were any fishing boats on the sea, they were far away. The pilots had chosen an opportune spot to set down as unnoticed as possible.

The giant aircraft rested on the water, out of sight of either islands or land.

The plane's turbofans feathered in their nacelles, adding an oily tinge to a fresh morning wind that ruffled hair and collars.

The passengers disembarked on an island ferry that chugged in close from Vulcano.

As soon as the last passenger went down the ramp to *MV Hercules*, men on board the ship pulled back the gangway, and the Beriev started taxiing away.

Passengers crowded the railings to watch her take off. She was, indeed, Jack thought, like an enormous motor boat leaving a long white wake that rocked the ferry.

On maximum thrust, the BE-200 raised her long nose into the air, and started climbing. In five minutes, she was entirely out of sight.

The ferry chugged toward Vulcano. Its engines were the only major sound now, except for the screaming of gulls who accompanied her.

On the vessel's high and low outer decks, and two lower decks, passengers refreshed themselves in the loos. They sought fresh Italian coffee and cellophane-wrapped pastries, courtesy Dr. Night.

Jack wandered about anonymously, looking for opportunities to get a message out to Rector or Claire, without getting anyone else killed.

He spotted Cartouche and Tissy clinging together on the bow deck, but stayed away from them. They were in enough trouble, and their huddled posture signaled as much.

Jack was tempted to send a message that Dr. Night was George Blechstein of Anaconda, and then throw the phone into the drink, but he hoped Camelback could continue tracking him wherever inside Vulcano BLUM was conducting the Pollux project.

Someone else had a similar idea.

The vessel appeared to be crewed by a half dozen men in Italian style sailor uniforms. They wore white bellbottom trousers, white tunics with dark blue collar trim, white (unbilled) saucer cap with dark blue band on which was embroidered, in gold, *MV Vulcani*. Jack spotted three officers as well, in white uniforms with black-billed, white-topped saucer caps, and black epaulets with gold piping.

Jack saw an opportunity when the complement were all on the top deck. In a small, off-limits corridor below decks, he read the legend Uffizio. That was an administrative office, probably belonging to the officers. It was locked, but Jack used a fire extinguisher to smash the shining brass handle. Once inside, he went straight for the desk phone, which was half-buried in papers, cardboard boxes, log books, and other incidentals. He got an outside line, cut through the crypto layers, and reached Claire.

"Jack!"

"No time to chat. Dr. Night is George Blechstein of Anaconda." He must confirm that they were tracking him via his phone GPS. It was almost entirely passive, only emitting a faint signal when pinged by satellite, and should not give him away for a while, at least. His next sentence was going to be "Location is Vulcano. Are you tracking?" He never got that far. As he finished the first sentence—as the last wind came out of his mouth—someone hit him over the back of the head. He pitched forward into darkness.

Sombra.

Minutes later, as he started to regain consciousness, he heard her voice. The phone cord bound his hands behind his back. The fire extinguisher, which he'd used to force the lock, and which she'd used to bash his head, lay nearby under a desk.

"Jack, you amaze me with your ability to stay alive and keep interfering." She straddled his back, with her black-clad knees on his shoulders. Lying face down, he was under her control. "I threw your phone overboard, Jack. Consider this: the corporate powers know that if anything happens to this project—say, commandos coming on shore—we will release a ton of highly radioactive materials over one of the world's busiest megalopolitan corridors—say, the U.S. northeast from Washington to New York City to Boston. Or maybe in Europe from London to Paris. Take your pick--tens of millions of lives, first immediately, then long term from cancer. Your superiors can't stop us, Jack."

"There is always room for a deal," Jack said.

"Oh yes," said another voice—silky, deadly, masculine—Dr. Night.

Jack groaned. "Blechie…and I do mean *blechh*…"

"Mr. Gray, you are a pain in the arse," Dr. Night said.

Sombra slapped Jack painfully across the cheek with a hard palm.

"I see you dug yourself another gopher hole here," Jack said.

"Let's not waste time on idle talk," Dr. Night said to Sombra.

Jack dreamed of sunshine and blue skies. What he would not give to lie on a deck chair maybe in Monaco, just above the beach, on the patio of a five-star hotel—reading news on his digital pad, while a freckled redhead in a bikini sauntered out holding drinks…tiny umbrellas topping the frosty, pearling, perspiring, dripping glasses…

"I agree," Sombra said to Dr. Night, as her black-gloved hand descended with a needle in it. A drop of spray flew from it. "Good night, Mr. Gray. Sweet dreams."

Jack could still see that mauve little paper parasol atop his—oh, make that a Campari and soda—before he passed out as the needle bit into his skin, drove down into a vein, and released a cloud of narcotics into his fast-pumping red life stream oddly and delightfully the color of Campari.

Vulcan's Forge

Descent into Avernus

Jack Gray awoke with a hangover and a pain in the neck.

At first, he could not move.

He was in the Underworld—ancient Roman Avernus, 'below,' usually reached through the secret cave near the deserted ancient Etruscan town of Cumae on the mainland of Italy, not far north of Naples. Hell as a burning place was a modern invention. Inferno referred not to heat, but to a place underneath. Hell was deep, absolute, frozen cold similar to that of outer space. The icy hell of Dante's Inferno had been a place of horror and darkness in which the shades of sinners—cardinals, princes, popes, gluttons, sex maniacs—suffered endless loops of shame, fear, and pain. It was already known to the Augustan poet Virgil thousands of years ago.

Jack had been thrown into Vulcan's forge.

Slowly, he got his aching body to move.

He was in a cell—no, a prison—with bars all around. There were a dozen cells in all. Half were on either side of a central corridor, half of the cells empty.

As he massaged the back of his neck, he managed to pull his feet close and sit up on a hard mattress. The sheets spread over it were clean. The rooms down here—inside Vulcano Island, he presumed—were clean though age-worn. Someone had refinished the raw cave walls by slathering them liberally in stucco and then whitewash over that. Salt and water stains ran down the walls where an older, perhaps 18th or 19th

Century finish still clung to older sections. The lighting overhead was muted—bioluminescent. Most of the long, cigarette-shaped bulbs had either burned out or been twisted into the off position.

The dim lighting was helpful to his traumatized nervous system.

"You are awake," a man's voice said. Someone—another Lysander-type brute—shuffled close carrying a tray. "Here's some coffee, toast, jam. Things to perk you up." The guard's voice sounded Slavic. He was a muscular person, in his 30s, with a round head. His head was scarred, like an old battered bed knob, with graying golden-brown teddy bear hair on top. *Igor.*

With a loud clang, Igor unlocked a steel feeding tray and laid it down within the door—just a small, crescent-shaped shelf. On this he placed Jack's breakfast and left.

Jack shook as he staggered toward the cell gate, retrieved the tray, and set it on the bunk beside him. He gingerly eased down some of the hot coffee, black, and welcomed its lava-like course through the deep crevices of his alimentary system. Slices of light pumpernickel with butter and apricot jam helped supply sugar and starches to his starved body.

As Jack ate, Igor returned and tossed a packet of headache medicine on the steel shelf.

Dr. Night's voice whispered in the cell from a hidden speaker. "Here you go. For your headache. I should warn you, Mr. Gray. Any more stunts, and you will be fed to the sharks off the island."

"Why am I being held?"

"A ridiculous question, from a ridiculous man. You won't waste any more of my time. Consider yourself warned. Oh, and don't try to commit suicide when you tire of cell life. I need you and your fellow guests as bargaining chips with those corporate Neanderthals."

With an audible click, the connection went dead. Jack looked up, all around, as he ate. He noticed a wire coming out of the wall, just under the ceiling. It ran to a steel plate the size of a book, bolted to the wall high up, from which a small spotlight, a speaker, and a camera protruded. Munching on his toast, with a blanket around his shoulders, Jack slowly paced up and down as far as his 15'x12' cell would allow. Sure enough, the camera swiveled on its neck to follow him.

He sat down and finished eating. As he ate, he noticed that a prisoner across the aisle had hung up a faded blanket for privacy.

In a cell in the far corner slept two miserable figures huddle together on one cot: Tissy and Cartouche.

Jack placed his tray on the shelf so Igor could take it away. *Good citizen*, he thought, *will impress the management; might get off after twenty years for good behavior. Yeah, fat rotten chance.*

Jack held the bars with his hands high, and leaned his head tiredly against the steel bars. Boredom would be his death sentence here.

It was up to Camelback Consortium to throw the full power and skills of the North American Treaty Organization (NATO) and the Pan-European Treaty Organization (PETO) to work stopping Dr. Night and Black Umbrella. But dammit, they were stymied by the threat to kill tens of millions of people. That prevented some elite fighting force—say, the French Foreign Legion, the Italian Carabinieri, or the European Strike Force—from landing here like D-Day and taking out this crackpot in under five minutes. No, Blechstein was a chess player. He had his opponents in check, and was moving toward mate.

As he stood at the bars, a figure stirred opposite, behind the blanket.

Jack hoped the man spoke English and was a good conversationalist.

"Good morning, Sir," Jack said. "Nice day, sort of."

The figure moved away from the blanket so he could see his cell neighbor. His eyes widened.

"Miranda."

The woman looked bleary. Dark patches around her eyes spoke of a beating, perhaps when they seized her from Pension Adler in Frankenstein.

"Are you alive, or a ghost?" he asked.

Miranda stared at him, uncomprehendingly, from cavernous eyes. She reached up and turned a fluoro so that its bluish-white light sparked to life and filled her cell. "Jack, is that you?"

"It's me—I thought you were dead."

"Why would they kidnap me and just kill me?"

"You got me." He reached down and pulled out his empty pockets. "Hoover pennants to the wind. I'm now as helpless as you are. Good idea with the lean-to."

She clutched her cell bars with grimy fingers. "I'm going crazy down here. No books to read, nothing. Not even a little music."

"It's a form of torture," Jack said. "BLUM demonstrating its love of people and the masses."

"Slogans," she said bitterly. "I've stayed sane the last few days by trying to remember the plots of Charles Dickens novels, chapter by chapter."

"I'll be doing the same, I imagine."

"I want to escape. Can you help, Jack?"

He remembered the watching cameras and microphones, and made a *shoosh* gesture with a finger over his lips.

She nodded and touched her lips similarly to signal she understood. "Well, Mr. Gray, perhaps we can play battleship."

"Good idea. I got the game for Christmas as a boy."

"You can make one up with a sheet of paper, a pencil, and a few scraps of cloth or paper for the ships."

"Give me a little time for my head to stop flashing on and off where they whacked me with a fire extinguisher. Sounds like a marvelous idea."

Down the corridor, Tissy stirred. She staggered sleepily to the free bunk in their cell, and hung a spare blanket to block all view of them—except the camera swiveling alertly over her head as she moved about. Probably went back to sleep, cuddling with Cartouche, Jack thought. What if they were a plant? What if it was one of Blechstein's tricks? Jack thought not, but was resolved to keep up his guard.

Pollux in Autumn

In his control room—another dome like that at Kisimul, but three times as large—Dr. Night ruled. As usual, he stayed out of sight except for rare appearances under a nondescript, fictitious corporate name—George Blechstein. It was actually the name of an Anaconda executive he had personally murdered on a business trip to Johannisberg a few years ago.

The real identity of Dr. Night was as elusive as his whispering voice that came from nowhere, and insinuated itself into cracks and dark corners.

His voice crackled through the air in yet another conference call to the top 1,000 corporations around the world.

"We are once again playing our exciting quiz show. Who will the next sacrificial offering be? Will it be the president of the United States, or of Canada, or of the European Union? Will it be the premier of China or the Great Elephant of Zimbabwe or the Supreme Sachem of the Copper Nations or the Lord Inca? Stick around, folks, and have fun with me."

As thousands of horrified CEOs and their staffs watched, a beautiful brunette paraded up and down in a side-slit dress displaying tanned, firm calves.

With wide smiles and round, graceful gestures, she pointed to the main prop on the set—a huge game board with squares for letters or numbers.

An unseen audience shouted rhythmically in the background: "Night! Night! Night!"

"Who will be the next sacrifice of the Underworld?"

Vulcano is a potato-shaped island, lying at an oblique northwest-southeast angle in the Tyrrhenian Sea.

Its permanent population consists of about 500 souls, who derive most of their income from tourism.

The island is about 25 km (15 miles) north of Sicily, not far from the Straits of Messina that divide Sicily from the Italian peninsula—more precisely, the toe of the boot.

Five of the Aeolian Isles—Vulcano, Lipari, and Salino, plus Filicudi and Alicudi—form a hint at a crescent shape whose curvature, if pursued with a pointing finger, leads south to one of the world's most active volcanoes—Mt. Etna, in east central Sicily.

An extension of this imaginary—or perhaps primordial and real—crescent is yet a larger crescent including Stromboli, a few dozen miles northeast of Vulcano, and Mt. Vesuvius

About 300 km (180 miles) north along the Tyrrhenian coast at Naples—and then the smaller volcanoes that ring Rome, including those in the Alban Hills and at the Sabatini caldera in southern Tuscany.

An examination for hidden patterns suggests that, millions of years ago, at least two global super-volcanoes blew at various times, probably inducing volcanic winters lasting millennia. By this conjecture, the fragmentary circles of Italy's highly volcanic coast line are hot spots along ancient clashes between the African and European plates. And Sicily, of course, at its southwest point, is only 131 miles (209 km) from the closest point in Africa—long-ago Carthage, home of Hannibal and menace to Rome—in modern Tunisia.

Vulcano itself is a composite of multiple volcanic caldera speaking of a violent past. The last eruption of the main Fossa volcano was 1888-1890.

It is surprising how close together the islands are. On misty morning or foggy evening, they resemble a flotilla of ghostly capital ships steaming toward an epochal battle among gods. From atop Fossa, hikers can look north across the luxurious hotels and yacht clubs of Porto Ponente, out over Vulcanello, and a few kilometers out see Lipari. At the same time, the hulking shadows of Salina and Stromboli can be seen on the horizon, along with lesser islands.

Seen from Lipari looking south, Vulcano looks like a collection of volcanic cones leaning against each other, covered with a green layer of peace, but mutely testifying to eons of horrific fire and violence.

While the islands have been inhabited by humans since the Old Stone Age, more than 10,000 years ago, they have been ghostly shadows along some of the major regional trade routes. The ancient Romans maintained mining and lumber towns on the island, hauling off trees, sulfur, and alum compounds.

The African and Eurasian plates abut each other for the most part along the North African coast from Gibraltar east, running through the narrowest point in the Mediterranean Sea (between Sicily and Tunisia, as mentioned), then making a northward pointer in to the Ionian Sea, almost into the Adriatic between Italy and the Balkans. From there, the fractured border swing south again in one large curve that takes it to its southernmost point roughly below Crete and the Aegean, and back up to touch the coast of Turkey in Asia Minor, and the coast of Cyprus. From there, it interacts with the Arabian Plate, and swings back around the coast of Africa.

In the 1st Century BCE, a new, small volcano exploded on the north shore of Vulcano, creating an island called Vulcanello, or little Vulcano. This island, which is the closest point to the major Aeolian Isle of Lipari, contains tourist hotels, harbor, and other accommodations for visitors from Lipari, itself a tourist destination. Vulcanello is joined to Vulcano by a rocky causeway, with a single road between the two islands along the northwestern beach.

On the south end of Vulcano are the anchorages of Scolaticci and Gelso, where traffic from Sicily more rarely lands. A single major road, with several forking branches among the forested valleys between volcanic cones, runs along the spine of Vulcano from southeast to northwest. This road winds for several miles. In the south, it runs switchback along extinct lava fields. In the north of the island, it makes a long detour around the base of the volcanic cone of Fossa. This volcano, now dormant but not extinct, occupies about a fourth of the northern hemisphere of Vulcano. All the action—hotels, discos, bars, restaurants—is at the north end as well as the add-on islet of Vulcanello, which is reached along a causeway from Vulcano.

The valleys of these islands are overgrown with trees and scrub. Not far above sea level, the dominant landscape is of tight brush littered with flint and loose tufa debris. On the slopes, and in the calderas, of the large volcanoes, the landscape is one of desolation—especially in Fossa's Gran Cratere (Great Crater),

Somewhere, deep in the guts of the island, was the command center of Project Pollux.

Like Hades (Greek, Doric, 'the Unseen'), Dr. Night ruled the underworld here. Sicily, originally land of the aboriginal Sicels, had been part Greek and part Phoenicians before the Romans came along. Another of Hades' Greek names was Plouton, god of wealth, which suited the more practical, mercenary Romans. Pluto, in Latin, became the chief god of the Roman underworld. No doubt, his hard-headed, fiscal ruthlessness appealed more to a practical man like Dr. Night, whose appetite for power and wealth was as voracious as his global ideas were grandiose, brutal, and unexpected to chieftains of the unsuspecting corporate world order.

"Who will it be?" intoned Dr. Night, while the clock ticked.

The brunette marched gorgeously and magnificently up and down the stage.

As she gestured roundly with her arms—making Flamenco-style *palomas* or doves of her hands—one by one, new letters fell into place.

Orchestral music blared softly in excited brasses.

Dr. Night knew how to stretch things out and build suspense.

The audience kept up their rhythmic, voodoo-like "Night! Night! Night!"

Meanwhile, on screens around the world, a series of images flashed and disappeared, each making way for the next to segue, sliding in from the sides, the top, or the bottom.

The presidents or premiers of the United States (Jefferson Memorial in autumn leaves);

Of Canada (Nunavut fields of snow and ice);

Of the U.K. (towers of Westminster under a gray, rainy London sky);

Of Japan (cherry blossoms around the imperial palace grounds).

And more…

"We have a loser!" Dr. Night cried out. "Give a big hand for today's target of the Underworld Game Show!"

"Night! Night! Night!" cried the feverish audience.

In orbit at 180 miles altitude, the Capricorn satellite rode steadily in orbit around the earth.

A silvery flap opened.

From the satellite's bowels, an object shot out like a cork from a champagne bottle.

It was pale white, ceramic, and shaped like a small space shuttle the size of a motorcycle.

Flying blind, guided by telemetry and GPS from the mother ship as well as signals from Vulcano and from certain mountain tops and deep forests around the world, the tiny shuttle began to glow from reentry into the atmosphere. Also tracking was Black Umbrella's new launch center on the equator, their answer to Kourou, but in the deepest jungles of the Congo.

The shuttled traveled at one mile per second—far slower than most meteors.

Its trajectory was a curve that started out steep in the thin upper atmosphere, or stratosphere (twenty to fifty km, or 12 to 30 miles).

It approached the earth's surface unnoticed by astronomical observatories and military radars, because it looked like one of the hundreds or thousands of random space rocks that burn up harmlessly in the earth's atmosphere every hour of day or night.

It leveled off to a slower descent in the lower atmosphere below six km (3.6 mi) altitude.

It entered the thick, turgid slush of the lower atmosphere, glowing like a fireball, and exploded when it dropped through the one mile high mark.

So far, it had traveled about four minutes and covered some 240 miles.

When the outer shell—the shuttle shape—shattered into unrecognizable fragments, a smaller cruise missile shape appeared at low cloud level. The inner vehicle was grayish ceramic, without markings. It contained very little metal to betray it to searchers once the mission was accomplished within the next minute.

Four tail fins popped out, pointing up, down, port, starboard. The sniper rifle wobbled a moment, then stabilized, seeking a lock on its target. A rapid exchange of data zoomed back and forth between the projectile and the Gemini satellite above. The satellite received a stream of GPS data down to a millionth of a arc-seconds accuracy in three spatial dimensions , as well as the corresponding ghost-dimensions along a time continuum. The system flashed infinitesimal mid-course corrections.

As the projectile reached a point some 250 meters (820 feet) horizontally from its target, the tip of its nose cone—the size of a coffee cup—sheared off at an oblique angle. A split second later, a bullet shot from the opening thus created. The bullet was already traveling at half a mile (2,600 ft) per second; the added explosive velocity was more for final approach guidance. Powered by the exhaust gas of the shot, the orbital sniper rifle shattered into many fine, nondescript pieces that would litter a wide area and escape detection by homicide investigators.

A split second later, as the sound of the gunshot flew over the heads of 100,000 spectators, the .50 caliber style bullet struck the torso of North Korea's Beloved Leader, instantly killing him.

The hit was catastrophic, taking the entire back of his body away in a splatter of blood, organs, vertebrae, and other detritus. His intact front side, with a fist-sized hole in the solar plexus area, crumbled to the wooden platform behind the podium, along with his limbs and head.

A scream rose from tens of thousands of fanatical followers, threatening the next world war.

"Bravo, Louis Cartouche, for creating this wonderful technology," whispered the voice of Dr. Night.

"Look up from counting your money and killing innocent middle class people, and gaze upon the new world order that makes your corporate empires obsolete.

"Black Umbrella is rising, Pollux is ascendant, and wondrous are the works of the righteous. See what imaginative thinking, forward technology, and rewarded genius can accomplish.

"I expect that you will assign 33.33% of your assets by noon tomorrow, or more signs like this will fall from orbit. After tomorrow, the figure will be 51%—an absolute, controlling majority in all of your corporations.

"As a final warning, remember that our satellite contains over a ton of highly radioactive material, not to mention deadly viruses. If it weren't for the threat of insurrection and chaos, it is clear you don't care if a million or a billion of your serfs die. Look at the hundred million your war industries slaughtered for profit during each world war alone. You have no choice but to care now, or your world will fall apart. If you force us to release these radioactive agents, we will be protected, and perhaps you will be also—but think of the chaos, the collapse of civilization, the shattering of your power base, and the emergence of your victims who will hunt you down and kill you as you cower in your shelters. In short, your money will evaporate."

Bottle in the Sea

"He's utterly insane," said Claire Lightfield.

"There is always a kernel of truth amid disinformation," said Rector. "This person, however, must be stopped." Rector was not in the habit of lowering himself to refer to a criminal as a man. A person or a creature—that would do.

Claire and Rector sat—among joint chiefs of North American Treaty Organization military, corporate, and Congressional staffs, and some thirty of their senior aides—in Sigma 2020's Situation Room Alfa.

These three dozen persons sat along the sides and ends of a very long, wide conference table. Electronic equipment sat stacked down the center, along with haphazardly situated water carafes and glasses, and many telephone land lines and other devices.

The president in rotation, Senator Bloviant, went *hem hem* and gruffled: "Ms. Lightfield, have you nothing more to offer than the obvious, that this Dr. Good-for-nothing is nutty as a fruitcake?"

"We have an agent on the ground, Senator. We were able to track him to the northern coast of Sicily before his GPS transponder went dead."

"So you don't really know if he is alive or dead?"

"That is correct."

"Lot of good that does us."

Senator Hawgbile added, while clearing his throat: "*Hem hem—gruffle gruffle*—but I understand he has put a name to Dr. Night."

Rector spoke up. "We tracked the name, Senator—dead end. An Anaconda executive named George Blechstein, from Transvaal, was murdered on a business trip in South Africa a few years ago. His body was only found two years ago. The remains were skeletal, and had been scattered by animals. Detectives from South Africa and Botswana are working the case, and we hope they will turn up some clues."

Hawgbile said: "You mean to tell me, Mr. Rector, that this Dr. Night managed to infiltrate the Anaconda organization and pose as one of their executives for the past several years?"

A representative from Anaconda spoke up. "Senator, that is all true. We only discovered the ruse a few days ago, when a senior project engineer named Blechstein failed to show up for a major corporate board meeting in Paris. Our Gamma security personnel did a check, thinking something had happened to him. In doing so, they found that the missing man's fingerprints on glasses and other objects in his office in Lagos, Nigeria did not match standard intake fingerprints from Anaconda Gamma."

"Intake…?"

"When we hired the real Mr. Blechstein twelve years ago, Senator." Gamma, they all knew, was Anaconda's security arm, equivalent to Camelback's Sigma 2020.

Claire leaned closer to Rector and whispered: "We are getting nowhere fast."

Rector raised one eyebrow a millimeter in reply, while keeping a pretend-attentive, pleasant face toward the important speakers.

"What if we nuke the whole island?" General Todstole barked. "Surprise them."

President of the United States Mrs. Helen Cameron said: "General, that will not be an option. We will solve this problem like rational, civilized adults."

President of Camelback Consortium M. A. Nifico interrupted her: "Mrs. Cameron, we will keep all options on the table. In deference to your political sensitivities, we will put General Todstole's nuclear option last in line. But I warn you—we may get there fast if we exhaust all other options."

Cameron, looking stung, clapped her mouth shut.

Nifico, the real power broker at the table, ignored her and looked around. "Any other suggestions, short of the atomic hammer?"

Rector coughed softly and said: "We're not done yet with Pathfinder. That's our agent on location—Jack Gray."

Claire backed her friend and associate immediately. "That's right. Jack Gray can be surprisingly resourceful. We are looking for some way to get back in touch with him."

"If he is alive," Senator Hawgbile barked.

"First things first," said Nifico. "Let's get our diplomats out there, smoothing feathers around eastern Asia. We'll send a low-ranking attaché to the Great and Wonderful Leader's funeral in Pyongyang. Mrs. Cameron, I trust your branch will take appropriate care of that."

"We are the best in the west," she said. "Bring on any mission, and we'll accomplish it."

Rector leaned close to Claire. "I have something to show you."

"What a bore these things always are," said Claire as she combed her dark blonde hair back into its frumpy helmet. She was in her mid-30s, and still had an attractive, athletic sort of school marm face—long, with straight lines for nose and mouth, and sympathetic gray eyes. There was something delightfully vulnerable and honest about her pale, lemonade freckles.

Rector drove as the sped along roads on which dead and dying leaves swirled. Lucky Tony, he thought—her husband, best friend, and life's love affair. There was a yin-yang balance here, in that Rector's wife was also his best friend and the great love affair of his own life. His friendship with Claire Lightfield was professional, but it extended into personal shadings. Call it fondness, he thought. Being around her was another reason to be in love with life. They had never spoken of their feelings, nor would they trespass on one another's marital trust. Things between them were just perfect as they were.

Washington never looked older or more broken, he thought, as he drove into Virginia. The city was a graveyard of slogans, promises, and betrayals. Only a complete corporate takeover, and an end to pretenses, had restored the economy. More people lived well than during the recent chaos, and most welcomed a firm new hand—as long as nobody stepped out of line.

Rector took the exit at Langley, while Claire lightly retouched her makeup.

Rector and Claire left the car to a valet at the front door of the Camelback Extension to CIA headquarters. They had checks on fingerprints, eye scans, and badges every few hundred feet. Riding up several stories in the secure, ultra-modern building, Rector led her down a wide floor of gleaming tiles. They walked past closed doors of blonde wood. The place smelled of floor polish, as well as candles from an upcoming Hallow E'en party for the employees' children.

Rector used his retinal scan, together with fingerprints and badge, to open a steel door marked top secret in red stencil letters on navy-gray.

Inside was a room stripped down room.

Rector turned lights on. "This was a forensics lab, but they moved it to CIA." He swept his hand around over empty lab benches, missing equipment, and a few abandoned glass titers. "Here is what I wanted to show you," he said.

Claire followed him around a lab bench with a tall central divider.

On a black countertop on the opposite side stood a plain glass bottle.

"That looks like a beer bottle," Claire said. It was empty, and dry. Its surfaces looked scratched. In a few places, including around the rim of the mouth, it was chipped. On its tapering neck hung a spidery metal pressure-holder, from which dangled a white glass cork that seated inside the bottle mouth with a red orange gasket.

"It is a beer bottle," Rector said. "To be precise, an empty Peroni bottle. Good Italian beer. That's a 250 ml bottle, if you care." He took a sheet of laminated paper from a drawer under the bottle. "Here's what you really want to see."

Claire read the scrawled note. "It's from Miranda Coldstream," she said. "Poor kid."

"No, we think she's still alive."

"You're kidding. That would be so wonderful. I hate losing agents."

"It happens, and it's always tragic, but this one was still alive, at least when she threw this message into the sea about a week ago. It drifted south from Vulcano, and was picked up by a fishing trawler out of Capo di Milazzo, on a little peninsula that sticks out from the northern Sicilian coast. They handed it over to the Italian coast guard, who passed it along to the Carabinieri, who passed it along to Europol, who passed it along to Interpol, and thus it came to rest in the gentle paws of Compass News, which is me. My associates high up in the Camelback Consortium of course passed a copy along to me, with instructions to share this with you."

In a pencil scrawl, made under duress on the face of a menu, was a brief note from Miranda: "Alive and well thus far. Vulcano in the Aeolians, Pollux HQ. Forget Castor, Gemini. Focus Dr. Night. Re: Fossa/"

Following this was a geographic coordinate, in metric form, using the World Geodetic System, that Claire took to be Miranda's location.

Rector already had a colored map-printout on the wall, which showed the islands nestled in a triangle formed by the peninsular and Sicilian coasts. The print was a meter-wide satellite hybrid combining visible topography (natural and man-made) with geographical grids and legal divisions.

Claire ran a fingertip across the blue sea with its whitecaps visible, and the great caldera, as well as the resort town on the opposite northern edge. "Fossa is the big volcano that is dormant, not extinct. Sounds like she is being held inside."

"I think they are under the northeast slope of the caldera—right near the coast. I have Italian police choppers and float planes from Messina reconnoitering every inch of the coastline, without hopefully being noticed. What we are after is any kind of cave inlet or other opening."

"What if he's using a submarine channel has he did at Kisimul?"

"Anything is possible."

"It's a clever setup," Claire said. "The northern end of Vulcano has two small ports, the western or Porto di Ponente, and the eastern called Porto di Levante. The setting and rising suns." She swept her fingers across the map image of the island. "There are beautiful beaches all around the island, with several docks for sailboats. Most of it is taken up by three large volcanoes."

Rector added: "And the Great Crater is still active. It still rumbles, and emits gouts of sulfurous steam from anyplace in the crater, including the upper edges."

Claire said: "Whatever noise they make will be covered up and will be thought of as fumaroles and seismic activity."

Rector grinned: "From what I hear, some of the most awesome young bodies throb to the discos along the northern region, including up into Vulcanello. There's the villa built by Stevenson over a century ago—today a tourist hotel with the Cantina Stevenson." He shook his head. "Poor Stevenson. Besides harvesting lumber, and mining the craters for sulfur and alum, as the Romans did two thousand years earlier, he thought he had a going thing with the region's most famous grape variety. He tried to grow the Malvasia grape, used to make Malmsey or Madeira wine. The volcano put an end to all such dreams in 1888-90. Now it's a secondary tourist spot after Lipari."

Claire tapped her finger on the 1,600 foot cone of Fossa, the largest and still active of the island's volcanoes. "I would bet that they also have Jack deep inside there someplace."

"We could have PETO run echo sondes on the ground, and side scan sonar on the sea shelf to look for evidence."

"But there is the time element," Claire said. "And I'm very much afraid—"

"—Yes?—"

"The corporations aren't going to sign anything over to Black Umbrella. That means the deadline will pass at noon European time tomorrow, just hours from now, and Dr. Night will dramatically up the ante."

"Meaning?"

"He will start threatening to destroy a major world population center with his dirty bomb, and I can't think of any way to stop him. It's just a question of—which greater conurbation will he choose for mass murder?"

Rector scratched his head. "There are about thirty metropolitan centers in the world with at least ten million residents. It ranges from Greater Chicago and Greater Paris around ten million, to Greater Tokyo at 35,000,000. He could pick any one of them."

She rattled off the names she remembered from the top of the city populations: "Mexico City, London, Tehran, Beijing, Cairo, Rio de Janeiro..."—not in that order, but part of the list Rector had mentioned. "He has his pick of a lot of juicy targets."

Rector said: "The whole list of cities with over a million accounts for close to a billion, or about 15% of the human population on earth. The biggest is Tokyo, with 32 million. If he hits even ten million men, women, and children, it would not only be a tragedy right away, but he would leave some major population center like New York City, London, Berlin, Moscow, Beijing...you name it...uninhabitable, as well as spreading death on rivers, bays, and in the rains."

Claire folded her arms over her chest, as if protecting herself from a terrible idea. "It almost makes sense to use General Todstole's method and nuke the Aeolian Islands. That would set off even bigger explosions from Stromboli and Etna, and definitely end the Black Umbrella problem."

"Let's home we can prevent it from coming to that. Come on, Jack, where are you when we need you?"

Carcer

Stretching to their utmost, Jack Gray and Miranda Coldstream they could just barely brush fingertips—but brush they did, several times.

"That feels so nice," she said in a low breath. "I want you to hold me."

"It's good to feel your touch again, Miranda. I was very worried about you."

" I thought they might have killed you."

" How did you end up here?"

"They beat me up, threw a blanket over my head, and a man carried me out to their van. I was afraid they were going to shoot you while you were in the shower."

"Hmm," Jack said. "I wondered about that, but Dr. Night made it clear I got three warnings. I think he likes keeping people around as pawns to trade."

"Like them," she said, pointing to Tissy and Louis.

"Yes, them especially. He's the inventor of the OST, and she's an Alecto defector. If anything, I would think she is in the most danger."

"He'd want to make an example of her for the other Alectos."

"Exactly."

"They take me out on the volcano for my exercise once a day. I hope we get to go together.'"

"I would love to exercise with you."

She waved him off. "Jack, you are incorrigible.'

"You've only known me a day or so in real time."

"It doesn't take much." She added. "To be honest, I'd love to exercise with you too."

"I'll do what I can." He raised his finger to his lips, and rolled his eyes toward the camera. Then he rolled them toward Tissy. They must save her first.

"I understand," Miranda said. She went to rest on her bed.

Jack rigged up a blanket for some privacy, as she had. That didn't shield him from the camera, but it answered a primordial human need for privacy.

Lying on his back behind the blanket, he crossed his hands behind his head, and crossed his legs at the ankles. He lay looking up at the camera and plotting his next move. He must do something—but what?

As he lay staring at the wall, a strange thing occurred to him.

That wiring came out of the wall. Had they drilled through yards of solid stone? Or was the wall at the foot of his bed a false front? The more he stared at it, the more he saw it.

He rose and pace about, examining the walls as far as he could see. The older, natural cave walls were bumpy and uneven. Over generations, people had created flat, stuccoed surfaces. What lay underneath? And where did the wires go?

He found three spare blankets folded up under his mattress. He pulled them out, and hung a blanket on the wall. The metal at the bottom of the camera plate had become partially detached, forming a catch. On this he hung the blanket, and stretched its wings out. Using two rusty nails thrown ages ago into dusty corners of the cell, he managed to dig through the stucco. As he hoped, he encountered brick underneath, rather than solid wall. With the two rusty nails, he dug into the mortar, creating two barely adequate hooks from which to suspend the blanket.

A voice startled him. "Hey, what's with the blankets."

At that point, lay resting on his cot. He turned to see Igor bringing another meal on a steel tray.

"A little privacy," he said. When Igor responded with a suspicious look, Jack stopped him. Pointing across the aisle, he said: "She's got her little privacy. Why can't I?"

Igor shrugged. His battered head, resembling an old wooden sock-darning ball, bobbed up and down like on turtle shoulders. Igor looked at the blanket on the wall. "You afraid the walls have eyes?" He burst out laughing at his own joke. He seemed an unpleasant, stupid, unshaven man whose tongue slightly protruded over his lower teeth when he breathed.

"Yes," Jack said. "I'm sorry. I can't help myself. Then I curl up in a ball and cry all night. It really annoys everyone, and I hope you don't make me do it. It will be so embarrassing."

Igor shook his head and rolled his eyes. "Just remember." He jabbed a heavy fist and pointy index finger at the end of the aisle. "There is always a guard up one flight of stairs at my desk. Anything you need to keep from howling, just let us know. We like to get our little snooze at night."

"On duty?" Jack looked horrified.

"Keep your fat nose in your own business, and don't make a racket or—." He patted the heavy black revolver in a holster at his hip.

"I get it. You'll kill me. That would be most unpleasant. I'll be quiet as a mouse."

"You do that." Igor placed other trays at the doors of Miranda and the pair down the aisle. Then he sniffed, hitched up his belt importantly, and strutted out of the cell area.

Jack got to work almost immediately.

At an angle beyond the foot of the bank, he was out of the camera's swivel range.

He peeled the blanket on the wall back and climbed on the foot of the bed. He probed around the hole in the wall where the wires came out to the plate on which the camera swiveled.

The hole in the wall was covered with crumbling white plaster. Using another nail, he scraped away at the hole until he exposed the mortared outline of the brick wall. Digging around, he found the mortar seam in the brick wall under the whitewash and plaster.

It seemed that Dr. Night's conversations were mostly monologues. He liked to talk, but not listen to people. Chances were he was not listening in on Jack's cell noises.

Jack climbed on the bed and turned off the bioluminescent stick above. Now he was in a gloomy light brightened only by another biolume in the ceiling over the aisle outside his cell. The blanket he'd hung from the bars, to shield the bed from view, added some shade from the hall light as well.

Using a nail head as a scraper, he began to work on mortar that must be 150 years old, dating to the time when wealthy Englishman Stevenson had tried to turn Vulcano into a fruitful wine growing place in addition to its age-old sulfur and alum mines. The volcanic eruptions of 1888-90 had sunk all such hopes.

Hearing a distant rattle, Jack threw himself on the bed. It turned out to be nothing, but it gave him an auditory range of where the guards had their station—down the hall, up a short flight of curving stairs, in a room or corridor large enough to have echoes.

Jack returned to his work. The Romans had invented concrete, and some of the best came from the fiery Phlegraean Fields and other seismically active ash fields along the coast north of Naples. The 19th Century mortar was strong, no doubt reinforced with extra cement, but had many cracks in it—some probably from many temblors over the past 150 years. He knew little about his location, other than it was a small island in the Aeolian chain just north of Sicily. It seemed likely that Dr. Night had one of his underground facilities here, unbeknownst to hundreds of young people discoing night and day in bars and resort hotels on the north coast. The only other thing he could surmise was that there was at least one huge volcano, that it was either dormant or extinct and not very famous, and that the discos would not be near it. He did know the island's name—Vulcano—which was indirectly famous in that all the world's volcanoes derived their generic name from it. And Vulcan was the Roman cognate of Greek Hēphaistos, the divine smith who pounded in his forge under the ground.

Once Jack got one brick loose—closest to the wire for the camera—the rest came loose with increasing ease. The bricklayers had placed them on top of each other in traditional staggered rows. As the opening grew, Jack was able to put considerable force to loosen each brick. Some of the loose bricks he stacked under the bed, and others he pushed so they fell back into a void behind the wall.

Miranda stayed up, watching him for a while. When he looked at her, she shook her head. They should not speak. She placed her finger over her lips, and surreptitiously eyeballed the camera. Jack nodded—best not to rouse any attention. The guards were probably watching his cell, and perhaps even Dr. Night cared enough to look in on his most irritating prisoner at times.

Jack labored on. He was increasingly jumpy, prepared to fly into bed at the slightest sound. Having it semidark helped diminish a view of the by now half-destroyed end wall. Two or three times, thinking a guard was coming, he hung the blanket. Quickly weighting the upper edge of the blanket down with a brick on each end, he jumped into bed and pretended to be asleep.

Surely, Sombra at least must be keeping an eye on him. But they were all busy with their threat to shoot the pope or whatever.

Jack picked up the pace as he kept picking at the wall.

Then, after a few hours, he could stand back, out of the camera's gaze, and behold his handiwork. He had exposed a four by four foot, squarish hole. The wall reached close to the cave roof near the top, where the wires came out. The wall dropped straight, while the cave walls sloped away by several feet.

Now or never.

He rolled up a blanket to make it look as if he were curled up, behind the hanging blanket, facing the wall.

Pulling off a few more bricks, he managed to crawl out in to a hallway full of cobwebs. He smelled a warm, sulfurous breeze. He hung the wall blanket and anchored it down with three bricks. If anyone walked by and shone a flashlight, they would obviously see that there was something amiss.

"I'll come back for you," he whispered to Miranda.

"I threw a bottle into the sea days ago," she said. "Maybe someone found it. It says where to find us."

"We'll go find them," Jack said bravely, feeling terrified inside.

At first, the passage was dark. It did, however, have a flat floor. Bending down to feel, he guessed that Stevenson's people—or someone in the island's long history, maybe gun runners in the age of the Bourbons, or of Napoleon, or during the Risorgimento leading to final Italian unity in 1871—had simply poured a lot of concrete. They'd poured it slightly more liquid, so that it oozed into any low-lying crevice and hardened to form a fairly even floor.

As he fumbled his way along, he noticed a faint light ahead.

He had the scare of his life when he began to see—and realized that he was surrounded by objects so ancient that a few turned to dust at his touch.

In wall niches were Roman and Greek statuettes. Dust roiled around small wood and clay figurines of Hercules, of Venus, and other deities as his fingers trawled by.

He saw former wooden furniture with decorative touches—spindly, turned legs—that had tipped over and gone past sawdust to shadowy triangles and squares amid piled dust.

Sacks holding long-ago alum had crumbled, leaving gray piles with shreds of woven hemp still sticking out. He saw a few small amphorae stack in a corner. Their black clay curvatures still bore faded reddish designs in glaze.

An iron scale had tumbled to the floor. It was still painted red, with just traces of rust along its curving edges—testimonial to the aridity of this place, which had preserved everything so well. He could make out the two pans, the piled chains, the broad stand, and a central figure of Mercury. The patron of commerce stood in a kind of dance step, wearing a sort of kilt. He held a sword in one hand and an upraised finger. On his head was the common ancient peasant sun hat for working in fields—a petasus—with wings.

He stopped in his tracks in the center of a small store room. For a delirious moment, it was as if a fat, tunica-clad accountant had just bustled from the room, holding a scroll, to check the cargo of a pentecounter of nine oars on each side, and a dingy white sail with an eye painted on it. That would be what the Arabs called a Nazar, and the Egyptians the Eye of Horus—an eye designed to trump the Evil Eye, which modern Italians called the Malocchio.

What a treasure trove for science! He stared with incredulity. Under the heavy dust lay countless objects. It was a miniature Pompeii, buried in dust and time instead of volcanic ash. This was a major discovery. He would come back here, perhaps write a scholarly book, or contribute to a collection of papers.

Other statues of Jupiter, Juno, Minerva, and Venus were made of copper or tin, and covered in scabs and patina. Their eyes followed him as he crept on. None of the statuettes was more than a foot tall. Some brandished spears or daggers at him. They were surrounded by hundreds of spent, clay votive lamps that had once cast their dim, flickering light in this cavern. Maybe it had been a store room for ancient Roman clerks or accountants, or a treasury long since emptied.

Thrilled, Jack walked more quickly into a growing light.

He stood on a ledge overlooking an underground channel that smelled of sea water—and diesel smoke and oil. Craning his neck around the corner of this entrance, he spied an old friend tied up at a subterranean loading dock—the submarine from Kisimul, or its twin. Some of Black Umbrella's casually clad sailors were busy carrying supplies or cargo into the sub. Did that mean they were about to sail away? Did that mean the island was being targeted? Whatever it was, Dr. Night had no doubt thought several chess moves ahead.

Looking the other way, Jack saw that a wall of raw, porous tufa stone curved down into the water. Same setup as Kisimul, except here the submarine had to submerge before entering or leaving. Probably a much bigger facility.

What in the hell to do? He had no idea where the Pollux project was being executed, or how to stop it. His best bet was to summon skilled help from Rector and Claire. He must get out of here and find a free telephone.

Jack was already down to Jeans, shirt, underpants, socks, and hiking boots. He had no watch, no wallet, no money, no phone—he must get to the outside, maybe to the rocking disco world. He'd take his chances from there.

He clambered carefully down the rock face to the water. This was about fifty feet, mostly too steep to climb, but there were fissured blocks of stone leaning against the sheer face at various heights, forming a rough stairway. Perhaps the Romans had had a wooden staircase here, and maybe a wooden loading crane with ropes and pulleys, block and tackle.

With about six death-defying jumps, Jack managed to get down to a tiny patch of beach little bigger than a child's sandbox. Sheer stone rose all around—tuff being porous, volcanic rock made from hardened lava. The water sloshing around smelled of diesel spillage and of dead, rotting kelp. There was not a ripe odor he'd associate with dead fish or garbage. That meant this place was not frequented by people, at last most of the time.

There were rainbow sheens of oil on the water. For the most part, nature was slowly cleansing itself.

Hearing voices, Jack pressed back and made himself small.

Just twenty feet away passed a rubber dinghy with three men on board. They wore scuba gear, with the lenses up and their tanks laid aside. They were laughing and talking—one man left a trail of cigarette smoke—as they paddled in the direction Jack wanted to take. When they reached the wall at the end of the passage, the smoker put his cigarette out. Two of the men pulled their masks in place, and donned their diving tanks and mouthpieces. The third man minded the rubber raft while the other two dove down.

For about ten minutes, there was silence.

Then the water bubbled as the two men rose and broke the surface.

One of them held aloft a tightly wrapped plastic package, and all three cheered. Jack made out the word marijuana. They clambered on board and sat around excitedly laughing as they prepared a pipe, lit it, and passed it around. The smell of marijuana smoke filled the close air.

Jack, who did not use drugs, held his nose and wished they would row away to oblivion.

He had learned what he needed to know.

They had been gone ten minutes. That meant swimming down, and out. It meant meeting someone and passing money along in return for weed. Then they had dived down and swum back. By a good guess, the passage underwater would take about two or three minutes—a hell of a feat, if he held his nose and hoped it wasn't too many seconds more. The idea of drowning terrified him—especially the last minute or two of panic, of struggling, of wasting precious oxygen all the faster. Not something he was up for today.

Jack got a better idea. He plotted his next move in the dim light that came from the industrial lighting about 200 feet away around the docks and the sub.

The men smoked until they were ready to fall off the raft. Apparently, they were sneaking some illegal dope behind Dr. Night's back. That meant this was not a well patrolled area, or they would not have used it for nefarious purposes. Looking around, and upward, Jack did not spot any security cameras—which did not mean there weren't any. Surely these dweebs must know something—probably this was a backwater, away from cameras, where you could get away with things.

When they finally began to paddle back toward the docking area, all had removed their heavy tanks. Two of them lay stoned on their backs, while the third man paddled effortfully. He alternated sides, since he had to do all the work himself. A spare paddle lay propped against the rear gunwale of the rubber boat.

Jack waited until he was directly opposite, and in the middle of the channel. He gathered a dozen small, hard stones of the natural granite underlying the volcanic stone.

At twenty feet, Jack tossed a sharp, flat stone the size of a small pancake. The first throw missed, but the rower barely noticed. When it splashed into the water, close to the opposite rock wall, he looked over but did not stop rowing. Perhaps he thought it was a fish surfacing. Or a rat.

The second rock stunned him and he stopped rowing. The third rock curved like a boomerang and hit him behind the ear. One of his stoned companions struggled to rise, but a rock stunned him as well. They still had plenty of play in them.

Jack stripped off his precious boots, and the heavy socks, and dove in like an arrow. It was a hard, straight dive that did not make much of a splash. In a few scissor strokes, he covered the distance and rose under the dark shadow of the boat.

Surfacing, shaking water from his head, Jack looked right into the shocked face of the third man. The man's cheek rested on the inflated gunwale, and his mouth was open in shock. Jack rose in the water, and snapped a short, hard, circular punch downward on his temple. If he killed him, too bad. These guys would think nothing of killing him. A second man stirred. Jack was half into the boat, and had the spare paddle in hand. Two good stabbing thrusts to the throat, and the man collapsed into the bottom of the boat, holding his neck. The other man was coming to as well, but Jack was fully in the violently rocking boat now. He swung the paddle to knock the waking man unconscious, and brought it down on the middle guy's head. He didn't want to kill any of them, but they needed a good knockout.

A swift current was pulling the boat back the way it had just come. Probably a good thing. Probably meant the tide was going out, and the entrance was not too deep. Bad thing might be if he got pulled out and bashed on some whitewater rocks. That was a chance he'd have to take.

What to do? He couldn't let them go. He was not a cold-hearted killer. Then he had an idea.

He paddled the boat close to his little hiding place and secured it. One by one, he dragged the dazed men head-first, belly down, onto the tiny beach.

He pushed the empty boat, now light, up onto a low shelf for safe keeping. He set the men's scuba gear, belts, knives, and other equipment near the water for his use in a moment.

Taking a knife from one of them, he cut open the wetsuit of each man over the rear end.

He took their drugs—about a half pound of marijuana and about an ounce of hashish or opium—out of the plastic container. In a tiny depression, he dumped the dope. He cupped several handfuls of water from the channel into the hole. Then he kneaded, pressed, squeezed, and kneaded some more. One of the men coughed and tried to sit up. Jack tapped him on the head with a rock, and all three were in repose. After developing a paste, about two coffee cups' worth, he divided it into three little mounds of goo. Straddling each man in turn, he gave each an enema of drugs. He saved a small quantity to stick under each man's tongue. Last, he tied their hands and legs together, using their belts. For three extremely stoned men with severe headaches, it would take a lot of work—and time—to eventually figure out their predicament, free themselves, and swim to the docks for help. Most likely, they would feel scared and humiliated and not tell anyone.

Jack washed his hands at the water's edge. He packed his socks and hiking boots in the plastic that had kept their dope dry—it was a large lunch bag with a self-locking zipper. Then he donned a mask, a tank, and breathing apparatus. He found a weight belt, which he put on so that he'd be able to submerge efficiently and stay submerged.

He pulled the remaining tanks and equipment to him, and shoved them into the water, where they disappeared. Checking out his breathing—worked great—he clutched the zip-bag in his right hand, tipped over forward, and entered the black watery night.

Immediately, he felt the current pulling him along. The water was relatively warm, having sat for hours around the docks. The current was powerful, and he sensed that he was moving fast—maybe too fast. He had no light, so he could not see anything.

He guessed he was about three fathoms down—a fathom being six feet, that might put him close to twenty feet. Judging by the pressure on his ears, it was not more than that.

The water went totally dark, which suggested he had entered the passage. The light from the docks was now totally lost.

Putting his feet before him, in case his turbulent rush took him down onto any bottom boulders, he relaxed and let the current sweep him along.

It took five minutes to bounce along rough sand and a few smooth stones on the bottom, and emerge on the other side. He'd been close in his estimations.

He came up in bright sunshine and blue skies. It was wonderful, fresh, and blinding. He just wished Miranda could be here with him, splashing in the warm sea, with her dazzling ring and long hair. "Wake you," she had murmured, rubbing it on his throat.

The current swept him along—there was an undertow below him, but he managed to swim laterally just fifteen feet out of its stream. He crawled up on a sandy little beach and lay on his back. He removed his breathing gear and inhaled fresh Mediterranean beach air.

A few feet from his head was the money the two divers had left in return for their dope. Jack counted fifty Euros—certainly enough for a phone call. "I'll owe you," he muttered as he stripped off his gear and hid it in a shallow tidal pool filled with floating kelp.

How to mark this location so he could find it again? He spotted a few landmarks nearby—a pier, a restaurant, and six small motorized sailboats anchored at a dock.

He began walking. His clothing would dry in the wind and sun. A wet young man hiking along on an Aeolian beach was probably nothing of note. When he had walked up, onto the dry sand and shells above the tide line, he found a rock. He sat down, opened his zip bag, and put on his socks and shoes. As he dressed, he gazed at the blunted 1,600-foot (500m) volcanic cone. That must be main volcano. A few miles across at the base, it dominated the small island.

The sun was stood middling in the sky, so it was mid to late afternoon. Shadows of rocks and other objects, including the volcanic cone, fell toward the water. He must be on the eastern side of the island, because the shadows increasingly pointed east as the sun headed west and downward for a relatively early autumn sunset.

Jack walked onto the wooden dock, and out to the last boat--a little fourteen foot toy with a single, triangular sail, and no more than a foot of freeboard. There was room for one or two passengers, and plenty of room for Jack. There wasn't time to blunder and climb about—that could cost hours. He must get help as soon as possible, to get Miranda, Tissy, and Cartouche out, and to stop Dr. Night from killing many people.

The sail was up on its aluminum mast. The sail hung loose, and luffed gently in a mellow breeze, making slow popping sounds in the lee of these cliffs. Judging by boats out on the water, and hard little white caps, he'd have plenty of wind. Jack stepped into the boat, sat down, cast loose its flimsy nylon mooring line, and yanked the sail taut. Immediately a wind came and pushed the free boat away from its dock. He expected some three hundred pound man to come running with a cleaver, bellowing to get back his boat. But nobody seemed to notice as the stranger in the stolen sailboat tacked out to sea and then on a bearing north to take him toward a mass of lights and civilization. The afternoon sun made hundreds of west-facing windows at Porto di Levante glow like one great, golden lighthouse, or a ring of many facets.

What a great time it would be to forget all his woes and cares, and just settle back with a glass of fine red wine and a beautiful woman—Miranda came to mind. What a nuisance it was, having to save the world instead.

Porto de Levante

Porto di Levante

As Jack beached the little sailboat, the sun was just setting over the western sea. The colors—mauve, yellow, red, with a flash of green—were spectacular, especially seen against the black hulk of the Fossa volcano to his left. The volcano's cone was uneven, and slightly tilted toward him so he could see a little bit of its sloping insides.

He heard one or two popping sounds, like a car backfiring—only the echoes traveled for miles. Tiny clouds of white and gray mist rolled over exhaust cracks in Fossa's guts and upper rim. Fossa was speaking. Vulcan was stirring in his forge.

To Jack's right were the lights of a few hotels on Vulcanello. The little volcanic peninsula rose from the sea, smoking and boiling lava, in the late Roman Republic. Jack had sailed into a little bay on the south shore of Porto di Levante. Several small jetties and one large pier jutted from land. The big pier was off to his right, while he was on the edge of the tiny town. To his north were a mix of people: families with small children, locals going about their business as the did anywhere in the world, and groups of young men and women who looked like college students on vacation. The swirl of languages drifting to his ears included Italian, Sicilian-Italian, English, German, Greek, Spanish, Turkish, and Arabic.

Rock music echoed from discos in Porto di Levante. This small town was the Eastern Port, or port of the rising sun. Jack smelled fresh bread, sizzling meat, and roasting coffee. He realized how hungry he was.

Families were just packing up to return from the beach to their hotel rooms. The beach was overgrown with trees at this southern end of the bay, and the large volcano rose up in a black before him. Young people— all lovely, the girls crisp and shapely in bikinis and broad-brimmed woven hats, the young men clean-cut and still half sober—headed off toward town to the north for dinner and a long night of drinks and dancing to wild music.

Jack spotted a light glowing among trees and headed in that direction. He passed a public latrine that looked very well kept with solid concrete-block walls like fallout shelters—in case, Jack supposed, the restaurants were serving the Italian equivalent of chili. He stepped from the beach onto a network of gravel roads, one of which took him a block inland to a wealthy villa. He rang the street bell and waited by a wide double gate. The gate was of black, lacy wrought iron with steel plates also painted black.

A voice challenged in Italian.

"I have an emergency. Need a telephone. My boat sank."

"Of course…come in," said a woman's voice in accented English.

At the sound of a buzzer, Jack pushed one side of the gate slightly open. He stepped into a well-kept yard that was part labyrinth, part cactus garden, and part swimming pool area. A wide gravel drive went off to the left in the direction of a four car garage with a clay tile roof. To the right, a narrower gravel path with flagstones led to the house itself—also clay tiled, with picture windows and a recessed door. Along the way, on the right, was a large swimming pool. Underwater lighting illumined the pool's long, aqua-colored basin, while wind-blown wavelets bounced around on the surface, glittering and throwing mesmeric flashes of light against the house walls and the trunks of surrounding trees.

A woman appeared in the doorway. She looked Italian, in her forties, with a squarish face and attractive eyes, a bit too much mouth and nose. But very friendly. "'Allo, did anyone die?"

"No, everyone is all right. We just lost our boat about 100 meters off shore, and luckily we had lifejackets so we swam to shore."

A white-haired man appeared behind her, holding her protectively. They led Jack into a white-tiled kitchen. The house smelled of an almond noodle casserole, whose aroma drove him insane. "Here is the phone," she said pointing to a black desk model. "Are you hungry?"

Jack rolled his eyes up and made his last-breath-on-earth face.

Moments later, the couple had him sitting at their kitchen table, eating noodles almandine with slivers of fresh Sicilian ham—this was legally part of Sicily—while he dialed out to reach Rector or Claire.

"You are the finest chef in Europe," Jack told the lady. She beamed. A moment later, she appeared carrying a little clay saucier of flan, while her husband brought a bottle of white wine and three glasses. Jack almost felt guilty about fibbing. But what could he say? *I am a secret agent from Compass News, and there is a mad genius in the bottom of your volcano who wants to destroy the world unless I stop hi, at least long enough for the Carabinieri and the 7th Cavalry to arrive on their horses with that famous bugle rally.* Definitely would not fly. They might take away this fine dinner. "My company will reimburse you for all time and trouble," Jack said and felt better.

"Jack," came Claire's voice on the phone. "We lost your signal."

"I'm in a house in Porto di Levante. I sailed here from a secret passage in the volcano."

"We think that's where BLUM is operating. Any idea where the control center for Pollux is?"

"I don't know directly, but I found their submarine along a channel of water, a tidal channel, inside the mountain. Rented a boat, sort of, and came this way. Cover is that I had two passengers on board and we all swam here after the boat sank." He spoke low and cryptically, hoping that his two hosts would not pick up on the fact that his story wasn't quite *halal* (the Islamic equivalent of kosher).

"Dr. Night is threatening to kill millions of people with radioactive waste in orbit. We've got your exact location now," she said. "I'll have some people outside in five minutes."

"The wonders of modern technology."

"Your hosts are...let me see...harmless...Heinz and Ingrid Ehrlich of Geneva. He is a banker. She is a professor of law. They own a vacation home on Vulcano."

"More like a vacation villa."

"Just so you know, Jack. This call may be picked up by BLUM, but I am just half a mile from your location."

"You're kidding."

"In Porto di Ponente. We haven't just been sitting around idly, Jack."

At that moment, a car horn tooted outside on the street.

Herr Ehrlich toddled to the window, pushed the drapes aside, and peeked outside. "Who did you say you work for, Mister—?"

"Gray, sir. Jack Gray. I'm a kind of traveling trouble shooter for global corporations, and of course the relevant governments."

"I see," Herr Ehrlich said. "Ingrid, *Liebchen*, come and look. I think the entire Italian army is on the street outside."

"Gotta run," Jack said, wiping his mouth. He kissed Frau Ehrlich on the cheek. "Best cook in Europe, you are. We'll send a check soon."

"No need," the couple both said, while clutching each other for safety. That was how Jack left them, on their porch, by the light of two cozy looking coach lights, as he jogged down the driveway to the street.

There were indeed a row of dark green and desert camo vehicles, bearing Carabinieri and Italian Army markings—federal military police, commandos, the elite. An officer snapped to attention and saluted. Beside him were a lieutenant and a sergeant major, who did the same. All wore dark fatigues, black combat boots, and dark berets. "Lieutenant Colonel Rocco Pavone, presenting. At your service.

Jack returned the salute in relaxed but military fashion. "Major Jack Gray, U.S. Army Special Forces, at your service, sir."

Behind the colonel were at least a dozen light, six-wheeled Puma 6x6 armored fighting vehicles, or troop carriers, each with eight soldiers on board and a full cache of sea and land combat equipment, including shoulder-fired rockets. Each of these heavily armed infantry combat vehicles was surmounted with a 12.7 mm machine gun on a 360 degree turret.

Operating in tandem with their protective Puma escorts were a row of amphibious attack vehicles, modified armored personnel carriers.

Behind those were a further row of hulky ACM90 light trucks and smaller field utility vehicles Jack had not seen before—an Italian made equivalent of the NATO Hummvee, with half those on the street before him resembling amphibious motorcycles capable of high speed and maneuverability. The latter carried one remote-controlled machine gun, so the operator did not have to take his hands off the motorcycle-style control bars.

The colonel informed Jack: "Two dozen fighting vehicles, two dozen support and light combat vehicles, half amphib, supported by a strike force of 200 men, including twenty officers and twenty NCOs. At your service, Major."

Jack conferred briefly with his new allies in arms. While several men held flashlights, he and the officers conferred over a map which someone had spread across a vehicle's bonnet or hood.

An aide brought a portable field phone to the colonel. Pavone held it to his ear and said sharply: "*Si?*"

Then, as Jack watched, the colonel's facial expression darkened.

Something vast and tragic was going on.

Jack was handed a phone, on which Claire spoke: "Jack, BLUM is taking it to the next level. The corporations again failed to agree to the demand for turning over their stock to BLUM. Dr. Night just made his latest announcement. We think it's true, because we tracked the launch of a three-ton satellite from a new, secret base in central Africa, of unknown nationality. Dr. Night has launched a satellite into orbit, which he claims contains two more tons of highly radioactive material, along with separate launch canisters of highly toxic, uniquely evolved flu virus. At noon tomorrow, they will bomb either Tokyo, New York, London, or a comparable megalopolis. Millions will die. Our only hope now is that we can stop Dr. Night dead in his tracks on Vulcano. There are four U.S. carrier groups steaming toward you, including one on duty in the Med and already on your doorstep. We can also launch ICBMs from nuclear submarines off Spain. But we would prefer to avoid the enormous loss of life, without even a guarantee that it will stop this madman. He has launch facilities in Equatorial Africa and maybe elsewhere. I'm just hoping Vulcano isn't a blind to divert us."

"I'll do my best to find out," Jack said.

He turned to Colonel Pavone. He explained his own history since arriving on Vulcano, which wasn't much. "The submarine was at Kisimul, and now it's here. My best guess is that Dr. Night has set up shop inside the volcano."

Pavone nodded, while holding his fingers to an earpiece. "I am in touch with my headquarters in Messina and Rome. I am just receiving instructions."

"Stay with Colonel Pavone, Jack. We're running several independent Camelback operations in parallel. Your mission now is to get Louis Cartouche safely out of that ant hill. Think you can do that?"

"Yes. I know where to find him."

"That makes you a number one asset as usual. Just forget the rest of it and extract him. We'll have a wider extraction situation ready. Just let us know."

"Right."

Pavone added: "I have instructions to help you extract this Monsieur Cartouche and his staff if any."

Tissy Fître. Jack wanted to see her rescued, particularly because she had unique insight into the BLUM organization. If Dr. Night had wind of this, he'd have her and Cartouche killed immediately. Besides, she was an extraordinarily beautiful woman—good things came in small packages, and Tissy was the daughter of all great candy bars. In a weird way, Jack wanted her to be happy with Cartouche. It neutralized the rogue scientist, and thus made the world a safer place if Cartouche was regularly getting laid and staying fat, dumb, and happy. It would keep Tissy out of trouble as well, and out of Dr. Night's clutches.

"I'll need minimum support," Jack said. "Let's not tip them off. What we could do with your splendid organization is organize a feint. We'll throw them off."

"Sounds like an excellent tactic," Pavone said. "Tell me more."

In a matter of minutes, Jack described the lay of the land inside the channel where sub was docked. He described the Roman cave from another age, reminding the colonel his men must not touch or disturb anything.

"We are Italian," the Colonel said proudly. "Antiquities are in our blood. We know what to do—and not to do."

Jack explained: "A large force would probably tip BLUM off. I suggest you take most of them across the island to Porto di Ponente, Port of the Descending Sun—"

"—How appropriate for Dr. Night—"

"—Yes, and for so much ancient history. Create a large diversion there. Call the local police and tell them a story…say that a boat load of dangerous refugees from somewhere has run aground, and your people are rounding them up. The local police should seal the main road leading south, as well as the beaches on both sides from the north side of the island to the south. Meanwhile, you send in a small team of all-purpose warfare specialists to help me extract the three people I have described— Louis Cartouche, Tissy Fître, and Miranda Coldstream."

"*Bravo*," the colonel said as he folded up the map and waved for his aides and commanders to gather around him. "We will focus on this mission, while our navy seals off the entire island, and our paratroopers do a mass landing on the south face of Fossa."

"Warn them that there are still active fumaroles all across the top and insides of the Gran Cratere. Very dangerous. Intoxicating, as the signs say."

"Ah yes," said Colonel Pavone. "Very much sulfur—the brimstone mentioned in the Bible, and a key part of *il polvere*, the gunpowder." He made a face and touched his ear piece. "*Si. Bene.*" He turned to Jack. "Your driver is here. She is apparently a liaison and interpreter between your Sigma and Compass News offices and the local police. Will you meet us in Porto di Ponente then?"

"Of course. I'll see what they want. Please get your team ready for the dive with me."

Pavone saluted. "With pleasure, Agent Jack Gray."

A dark blue Alfa Romeo Brera with Carabinieri markings pulled up, and the colonel held open the passenger door for Jack. Jack thanked him and got in. Immediately he loved its smell of leather and machine oil. This car was one of a variety used by the elite police. Their fast pursuit cars were called *gazelle*, gazelles, and this was no exception. With the 3.2 V6 FWD engine, a fairly recent production model could hit 100 kph (60 mph) in seven seconds, and cruise at 250 kph (155 mph) top speed. Jack's attention was focused on the beautiful lines of the car.

Pavone laughed as he pushed the door shut. "You ride like a general now!"

"*Arrividerci!*" Jack said.

As the car pulled away, he felt something cold and hard on the back of his neck.

The driver, a female in black leather Carabinieri motorcycle uniform, pulled back the hoodie that had veiled her face. She turned with that broad, crazy laugh and stark eyeballs, and said: "Hello again, Jack."

"Sombra," he said. "And who is that charming someone holding the cannon on my neck?"

"There are two someones in the back seat. Take a look."

Jack twisted his neck and stared into the muzzle of a 9mm Glock.

"The one behind you is Granato, the Grenade," she said as she propelled the car too quickly over the island's gravel roads. "The other gentleman is Urso, the Bear. You are such a royal pain in the ass, Mr. Gray, that I felt it would take three of us to make sure you do not escape again."

"Did you notice my fifty-car special forces escort back there by any chance?"

"Oh, they are all idiots," she said. "Not to be taken seriously. Their commanding officer held the door open as I kidnapped you from under their noses. You, on the other hand, are as persistent as butt trash."

"Is that a polite way of saying butt rash?"

"You are a third grade boy with a dirty mind. Changing the subject, Mr. Gray, we want you as a bargaining chip. Also, if we know where you are, we feel much more at ease."

"And what good am I as a bargaining chip when, the latest I hear, millions of people's lives are at stake?"

"Oh, that."

"And where do you folks hide while you are atomizing Atlanta or nuking Delhi or whatever your latest nutty gambit may be?"

She smiled. "Try harder, Mr. Gray. You were stimulating for a while on top of Heave-Ho or whatever the mountain is over Castlebay, but you became boring right after that."

"When you tried to drop me half a kilometer to my death down that shaft?"

"You dramatize too much. I knew you would make it down hand over hand."

"You were quite stimulating yourself," Jack said. "Now you are simply terrifying."

"Good. Then you do have the capacity to feel fear."

"But do you have the capacity to have any human feelings at all?"

Sombra made a face. Granato tapped the hard, blunt tip of the weapon painfully against the bump at the back of Jack's skull. She said: "Shut up, Jack. You are boring."

"I'm sorry." He was angry. Anything to annoy her.

"If you want to live longer, Jack, take my advice. Put a push-pin in your tongue. Staple it to the bottom of your mouth. Silence will earn you survival points. Vapid conversation will get you a brief stop by the road, we blow your head all over the dirt, we drive on with our lives, and you are road kill. Do you want that?"

"That's okay, I'll be quiet. The invasion force is about to land."

"Okay, you can talk a little. What invasion force? Or farce?"

"Just the entire armies of about fifty nations. You think that they're going to hear your leader talk about killing tens of millions of innocent people? Corporations may rule, but people can still riot, burn buildings, and lynch CEOs. The Roman emperors were acutely aware of this, and built giant playpens like the Colosseum to keep the street mobs busy with free wine, booze, and gruesome games."

"I did not ask for a history of the world, Jack."

"I'm a history professor. I can't help it."

"Don't you people get it? Dr. Night planned for all eventualities. He knew you'd swarm over Vulcano like stink on kimchee. By the way—we of course discovered your juvenile trick with the blanket over the wall. We assume you'll send idiots to save the three people in their cells. We'll be waiting for them. It will be a massacre."

Jack sat back. "I'm going to be a good boy and keep my mouth shut."

"You have wasted plenty of my time. Enough!" She pressed her lips together in fury, and did not reply. Her gloved hands spun the wheel so that the car sped through turns. Her eyes had that manic look, diagnosed when people show the whites of their eyes all around the pupil, especially along the top of the iris.

Their drive took them through the suburbs of the tiny eastern port town. Jack could smell fish and steak cooking, along with wafting smells of wine and perfume and men's heavy cologne. Women shrieked, men laughed, and music pounded from a half dozen bars and nightclubs.

"Wouldn't you like to stop for a samba, Sombra?"

She ignored him. The car sped on, turning south along the beach road. She raced through Porto di Ponente—port or gate of the setting sun—leaving a cloud of road dust. There were bright lights along a stretch of beach, where at least two other bars pounded under the starlight. Jack could see excited secretaries from London, nurses from Frankfurt, stock brokers from Paris, and probably a few clerics from Rome—and U.S. evangelists—waving their arms in a conga chain, and shrieking to the hypnotic blast of Lambada at top volume.

The car downshifted and roared down into a dark dip beyond the beach. If there were street lights here, they had been disabled.

Jack caught a glimpse of lights approaching from out at sea—probably naval landing craft ferrying Italian and PETO marines. How ironic. He wished he could get a message to Pavone—*Advise: not an exercise; look for real BLUM entrance.*

Sombra turned left on two wheels and headed along a private road perpendicular to the beach road. Heading directly away from the water, she accelerated. For a moment, Jack thought she was going to commit group suicide by driving directly into a whitewashed farm house at the end of the drive. He was already pressing his left foot down, amid twisty body language, trying to stomp on an imaginary brake.

The farm house turned out to be the gateway to an abandoned, underground NATO airbase from the most terrifying, dark ages of the Cold War. The farm house was an empty wooden box on giant hinges. It opened up like a cell phone. More accurately, like a giant mouth, tilting along its far edge to open like a clam shell or an alligator's mouth. The interior was vast and well lit. It was a wide, concrete roadway illumined with bluish daylight arc lights. The car raced through, entered a giant set of tonsils, and screamed along an underground highway four lanes wide. Behind them the house rolled back down and locked into place. It would look for all intents and purposes like a private resort residence locked down and dark for the off-season.

The gun muzzle tapped against his skull once again, as a periodic reminder to be quiet and not try anything foolish.

"I get the message," he said over his shoulder. "You can stop tapping me with your bone, Fido."

"Welcome to Operation Pollux," Sombra said. She had regained her calm.

Pollux Ascendant

The car roared along an underground highway. The sound of its powerful engine reverberated from distant walls on either side, and a ceiling some 300 feet above. The strip was lit by street lights, just like a surface road. Rows of dusty vehicles stood parked along either side.

If he had to guess, Jack was sure they were driving deep under the volcano—presumably sealed off from fumaroles, and deep down, the magma chamber.

The drive took only ten minutes. Along the way, Jack noticed that a heavy dust of fine particles followed the car in a plume. He also noticed shadowy aircraft parked along either side, beyond the twin narrow sidewalks and their streetlights, and the rows of parked cars. Some of the aircraft were missing wings or nose cones. A lot of spare parts lay about. They were very old aircraft, which had not flown in half a century.

Jack had his insight. On several walls was painted a flag or design: a blue square with a four-pointed silvery star in a circle. This must be an old emergency strip, hidden from the world, of NATO, when it was the old North Atlantic Treaty Organization. The base had been built so its departure strip aimed over the western beach of Vulcano. Nobody—not the local people, not the Soviet Union, had known about it. It had been dug out of soft volcanic tuff during a legitimate, above-ground road building or other large construction operation. At some time, NATO shed the base. The old NATO became PETO and went off to other duties, with the Warsaw Pact and the Soviet Union long gone. The Italians took over the base, and ultimately sold it to some bland subsidiary of BLUM, complete with the hokey farm house on hinges.

The car whisked to a stop along a circular driveway at the main underground entrance. The place looked like the entrance to a fine hotel, except for the dust and decay. At one time, generals and admirals had covertly arrived by limousine here, wearing fatigues, accompanied by pet senators and parliamentarians (still tingling from their nights with top-flight call girls flown in from around the world to these islands), all looking over their shoulders like gangsters in sunglasses. Today, instead of valets, doormen, and bellhops, black-uniformed BLUM troopers stood around with compact assault rifles.

"Just remember to keep your ideas and your hands to yourself," Sombra said, "and you won't be instantly killed by Granato and Urso.

As Jack stepped from the car, he looked about. No signs of an escape route. Sombra got out, and a black-clad valet climbed in to take the wheel. Now Jack got his first glimpse of Urso and Granato. They were two huge hoods resembling twin volcanic plugs guarding the doors of hell. Each man was scarred from acne and combat. Each carried his Glock openly, with his hands folded at the bottom of his torso. It looked almost as if they were holding their manhood, which consisted not so much of a one-inch pickle, but of a powerful gun. Jack guessed that a proverbial swift kick in their grapes would only result in his foot being injured.

An uneasy quartet, they went into the former NATO reception lobby. They walked past the ghostly reception desk, and to a pair of elevators framed in marble and dull brass. Leave it to the Italians to endow even a secret, underground facility in pomp and splendor, as if gladiators and lions were about to appear before a roaring crowd and the imperial box.

The elevator ride took them upward as Grunt and Grant (Jack's new names for his guardians) flanked him like obelisks. Sombra stood to one side with one hand covertly on a gun. She was taking no chances, Jack could see. For his part, he was ready to seem very bland, to look around, and to learn everything he could. A clock was ticking—potentially, the madman could either shoot the pope or some other dignitary, or unleash hell in the form of a thousand Hiroshimas on millions of innocent people.

"Hello, Mr. Gray!" whispered the voice of Dr. Night.

Jack stood in a control center dome like that he'd seen under Kisimul. This one was about three times as large. A hundred or more technicians in silvery jumpsuits sat at terminals. Everywhere, Jack saw digital terminals, analog displays, and video screens. The ten foot band of wall supporting the actual tufa dome was covered with view screens and various mutations of sine waves moving according to mathematical, almost astrological, designs. Two dozen voices spoke into microphones or listened to other voices on speakers. This entire apparatus meshed into what Jack recognized must have been the control network that hijacked Anaconda's Capricorn satellite and morphed it into BLUM's Pollux craft.

In the center of the dome was a large table. On it, amid surgical linens, silvery tools, and exposed parts, was the clone of the Castor and Pollux control units. Evidently, Louis Cartouche had looped some virtual circuits of Castor through an additional copy, Pollux, to prevent anyone who managed to steal the one control from operating the satellite without running the other in parallel. This gave Jack the kernel of a wild idea.

"Don't worry, Mr. Gray. Nobody can bomb us or hurt us here. Since you will not leave here alive, you won't be able to send your friends with the berets. If you behave yourself, I won't have you killed immediately. You can hang around, enjoy yourself, eat well, and watch the success of our operation."

Sombra shoved him. "Go on." With Grunt and Grant trailing, Jack followed Sombra out of the main dome. The design here was similar to that at Kisimul. Perhaps the BLUM engineers at Kisimul had copied this as their template. Why not? NATO had done all the work, not far shy of a century ago.

As they left the room, Dr. Night's voice echoed softly all around them. The megalomaniac was speaking to the world at large, and nobody in particular. In a godlike fugue, he must feel the corporate security apparatuses were listening—and no doubt they were. "Today, I will give you one last warning. Somebody very important will die today. Let's get our game show running, shall we? I like this so much, I may go into show business yet. Who are our contestants today, Honey? The pope? The British monarch? The Chief CEO of Corporate USA? Roll the drum and let's see our ten best contestants. As we speak, the Pollux craft is ready to launch the next OST…

As Dr. Night spoke, Sombra led her group down a long corridor, like a 1,000 foot Quonset hut. There was, along each wall, a row of rounded doorways. Most were closed and opaque, revealing nothing of their purpose. Each was numbered in faded old large stencil-type letters in dark green paint upon the whitewash.

The tunnel was well lit by overhead bioluminescent tubes, but deadly quiet. The hive of activity from NATO times was gone. Everything today was miniaturized, efficient, digital, and deadly. You could do frightening things with a few dozen people, where the old bomber command might have had over a thousand souls working here. As with Groom Lake and other secret facilities, the workers and navy technicians were probably brought in by submarine or even a disguised tourism boat, and led into the volcano without having any idea where they were. If the number of rumbles heard in the walls was more frequent than the number of thunderous take-offs, it was probably due to fumaroles, but these would be explained away as cargo stacking in remote warehouses. Long gone now, forgotten, relegated to the UFO and other conspiracy blinds created during the Cold War.

The tunnel walls were of natural volcanic stone that had been hollowed out—probably to wheel NATO atomic weapons to the planes, one by one. That meant—the submarine channel on the eastern side of the island was the abandoned weapons delivery base, where Jack had emerged from his earlier captivity to steal the sailboat.

Laid across a steel gurney, each bomb or missile would have been wheeled west for attachment to the bomb bay of an old Vulcan bomber. Perhaps the U.K.'s Avro-Vulcan program had gotten its name right here. That was not so unlikely, given that every volcano on earth got its name from the one Jack was inside of right now.

The delta-wing Vulcan aircraft, almost resembling a flying wing like the U.S. B-2, had been one of the world's most advanced aircraft from the 1950s to the 1970s. It had been capable of delivering death to Josef Stalin's front door, had the Soviet dictator decided to let loose his useful fools on those of the West. It was the age-old story of warfare, Jack thought, being a soldier and secret agent himself. His vague philosophies stopped at the end of the walk.

Sombra led them into doorway number 85, in the sequence of odd numbers along the left wall. They entered a circular stairwell, and went up. Two stories above, in the utilitarian world of concrete, tufa, and cold lighting, they emerged into a hallway that Jack recognized. He nodded to his old guard, who sat at a bank of closed circuit video screens. A second guard accompanied them now. Down the curving stairway they went, and Sombra supervised as Jack was put back into his old cell. The guard locked him into his cell.

Sombra grinned, and her eyelids parted to reveal white all around her pupils. "We fixed your wall, Jack. Not only did we brick it back up, but it now carries over 10,000 volts that will fry you if you try to break the circuit by scratching the mortar as you did before." Turning, she said over her shoulder: "Rot tight."

After she and her monoliths had left, Jack stood at his same old cell door. Miranda rose to speak with him. In their corner, Tissy and Louis stood as well to greet him.

"Everyone okay?" he asked.

They murmured unhappily, but appeared to be well fed and hydrated.

"Let me get this straight," Jack said. "There is a satellite in orbit."

"Pollux," Louis said. "Meant to be Anaconda's Capricorn, but became BLUM's Pollux."

"With our help," Tissy said. "I could kick myself."

"As could I," Louis said. "They eliminated Castor from the equation, once they got the satellite into orbit."

"Where did you come up with all this on your own?" Jack asked. He looked at Miranda, whose knowing expression signaled that she had already gone over this with Cartouche.

Louis explained: "When I was young, I wondered if we could simply assassinate someone like Saddam Hussein and avoid full-blown war. Of course, the CIA and other agencies were hot on his trail for that purpose. Like other dictators of his type, like Manuel Noriega of Panama before the U.S. military captured him, Saddam moved around every night. He would arrive suddenly in a fleet of cars with tough boys, commandeer a family's home, and make himself at home while the family cowered in a back room. By morning, he'd be gone. The U.S. could never quite track him down. And when they did try to hit him with a few rocket attacks, it was a provocation from his part to embarrass the West. Several times, they wiped out innocent people with their attacks. So I thought to myself—thinking of blow-hards like Castro, or Mussolini, or Hitler, or Milosevic, or Ghaddafi, or any of them—when is such a person most vulnerable? Of course it is while they give their long, blustering, maniacal speeches. Castro, for example, in his younger years as dictator of Cuba, was known to ramble on, pounding his podium, for eight hours straight on. These guys hardly pause to drink, pee, or take a breath. Anyone who wants to leave will be shot, so people stay and pee their seats while pretending to rapturously listen. So that solved my first problem, which is getting the target to stand still for at least four minutes, which is typically the time it takes for my reentry vehicles to go through their full cycle."

"But the technology," Jack said. "Where did you come up with that?"

"Before digital and advanced telemetry, the U.S. used aircraft surveillance photography developed in World War II and Korea. The SIGINT satellites of the U.S. from the 1950s on until the 1970s. The CIA had one version, called the Keyhole series. The Air Force had a parallel program called Corona. These satellites would hover above Low Earth Orbit, over 200 miles or 300 km altitude. They used small rocket thrusters to lower themselves to 165-180 miles, as needed, to shoot their film. They shot still photos of very high quality, or even movies, on actual film. The satellite rolled these up, the way the old-fashioned roll of film would be in a little light-safe roll and then in a rubber tube. It would then drop the film canister from LEO before returning the craft to a higher, more stable orbit."

Miranda said: "You can't maintain a stable, unassisted orbit under 200 miles at best, or the atmosphere will start tumbling your craft. As it loses momentum, it will drop below 17,500 centripetal equilibrium. It will go into unplanned reentry and burn up before its mission is complete."

"I loved that whole concept," Louis said. "I thought about it endlessly as I wasted my college years. Instead of adapting to a solid engineering program, I took random classes in the arts as well as mathematics. I went out drinking all night, often alone, and ended up being expelled from McGill University. I went underground, so to speak, and wasted two decades at the periphery of the real world. Meanwhile, as a student, this spy satellite technology captured my imagination. Perhaps I already knew that my destiny would be caught up in such a thing. If only—"

Miranda said: "Think again, Louis. Your invention may yet be used by real governments to kill pests in the tradition of Milosevic or Saddam."

He grinned self-effacingly. "Or worse. But yes—I have a lot to live for." He squeezed Tissy, who stood at his side.

Tissy said: "We both made terrible mistakes. I am really Genevieve Bertrand, of a very wealthy Belgian family. My father made countless millions in huge projects of civil engineering—roads, palaces, corporate skyscrapers. I went to the best schools and could have married into more money—but those shallow young men did not interest me. Maybe it's because my father was gone too much, and my mother was not much of a mother, always out at parties or giving parties to effete snobs. I look for stability in an accomplished older man." She looked up at Louis and smiled, rubbing his chest with her hand. "I thought I had ensnared Louis for Black Umbrella, but he ensnared my heart instead."

"But you did capture me," Louis said. "You captured my heart the way Artemis brings down a lamb on a springtime meadow—not to kill, but to rejuvenate. It is always spring when we are together."

Charming as this display of love and poetry might be, and Jack appreciate it full well—the clock was ticking for mass murder by Dr. Night. "Louis, keep talking. How did you construct this thing in your imagination and then in reality?"

"Well," Cartouche said, "it all boils down to a very simple idea that struck me as a nineteen year old student holding a mug of Labatt in a Montreal bar one night, and I have never let go of it. What if, instead of snapping a photograph, you could shoot a bullet? There was this rumor that the CIA could snap a picture of a Soviet staff car from 180 miles up, and read the numbers on the license plate. This was probably true by the 1970s, as the technology was refined. Then, as the space programs became a reality of the Cold War—and largely dropped away for two generations afterward—more advanced digital telemetry made the SIGINT or Signals Intelligence of the Keyholes and Coronas as such unnecessary. The world became covered in weather and communications satellites. Instead of dropping a canister of film, and a little parachute opens, and a Flying Boxcar drones past to snatch it from the air, and then it's flown to a lab for analysis—today it's called DIGINT—Digital Intelligence. You capture endless, cheap, accurate images and relay them to a transponder on the lab's rooftop, for analysis within seconds by automated pattern recognition, followed by expert human interpretation. The CIA and the Air Force shelved their wonderful technologies. Also, after the debacle of the Diem and other South Vietnam assassinations of the 1960s, Presidents Ford and Reagan outlawed assassination of foreign heads of state. That put the final kibosh on it. These wonderful technologies went into hibernation. "But I persevered. I was on the fringes of science and technology, even as I developed the Project David technology that I sold to Anaconda."

"Let me guess," Jack said. "The Chinese sniper rifle was a cover, a blind."

"Of course," Louis said. "Once I made my deal with Anaconda, they took care of the marketing, so to speak. They created a bogus Chinese company with a project called David. This was allegedly imported into Europe—all a fake and a shell game. There was nothing under the shells. We need not dwell on how BLUM recruited me in Palermo and Agrigento." He hugged Tissy close. After a pause, he continued: "I managed to buy parts and plans, and eventually assembled a reasonable facsimile of a Corona satellite in my warehouse in Montreal."

"You built in a safeguard," Miranda prodded.

"Yes," Louis said. "Knowing I'd have to market OST myself—and I am terrible at people skills—I protected myself by creating a second machine, a clone. I made it necessary to run both the Castor and Pollux machines to control the orbiting satellite. Once Anaconda got my plans and my prototypes, over the next two years they put several hundred million Euros into developing their Capricorn machine. With Capricorn in operational orbit, you'd only need one control unit (Castor or Pollux, but not both) once I got paid and left for some remote South Pacific Island.

"In the end, the OST does what I dreamed of as a nineteen year old boy holding a beer mug, alone and passionately lost in dreams, in some brick corner in this or that Montreal tavern. Just as I dreamed, my invention drops down into ultra-LEO at 180 miles up, and shoots a near-magical sniper bullet that kills, oh, say, a bloviator standing behind a podium on schedule, giving a windy speech."

"And now it's fallen into the worst imaginable hands," Jack said. Tissy and Cartouche clung to each other. Jack wished he could hug Miranda.

Cauldron

Claire and Rector had flown to Italy, landing at an experimental two mile (3 km) long strip at the big PETO air base at Aviano. They'd had a ninety-minute, rocket-assisted flight from Washington's Rosa Parks International Airport.

A small corporate jet of the Italian Air Force flew them to Lipari, and an Italian naval speed craft on skis whisked them to Vulcanello. They were now staying on demurely different floors in the same hotel on Vulcano. They spent hardly any time in their rooms, but were fixtures in the large conference room set up on the first floor. The Italian army had cleared the hotel of guests, relocating many to Lipari or the many other resorts along the Sicilian and Calabrian coasts. Tourists were evacuated in civilian ferries. Hotels and cantinas were eerily gloomy and morose.

Rector and Claire were set up for a constant, live conference call with the Camelback Consortium's Virginia headquarters, including the CIA and Sigma 2020 at Langley, and Compass News in San Diego. Since the White House and Congress were part of the Camelback Consortium, the President's and the Hawgbile-Bloviant Committee of Congress were slaved to the network as well. Rector and his wife were key figures in Compass News, so the San Diego feed was mainly for recording purposes. At Vulcano were a limited number of key field managers of intelligence, military, police agencies of Italy, PETO, and Camelback.

Information and data flooded in from many directions.

"Claire," Rector said, "I have a screen showing a message from Italian Navy Directorate in Rome. Apparently, there was an old NATO base here."

"Really?"

"Yes, I was wondering—where would you hide such a thing? Nobody on Vulcano or anywhere in the region has a clue, although there have been major allied navy and air bases across the region."

"Buried in the volcano itself," Rector said. "The magma chamber is many miles below the surface. Natural steam vents rise through the granite bedrock and the volcanic tufa. NATO created a heavily reinforced interior concrete structure from which to launch early jet bombers, before they had intercontinental ballistic missiles."

"ICBMs. Yes."

"It was so top secret that all mention of it was buried in government cellars and what not. When the Carabinieri at Bolsano pulled all available data before their recent landing on Vulcano, a lot of extraneous information floated to the surface, including about the secret bomber base. Get this—the takeoff gate was located on the west side, as added insurance during the critical moments of World War III starting, to give the Soviets one less chance to spot the jet tail exhausts and counter-attack. The NATO planes would have lost several minutes turning to head east, but they would have prevented an easy strike on their home base. In fact, I imagine they would have scrambled older machines from Sicily or Campania to drop chaff and flares to further confuse the Evil Empire. Remember, this was during the years immediately after World War II, when the world was still off its balance, and anything was possible. It's before ICBMs. It's before even the B-52 jet bomber—the U.S. was planning an enormous rotary-engine bomber, the B-39, to drop atomic bombs on the U.S.S.R."

"The Dark Ages again," Claire said.

"Yes. Luckily, World War III never happened—instead, nearly half a century of Cold War."

"So what are you saying, Rector? BLUM got their hands on the old, defunct NATO base?"

"Right. Through Dr. Night's usual corrupt network of secondary and tertiary contractors and sub-contractors, he was able to fake a dredging project or something—as he did in Scotland—to make the necessary updates to the Vulcano base."

"So we not only know where Dr. Night is conducting his main operations, not withstanding new orbital launches from central Africa, but we have a diagram of his facilities."

"Right. Bear in mind, he's only using a tiny area of the original vast facility, Claire."

Minutes later, as they labored over their terminals and viewing screens, Claire took a call from her chain of command in Washington, D.C. Rector was just returning from the coffee bar with two steaming cups of the brew of life. She waved to him. "Rector."

He served her coffee. "Mmm?"

"The Italian navy has taken over all operations, putting the army and the police under them. They have already evacuated 95% of residents (that's about 500 people) and tourists. They are also evacuating all ground troops, including Carabinieri and Alpini special forces. I think they are going to drop something down a shaft they found in the side of the Fossa volcano."

"Like a bomb?"

"Possibly."

"Didn't I read in my copious message traffic that the main NATO facility is about fifty feet above sea level, meaning it cannot be flooded in an attack."

"Yes," she said, "but if you dropped some of those giant old U.S. vacuum bombs…"

"Oh yes." Rector reminisced, sitting with his head back and his eyes closed. "They tried to flush Osama bin Laden out of his caves in Afghanistan with these huge implosion devices that literally suck all the air out, causing people to suffocate while their eyeballs pop out and their lungs rise up into their mouths."

"What about Jack and the other three we know are being held captive?"

"Unless we get them out, they'll be as just mentioned. I would hope it's a quick death, because it sounds incredibly gruesome."

"Rector!"

"Just sayin', Claire. Don't shoot me—I'm just the messenger. Got any ideas?"

"I wish we could contact Jack. If we were talking with him, that would be half the battle."

"Right…" Rector studied some plans, transferring them from his pad to a much larger wall screen in the converted ballroom. "Looks like there is an old take-off strip heading over the western beach, south of Porto di Ponente. The planes would be airborne, maybe just 200 feet, and roar away over the beach, and across the Med, north of Sicily, before hooking back and streaking toward what used to be Communist Czechoslovakia and the former Yugoslavia, or even a little further into the USSR. It would have been a flight of under an hour before they dropped their bombs and attempted to return to base, or if those were bombed out, ditch in the sea or land on a beach along the Tyrrhenian Sea. Never happened, thank God..."

"Rector!"

"Sorry, I meander. Don't forget, we are constrained by the fact that, if we attack him in his lair, he nukes ten or twenty million people."

"All we can do," she said, "is be little gnats and hope to suck him to death one sting at a time."

"I'm thinking—what if we put a guy in there to meet up with Jack and Miranda?"

With not a minute to waste, Operation Cauldron or Caldera launched within the hour. It was a project using Italian resources, but under Sigma 2020 control, and totally independent of the much larger Italian military operations in progress. Claire, standing in for Camelback, was nominally in charge, with a PETO liaison at the Italian armed forces joint command near Aviano.

OpCal was a two-prong operation. One was to go tragically wrong, while the second had some hope of success.

OpCal-1—Ultimatum Final

Prong 1 of OpCal: Carabinieri diving specialists and submarine warfare troops made a glorious sortie out of Porto di Levante on the northwest side of the island. Racing in three converted cigarette boats, they covered the few miles from the port to the south side of the volcano in a few minutes.

Working from Claire's estimate of where Jack had said he had emerged from an underwater submarine channel, each cigarette boat dropped three sea-land commandos (men and women) overboard, each with their own small dive or skimmer craft. They wore black wetsuits and tanks, along with small, waterproof equipment backpacks containing Uzis and ammo. They roared toward the shore on three skimmer craft. These were handle-bar controlled, amphibious three-wheelers that converted into a military version of the common ski-scooters seen at resorts around the world.

For an exhilarating ten minutes, the three craft created white, spongy wakes that threaded in and around each other on the heaving seas as they streaked toward the hidden submarine channel.

They crashed through the breakers and throbbed to silent halt on a little beach. From Jack's description over the phone from the Ehrlich house, and from subsequent surveillance by patrol boats with huge binocular telescopes, this must be the place where Jack had emerged and sat to strap his boots on, and where he had found fifty Euros of loose drug change.

The appointed action team of three divers—one female sergeant and two male sergeants—stripped their craft, peeling away layers of structure, until all that was left of each skimmer was one torpedo-shaped underwater machine with a small windshield, handlebars, a saddle, and in the rear a pair of propellers on dive planes, as well as a little yaw-controlling tail fin. Silently, the three divers disappeared into the water. Using high-powered lights, they found the opening—a channel about 8 meters (26 ft) wide and just as high. It took traveling at full power to overcome a strong receding tidal flow that made green growing things on the sea floor lean eastward. The fierce tide created an undertow further out.

Fighting their way in took about fifteen minutes, before they emerged in the submarine channel. Cautiously rising to the surface, so that just three pairs of diving masks showed, they could smell the diesel smoke in the air, and a distasteful film of oil on the water.

The immediate, seaward end of the channel was shrouded in gloom, except for light leaking from the submarine dock a quarter kilometer inland. After anchoring their vehicles, the divers swam toward the lights, but not all the way. They went ashore on a little sandy square on their left, as described by Jack. They found evidence of recent human occupation— including abandoned diving fins and other equipment. Either a large animal in distress had defecated in a spot to one side, or a succession of men had squatted to firehose in the same spot, leaving a weedy odor amid human waste.

Leaving their fins and other gear on the sand, the three commandos began to ascend the ancient Roman loading dock. Traces of ancient, collapsed wooden cranes lay by the side of the cave mouth. The divers wore extremely lightweight leather-soled, cloth footgear. Each diver wore only bathing clothes and wet suits, and carried a diving watch and a serrated knife. They wore nylon, olive-green web belts with the diving weights removed, but compact NATO standard Beretta Nano semi-automatic pistols of 9mm Parabellum/9x19mm caliber dangling from nylon holsters.

Climbing from ledge to ledge, sometimes helping each other with cupped hands or shoulders to step up with, they arrived at the ledge above. Their orders were to touch nothing, but to penetrate into the BLUM jail cells and rescue the three occupants. Each diver carried a pouch containing a shaped charge and a timed fuse run with an electric igniter. The explosive was venerable Italian army T-4 *plastico*, developed along the same lines during World War II as C-4 in the USA, and the 1950s Czech explosive Semtex of the Stalin era, named after the small town of Semtin in the modern Czech Republic.

When the three commandos reached the end of the tunnel, they found a newly installed brick wall. A V-shaped upper section was brand new, fitting into a much older segment. Someone had knocked loose the top of the wall.

As the commandos approached, they barely noticed a broad puddle of water at the base of the wall. Having just emerged from the sea, they did not pay attention to this. They also did not see the electrical cords hanging down the wall and onto the floor, terminating in bare copper claws like car battery jump starters.

One of the two men knelt down to prepare a shaped charge.

The woman and the other man approached the wall, and were instantly electrocuted before they could touch it. The air filled with bluish arcs of light, and loud booming sounds.

The survivor jumped back as he watched his compatriots twitching in their final moments, and acrid smoke rose from the water. A horrid smell filled the air, of burned hair and rubber.

The survivor wanted to check for a pulse, but he knew there would not be any. To step into the water would have meant his death as well.

Horrified, the man sat staring at this turn of events, yet gathered his courage back together. In their line of work, the commandos regularly faced extraordinary situations from which they might not walk away. He was the last one left, but the mission still existed. He continued shaping the P-45 plastic explosive charge. It was a small one, just enough to make a little noise and take out a one-course brick wall. As he worked, he watched two rats from sniffing out of nowhere. They climbed over the bodies of his dead companions and snuffled around their mouths—perhaps trying to figure out their most recent meal—and as they did so, their pink, splayed feet plashed in the water without harm. The circuit must have become fried during his companions' sudden deaths.

"*Grazie, amici,*" he whispered as he nudged the animals aside. "Thanks, friends."

Carefully, he advanced through the water. He respectfully pulled the two corpses clear of further harm. He pressed the charge against the middle of the brick wall, above the dip in the V. Activating the electric fuze, he hurried backward. He threw himself on the concrete floor, facing away from the death scene. Lying against the foot of the wall, he shielded his eyes with his arm. Even at that, the spray of tiny silica particles peppered him on his bare neck and through his clothing. As the deafening noise of the explosion reverberated around him, he rose and went to the wall.

There, through drifting dust, he saw a surprised looking dark-haired man in his mid-30s looking at him over the wall. They were visible to each other at chest height.

"Mr. Gray?"

"Yes," the rather athletic looking and self-composed man said.

"Special Operations at your command. I want to get you and your companions out."

As he spoke, he held a Beretta in one hand and twin packages of plastic explosives in the other.

The diver started to climb into the cell with the U.S. secret agent Jack Gray. His head was over the brick wall, when a gunshot thundered in the air, and a reddish hole appeared in the man's forehead.

OpCal-2

The second prong of Operation Caldera went slightly better.

An Italian navy ordnance team exploded the wooden barn or farm house on the western flank of the Fossa volcano. Tons of ripped planks, spinning slate roof tiles, and powdered glass flew sky-high in a brief, reddish flash followed by roiling gray and then black smoke.

Four large bulldozers with military markings roared into the smoke and began clearing debris away for Pavone's amphibious vehicles just then emerging in a double column from the sea.

The vehicles came up a sandy shore between looming cliffs, entered a tidal cave, and ran underground over a two-lane blacktop for about a kilometer. From there, they emerged into the mountain itself, and onto the NATO airstrip broadly paved in concrete. With the concealing structures blasted, the secret underground facility lay open to the air for the first time since its construction during the age of fear in the 1950s, during the Stalinist Red Scare.

Lt. Col. Pavone's assault group headed into the maw of Dr. Night's underground lair amid roars and diesel exhaust.

The last broadcast from Dr. Night whispered over the satellite airways and thus across the globe. "You disappoint me, Ladies and Gentlemen, but you do not surprise me. Your desperate tactics will not slow the growing power of Black Umbrella.

"For now, a chapter in our relations comes to an end. By no means have you defeated Black Umbrella. Call it the end of Phase One of our world takeover.

"I offered you a series of peaceful—and relatively painless—ways to coexist with the new world order imposed by Black Umbrella. We asked for 20% of your stock, and you said no. We asked for a third, and you said no. We asked for half, and you ignored us. That game is now over, and you lose. Now, I am afraid I must take it to a much higher level.

"I will leave you with an unforgettable chapter in world history. No more game shows for now. No more frivolity and good times. As of now, be on notice that the great city of New York, and its environs, a total of 22,000,000 human beings, will be irradiated with several tons of highly radioactive materials in just a few hours. If you decide to attack the satellite and take it out, think of it as opening a huge paint can that is orbiting the earth. If you take the lid off, its contents will spread over millions of square miles of your already polluted terrain. Entire species will become extinct, and vast areas will be uninhabitable. There is nothing left for you to do but wait for New York City to cease to exist as a viable human habitation.

"From New England to Washington, D. C. and inland as far as Ohio, over fifty million U.S. citizens will feel the deadly lash of Dr. Night's power. The destruction and death will be unimaginable.

"By all means, invade Vulcano. Bomb the island out of existence. My operation in orbit will proceed on autopilot. Neither I nor you can cancel its deadly progress. You have only yourselves, and your greed, to thank for this.

"We have already duplicated the OST, and plan to deploy it from one of our newly unveiled launch centers. But that is a page yet to be written, in a future calendar.

"Goodbye for now, corporate leaders. Count this as the opening salvo in your termination coming soon." He laughed. "You're fired!"

Lt. Col. Pavone's column of vehicles pushed resolutely in to the heart of the former NATO airbase amid clouds of dust.

A great roar issued from deep inside the facility.

For a moment, Pavone thought Dr. Night had figured out a way for the volcano itself to blow. He signaled for all his vehicles to halt. He, and dozens of vehicle commanders and machine gunners, stood in the turrets looking head.

While their collective headlights created cones of haze ahead, a pair of blazing white-blue lights rushed toward them.

Several aeronautical specialists among the Italian officers recognized the onrushing jet as a Brazilian-made Embraer Phenom 300, a medium-light business jet carrying one pilot and up to six passengers. The jet had wing and fuselage spans at approximately 15x15m or c52x52 ft, with a parked height of 5 m (c16 ft). It was powered by two Canadian-made Pratt & Whitney PW535E turbofan jet engines that were tucked high and close under a T-shaped tail fin.

During a flash second, a few of those on the ground recognized certain heads in the plane's windows—a shadowy man, an Asian woman with short, flying black hair, and several other figures. The woman looked out with manic black eyes surrounded by white rings.

Before anyone could react, much less shoot, the plane's wheels left the ground.

Landing gear folded up underneath.

Seconds later, the dart-like craft rose over the Mediterranean Sea on a southward roll in the direction of Africa. The turbulent exhaust of its twin thundering jet engines glittered in partial moonlight.

As Pavone's column pulled up near the defunct NATO entrance, they found a number of black-dressed figures lying around, plus two male monoliths in black suits. All had been summarily executed by Sombra to leave no witnesses. A faint cordite smell of gunpowder lingered on the air.

Dr. Night, Sombra, and several key companions were on their way to the next Black Umbrella base of global operations. At a speed of about 800 kph (480 mph), it could reach its maximum range (without drop tanks) of 3,600 km (2,160 miles) within about four hours' flight time. They would be tracked by scrambled NATO and North African radars and pursuit craft, but no doubt the ever canny Dr. Night would figure out a way to handily evade his enemies.

He left a global disaster waiting to unfold, without remedy or defense.

Corona Finale

Eternal Vigilance

Jack managed to grab the gun and explosives held by the Carabinieri expert in the second before the man fell dead from a fatal head shot.

Falling in a spin, Jack saw that Igor, the guard who normally fed him, had grown a gun and knew how to use it.

Moving fast—knowing it was his only chance—Jack whirled, holding the Beretta Nano.

A shot rang out toward him, and the brick wall above his head radiated splatters of whitewash from a brand-new pock mark.

Jack aimed his gun and squeezed.

Just as a third shot nicked his collar, Jack fired and dropped Igor, or Mr. Lunch. Extracting the gun and rolling sideways, Jack put another 9mm Parabellum slug into the recumbent porridge maestro.

Jack rose and moved quickly to the cell door. "Everyone okay?"

"Yes," sounded three voices.

Jack pulled the dead Igor close, and fumbled until he found the master key that opened all the cell doors. Within a minute, he was in the corridor, unlocking doors. For the first time in a week, Miranda Coldstream was free. She threw herself in Jack's arms and hugged him fiercely.

Jack relished the feel of her solid, warm body in his arms. "We have a lot of catching up to do, sweetheart."

Miranda gripped him tightly and laid her cheek against his chest. "I'm going to tuck you in and never let you out of my bed, at least for a week."

They released each other and hurried to the cell down the hallway. Jack opened the door and hugged Cartouche and Tissy—Genevieve Bertrand—as they emerged from their prison.

"You have saved our lives," Cartouche said.

"Let's rejoice when we can disco on Lipari—or better yet, in London or someplace far from here."

"For me, Montreal," Louis said.

Tissy added: "For me, wherever he goes. If we go to Quebec, I can speak naturally—being a Walloon, or French-speaking Belgian."

"We've been given a great chance," Jack said. "Several people died to hand us this key. Let's make the most of it. We can start by being very brave."

"If we die, we die free," Tissy said.

"Good idea," Miranda said. "Better yet, let's live free."

"Good thinking," they all said in unison.

"Okay," Jack said, "here's the plan. First of all, Louis and Tissy, we have to get you out of here and into Sigma 2020 hands. You can tell them all you know about Dr. Night and Mrs. Fright or whatever her real name is. Sombra." He put his arm around Miranda's shoulder. "Then, Miss Secret Agent, it's time for us to go to work."

"I'm ready," Miranda said sternly, pushing his arm away. "Play later."

Together, they pushed more bricks from the wall.

Stepping outside, they were horrified at the sight of the three brave commandos who had died. The Italians would send a recovery team for a dignified funeral and interment. No time for such honors at this moment.

As they exited, they heard distant klaxons. The sound eerily reminded Jack of the final hour at Kisimul. He could imagine technicians running for the exits; running for their very lives.

Jack collected watches and handguns, which he distributed. One went to Tissy and Louis, and a second to Miranda. He snapped one of the solid, rubber-coated chronographs to his wrist. He handed the Nano to Miranda, and kept Igor's cannon for himself.

"Don't touch anything," Jack cautioned as they walked down the tunnel—which was now illumined by the biolumes from the cells—and through the ancient Roman stock room.

Coming to the cliff, they were startled at a remarkable sight.

The black diesel submarine was just about to dive on her way out—probably loaded with escaping technicals, if BLUM was allowing these to get out.

The sight of the rapidly passing submarine was breath-taking.

Jack could almost have reached out and touched the conning tower, with its matte-black riveted plates and dimly lit windows as they passed by. The conning tower was a small, contained observation deck under the top hatch of the sail on a submarine. Jack glimpsed grim, pale faces with beards as the officers guided Dr. Night's submarine out into the sea. The boat evacuated outer air and took on water ballast as it sank down to the floor of the channel. Without slowing down, she would let the tidal flow pull her out, without minimal assist from her screw. Hopefully, the Italians would be waiting outside with their own submarines and ships to make it a short voyage for *SS Fright* or whatever they were calling the sub nowadays.

"There's the equipment," Jack said. "Let's climb down."

As he had anticipated, the commandos had left diving equipment on the little sandy recess. Would BLUM explode the docks? Probably not. They had been there for generations, were atomic bomb proof, and would be there thousands of years unless Fossa went ballistic and tore apart the island in some final Plinian rage of the gods. Not even a large hydrogen bomb could send that much molten rock, pumice, and smoke so high into the stratosphere.

"Miranda," he said. "Change of plans. There are three diving apparatus. No wet suits, and I don't want to spend time retrieving them from the dead people up top. I want you to get these two people out of here alive, and deliver them to Colonel Pavone or whoever is in charge up there. They may be able to help the world apprehend Dr. Blight and put an end to his insane schemes."

"No, no!" Louis said. "I must come with you, Jack. I think I know how to save all those people from death."

"You sure, Louis? This is your chance to get out alive."

"99%. Where you go, I go."

"Good enough for me. Tissy, you go with Claire."

"Bring my Louis back to me alive."

Jack said: "I plan to get out alive, and will bring your man along."

Tissy and Louis kissed long and hard. Then Louis let her go. She looked overwhelmed by her massive tank and oversized mask as Miranda helped her into the water. Tissy was a tough bird. She swam away like a trooper, with Miranda following.

Louis clutched Jack's shirt collar. "There is one chance that I can think of." He told Jack.

"That's as good as anything," Jack said. "Let's get within radio or telephone range of my chain of command."

They clambered back up the steep rock face—trough the Roman area again—amid leering drama masks and pensive statuettes still crated for delivery to some toga-clad tycoon—and down the hall until they could pile back over the wall and into the open cells.

Racing up the stairs, with Louis behind him, Jack came to the guard station.

With Igor—Mr. Lunch—dead, and the others gone, Jack unhesitatingly picked up a land phone and sought an outside connection. To his amazement, he instantly reached Claire.

"Jack."

"Claire—where are you?"

"We are in the Blue Bar Hotel on Vulcanello, eating tuna salad sandwiches, drinking *Sprudelwasser*, and watching the world fall apart. Where are you?"

"Three good commandos just died springing us loose from Dr. Night's jail in the volcano."

"I am so sorry. Pavone just informed us that Dr. Night and his female sidekick escaped in a small private jet. He's set the dirty bomb to drop on New York City in the next ten hours or so. We are frantic—we don't know of any way to stop it. The footprint could endanger up to fifty million people, Jack."

"Are they evacuating?"

"No, the government decided that it would cause more harm than good. Rather than have people fighting and in traffic jams, while that stuff rains down on them, the city has ordered everyone to stay where they are, close the doors and windows, and avoid breathing outside air.'

"What else can they do?" Jack was glad he did not have to make such decisions. "Nothing, I guess. I have Louis Cartouche with me. He invented the damn thing. He says he has an idea for stopping it. I'll put him on." Jack handed to phone over.

"Hello," Louis said without preamble. "Madame, years ago, I put together my own version of a Corona satellite, using a lot of bought, borrowed, and stolen parts. For the software, I hired a crew of hackers, who basically lifted the code from a museum version."

Claire spoke, and he listened briefly. "Yes, Madame. In the Smithsonian. Nobody ever bothered to wipe the code, but I'm sure the core memory stacks and executable binaries are blank by now. It's all long gone from the museum machine, but we can port my version and load it back in there. What I mean is, my code is based on it, so it is not the same, but we can get around the protocols and make it work again. For this, I will need your utmost cooperation. Is the machine at Kisimul gone?" He paused to hear her answer. "Yes? Too bad. It would have been so much simpler, or maybe not. Anyway, this is all we have to work with. Now I will tell you what we need to do."

After explaining to her, Jack and Louis found a motorized scooter. They rode down the long hallway to Dr. Night's control room. Along the way, many of the doors were still closed as they had been since NATO's abandonment of the base in the 1970s. Doors opening on BLUM operations stood open to reveal empty rooms with orderly rows of numbers.

When Jack and Louis came to the main control center, they found the domed room empty. Everything had been abandoned in place—computers still running, power and lights on, copiers humming, screens flickering, displays languidly rolling on the walls.

"I know why he didn't leave anyone here," Jack said. "It's because something can still be done from here. It's not over yet. He did not want anyone here who might stumble around in a rage, smashing things, after being left to die like those people in Kisimul."

"Thanks to you, they were saved, Jack," Louis said humbly. "Let me see if I can undo the damage I created, and save millions of lives."

"Let's get on it," Jack said. He found a portable phone, dialed up Claire, and paced about. Meanwhile, Louis bent over his creation—Pollux—and studied it. He began relaying instructions to Claire Lightfield and Rector.

Under Claire's direction, and with help from Rector, events unfolded quickly.

At the Smithsonian Institution, by the National Mall in Washington, D.C., all lights blazed inside and outside. Smithsonian Police, a branch of Federal Police, rushed about on orders from their bosses and the Chief of Staff at the White House.

A team of Smithsonian duty officers, all Ph.D. scientists or graduate assistants, were on the premises. Accompanied by security officers, the professors unlocked a room containing historical satellites—including a retired Corona of ancient Air Force vintage. The official in charge that night, a Dr. Grolich, who happened to also teach Physics at George Washington University evenings and weekends, conferred with Louis Cartouche on a phone relay.

"Forget the program," Louis said. "Get the thing powered up. A 240 volt power line should accomplish what we need—getting the CPU fired up on the security buses I will specify from the drawings here in Sicily. What we need on that table is an exact working duplicate of the Pollux operational system in orbit. Everything we do to it will happen to the real-time Pollux in space."

A cardboard sign, not far from the Corona satellite in the Smithsonian, retrieved for a related purpose from the NORAD defense center of Cold War vintage read: "The price of freedom is eternal vigilance."

As they conferred, a row of executive black limousines pulled up in the circular driveway of the White House. Into the cars poured a small army of computer specialists already on duty on the night shift at the executive mansion. The president had been summoned from bed, and sat in the situation room being briefed by men and women wearing a lot of brass and ribbons.

With light flashing and sirens screaming, the convoy headed from the White House to the Smithsonian. Along the way, they picked up an escort of eight police motorcycles, whose keening sirens and flashing blue lights warned pedestrians out of the way as the convoy cut through the National Mall.

Helicopters rattled in the air above, and all but military jets had been grounded at every regional airport.

The cavalcade came to a screeching, plowing stop around the Smithsonian's National Air and Space Museum. About thirty programmers, analysts, technicians, and computer scientists piled out and ran into the building. Fresh from their cutting edge, top secret ops center in the White House, they were now to work on a long-dead satellite hanging by wires from the ceiling, along with a Mercury capsule, a Ford Trimotor of 1920s vintage, and a DC-3 of the 1930s.

Technicians disconnected all terminals they could find and wheeled them under the satellite. Within minutes, men and women on ladders strung up networks of coaxial data cables, as well as power lines. Under the careful ministrations of scholarly looking men and women, a local area network took shape within fifteen minutes. As soon as it was peripherally operational, technicians started operating computer terminals, laptops, pads, and all manner of peripherals. Other techs combed out the kinks to build out a fully working LAN.

Dr. Grolich called out: "All talk at a minimum. Let's not drown each other out. Do not talk except to save your life—and only if no other alternatives exist. We are porting a massive virtual software engine, by satellite relay, from Italy. Database managers, are you loaded and compatible? Com, are your connections shaking hands? Systems operations, what is your status? Storage, are you ready to receive data on the south end? There are something like fifty terrabytes of operational records on the way—make sure nothing falls off the edge."

Within two hours, Louis Cartouche had relayed the entire Black Umbrella Pollux data core across the ocean, via satellites and transponders, while he was agonizing in the control room at Vulcano.

All the while, BLUM's satellite of death streaked ever closer to its fatal rendez-vous, when a silent stream of radioactivity would shimmer in the starry night sky.

Jack was on the phone with Claire. "Did you get Tissy and Miranda?"

"The Italian coast guard retrieved her and Miranda from the water—they were half frozen with hypothermia, but are nicely recovering."

"What about the submarine?"

"I'll let Rector brief you." She put Rector on.

"Jack, the Italians are stalking the sub. They'll depth charge her if she tries to escape from Italian waters. I think they'll surrender shortly."

"You'll only catch some small fry. I'm here with Louis Cartouche. With any luck, he'll work a miracle if everyone helps him out."

Cartouche cried out. "Jack. I am ready to make a try."

In Washington, the satellite LAN in the Smithsonian glittered like a galaxy of stars under the echoing ceiling. At least a hundred other experts had arrived by now from local universities and top Federal government cyber fortresses, and more were coming in by the minute. The Red Cross opened a kitchen and started serving coffee, tea, soft drinks, and hot tomato soup with soda crackers. It was going to be a long night. Dozens of young military men and women in fatigues or BDUs hurried about on technical errands.

Before long, press vans started rolling up outside. From the ad hoc computer center, one could look out through windows over a forest of relay towers atop vans, with dishes and antennas.

"I have the satellite," Louis said as he gazed over his Pollux controls inside Fossa on Vulcano.

"I see it," said Dr. Grolich in the Air and Space Museum. He was looking at its twin—the new Castor.

Between Castor and Pollux, they now had one complete, operational set of controls to manage the orbiting Gemini spacecraft.

"Is it too late?" Claire asked over the airwaves. "Dr. Night said the program can't be hacked or stopped."

"We'll see," said Louis.

Cartouche and Grolich ran tedious, nail-biting tests to synchronize the Washington and Vulcano ghost satellites in real-time with the deadly orbiter.

One cautious step at a time, the two men began a complex and touchy sequence to snare the orbiting satellite into the same synchronous command stream.

One wrong step, and they might lose Pollux. Then they'd be helpless to stop history's most horrible massacre.

Or, if Dr. Night had built in some fail-safes to override hacks, it could come to that as well.

"Don't worry," Louis muttered under his breath, "Dr. Shyte didn't take the time or have the brains. But wait—what's this?" His tone changed from contempt to fear and stress.

"It's stuck in a loop," Louis told Jack and Grolich finally. "We're dead in the water. I cannot reach the control program at the core to change it. It is set to release its load over Greater New York City within the next four hours."

"Let me see," Jack said. Together, they stared at a monitoring screen from a Jengdu military satellite about fifty miles away, which the Chinese government had managed to sneak near the Pollux under Dr. Night's nose. The satellite—seen in telescopic range, with optical and digital enhancement—looked like the typical complex of exposed wires and sensors. It was wrapped in a thermal blanket of golden-copper that shone in reflected sunlight and moonlight.

Louis pointed. See that big boxy looking part on the left? That has eighteen OST reentry vehicles stored for dropping, minus the two he's already used."

"Like a clip of rounds in a gun," Jack said.

"Right. They've shot two, so they should have sixteen left."

"You created all this..."

"Don't remind me, please. I will have nightmares every night for the rest of my life—even if we succeed in disabling this thing, which looks less and less likely now. You see that big box trailing on a long boom about 120 feet behind? That's the storage container for the radioactive material."

"And they just launched another box like it in a separate orbit."

"Yes," Louis said. "Into orbit at 300 miles, which, once they drop this one, will automatically descend to 165 miles and release its second cloud of strontium, plutonium, and whatever other dirty bomb materials they could scratch together."

"If we disable the main one, will it kill the second one?"

Louis shook his head. "I can only guess. Maybe yes, maybe no. The only way to know for sure is if it doesn't perform its task sequence."

Dr. Grolich said: "I'm detecting activity. I think it's running through its live launch sequence. Right on time, from what I can see. It will make two more passes around the globe and then dump up to three tons of radioactive hell all over the New York City area."

"How long would you say?" Jack asked.

"Two hours at the outside, depending on factors beyond our control. We're making a heroic effort here, but it's a pathetic struggle. And the switchboards are breaking down all over the D.C. region with frantic, angry, terrified calls from the New York area. And nuts from all over the country are calling in, saying they are going to take up arms against the government."

Louis straightened up. "Damn! I am defeated, Jack. I cannot break through this feedback loop that Dr. Night's engineers put in place to prevent anyone from deactivating his monstrous scheme."

"All right," Jack said. "Time for one last desperate effort. Dr. Grolich , are you with us?"

"On line, on board, and on pins and needles."

"We're going to try a desperate measure." When he suggested it, there was a pause, followed by weary sighs. It was about the only option left, all things considered.

In orbit, the Gemini satellite behaved exactly as it should.

It looked immobile, traveling about 17,750 mph against a black background on which the cosmic divine had spattered a zillion gallons of luminescent watch-dial radium.

Grolich and Cartouche and their aides made delicate adjustments while biting their tongues and pouring out profuse sweat.

For a while, nothing at all happened.

In an hour, the satellite was designed to cast loose its cargo trailer. Reverse thrusters would slow it for reentry. Its newly launched companion satellite would do the same, exactly in tandem only a mile away. Three tons of radioactive material would begin raining down, starting over Pennsylvania, and reaching full dumping volume over Newark, New York, and Fairfield among other population centers of Greater New York City.

For a little while longer, nothing happened.

The Gemini system was about fifteen minutes from D-Hour, or Death Hour.

Then, a ceramic lander detached from its torpedo tube in the OST rack.

As the little orbital sniper rifle popped out, it did not immediately begin its four minute descent to kill someone standing at a podium.

Instead, it did a neat little somersault, so that it faced the main control module aboard the Pollux craft.

Controlled by Cartouche on Vulcano, and shooting its instruction stream through the Smithsonian satellite and back to the Aeolian Islands to complete the action sequences, the tiny shuttle made a soundless pop. Its shell flew away, leaving the rifle itself, which normally would not open until within a mile or less of the earth's surface. Here, at 180 miles up, it fired a powerful .50 caliber round that instantly shredded the controls and killed the entire satellite.

A remote miniature camera recorded the brief sequence.

The satellite continued drifting in orbit, but without power.

Looking closely, one could see burned out panels, and torn, twisted wiring fragments.

"Jack," Cartouche whispered through a shower of sweat, with sorrowful eyes.

"Jack," echoed Dr. Grolich over 6,000 miles away.

"You did it," Cartouche said.

"We did it," said Jack.

Grolich said: "You just saved the world—at least, a good chunk of it."

Louis said: "I feel like a man reborn—a felon reprieved."

"Good job, Mr. Cartouche," Grolich said. "The scientific community will ignore you no longer." He added: "We'll send up a cargo craft to bring back the OST modules."

Cartouche said. "Maybe they can really be used to stop the next Hitler or Mussolini before the entire world has to go to war, and countless lives are lost for a single crazy man's testosterone foolishness."

"History stinks," Jack agreed, "for that reason above all others."

"The satellite itself will bump up well over 400 miles, until we can get a booster around it and send it harmlessly diving into the sun," said Grolich.

Jack added: "We'll start looking hard for Dr. Night and Mrs. Fright. They are probably already hatching their next insane scheme."

"Good work, Jack," said Rector.

"All's well that ends well," said Claire Lightfield.

"Amen to that," Jack said sincerely.

Rector said: "Come over for a drink and a walk on the beach some time, Jack." It as a veiled allusion to the fact that he lived in the hills of exclusive Loma Portal, overlooking the blue Pacific, while Jack was not much over an hour away in the back country on the D Ranch near Riverside.

"I'll take you up on that," Jack said. "If you get the urge to do some horseback riding among the fall foliage, bring the missus on by."

Exeunt

A few days later, Jack called his sister Janet at the D Ranch on a secure Air Force crypto satellite hookup.

"Jack, how are you? I was worried to death."

"I know you were. You always are, even though I'm perfectly fine. But I do apologize for that, sis."

"Where are you? I hear birds or something."

"Lots of birds and fresh air here. How are the kids?"

"We're all fine. Mark is on a business trip in Los Angeles. The kids are all in school. And I'm trying to hire some high school kids to pick apples in the back twenty."

"Save me a few apples. I'll be home soon."

"Where are you again, Jack?"

"Taking a little R&R with some nice friends. We decided to get away from it all for a few days."

"Did you hear about that scare about an old Soviet satellite breaking up and almost showering down radioactive material?"

"Yes, I heard about it. Sounds like a messy deal. Glad the people in charge figured out how to deal with it."

There was the usual awkward pause, where she wanted to remind him to wear his sweater, and he wanted to tell her the truth but simply couldn't.

"Okay, Jack."

He wanted to ask about Molly, but decided not to. Or Roberta. Then he asked anyway.

"Molly is doing fine. Roberta comes over every day to do homework with Gail and Marcia. And of course the boys are running around. Molly comes over to pick up Roberta, and stays for tea. She asks about you, Jack. With big eyes. She's waiting for you. As is Roberta—she's your greatest admirer."

"Well, like I said, I'll be home in a few days. Give Gail and Marcia my love. And the boys. We can go horseback riding and see the autumn leaves, you and I."

"I'd love that, Jack."

"Like old times," he said and rang off.

Jack slipped the little phone back into the suspender pocket of his fishing waders. Beside him, Miranda Coldstream's face looked flushed and happy in the sharp, cold wind. Across the babbling river, an 800 pound grizzly mother was teaching her baby to fish.

The chilly air of autumnal Alaska smelled fresh, with a tinge of wood smoke from the log cabin up the gravel path.

Genevieve—Tissy—and Cartouche were just walking down to the water, hand in hand, probably after a long, cozy sojourn in the warm cabin.

"I am making dinner," Tissy called out.

"What are you making?"

"Salmon!" Tissy said.

"Surprise," Miranda said, and Jack laughed. It was all they had to eat the past few days. Tissy, who came from a small country in Europe that made some of the best chocolate in the world, but no salmon, was learning some of the 1,000 tasty ways to prepare the orange fish.

Cartouche looked ten years younger. He was a man reprieved from years of prison and at least one near-death experience. His graying hair made a long streamer in the fresh wind as he stood on the bank with his hands in his pockets. For a man who had just helped save the world, he looked not excited, but remarkably calm and composed.

Their information, delivered during hours of friendly debriefing at Langley, shed surprisingly little light on the identity and plans of the man who called himself Dr. Night. In any case, Jack reflected, it was not his department or pay grade to laboriously sift through reams of elusive data. Let others do that. His mission was accomplished, and he deserved a rest.

Miranda laughed and chased in circles with Tissy. They splashed their boots in shallow water—utterly ignored by the bears just across the water.

Jack swept his long fishing rod back for a generously wide, arcing throw. His gesture was framed by the long, snowy expanse of the Coast Mountains of the Boundary Range, with their bluish wrinkles and broad white snow cover. Fog rolled slowly over dark green forests that made this area, an hour's drive north of Ketchikan, the Yosemite of the North. The four friends were camping on a reserved FBI federal hideout for persons transitioning into the witness protection program. The official name of the pristine area was Misty Fjords National Monument. The FBI refuge had no name. It was just a long cypher string in a distant database.

The air was so sweet and fresh that its oxygen-laden dampness was like a narcotic, laced with the scent of spruce and pines, putting you to sleep in your fresh sheets at night.

That evening, with Miranda Coldstream to warm the bed, Jack could not decide if he should yell or snore, so he did both, while Miranda laughed and clapped, sitting nakedly on her knees. They did not think about the moment, two or three days hence, when she would return to her family in London for a visit, before flying on to her duty station in Frankfurt. It would be dull, boring duty without him, she lamented. He promised to visit her on his return trips to Europe. But first, he would fly home to San Diego and Temecula to step back into his real life—until Claire Lightfield and Rector called him back to duty.

In the next cabin over, Louis Cartouche and Genevieve Bertrand-Cartouche were just getting their start as a married couple. The wedding had been a very private affair in a small church in Ketchikan. Jack and Miranda had been more than happy to offer their services as witnesses, as well as best man and bridesmaid. Louis had accepted a well-paying corporate engineering job on a project developing his OST—with

Camelback, not Anaconda, signing his paychecks. And Tissy was to work for a Quebec-based publisher, creating French and English language tourist brochures aimed at Belgian and other European visitors.

In three days, the De Havilland Twin Otter float plane—a hard-to-miss red and white explosion of colors based in Ketchikan, 'Salmon Capital of the World'—would remove the four to Juneau and civilization.

Until then, they played like children in a land that time forgot.

 END

Author Info, More Books

John T. Cullen's main web presence (begun in 1996) is:
www.johntcullen.com/
The author is a novelist, journalist, essayist, and science and history writer living in San Diego, California.

He has written at least 40 books (including two nonfiction titles, plus many novels). His work includes many scholarly, interesting articles (nonfiction) and short stories (fiction).

He has written at least one scholarly paper for peer review, about the ancient Sator Rebus—an enigma for which he has provided the first plausible translation as well as explanation. At least one primary academic expert on the subject has acclaimed his achievement.

He has lived in various countries across North America and Europe, and is conversant in a number of languages including English, German, and Luxembourgeois. He translated Goethe's Faust (Part I) from German into English in an edition to appear from Clocktower Books in 2012-2013.

Appearing as a Clocktower Books original (first authorized) edition in 2020-2012 will be his ground-breaking popular work of ancient history, <u>A Walk in Ancient Rome</u> (1st Authorized Print Edition)—a readable, accessible topological tour of ancient Rome in the age of Constantine. It goes far beyond other guides that only hit the highlights, usually in a random and surface manner, which only leaves readers confused and no wiser. This virtual tour guide takes the lay or student reader to all fourteen Augustan districts of the imperial capital, often visiting areas known only to experts, for an in-depth understanding of a lost world that was the template for our own. The author vividly explains the history and religious significance of the monuments, streets, parks, temples, and other sites in a structured, disciplined manner like no other book of its type.

In San Diego, he is the first to plausibly explain one of the region's (and nation's) most intriguing puzzle—the ghost story at the Hotel del Coronado, associated with Kate Morgan; but more importantly from his standpoint, the true crime of 1892 that led to the so-called Beautiful Stranger's dark and violent death amid allegations of foul play and sexual dalliances with men in the highest places. The owner of the Hotel del Coronado at the time was John Spreckels, one of the nation's wealthiest men. Spreckels was in the White House with President

Benjamin Harrison, negotiating the future of the sovereign Monarchy of Hawai'i, when in the author's opinion Kate Morgan and her accomplices attempted to pull of a blackmail attempt gone horribly wrong. The result was a cover-up, and a murky, colorful legend that has intrigued the world for over 120 years. The author has written Dead Move: Kate Morgan and the Haunting Mystery of Coronado, 2nd Edition (Nonfiction) as a scholarly analysis with over 120 footnotes. He followed this up with Lethal Journey, a noir mystery thriller based on his notes and the most gripping elements of the long-standing myth.

John T. Cullen holds a B.A. in English (University of Connecticut, Storrs), a B.B.A. in Computer Information Systems (National University, San Diego), and an M.S. in Business Administration (Boston University). He earned his M.S. while serving honorably with the U.S. Army in Cold War Germany for five years, attending graduate level classes in various West German cities under auspices of Boston University's Metropolitan College Overseas Division in Heidelberg FRG.

Visit his webplex anchored at www.johntcullen.com, and look for the tabs along the top that link other sites in his webplex. Among those linked sites are Galley City (sample chapters); Galley City Café (nonfiction); and special websites for his fiction, poetry, Clocktower Books, and the Clocktower Books Museum.

He has been an Internet pioneer—the world's sixth digital publisher (Clocktower Books, 1996+). He was for years author of the acclaimed Sharpwriter.com (in 1999 named by Writer's Digest as one of the top 101 resource websites for authors). He was also, for nearly a decade, publisher and editor of Far Sector SFFH—during its heyday, the world's oldest professional web magazine of science fiction, dark fantasy, and horror.

He is being recognized as the first person to ever decipher the mysterious ancient Sator Square, an enigma that has puzzled historians and archeologists for centuries. As an Active Member of International Thriller Writers, at a recent annual convention in New York City, he was probably the only author present who had ever actually deciphered a mysterious, ancient inscription of great importance, found all over ancient Roman empire—and lived to tell about it.